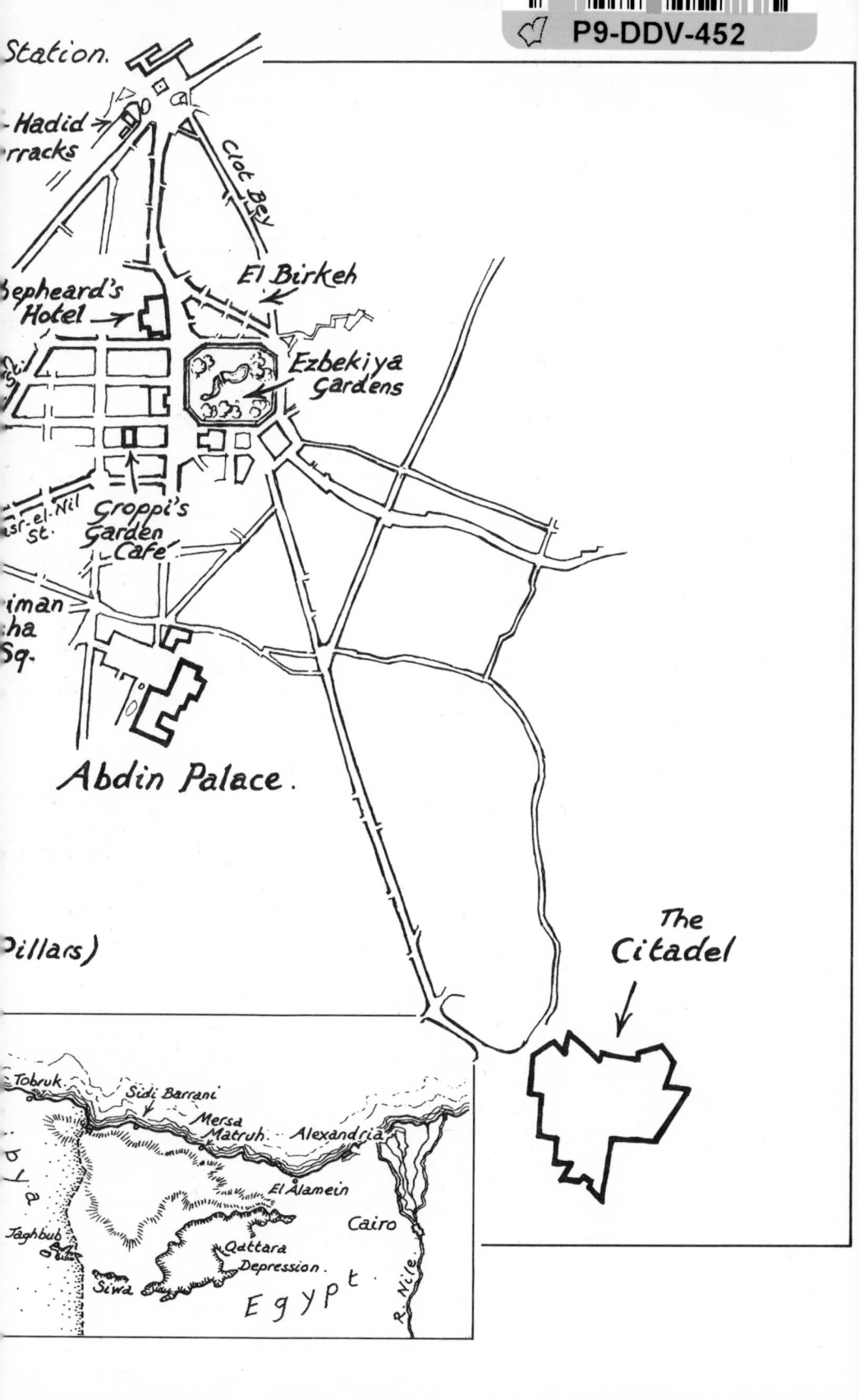

Station.

-Hadid
rracks

Clot Bey

El Birkeh

Bepheard's
Hotel

Ezbekiya
Gardens

Croppi's
Garden
Cafe

asr-el-Nil
St.

iman
ha
Sq.

Abdin Palace.

(Pillars)

The
Citadel

Tobruk.
Sidi Barrani
Mersa
Matruh
Alexandria
El Alamein
Cairo
Jaghbub
Qattara
Depression.
Siwa
R. Nile

E g y p t

CITY OF GOLD

ALSO BY LEN DEIGHTON

LEN DEIGHTON

CITY OF GOLD

HarperCollins*Publishers*

HarperCollins books may be purchased for educational, business, or sales promotional use. For information, please call or write: Special Markets Department, HarperCollins Publishers, Inc., 10 East 53rd Street, New York, NY 10022. Telephone: (212) 207-7528; Fax: (212) 207-7222.

FIRST EDITION

Designed by C. Linda Dingler

Library of Congress Cataloging-in-Publication Data

Deighton, Len, 1929–
    City of gold / by Len Deighton.—1st ed.
        p.   cm.
    ISBN 0-06-017937-6 (cloth)
    1. World War, 1939–1945—Egypt—Cairo—Fiction.   I. Title.
PR6054.E37C5   1992
823'.914—dc20   92-52565

---

92 93 94 95 96 CC/HC 10 9 8 7 6 5 4 3 2 1

Prologue

In the final months of 1941, General Erwin Rommel—commander of the Axis armies in North Africa—began to receive secret messages about the British armies that faced him. The source of this secret intelligence was not identified to Rommel. In fact, the contents of the messages sent to him were carefully rewritten to prevent anyone's guessing the source of these secrets and how they were obtained. But the messages were startling in their completeness; the dates of arrival of supply ships and their cargoes, the disposition of the Allied armies and air forces, the state of their morale and their equipment, and even what their next operations might be were provided promptly and regularly to Rommel's intelligence officer.

Said one specialist historian, "And what messages they were! They provided Rommel with undoubtedly the broadest and clearest picture of enemy forces and intentions available to any Axis commander throughout the whole war. . . . In the see-saw North African warfare, Rommel had been driven back across the desert by the British . . . but beginning on January 21, 1942, he rebounded with such vigour that in seventeen days he had thrown the British back 300 miles."*

*David Kahn, *The Codebreakers* (London: Weidenfeld & Nicolson, 1966).

=1=

They say that the sergeant's a very nice chap,
Oh, what a tale to tell.
Ask him for leave on a Saturday night—
He'll pay your fare home as well.
There's many a soldier has blighted his life
Thro' writing rude words on the wall,
You'll get no promotion this side of the ocean,
So cheer up, my lads. Bless 'em all!

TROOPING SONG

Cairo: January 1942

"I like escorting prisoners," said Captain Albert Cutler, settling back and stretching out his legs along the empty seats. He was wearing a cream-colored linen suit that had become rumpled during the journey. "When I face a long train journey, I try and arrange to do it."

He was a florid-faced man with a pronounced Glasgow accent. There was no mistaking where he came from. It was obvious right from the moment he first opened his mouth.

The other man was Jimmy Ross. He was in khaki, with corporal's stripes on his sleeves. He was that rarest of Scots, a Highlander: from a village in Wester Ross. But they'd tacitly agreed to bury their regional differences for this brief period of their acquaintanceship. It was Ross's pocket chess set that had cemented their relationship. They were both at about the same level of skill. During the journey they must have played fifty games. At least fifty. And that was not counting the little demonstrations that Cutler had pedantically given him: openings and endings from some of the great games of the chess masters. He could remember them. He had a wonderful memory. He said that was what made him such a good detective.

It was an old train, with all the elaborate bobbins and fretwork that the Edwardians loved. The luggage rack was of polished brass with tassels at each end. There was even a small beveled mirror in a mahogany frame. In the roof there was a fan that didn't work very well. According to the wind and the direction of the train, the ventilator emitted gusts of sooty smoke from the locomotive. It did it now, and Ross coughed.

There came the sounds of passengers picking their way along the corridor. They stumbled past with their kit and baggage and rifles and equipment. They spoke in the tired voices of men who have not slept; the train was very crowded. They couldn't see in. All the blinds were kept lowered on this compartment, but there was enough sunlight getting through the linen. It made a curious shadowless light.

"Why would you like that?" said Jimmy Ross. "Escorting prisoners. Why would you like that?" He had a soft Scots accent that you'd only notice if you were looking for it. Jimmy Ross was slim and dark and more athletic than Cutler, but both men were much the same. Their similarities of upbringing—bright, working-class, grammar school graduates without money enough to go up to university—had more than once made them exchange looks that said, There but for the grace of God go I, or words to that effect.

"I wear my nice civvy clothes, and I get a compartment to myself. Room to put my feet up. Room to stretch out and sleep. No one's bothered us, have they? I like it like that, especially on these trains." Cutler tugged at the window blind and raised it a few inches to look out at the scenery. On the glass, as on the windows to the corridor, there were large gummed-paper notices that bore the royal coat of arms, smudged rubber stamps, the scrawled signatures of a representative of the provost marshal, and the words RESERVED COMPARTMENT in big black letters. No one with any sense would have intruded upon them.

Bright sunlight came into the compartment as he raised the blind. So did the smell of excrement, which was spread on the fields as fertilizer. Cutler blinked. Outside, the countryside was green: dusty, of course, like everything in this part of the world, but very green. This was Egypt in winter: the fertile region.

The train clattered and groaned. It was not going fast; Egyptian trains never went fast. Scrawny dark-skinned men, riding donkeys alongside the track, stared back at them. In the fields, women were bending to weed a row of crops. They stepped forward, still in line, like soldiers. "A long time yet," pronounced Cutler, looking at his watch. He lowered the blind again. When the train reached Cairo the two men would part. Cutler, the army policeman, would take up his nice new appointment with Special Investigation Branch Headquarters, Middle East. Jimmy Ross would be thrown into a stinking army "glasshouse." He knew he could expect a very rough time while awaiting court-martial. The military prison in Cairo had a bad reputation. After he'd been tried and found guilty, he might be sent to one of the army prisons in the desert. Ross smiled sadly, and Cutler felt sorry for him. It hadn't been a bad journey; two Scotsmen can always find something in common.

"Have you never been attacked?" said Ross.

"Attacked?"

"By prisoners. Don't men get desperate when they are under arrest?"

Cutler chuckled. "You wouldn't hurt me, would you?" There was not much difference in their ages or their builds. Cutler wasn't frightened of the prisoner. Potbellied as he was, he felt physically superior to him. In Glasgow, as a young copper on the beat, he'd learned how to look after himself in any sort of rough-house.

"I'm not a violent man," said Ross.

"You're not?" Cutler laughed. Ross was charged with murder.

Reading his thoughts, Jimmy Ross said, "He had it coming to him. He was a rotten bastard."

"I know, laddie." He could see that Jimmy Ross was a decent enough fellow. He'd read Ross's statement and those of the witnesses. Ross was the only NCO there. The officer was an idiot who would have got them all killed. And he'd pulled a gun on his men. That was never a good idea. But Cutler was tempted to add that his victim's being a bastard would count for nothing. Ross was an "other rank," and he'd killed an officer. That's what would count. In wartime on active service they would throw the book at him. He'd be lucky to get away with twenty years hard labor. Very lucky. He might get a death sentence.

Jimmy Ross read his thoughts. He was sitting handcuffed, looking down at the khaki uniform he was wearing. He fingered the rough material. When he looked up he could see the other man was grimacing. "Are you all right, captain?"

Cutler did not feel all right. "Did you have that cold chicken, laddie?" Cutler had grown into the habit of calling people laddie. As a police detective-inspector in Glasgow it was his favored form of address. He never addressed prisoners by their first names; it heightened expectations. Other Glasgow coppers used to say sir to the public, but Cutler was not that deferential.

"You know what I had," said Ross. "I had a cheese sandwich."

"Something's giving me a pain in the guts," said Cutler.

"It was the bottle of whisky that did it."

Cutler grinned ruefully. He'd not had a drink for nearly a week. That was the bad part of escorting a prisoner. "Get my bag down from the rack, laddie." Cutler rubbed his chest. "I'll take a couple of my tablets. I don't want to arrive at a new job and report sick the first minute I get there." He stretched out on the seat, extending his legs as far as they would go. His face had suddenly changed to an awful shade of gray. Even his lips were pale. His forehead was wet with perspiration, and he looked as if he might vomit.

"It's a good job, is it?" Jimmy Ross pretended he could see nothing wrong. He got to his feet and, with his hands still cuffed, got the leather case. He watched Cutler as he opened it.

Cutler's hands were trembling so much he had trouble fitting the key into the locks. With the lid open Ross reached across, got the bottle, and shook tablets out of it. Cutler opened his palm to catch two of them. He threw them into his mouth and swallowed them without water. He seemed to have trouble getting the second one down. His face hardened as if he was going to choke on it. He frowned and swallowed hard. Then he rubbed his chest and gave a brief bleak smile, trying to show he was all right. He'd said he often got indigestion; it was the worry of the job. Ross stood there for a moment looking at him. It would be easy to crack him over the head with his hands. He could bring the steel cuffs down together onto his head. He'd seen someone do it on stage in a play.

For a moment or two Cutler seemed better. He tried to overcome his pain. "I've got to find a spy in Cairo. I won't be able to find him, of course, but I'll go through the motions." He closed the leather case. "You can leave it there. I'll be changing my trousers before we arrive. That's the trouble with linen; it gets wrinkled. And I want to look my best. First impressions count."

Ross sat down and watched him with that curiosity and concerned detachment with which the healthy always observe the sick. "Why won't you be able to find him?" Being under arrest had not lessened his determined hope that Britain would win the war, and this fellow Cutler should be trying harder. "You said you were a detective."

"Ah! In Glasgow before the war, I was. CID. A bloody good

one. That's why the army gave me the rank straight from the force. I never did an officer's training course. They were short of trained investigators. They sent me to Corps of Military Police Depot at Mytchett. Two weeks to learn to march, salute, and be lectured on military law and court-martial routines. That's all I got. I came straight out here."

"I see."

Cutler became defensive. "What chance do I stand? What chance would anyone stand? They can't find him with radio detectors. They don't think he's one of the refugees. They've exhausted all the usual lines of investigation." Cutler was speaking frankly in a way he hadn't spoken to anyone for a long time. You could speak like that to a man you'd never see again. "It's a strange town, full of Arabs. This place they're sending me to: Bab-el-Hadid barracks—there's no one there. . . . I mean there are no names I recognize, and I know the names of all the good coppers. They're all soldiers." He said it disgustedly; he didn't think much of the army. "Conscripts . . . a couple of lawyers. There are no real policemen there at all; that's my impression, anyway. And I don't even speak the language. Arabic: just a lot of gibberish. How can I take a statement or do anything?" Very slowly and carefully Cutler swung his legs around so he could put his feet back on the floor again. He leaned forward and sighed. He seemed to feel a bit better. But Ross could see that having bared his heart to a stranger, Cutler now regretted it.

"So why did they send for you?" said Ross.

"You know what the army's like. I'm a detective; that's all they know. For the top brass, detectives are like gunners or bakers or sheet-metal workers. One is much like the other. They don't understand that investigation is an art."

"Yes. In the army, you're just a number," said Ross.

"They think finding spies is like finding thieves or finding lost wallets. It's no good trying to tell them different. These army people think they know it all." A sudden thought struck him. "Not a regular, are you?"

"No."

"No, of course not. What did you do before the war?"

"I was in the theater."

"Actor?"

"I wanted to be an actor. But I settled for stage managing. Before that I was a clerk in a solicitor's office."

"An actor. Everyone's an actor, I can tell you that from personal experience," said Cutler. He suddenly grimaced again and rubbed his arms, as if at a sudden pain. "But they don't know that. . . . Jesus! Jesus!" and then, more quietly, "That chicken must have been off." His voice had become very hoarse. "Listen, laddie. . . . Oh, my God!" He'd hunched his shoulders very small and pulled up his feet from the floor, like an old woman frightened of a mouse. Then he hugged himself; with his mouth half open, he dribbled saliva and let out a series of little moaning sounds.

Jimmy Ross sat there watching him. Was it a heart attack? He didn't know what to do. There was no one to whom he could go for assistance; they had kept apart from the other passengers. "Shall I pull the emergency cord?" Cutler didn't seem to hear him. Ross looked up, but there was no emergency cord.

Cutler's eyes had opened very wide. "I think I need . . ." He was hugging himself very tightly and swaying from side to side. All the spirit had gone out of him. There was none of the prisoner-and-guard relationship now; he was a supplicant. It was pitiful to see him so crushed. "Don't run away."

"I won't run away."

"I need a doctor. . . ."

Ross stood up to lean over him.

"Awwww!"

Hands still cuffed together, Ross reached out to him. By that time it was too late. The policeman toppled slightly, his forehead banged against the woodwork with a sharp crack, and then his head settled back against the window. His eyes were staring, and his face was colored green by the light coming through the linen blind.

Ross held him by the sleeve and stopped him from falling over completely. Hands still cuffed, he touched Cutler's forehead. It was cold and clammy, the way they always described it in detective stories. Cutler's eyes remained wide open. The dead man looked very old and small.

Suddenly Ross stopped feeling sorry. He felt a pang of fear. They would say he'd done it, he'd murdered this military policeman: Captain Cutler. They'd say he'd fed him poison or hit him the way he'd hit that cowardly bastard he'd killed. He tried to still his fears, telling himself that they couldn't hang you twice. Telling himself he'd look forward to seeing their faces when they found him with a corpse. It was no good; he was scared.

He stared down at the handcuffs. His wrists had become chafed. He might as well unlock them. That was the first thing to do, and then perhaps he'd get help. Cutler kept the key in his right-side jacket pocket, and it was easy to find. There were other keys on the same ring, including the little keys to Cutler's other luggage that was in the baggage car. He rubbed his wrists. It was good to get the cuffs off. Cutler had been decent enough about the handcuffing. One couldn't blame a man for taking precautions with a murderer.

With the handcuffs removed, Jimmy Ross felt different. He juggled the keys in the palm of his hand and on an impulse unlocked Cutler's leather bag and opened it. There were papers there: official papers. Ross wanted to see what the authorities had written about his case.

It was amazing what people carried around with them: a bottle of shampoo, a silver locket with the photo of an older woman, a silver-backed hairbrush, and a letter from a Glasgow branch of the Royal Bank of Scotland acknowledging that he'd closed his mother's account with them. It was dated three months before. Now that the mail from Britain went around Africa, it was old by the time it arrived. There was a green cardboard file of papers about Cutler's job in Cairo. "Albert George Cutler . . . to become a major with effect the first December 1941." So the new job brought him promotion too. Acting and unpaid, of course; promotions were usually like that, as he knew from working in the orderly room. But a major: a major was somebody.

He looked at the other papers in the case, but he could find nothing about himself. Travel warrant, movement order, a brown envelope containing six big white five-pound notes and seven one-pound notes. A tiny handyman's diary with tooled leather cover and a neat little pencil in a holder in its spine. Then he found the amazing identity pass that all the special investigation staff carried, a pink-colored SIB warrant card. He'd heard rumors about these passes, but he didn't think he'd ever hold one in his hands. It was a carte blanche. The rights accorded the bearer of the pass were all-embracing. Captain Cutler could wear any uniform or civilian clothes he chose, assume any rank, go anywhere, and do anything he wished.

A pass like this would be worth a thousand pounds on the black market. He looked at the photograph of Cutler. It was a poor one, hurriedly snapped by some conscripted photographer and insufficiently fixed so that the print was already turning yellow. It was undoubtedly Cutler, but it could have been any one of a thousand other men.

It was then that the thought came to him that he could pass himself off as Cutler. Cutler's hair was described as straight and Ross's hair was wavy, but with short army haircuts there was little difference to be seen. When alive Cutler had been red complexioned, while Ross was tanned and more healthy looking. But the black-and-white photograph revealed nothing of this. Their heights were different, Cutler shorter by two inches, but it seemed unlikely that anyone would approach him with a tape measure and check it out. He stood up and looked in the little mirror and held in view the photo to compare it. It was not a really close likeness, but how many people asked a military police major to prove his identity? Not many.

Then his heart sank as he realized that the clothes would give them away. He'd have to arrive wearing the white linen suit.

Changing clothes with a corpse would be too much; he couldn't go through with that. He opened Cutler's other bag. It was a fine green canvas bag of the sort that equipped safaris. Inside, right at the top, was the pair of white canvas trousers. Ross made sure that the blinds were down and then he changed into the trousers. Damn! They were a couple of inches too short.

Then he had another idea. He'd get off the train in his corporal's uniform and use the SIB pass. But that would leave the corpse wearing mufti. Would they believe an army corporal would arrive in civilian clothes? Why not? They'd arrested Ross in the corporal's uniform he was wearing. Had he been wearing a civilian suit, they would not have equipped him with a uniform for the journey, would they?

He looked at himself again. Certainly those white trousers would not do. With an overcoat he might have been able to let the waist of the trousers go low enough for them to look normal. But without an overcoat he'd look like a circus clown. Shit! He could have sobbed with frustration.

Well, it was the corporal's uniform or nothing. He looked at himself in the little mirror and tried imitating Cutler's Glasgow accent. It wasn't difficult. To his reflection he said, "This is the chance you've always prayed for, Jimmy. The star has collapsed and you're going on in his place. Just make sure you get your bloody lines right."

It was worth a try. But he wouldn't need the voice. All he wanted to do was just get off the train and disappear into the crowd. He'd find someplace to hide for a few days. Then he'd figure out where to go. In a big town like Cairo he'd have a chance to get clear away. Rumor said the town was alive with military criminals and deserters and black-market crooks. What about money? If he could find some little army unit in the back of beyond, he'd bowl in and ask for a casual pay parade. He knew how that was done; transient personnel were always wanting pay. Meanwhile, he had nearly forty pounds. In a place like Cairo that would be enough for a week or two: maybe a month. He'd have to find a hotel. Such places as the YMCA and the hostels and other institutions were regularly checked for deserters. The real trouble would be the railway station and getting past the military police patrols. Those red-capped bastards hung around stations like wasps around a jam jar. He had Cutler's pass, but would they believe he was a SIB officer? More likely they'd believe he was a corporal without a leave pass.

He sat down and tried to think objectively. When he looked up he was startled to find the dead eyes of Cutler staring straight at him. He reached out and gently touched his face, half expecting the dead man to smile or speak. But Cutler was dead, very dead. Damn him! Jimmy Ross got up and went to another seat. He had to think.

About five minutes later he started. He had to be very methodical. First he would empty his own pockets, and then he would empty Cutler's pockets. They had to completely change identity. Don't forget the signet ring his mother had given him; it would be a shame to lose it but it might be convincing. He'd have to strip the body. He must look inside shirts and socks for name tapes and laundry labels too. Officers didn't do their own washing: they were likely to have their names on every last thing. There was an Agatha Christie yarn in which the laundry label was the most incriminating clue. One slip could bring disaster.

As the train clattered over the points to come into Cairo station, Ross undid the heavy leather strap that lowered the window. Everyone else on the train seemed to have the same idea. There were heads bobbing from every compartment. The smell of the engine smoke was strong but not so powerful as to conceal the smell of the city itself. Other cities smelled of beer or garlic or stale tobacco. Cairo's characteristic smell was none of those. Here was a more intriguing mix: jasmine flowers, spices, sewage, burning charcoal, and desert dust. Ross leaned forward to see better.

He need not have bothered. They would have found the compartment; they were looking for the distinctive RESERVED signs. There were two military policemen complete with red-topped caps and beautifully blancoed webbing belts and revolver holsters. With them was a captain wearing his best uniform: starched shirt, knitted tie, and a smart peaked cap. A military police officer! The only other time he'd ever seen one of those was when he was formally arrested.

It was the officer who noticed Ross leaning out of the window of the train and called to him. "Major Cutler! Major Cutler!"

The train came to a complete halt with a great burst of steam and the shriek of applied brakes. The sounds echoed within the great hall.

"Major Cutler?" The officer didn't know whether to salute this man in corporal's uniform.

"Yes. I'm Cutler. An investigation. I haven't had a chance to change," said Ross, as casually as he could. He was nervous; could they hear it in his voice? "I'm stuck with this uniform for the time being." He wondered whether he should bring out his identity papers but decided that doing so might look odd. He hadn't reckoned on anyone's coming to meet him. It had given him a jolt.

"Good journey, sir? I'm Captain Marker, your number one." Marker smiled. He'd heard that some of these civvy detectives liked to demonstrate their eccentricities. He supposed that wearing "other ranks" uniforms was one of them. He realized his new master might take some getting used to.

Jimmy Ross stayed at the window without opening the train door. "We've got a problem, Marker. I've got a prisoner here. He's been taken sick."

"We'll take care of that, sir."

"Very sick," said Ross hastily. "You're going to need a stretcher. He was taken ill during the journey." With Marker still looking up at him quizzically, Ross improvised. "His heart, I think. He told me he'd had heart trouble, but I didn't realize how bad he was."

Marker stepped up on the running board of the train and bent his head to see the figure hunched in his corner seat. Civilian clothes: a white linen suit. Why did these deserters always want to get into civilian clothes? Khaki was the best protective coloring. Then Marker looked at his new boss. For a moment he was wondering if he'd beaten the prisoner. There was no blood or marks anywhere to be seen, but men who beat prisoners make sure there is no such evidence.

Ross saw what he was thinking. "Nothing like that, Captain Marker. I don't hit handcuffed men. Anyway, he's been a perfect prisoner. I don't want the army blamed for ill-treating him. I think we should do it all according to the rule book. Get him on a stretcher and get him to hospital for examination."

"There's no need for you to be concerned with that, sir." Marker turned to one of his MPs. "One of you stay with the prisoner. The other, go and phone the hospital."

"He's still handcuffed," said Ross, who'd put the steel cuffs on the dead man's wrists to reinforce his identity as the prisoner. "You'll need the key."

"Just leave it to my coppers," said Marker, taking it from him and passing it to the remaining red cap. "We'd better hurry along and sort out your baggage. The thieves in this town can whisk a ten-ton truck into thin air and then come back for the logbook." Marker looked at him; Ross smiled.

Ten billion particles of dust in the air picked up the light of the dying sun that afternoon, so that the slanting beams gleamed like bars of gold. So did the smoke and steam and the back-lit figures hurrying in all directions. Even Marker was struck by the scene.

"They call it the city of gold," he said. There was another

train departing. It shrieked and whistled in the background while crowds of soldiers and officers were fussing around the mountains of kit bags and boxes and steamer trunks that were piling up high on the platforms.

"Yes, I used to know a poem about it," said Ross. "A wonderful poem."

"A poem?" Marker was surprised to hear that this man was a devotee of poetry. In fact he was astonished to learn that any SIB major, particularly one who'd risen to this position through the ranks of the Glasgow force, would like any poem. "Which one was that, sir?"

Ross was suddenly embarrassed. "Oh, I don't remember exactly. Something about Cairo's buildings and mud huts looking like the beaten gold the thieves plunder from the ancient tombs." He'd been about to recite the poem, but suddenly the life was knocked out of him as he remembered that his own kit bag was there too. His first impulse was to ignore it, but then it would go to Lost Luggage and they'd track it back to a prisoner named James Ross. What should he do?

"I should have brought three men," said Marker apologetically as they stood near the baggage car, looking at the luggage. "I wasn't calculating on us having to sort out your own gear."

"Just one more bag," said Ross. "Green canvas, with a leather strap round it. There it is." Then he saw his kit bag. Luckily it had suffered wear and tear over the months since his enlistment. The stenciled name ROSS and his regimental number had faded. "And the brown kit bag."

"Porter," called Marker to a native with a trolley. "Bring these bags." He kicked them with his toe. "Follow us." To his superior he explained, "You must always get one with a metal badge and remember his number." He politely took Cutler's leather briefcase. "It's not worth bringing a car here," explained Marker. "We're in the Bab-el-Hadid barracks. It's just across the midan."

Marker kept walking, out through the ticket barrier and

across the crowded concourse and the station forecourt. The porter followed. Once outside the station, there was all the bustle of a big city. It was the sort of day that Europeans relished. It was winter, the air was silky, and the sun was going down in a hazy blue sky.

So this was Cairo. Ross was looking around for a way of escape but Marker was determined to play the perfect subordinate. "You'll find you've got a pretty good team," said Marker. "And what a brief! Go anywhere, interrogate anyone, and arrest almost anyone. 'You're a sort of British Gestapo,' the brigadier told us the other day. The brigadier's a decent old cove too; you'll like him. He'll support you to the end. All you have to worry about is catching Rommel's spy."

Ross grunted his affirmation.

Marker froze. Suddenly he realized that this probably wasn't the way the army treated a newly arrived superior. And not the way to describe a brigadier. Marker had been junior partner in a law office before volunteering for the army. It was the way he treated his colleagues back home, but perhaps this fellow Cutler was expecting something more formal and military.

They walked on in silence, brushing aside hordes of people. All of them seemed to be selling something. They brandished trays upon which were arrayed shoelaces, flyswatters, sweet cakes, pencils, and guidebooks. The great open space before the station was alive with peddlers. And there was Englishness too: little trees, neat little patches of flowers, and even green grass.

"That's the barracks," said Marker. "Not far now."

In the distance, Ross saw a grim-looking crusader castle of ocher-colored stone. The low rays of the sun caught the sandstone tower so that it too gleamed like gold.

Ross looked around. He didn't want to go into the barracks; he wanted to get away. There were too many policemen in evidence for him to run. Half a dozen men of the Cairo force came riding past, mounted on well-groomed horses. The British army's policemen were not to be seen on horses. With their red-topped peaked caps they stood in pairs, feet lightly apart and hands loosely clasped behind their backs. They were everywhere, and all of them were armed.

Back at the train compartment, the two MPs were waiting for the doctor to arrive. The elder of the two men assumed seniority. He wore World War I ribbons on his chest. He'd leaned into the compartment and spoken to the dead man a couple of times and got no response. Now he said, "Dead."

"Are you sure?"

"Stone cold. In France I saw more dead men than you could count."

"What will we do?"

"Do? Nothing. The officer says he's sick; he's sick. Let the doctor decide he's dead. That's what he's paid for, ain't it?"

He got down from the compartment, and they both stood alongside the open train door and waited.

The younger red cap did not relish the prospect of moving the body. He changed the subject and said to his companion, "I reckon that's the one they've sent to take over from the major with the big walrus mustache."

"Well, that bastard lost a pip and was booted out to Aden or somewhere."

They watched a civilian coming through the crowd. They hoped it might be the doctor, but when he stopped for a moment at the sight of the snake charmers they knew it couldn't be. Only tourists and newcomers stopped to see the magicians and snake charmers and acrobats. "I heard the new bloke was coming today. Some sort of detective from Blighty, according to what the rumors say."

"Well, that one won't last long," said the elder man. "He obviously doesn't know Cairo from a hole in the ground. How's he going to start finding a bloody spy here?"

"Nice disguise, though."

"The corporal's uniform?"

"Yes, the corporal stunt."

"You get the idea, don't you?" said the elder man bitterly. "If Captain Marker hadn't brought us over here to sort him out, that bastard would have ambled over to the barracks, and if he'd got through improperly dressed and no one asking him for his leave pass, we'd all be for the high jump for dereliction of duty and suchlike."

"I suppose. Where's that bloody doctor?" said the young one. He'd phoned. "They said straightaway. We're back on duty tonight again, aren't we?"

"Too right. It's El Birkeh tonight, my old pal. I hope you're feeling up to it."

"I dread that rotten poxy place. It stinks. I've asked to go back on traffic duties. I'm sick of patrolling whorehouses."

Ross had been completely accepted in his corporal's uniform. Marker showed no suspicion at all. But there just seemed to be no way of escaping his amiable friendliness.

When they got to the gate of Bab-el-Hadid barracks there was an armed sentry there. The porter dumped the bags and Marker paid him off. Ross offered him his identity card but the sentry gave it no attention. His eyes were staring straight ahead as he gave the two men a punctilious salute.

"The staff all know you are coming," explained Marker. He flipped open the special card issued by SIB Middle East, so that his superior saw it. "Your pass is no use to you here. We don't let people in and out with ordinary passes and so forth, not even SIB people. We have our own identity cards. I think we should get you photographed today, sir, if you can spare the time. It's difficult to keep the sentries on their toes unless we set an example."

"Yes, of course," said Ross.

"And then you will have your new pass and identity document tomorrow." He led the way up the stone steps.

"Very efficient," said Ross. His voice echoed. This place was just like an ancient castle, but no doubt the coolness of the stone would be welcome when summer came.

Marker didn't respond to the compliment. "The routine is to close all Cairo offices between one P.M. and five P.M. I've asked your staff to be at their desks early. I thought you might like to meet them. Then you could cut away and see your quarters."

"I'll take your advice, Marker."

"Unless you want to go through the files, sir. I told your clerk—if you decide to keep the same clerk as your predecessor—to have all current files ready for you to examine. Or I can take you through them verbally."

"Are you always like this, Marker?"

"Like what, sir?"

"Super bloody efficient."

Marker looked at him, trying to decide if he was being sarcastic. He couldn't tell. This new man knew how to keep an inscrutable face. "In civvy street I worked for myself, sir."

"You're beginning to give me an inferiority complex, Marker. Do you know that?"

"I'm sorry, sir." How much was Major Cutler joking? It was hard to know. They were walking along the open balcony overlooking the parade ground. A dozen red caps were being paraded and inspected before going off on their patrols through the streets of the town.

"This way, sir. This is your office."

The department that Cutler had been assigned to take over had its offices on this floor. This part of the building was only one room deep. The offices that were reached from the balcony overlooked the midan and the railway station beyond it.

They were all lined up waiting for him: privates, corporals, and a sergeant plus four radio room staff and their corporal in charge. There was even a cunning-looking old soldier who was assigned to be his clerk.

"Organize a photographer right away," said Marker to one

of the clerks. "Identity photo for the major, double quick."

"We'll get to know each other soon enough," said Ross, trying to remember other clichés he'd come across during his duties in the orderly room. Marker introduced each of them and described their duties, their accomplishments, and, where applicable, their previously held civilian jobs. None of them were ex-policemen. Poor old Cutler had guessed right about that.

"Is that everyone?"

Marker hesitated.

"Well, is it?" said Ross.

"There is one member of your staff not here yet," said Marker. "A female clerk: Alice Stanhope. I'm sure she'll be here any minute."

"Where is she?"

"She went to see her mother in Alexandria."

"Is she sick?"

"Her mother? No. No, not as far as I know."

"Why isn't she at work then?"

Marker hesitated. It was difficult to explain about Alice Stanhope. "Her mother . . . that is to say, her family are good friends with the brigadier. That's really how she came to be working here."

"I see."

"Oh, don't get me wrong, sir. Alice Stanhope is a highly intelligent young woman. She speaks several languages and knows more about this wretched country than any other European I've met."

"But?"

"Well, her mother knows everyone. I mean everyone." He went to the door and looked over the balcony. Then he came back. "Yes, I thought that was her car. It's an MG sports car, I recognized the sound of the engine."

"Do you mean to say she parks her car on the parade ground?" said Ross incredulously.

"Her mother arranged it with the brigadier," said Marker. In a way Marker enjoyed explaining the situation to his boss, just to watch his face.

"I can't wait to meet her," said Ross.

"You won't be disappointed," said Captain Marker.

He guessed of course that the big surprise was yet to come, so he was watching very carefully when Alice Stanhope came down the exterior balcony and swung in through the door. "I'm so sorry I'm late, sir," she said. Then, remembering she should have saluted, she came to attention and put her hat back on.

"That's quite all right," said Ross. Until that moment he'd firmly intended to leave his quarters that evening and disappear, thanking his lucky stars for preserving him. Now his plans, and indeed his life, changed. He would have to come back to the office tomorrow.

Alice Stanhope was the most beautiful woman he had ever seen. He must see her again, if only just once.

2

The region called El Birkeh, where so many of Cairo's brothels were found, stretched from the railway station almost to Ezbekiya Gardens. This forbidden area—marked OUT OF BOUNDS by means of circular signs bearing a black cross—was constantly patrolled by red-capped military policemen. Its main streets were Clot Bey, named after a physician who did notable work on venereal disease, and Wagh El Birkeh, after which the whole Birkeh district was named. For centuries this pleasure district had been spoken of with wonder throughout the Arab world, from Casablanca to Zanzibar.

The extreme western edge of El Birkeh was a maze of narrow alleys, twisting and turning between low mud-brick buildings. Day and night it was always populous, rowdy, and predatory. Once musicians, magicians, soothsayers, and dancers had plied their trades along with the whores. Now, in January 1942, the cabarets, peep shows, and whores predominated. Women of all colors, all sizes, all shapes, and all nationalities were to be had here. There were women for the rich and women for the poor. They sat on their tiny balconies calling down to men in the streets below. They were available in accommodations that varied from curtained alcoves in mud-wall huts to ornate rooms in palatial houses.

One of the more expensive establishments in El Birkeh was

the brothel the soldiers called Lady Fitzherbert's, after the heroine in a ribald army song. The woman they called Lady Fitz was a fifty-year-old Greek dentist who'd arrived in Cairo penniless in 1939. The war, and the buildup of the army, was making her rich. She had already become one of the most influential people in Cairo. Lady Fitz ran her establishment with all the managerial skills of a Swiss hotelier. She sent gold coins to the ministers and provided the choicest young women for the Cairo police inspectors and gallons of whisky for the British red caps.

It was a cardinal rule with Lady Fitz that she did business only with those she knew. She knew the two soldiers who were using one of her best upstairs rooms. They came regularly. She knew them as Sergeant Smith and Sergeant Percy. What their real names were she did not care; the money they paid was genuine and they never gave her any trouble. She looked at her watch. The expensive Longines wristwatch was one of her few concessions to luxury, for her hair was simply combed, her makeup minimal, her dark blue cotton dress simple, and her flat-heeled shoes purchased in the souk. It was almost time; she made a signal to one of her girls.

The two soldiers had been upstairs for almost an hour. Soon Lady Fitz would send the girl up to them. She was a beautiful half-Tunisian child who didn't know the date of her own birth. She knew only that all her family had been killed during the fighting in Sidi Barrani in December 1940. From there she had walked about 350 miles to Cairo. Lady Fitz had found her begging outside the great al Azhar mosque. She'd looked after her well and was saving her for someone special, which meant someone who could pay.

Sergeant Percy always paid for everything well in advance, and without argument or complaint. Percy was different from all the others. He wore South African badges, but she was not convinced that he was from South Africa. She didn't inquire. The important thing to her was that he was quiet, sober, and polite. He seldom smiled, never made a joke, and always wanted a different girl. It was the sort of behavior that Lady Fitz expected of men, and she liked him. The other one, Smith, was sober too but fat, flashy, and arrogant and too ready with sarcastic jokes. He ordered everyone around as though they were his subordinates, but for Lady Fitz his worst fault was in showing a complete indifference to her girls. Sometimes she wondered whether he was a homosexual. She could have offered him boys, men, anything he wanted, but he showed no interest in her offerings. She'd never fathomed him.

"Get ready now," she told the girl. "Prepare the tea. It will soon be time to go to them. Do exactly as I told you."

The girl had that earnest expression with which many children face the world of grown-ups. She looked at Lady Fitz and nodded solemnly.

The rough surfaces of the khaki uniforms the two soldiers wore, and even their tanned flesh, was made into gold by the light of the oil lamp. The big brass bedstead glinted like gold, and across it a lace shawl had been draped. The polished metal fittings on the chest of drawers glittered, and the flame of the oil lamp was seen again in the swiveled vanity mirror that reflected the room. To a casual observer they could have been old friends getting drunk together, but a closer look would reveal the sort of tension that comes from arguing and bargaining, for when the two men met here it was for business, not for pleasure. A brothel provides a discreet rendezvous for men who want their meetings to remain secret.

Sergeant Smith was on the bed. At first his feet had been resting on the large oriental carpet but, having stubbed out his cigarette, he untied his laces, eased off his boots, and swung his stockinged feet up onto the bed. "Ahh!" he said, wriggling his toes and delighting in the feeling of resting full length on the freshly laundered bedding.

Smith was thirty-three years old. His cheerful face was made memorable by a waxed mustache, its ends twisted into sharp points. The Grenadier Guards drill sergeant who had taught him, and his recruit intake, to march had had a mustache like that, and Smith had immediately decided to grow one for the duration of the war.

Smith glanced at the mirror to see himself and the big bed reflected there, and then he sipped his glass of lemonade. On his eighteenth birthday he had promised his father he would never touch alcohol, and he had kept his promise. Even at his wedding he'd stuck to soft drinks. That was long ago. Now his wife and two daughters lived in the upstairs part of his mother-in-law's house near the big railway depot at Crewe in Cheshire, England. Although he missed his family, Smith did not brood about things he could not change. Before the war he'd worked for the railway as a senior storeroom clerk, and they were holding his job open for him. Meanwhile he was making a great deal of money, and his work did not entail exposure to enemy bombs, bullets, or shells. As Smith repeatedly said in his letters home, he was a very lucky man.

The other soldier, Percy, was sitting in a large wicker armchair. He was younger, twenty-seven years old, and exceptionally neat and tidy. He'd sewed on his buttons, the South African shoulder flashes, and the white coiled-snake unit badges with the same meticulous care that he serviced the engine of his truck and oiled the guns he used. The tight webbing belt he wore was perfectly brushed, and its brasswork was fastidiously polished so as to leave no stains on the webbing. The only jarring note in Percy's uniformed appearance was the dagger attached to his belt. It was a German army trench knife. Some people said that Percy had killed its previous owner.

Percy was not his real name. He'd adopted the name Percy on the battlefield when he deserted. That's why he liked to call it his nom de guerre. He was very adaptable. He told anyone interested that he had made the transition from civilian to soldier by the same sort of effort that he'd devoted to getting good exam results at university. Percy's whole life had been marked by his willingness to accept new circumstances and adapt to them. One of Percy's lecturers had said that *Homo sapiens* survived and came to control the planet only because he'd adapted more completely and more quickly than had other species to changing climates and environments. Percy took that lesson to heart.

Now he looked at Sergeant Smith without admiration. Smith's hair was dark, wavy, and somewhat disheveled; Percy's hair was fair, bleached by the sun, and cut short in military style. The sergeant was at least ten pounds overweight; Percy was slim and athletic. Percy's khaki shirt was starched and ironed; Smith's shirt was marked by a few drips of lemonade. For Smith the abundance of native labor meant he could change his shirt as many times as he liked, and such marks and stains were of no importance. But Percy was fussy about his clothes and often ironed them himself.

There had been a long silence. Sergeant Smith said, "All good things come to an end, Percy." And as if savoring his own keen wit he gave a brief smile.

"It is your loss," said Percy. His voice was throaty, and his English had that hard accent that was not unlike the one that distinguished many of the South Africans, especially the ones from the farms. "I thought a family man like you would want a nest egg for after the war." He drank some beer. It was local beer, little more than chilled colored water, but that suited him. He had to keep a clear head.

"Who told you I was a family man?" said Smith, as though a dark secret had been unearthed.

"It was a manner of speaking," said Percy. He was unruffled and his cane armchair creaked as he sat well back in it, his legs extended in front of him as if he had not a care in the world.

"You don't mind, then?"

Percy put his hand into his shirt. After unbuttoning a secret pocket, which he'd sewn there, he brandished a bundle of paper money. "What is it we owe you, nine hundred Egyptian? I have it written down somewhere."

"What's it matter how much money?" said Smith, and a note of anxiety came into his voice. "I can't get the bloody stuff back to England. I'm up to my ears in Egyptian money. The sergeant in the cashier's office promised to fix it, but suddenly he's scared shitless."

"Is that the problem? Getting the money back to England?" Percy leaned forward and passed the money to Smith.

Smith took it. "I told you. I don't want to do any more deals. We've got a new young officer. Instead of just signing the inventory on the dotted line, he wants to see everything he's signing for." Smith shuffled the money in his hands, as though counting it. Then he slipped it inside his paybook, but he didn't put it away. He shuffled the money around in the pages of his paybook as if comparing the two, weighing the bundle of money as if still trying to make up his mind.

"Because I might be able to get your money to England."

Smith looked up suddenly. "Are you listening to me, you prick? Every item! My officer wants to see every item before he signs. If he goes raking through all my stores, he'll soon discover that half the stuff is missing."

"But that is no trouble. You can write it off as damaged or lost to enemy action or beyond local repair or whatever."

Smith was angry now. "Not tons and tons and bloody tons of 'warlike stores' . . . not in the week or so I've got before he signs the inventory!"

"Pull yourself together, Smith!"

"Don't tell me to pull myself together, you ugly little bastard. I just don't want to do business with you people, that's at the root of it. I don't trust you. Where is all this stuff going? Who are you selling it to?" He sniffed and pushed out his legs on the bed. "South African, are you? You sound like a bloody German to me." He still held the money on his lap, holding it tightly enough to reveal that he was not as indifferent to it as he pretended.

Percy said nothing.

Percy's silence made Smith more angry. He thought he saw a look of amused contempt on the younger man's face. For two pins he'd pick up this fellow bodily and shake the life out of him. Although Smith's affluence had encouraged him to put on weight, it was not so long since he'd been a heavyweight on the railway boxing team. On one memorable occasion he'd knocked out the reigning champion from the locomotive works. The loco men were big brawny fellows, and this one had weighed in seven pounds heavier than Smith.

"Let me tell you a little secret," Smith said. "Last time we met, I was a little late getting here, remember? The reason being, I was taking a closer look at that truck of yours. I took a note of the engine number. You changed the license plate number, but you didn't think of the engine number, did you? Back at the depot I got my corporal to look that number up in the records. Stolen: well, I expected that. When stolen it was loaded with small generators. Generators are like gold dust round here, everyone knows that. But what I wasn't ready for was hearing that the driver was killed, murdered; the truck ran right over him." He looked Percy full in the eyes. "Run over! The death certificate said the cause of death was 'accidental,' but no one explained how he came to lay himself down in the road and run over himself. Any ideas?"

Percy made no response.

Smith bared his teeth. "Now perhaps you see why I don't want to do any more business with you."

"You took a long time deciding," said Percy. The variety of objections that Smith had offered had still not convinced Percy; there was something else. "What is your real reason? Forget the bullshit for a minute or two. Tell me the real reason."

Smith gritted his teeth. He'd been bursting to tell the real reason, and now he could no longer resist it. "You're selling all this gear to the Jews, aren't you?" His smile was fixed and challenging.

"Jews?"

"Come off it, you little bastard. This stuff is all going to the Jew boys in Palestine. They're getting ready for the big show-down with the Arabs. That's where the money is, and you lot know where the dough's to be got." He looked down at the notes and said it again. "You know where the money is, all right. What I get is probably just a spit in the ocean."

Percy looked at him soberly and without expression.

"I was stationed in bloody Haifa, mate," Smith said. "I know what they are up to. Those Jews are worse than the bloody Arabs. They'll skin you alive for a handful of small change. Don't lie to me; I've heard them all. One of my mates was beaten up by a gang of them—"

There was a tentative knock at the door. "Come in!" called Percy. Now was the time when Percy had to make his decision. Could Smith be made to see reason, or had he gone off the rails? A malicious blabbermouth could betray them all.

The young Tunisian girl came in with a brass tray. On it was a pot of mint tea and a selection of small oriental pastries, over which rose water and thin dribbles of honey had been poured. She wore ornamental slippers and a brightly patterned cotton cloth that was tucked in and held only by the shape of her body. She eyed the two men with placid curiosity. She did not seem frightened or intimidated. Working for Lady Fitz had shown her men in all their many moods and tempers. It would be hard to surprise her. She put the tray on the bedside table and poured two cups of tea. She gave one to Percy. He nodded to her, and she gave a slight movement of the head that acknowledged his signal. Then she offered the other cup of tea to Smith, wafting the steam toward him with the side of her hand, inviting him to smell the fragrance of the mint. Smith sniffed it as he was ex-pected to do, keeping his feet stretched out on the bed and letting his head relax against the pillow.

"I think she likes you," said Percy. "Why not take a little tumble with her? It will put you in a better mood. We will talk again later." He got up as if to leave the two of them in privacy.

"No, no. Stay where you are," said Smith, but Percy could detect a lack of resolution in his voice.

The girl lightly stroked Smith's arm and walked her fingers across his body. Smith shivered. "What is your secret, Smith? She wants to get into bed with you, you can see she does."

The bed creaked as Smith laboriously sat up on it, brushing the girl's hand away. "You never give up, do you, Percy?"

"What are you talking about? Have you never had the full treatment at Lady Fitz?" said Percy with good-natured interest. "It is not the hurried gallop you are used to back home. This girl will anoint you with perfumed oils, smoke a little hashish with you to get you into the right mood, and afterward she will bathe you. An hour in paradise: this is the way it is done in the East. You should try it. By God, she is a beautiful young creature!"

"She's just a kid. She can't be more than fifteen."

"In a country where life expectancy is thirty years, fifteen is middle-aged. Look at her face; she wants you."

"And she must have cost you a packet," said Smith.

Undaunted by Smith's words of rejection, the girl had opened his shirt and put her hand against his chest. Smith sat very still. His good sense told him that the behavior of the girl was something of Percy's devising, but his ego, fed by his desire, was overcoming that belief. He could smell the sweet lotions that the girl had used. Temptation, after months of celibacy, was fast overwhelming him.

Percy stepped over to the tray and helped himself to a pastry. "You cannot get this Turkish delight anywhere but Cairo," he said conversationally. He held it up to show Smith: dusted with powdered sugar, it shone in the lamplight. Percy popped it into his mouth and chewed it with studied relish.

As if following this exchange, the young girl got a cube from the same plate and brought it close to Smith's lips. She'd completely unbuttoned his shirt to expose his hairy chest, and now with her left hand she stroked him gently.

"Open your mouth and shut your eyes, you lucky bastard," said Percy amiably.

Smith could smell the rose water and taste the dusted sugar as he bit down hard upon what turned out to be a cube of softened mutton fat. "Ugh!" But the tepid fat clung to his teeth. He could not scream. It clogged his mouth and tongue and would not budge. Before he could spit it out he felt a strong hand clamped across his face. Unable to breathe through his mouth, he snorted violently like a frightened horse.

"*Imshi!*" said Percy.

The girl drew back. As she slid aside from the reclining figure, Percy brought a dagger down fiercely into Smith's bared chest. Smith gave a mighty heave, but with his heart pierced the violent movement served only to pump blood and hasten his end. Still pressing down on the thrashing body, Percy glanced at the girl. She held her hand to her face, palm outward, splaying her fingers wide so that she could see between them. Her lips were moving, and he wondered if she would scream. Even if she did, it would not matter in a place like this, where screams and groans and gasps were commonplace.

But she did not scream. She watched the scene from behind her spread fingers as Percy twisted the knife a little, keeping his other hand pressing down upon Smith's face.

Expiring through his nose, the dying man arched his trunk, gave one heave, and vomited fiercely through Percy's fingers but did not break free. One leg shook violently, scattering the money across the bed. He writhed and seemed to shrink and then was still. Percy waited a minute or two before letting go of him. For a moment he stood looking down at the body. The bedding was marked by blood and smelly vomit. Dozens of tiny splashes of blood made a pattern on the bed cover, the pillows, and the wall. His military training had taught him to kill sentries quickly and silently, but they'd given no advice about not leaving a mess behind. He wondered how much more blood would spurt if he removed the dagger. For the time being he left it there. As if reading his thought, the girl brought a towel and wrapped it around the handle of the dagger. Then she began to remove the pillows from the bed.

"As soon as I have gone, go quickly and get the men," he told her. They would know what to do. "Do you hear?" He recognized the splayed fingers and the other gestures she was making with her hand as a sign to give protection against the evil eye. She was moving her lips, soundlessly reciting verses from the Koran. He did not laugh at her; he felt like seeking the same sort of protection.

After a moment to catch his breath, he lifted Smith's heavy body from the bed and thankfully dumped it onto the carpet. He flapped the ends of the carpet over Smith's mortal remains.

At that moment the door opened. "All done, Percy, old bean?"

A slight young man was standing in the doorway. He was hatless, dressed in khaki shirt and officer's-style khaki gabardine trousers, without any sign of rank or unit. The tone of voice, accent, and confident manner were unmistakably the product of some exclusive school in England.

"It is done," said Percy, without looking at him. "He had cracked. He even checked the engine number of the truck. And he started on about the Jews. It was only a matter of time before he betrayed us."

Percy gathered together the money that littered the bed. He went through the bundle of Egyptian notes. There were flecks of blood on them, but money was money. He took a couple of notes from the bundle and held them out to the girl. She took them without a change of expression, tucked them away, and went on changing the bed cover. Irritated at the way she failed to thank him, Percy put the rest of the money back into his inner pocket.

"All for one and one for all," said the newcomer. He said it solemnly, as he might repeat on oath. Then: "Phew, what a smell!" He looked at the dead man and then at the young girl as she began to remove the soiled bedclothes. She lowered her eyes as she felt his gaze. "Wow! I see what you mean about the bint: what a lovely piece of ass." And then in a brisker voice he said, "Give me the cash, old boy. We mustn't forget that, must we?" He took it and stuffed it into his pocket without counting it. "Let's go. Mahmoud's men will do the rest."

═3═

At Cairo the water of the Nile divides to make the island of Gezira the coolest and most desirable residential area in the city. The moorings on the western side of the island had by 1942 become crowded with houseboats. They were mostly rented to visitors who liked the noisy parties and bohemian atmosphere. This too was part of the city of gold.

With a small effort of the imagination, even the brown shiny ripples in the sluggish waters of the river Nile became gilding on a dark bronze underlay. There was something golden about the music too: subtle, reedy Arab dissonances that came across the water mingled with the traffic and street cries and other sounds of the city to make a hum like that from a swarming beehive. Wartime Cairo *was* like a beehive, thought Peggy West: a golden beehive frantically active, dribbling with honey, and always ready with a thousand stings. It was an inclement habitat for any unprotected woman. Peggy had no other home; seeing the city like this, at night across the waters of the Nile, she felt lonely and afraid.

"My master will receive you soon, madam. May I bring you coffee?"

"Yes, please."

"*Sukkar ziada,* madam?" Only Cairo's wealthy residents could afford servants who spoke clear English. This one—Yusef—did, but he persisted in using Arabic phrases as if to test her.

"No, thank you, no sugar; *saada.*"

The servant stared at her and smiled insolently. He was very thin. His face was hard, with hollow cheeks and large brown eyes. He had a slight limp but was without the warped stance that is the product of malnourishment. Once he must have been very handsome. Now a broken nose marred the servant's looks, giving to his unsmiling face a fierceness that did not reassure her.

She had told him on previous visits to the houseboat that she didn't like the sweet coffee they always served to women. But women counted for nothing in Egypt. Girl children were unwanted. Women wore the veil, held their tongues, and kept out of sight; women belonged to their husbands and took sweet coffee. He bowed his head to acknowledge her and soon brought coffee for her. It was in a tiny china cup decorated with flowers. He placed it on a brass tray that formed the top of the side table where she was sitting.

"The master will not keep you waiting much longer," he said. He bowed again and departed without waiting for a reply. There was nothing to be said. Women—even educated European women like Peggy West, a highly respected nursing sister at the Base Hospital—could not expect to be treated like men. When Peggy West visited the boat she often had to wait here on the upper deck and drink coffee. It was arranged like this; important men made people wait.

She picked up the coffee cup. Even before she put it to her lips she could smell the heavy sugar syrup with which it had been made. She swore and resolved to complain about the wretched man. But she drank it anyway as he knew she would. As she sipped it she stared at the river. Coming to the island over the Khedive Ismail bridge, she'd noticed that the old Semiramis Hotel was fully lit. The once grand Semiramis was now taken over as the headquarters of "British Troops in Egypt." The electric lights made the windows into yellow rectangles. Every room was lit; it was almost unprecedented for the British army to be working so late. Rommel was on the move again. The army that the British had chased to a standstill in the desert had suddenly revived itself and lunged forward. Cairo was in danger.

She buttoned her coat. There were rumbling sounds that might have been gunfire, and then a truck, with headlights on, went rattling over the nearby English Bridge and two more followed it as if trying to keep up. She recognized them as Morris Quads, curious-looking humpbacked vehicles used to tow 25-pounder field guns. The artillerymen were in a hurry, and they were heading for the Western Desert. Rommel's soldiers were rushing to meet them. No one could guess where the big battle would take place.

It was easy to sit here and fancy she could hear the gunfire or smell the desolate space that started only a few miles down the road, but that was the sort of silly imagining that newcomers were prone to: flashy English reporters and pink-faced officers straight out of school, who desperately wanted to become the heroes they'd so recently read about in their comic books.

Peggy always thought of her husband, Karl, when she came out here to see Solomon and collect her money. It was natural that she should; Solomon was a close friend of her husband, or so he said. She sighed as she thought about it. You could not depend upon anyone here to tell the truth. The army, the Arabs, and even the BBC all lied like troopers when it suited their purposes.

She'd lived in this part of the world for a long time. She'd proved to her own satisfaction that a young Englishwoman with an ordinary suburban background could work and wander in the same casual carefree style that men so frequently did. She knew the southern Mediterranean coast all the way to Tunis, where she'd first arrived, armed only with her nursing qualification and the promise of a job in a hospital supported by the funds of local European fruit farmers. Soon she discovered that an experienced nurse with a European certificate could get a job almost anywhere along that coast.

Even after she fell in love and got married, her traveling did not end. Her husband liked to joke about his Italian mother and Canadian father; that's how spaghetti with meatballs was invented, he said. Karl was an engineer working for an oil company. In the autumn of 1937, he had taken her on a long-delayed honeymoon in Cyrenaica. He had close friends there, and he spoke wonderful Italian. Little Italy, they called it. They'd celebrated with sweet local champagne and *paradiso* cake—made from almonds—for their wedding feast. The scenery was breathtaking: so green and beautiful, the Mediterranean had never been such a radiant blue as it was that day from the balcony outside their bedroom window. Seven glorious days, and then they'd driven their beloved V8 Ford all the way back to Cairo. Or almost back to Cairo. The poor old car had served them faithfully, but without warning it expired. Its gearbox gave out, and with great sadness they abandoned it. They lugged their suitcases to the nearest village—little more than a railway station and a dozen primitive dwellings—and drank chilled beer and untold cups of coffee while they waited five hours for the Cairo train.

They'd been so in love it had seemed like a heaven-sent opportunity to talk. They talked about everything in the world. She'd told Karl her whole life story: her loving and constantly worrying parents in England, her craving to travel. She remembered that stopover so vividly: the railway station at El Alamein, the flea-bitten spot where they'd spent half the night. That honeymoon was a long time ago: four, or was it five years? Now Karl was working out a five-year contract, assigned to one of the oil exploration teams that ranged through the deserts of Iraq. It was eighteen months since he'd last had leave. She wondered if Karl thought about her as much as she thought about him. He sent the money without fail; he must love her, surely? In some ways she had to be thankful. After marrying her, Karl had obtained a

British passport. Had they stayed in England he might now be in one of those trucks going up to the battlefront. She would have been worried sick. So many of the men who went to the desert would never come back. Sometimes she had nightmares in which she watched Karl being sewn together on the operating table.

She shivered. January was always the coldest month in Cairo's year. At night she had two blankets on her bed. She wondered why Solomon, the man she'd come to see, didn't live somewhere more comfortable and permanent. He had prevaricated about that when once she asked him. Solomon liked to call himself Solomon al-Masri—Solomon the Cairene or Solomon the Egyptian; the language made no distinction. It sounded like an assumed name, but so did many genuine ones. This man had an almost pathological obsession with secrecy. To arrange the first few visits to him she'd had to phone an Austrian dentist in Alexandria and say she needed treatment. She didn't object. She knew some men liked to cloak everything they did in mystery. Karl was like that. At first she'd thought he was keeping a mistress, but later she decided it was just the way he'd always behaved. Perhaps it was something to do with his upbringing; perhaps all men were like that when you wanted to know more about them.

She looked around her. Yellow lights from the boats moored along this stretch of riverbank made patterns on the water. One boat nearby had its windows open to let in the night air. Through them came loud voices, with posh English accents, and the sound of a scratchy record on a wind-up record player: Bing Crosby singing "Just a Gigolo."

She consulted her watch; it was almost midnight. She wondered how long Solomon would keep her waiting. There was someone with him. She knew that from the silver tray with its half-eaten sandwiches, used plates, and coffee cups that she'd spied in the galley on her way past. Judging by the remains it must have been a long session: negotiations of some sort. He'd told her he liked making deals. I was born in a bazaar, he'd said.

She didn't know whether he meant it literally, for he'd once told her his father had been a wealthy resident of Cairo. Whatever the details of his birth, Solomon was a Jew, but of that he'd made no secret. Otherwise she knew little except what was obvious: that he was a highly intelligent, much-traveled businessman who spoke a dozen languages, including excellent Egyptian Arabic and English that was distinctly American in syntax and accent. She knew nothing else about him, and she took care not to appear inquisitive. Solomon had offered to bring for her each month the money that her absent husband sent from faraway places. The wartime British restrictions on money transfers of any kind made her wonder how she would have managed without Solomon's unofficial courier service. The money she earned working for the British army in the Base Hospital was not enough for even her modest lifestyle. Almost all the others were young, inexperienced army nurses from England, living in quarters and glad of a chance to be in a city full of woman-chasing men. They didn't need any money. But Peggy lived in a hotel and had so far resisted the temptations and propositions. Peggy needed Karl's money, so it was necessary to put up with Solomon's quirks and eccentricities.

Solomon had even renamed this boat *Medina al Dahabiya: City of Gold.* It was a pun. *Dahabiya* means shallow-draft Nile houseboat, as well as meaning gold. Before he took it over and refitted it, it had been little more than a hulk owned by a drunken South African airline pilot and appropriately named *Flying Fish.* Houseboats moored along the west side of Gezira Island had acquired a new chic reputation since the war started. The boats were of all shapes and sizes; some—like this one— were in good condition while others were leaking and derelict. Everyone had colorful stories about this weird fleet. Black marketeers, British army deserters, and even Italian prisoners of war were said to be here, throwing amazing parties with every variety of drink and drug freely available. But Cairo loved rumors, the more flamboyant the better.

"Will you come this way, madam."

"Yes." She never called him Yusef. He was familiar enough already.

When she was finally invited down into the well-appointed drawing room on the deck below, Solomon greeted her warmly. The irritation that had built up while she was being kept waiting disappeared. She came under his spell. If Solomon al-Masri was rich, he was certainly not one of the well-bred, well-spoken, cultured figures so frequently found in Cairo's best hotels, bars, and nightclubs. Solomon was good-looking in the tough-guy way that Hollywood had recently discovered in Cagney and Bogart. He was short and muscular, with a tanned, weathered face, black mustache and bushy eyebrows, and wavy black hair that resisted his efforts with comb and brush. His custom-made silk shirt and trousers fitted perfectly, unlike so much of the clothing produced by Cairo's tailors. Anyone could see he was a man who demanded things done exactly the way he wanted them. In everything he did she recognized the single-minded drive she'd found in other self-made men, her father for one.

Now Solomon sat her down and fussed over her as if this was the moment he'd waited all day to enjoy. "You'll have some whisky?" He remembered exactly how she liked it—soda and whisky in equal amounts, no ice—and selected a heavy cut-glass tumbler for it. He brandished the Johnnie Walker bottle as if to prove it was not one of the bogus local distillations that were now in such abundance.

He watched her, as she sat down and crossed her legs, and handed her the drink. "Are you cold, Peggy?" She felt better now. She caught a glimpse of herself in the mirror: smooth skin, reddish hair, and large green eyes. She was reassured. She still looked fresh and young; few of the younger nurses outshone her.

The room was warm and hazy with cigar smoke. "No, not now," she said. "But boats are never warm, are they? I don't know how you bear it on the water in winter."

"You get used to it, Peggy. My father had a fine house here

on the island. Each morning, having said his prayers, he looked at the water flowing past. The Nile is long, he used to tell me, as long as our people's exile."

"And what did you say?" She wondered how many of the Arabs with whom he had dealings recognized him as a Jew. Perhaps, if there were goods to be traded and money to be made, they did not care. Money speaks all tongues; that was what they said in the Cairo souks.

"I would tell my father to look north and remember that, here in Cairo, we are almost at the end of the Nile," Solomon said. He smiled briefly as he suddenly recalled telling her this little parable before: he liked parables. She had dutifully provided him with his cue.

"You are a Jew, Peggy." It wasn't a question; it was a statement of fact, a reminder.

"My father was—"

"I don't want to know about your father. I want to know about you." He said it firmly and sat down on the sofa and looked at her as if expecting a long answer.

She knew what he was expecting. He was very like Karl in some ways, and Karl loved to discuss his roots and the essence of race and religion: the Jewish homeland and the pioneers who struggled to create it.

"I suppose I am," she said. She'd grown up in a family where religion was never mentioned. She had been about to say that her father was an atheist until Solomon interrupted her. She knew little or nothing about religion before meeting Karl. Her father had told her that Jewish descent goes through the female line, and anyway Peggy found it difficult to become a believer in any sort of God. Lately her work at the hospital watching so many young men bleed and die had made her less, rather than more, religious. But she didn't want to argue. "Karl is a Jew. Once, long ago, I promised that if we ever had any children they would be brought up as Karl wished."

"Exactly. Karl told me the same thing. Karl said you would say that."

"When is Karl coming back?"

"Not yet. He still has a lot of work to do." Solomon got up and walked to the electric fan and moved it so that its airflow rippled the curtain. It was stuffy in the room, and the smell of cigar smoke remained faintly in the air. He could have cleared the air by opening one of the windows, but she knew he didn't want to risk being overheard. The noisy fan was no doubt part of his desire for privacy. He turned to her and said casually, "In fact, Karl has run afoul of the British authorities in Baghdad. Until we can sort it out for him, it is better if he is not anywhere where he'd be recognized."

"What do you mean?" She could not keep the alarm from her voice. "What has he done?"

Solomon chuckled. There was a certain brutality in his laugh that did not encourage her to join in. He looked at his watch. "Why should you think he has done anything? Karl will be all right." He got up again and switched on the radio. He had judged it perfectly: he was a man of method. The time signal sounded and then came the BBC news. It was an hour earlier in London—11 P.M. She could never get over the fact that the man reading the news would afterward go outside and be in Langham Place, sniff the London air, and be able to see the red double-decker buses going across Oxford Circus.

They listened to the news. The voice of the BBC announcer was dry and solemn. There was only a perfunctory reference to Rommel's advance. Soon the man was telling of the Red Army's valiant counterattacks, but even on that subject his buoyant tones could not make up for the fact that the Germans were close to occupying both Moscow and Leningrad. The Japanese advances across the Pacific continued unabated. All the news was ominous. After the first few minutes, Solomon switched it off and went to sit beside her. She could smell the cologne he'd used and see the talc on his chin. He was drinking some sort of fizzy water with a lemon slice in it. She'd never seen him drink alcohol.

"I love the smell in the air. Can you smell it, Peggy?"

She had no idea what he might be talking about. She could see he was in an excited mood and guessed it was something to do with the work he did. "The desert?"

"The desert, huh. You romantic. I'm talking about the stench of betrayal." He leaned back in his seat. "I sniffed that same stink in Madrid in 'thirty-seven. That hoodlum Franco was at the gates, as Rommel will soon be at the gates of Cairo. An anarchist patrol had murdered a Communist leader named Cortada. The Communists were giving the police their orders; the police were fabricating evidence to convict the Falangists. The Russian secret policemen were murdering the Trotskyite POUMists, and the Radicalists and other riffraff were fighting one another. It was easy; the Fascists didn't have to fight. They had only to march in and win the war."

She'd heard too much about the Spanish Civil War from her husband. For these men, who'd been on the losing side, it had become an obsession. "Yes, I know. We lost; Franco won."

"Don't play the silly old woman with me, Peggy. We've known each other too long for that. You know what's going on here."

"Young Egyptian hotheads want to overthrow the British. Is that what you mean?" she asked. Her voice revealed that she was British enough to scorn their chances of succeeding.

He regretted having revealed his feelings. Now he answered her in a mocking drawl as if he were nothing but an impartial observer of local events. "That's part of it. Some young Egyptian officers are planning a palace coup. This wonderful town is full of people feathering their own nest while Rommel gets ready to send his tanks in to take it over."

"Rommel will never get here. He's a long way away."

"Yes. And if he does get here, Rommel is not going to hand over his prize to crazy young Egyptians. Exactly. The very fact that they expect him to shows how naïve they are. But my masters keep asking me what exactly is going on here."

"Your masters?"

"And Karl's masters. Yes." There was a serious note in his voice now.

She was going to ask him who his masters were, but instead she said discreetly, "How do I fit in?"

"You live in the little hotel where that fascistic old bastard Prince Piotr holds court. Drink up."

"Yes?"

"For God's sake, Peggy, wake up! Are you going to tell me you don't know Piotr?" He poured more whisky into her glass.

"Of course I know him. . . . Thank you, that's enough. . . . Everyone in Cairo knows him. He's a White Russian prince who just loves what Hitler's armies are doing to Stalin. Here in Cairo he has good friends in the palace. . . . Some say he plays cards with Farouk. What is it you want to know?" She helped herself to more water.

"I'm not stupid, Peggy. The messages I send to Tel Aviv don't retail stories got from the gossipers in the souks. I want to know what our princely friend really thinks and does and meets and talks about. Does that make sense to you?"

"No. It doesn't make much sense to anyone who has ever met him. He's ancient. He's an egotistical, name-dropping old snob, full of boring stories of long ago. He's not a high-level go-between for Hitler and Farouk, if that's what you're suggesting."

Solomon smiled grimly; he liked a little sparring. "I'm suggesting nothing. I'm simply asking you to take a closer look at him so we can be sure."

"I hardly know him."

"You told me you have drinks with him every week."

"Everyone does; his apartment is an open house."

"Open house, eh? That would be a smart move for a Nazi spy."

She looked at him: at one time she'd thought these earnest

stares were a sign that he was attracted to her. But since then she'd decided that Solomon was too self-centered to fall in love with anyone. Those looks he gave her may have been demands for respect and admiration, but they were not the masculine pleas for respect and admiration that constitute a prelude to love. Solomon was a loner. "I thought you were more sophisticated than that, Solomon," she said.

"Don't go with closed ears," he said.

"I shall report to you every last little drunken exchange I hear."

"Prince Piotr tells everyone he has an American shortwave radio. I want you to look at it carefully and tell me what name it has and which wave bands it can receive."

"Why?"

"Everyone in this town knows there is a big security leak. The British top brass are running around in circles trying to find out where Rommel is getting his information about British strengths and positions."

"Where would Prince Piotr get such secrets?" she said scornfully.

He wasn't going to debate with her. "We have to look into the future, Peggy. Whatever happens between the German and the British armies, we Jews will still have to defend ourselves against the Arabs. To do that we must have guns. Violence is the only language an Arab understands. There will be no negotiations when the day comes. It will be a fight to the death."

"Whose death? Do you know how many million Arabs there are?"

He dismissed this with a flick of the fingers and a deep inhalation on his cigarette. She wondered how much of this stirring rhetoric he believed. "Are you familiar with the word *tzedaka*, Peggy?"

"Charity?"

"My father used to say it means, If we Jews don't look after ourselves, we can be sure no one else will." He blew smoke in a studied way, as if demonstrating that he had his feelings completely under control. "You're an old-timer, Peggy. We both know Cairo is a snake pit of conspiracy and betrayal. There are so many factions fighting for control of their particular little backyard that no one can see the true picture."

"Except you?" She tried not to show her resentment at the way he liked to call her an old-timer. He only did it to ruffle her.

"Except Tel Aviv."

There was a knock at the door. Four knocks sounded in rapid succession, and in a rhythm that denotes urgency in any language.

"I'm busy!"

Despite this response, the thin servant came into the room and said without pause, "There are soldiers, sir, searching all the houseboats."

"British soldiers?" Solomon asked calmly.

"Yes, British soldiers."

"Yes, British soldiers," said another voice, and a man in the uniform of a British captain pushed the servant aside with a firm and practiced movement of arm and body. He was in his middle thirties, a clean-shaven man with quick eyes. "And Egyptian policemen too. This is my colleague, Inspector Khalil, should you want to know more." He ushered a slim young Egyptian police officer past him into the room. The Egyptian was dressed in the black wool winter uniform with shiny buttons. Despite the deference shown him, his presence was only to keep the legal niceties intact.

Solomon got to his feet. "My name is Solomon al-Masri." He put on a calm and ingratiating smile. "May I offer you a drink, major?" He didn't ask Khalil, politely assuming that he observed the Muslim strictures on alcohol.

"Captain, actually. Captain Marker. Field Security Police. No, thank you, sir."

"Captain, is it? How stupid of me. I can never remember

your British rank insignia. Your face is familiar. Have I seen you at the Turf Club, Captain Marker?"

"No, I'm not a member," said Captain Marker, without giving an inch. Marker's voice was soft and educated, but his eyes were hard and unblinking. Solomon had spent a lot of his life under British rule, but for the moment he could not decide whether this man was one of the regular soldiers from BTE— British Troops in Egypt, the peacetime occupying army—or one of the senior British policemen who'd been put into khaki and sent here, there, and everywhere to cope with the flood of serious crime that the war had brought to the Middle East.

"The Sweet Melody Club, perhaps?" said Solomon. It was a joke; the Melody was a notorious place where every evening's performance ended with the Egyptian national anthem, to which British soldiers bellowed obscene words. A riot always ensued. Lately the band had been protected behind barbed wire.

Marker looked at him for a moment and then sniffed. "Inspector Khalil's men will search your boat." Through the wooden bulkheads and deck came noises made by men opening and closing cupboards and containers. Solomon recognized the sounds as those made by police specially trained to search carefully and thoroughly. Sometimes the British brought men who were encouraged to break furniture and chinaware and do as much damage as possible.

"Of course," said Solomon. "Search. Yes. I insist. Please treat this boat in the same way as any other. I want no special treatment. It is my privilege to cooperate with the security forces in any way possible."

"May I see your papers, miss?" said Captain Marker. He was looking at Peggy.

Solomon answered. "I can vouch for Peggy West. She is one of Cairo's fairest and firmest fixtures."

Captain Marker still looked at Peggy as if he'd not heard Solomon. "Is that your 1938 Studebaker parked under the trees, Miss West?"

"Mrs. West. No, I don't have a car. I walked here."

"It's a chilly night for a stroll. Do you have your passport, Mrs. West?"

"I don't have it with me. It's at the Hotel Magnifico. I live there."

Solomon said, "She drops in on me once a week. I let her have recent English newspapers. We were just saying good night."

"Recent newspapers?" said Marker, raising his eyes to give all his attention to Solomon.

"The planes come via Gibraltar—sometimes ships too. One of the senior customs officials lets me have them."

Solomon turned away from the Englishman's stare. He got his passport from a drawer and handed it to the captain. The cover announced that it was a U.S. passport.

"We're in the war together now, captain," said Solomon, as he passed the American passport to him. "We're friends and allies now, right?"

Marker studied the cover, then the photo, and then looked at Solomon. The passport was in the name of Solomon Marx. "We always have been, Mr. Marx." He gave the passport back. "Thank you, sir. My men will not take long. Since you're just saying good night, I'll take you back to your hotel, Mrs. West. You'll be able to formally identify yourself."

She hesitated but then agreed. There was no alternative. It was wartime. Egypt was a sovereign state and technically neutral, but any order of the British military police here was law.

When Peggy West, Captain Marker, and all the policemen had departed, Solomon sat down with a large bottle of beer. His manservant shed a measure of his deference. "What was that all about, then?" he asked Solomon. The servant was in fact his partner, a Palestinian Jew named Yigal Arad. He'd lived among Arabs all his life and had no difficulty in passing himself off as one. For a year or more he'd been an officer of the Haganah, an armed Jewish force. He collected a British army commendation and a gunshot wound in the knee from a Châtellerault machine gun, when guiding British troops across the Syrian border to attack the Vichy French forces the previous summer. The 7.5mm round, now a bent and twisted talisman, hung from a cord around his neck.

"What was that all about?" repeated Solomon as he thought about the question. "The British simply want to let us know they have their eye on us."

Solomon was the leader of this two-man Cairo mission. Solomon al-Masri—or, to those who knew him well or got a look at his U.S. passport, Solly Marx—had also been born in Palestine, the son of a Russian Jew. His father had lost all his relatives in a pogrom and had never come to terms with the strange and sunny land to which he'd escaped, except to marry a young Arab woman who gave birth to Solomon and five other children. When his father became bedridden, it was Solomon who'd found ways of keeping the family clothed and fed. Some of those ways he now preferred to forget. That's why he had taken the first opportunity to leave his homeland. Never now would he discuss his early life, and yet the key to all Solomon's thoughts and actions could be found in the pity and disgust he felt for that child he'd once been.

"That's all?" Yigal persisted.

Solomon yawned. It was an affectation, like his languid manner and the fictitious stories about his father and the sumptuous Cairo mansion that he liked to pretend had been his family home. "There are not many real secrets in this town. We must let the British discover some of our little secrets in order to keep our big secrets intact."

"She always wants unsweetened coffee."

"Perhaps she doesn't want to get fat."

"At home we drink it sweet. Unsweetened coffee is only served for funerals."

"Because your people are all peasants," said Solomon without rancor. "Here in Cairo people are more sophisticated."

"Will you confide in the woman?" He poured a beer for himself.

"Peggy West? I might have to."

"And take her with us when we leave?"

"You know that would be impossible."

"She'll talk."

Solomon looked at him but didn't reply.

"She'll talk, Solomon. The British will squeeze her, and she'll tell them everything she knows."

"Don't rush your fences, Yigal. I'll tell her nothing until I'm quite certain that she's not already spying for the British."

"Peggy West?"

"Figure it out for yourself. The British must be curious about the prince for the same reasons we are. Peggy was here before the war. She must be registered with the embassy, with the Hotel Magnifico as her permanent address. It would be sensible of them to ask Peggy to report on what the prince is saying at his parties."

"You have a devious mind, Solomon."

"I am logical. That is why Tel Aviv gave me this job."

"You are cynical, and that is quite different."

"All men serve two masters; that is human nature."

"Two masters?"

"We both know British soldiers who salute the union jack but who are also Jews. I know some British soldiers who even combine loyalty to their king with a faith in Soviet communism. Prince Piotr no doubt has a love for Mother Russia, but he detests Uncle Stalin and might well be helping the Germans. We know proud Egyptians who faithfully obey the British. It is a lucky man indeed who works for only one master."

"You like riddles; I like straight answers."

"There are no straight answers, Yigal."

"You have avoided my questions. Eventually you will have to confide in Peggy West. When we leave what will you do?"

"I know how to handle such things, Yigal."

"Does that mean you'll silence her?"

"It will be all right."

Despite Solomon's angry tone, Yigal persisted. "She's one of us. She's Karl's wife. I'll have no part in killing her. Don't say I haven't warned you."

Solomon gave him a cold smile. "Teach us, Lord, to meet adversity; but not before it arrives."

"Spare me another of your lessons from the Talmud."

"Why do you scorn the lessons of the Talmud?" asked Solomon affably. He was pleased at what looked like a chance to change the subject.

"Would it teach me about your devious schemes for Peggy West?"

Solomon sipped his beer. For a moment it seemed as if he would not reply. Then he said, "Many years ago there lived a scholar who asked an old rabbi what could be learned from the Talmud. The rabbi told him of two men who fell down a chimney. One man arrived at the bottom dirty, while the other arrived clean. Is that the lesson of the Talmud? the scholar asked. No, replied the old rabbi, listen to me: the dirty man looked at the clean man and thought himself clean. Is that the lesson of the Talmud? asked the scholar. No, replied the rabbi, for the dirtied man looked at his own hands and seeing them sooty knew he'd been dirtied. This then is the lesson of the Talmud? said the scholar. No, said the rabbi. Then what am I to learn from the Talmud? asked the scholar. The rabbi told him: You will learn nothing from the Talmud if you start by believing that two men can fall down a chimney and not both be dirtied."

≡4≡

They'd given Jimmy Ross his predecessor's quarters. He was in the massive Citadel of Muhammad Ali, which overlooked the whole city. In this ancient fortification the British garrison had long made their home. Within its bounds there were a military hospital, swimming pool, tennis courts, stables, and extensive parade grounds. He'd been assigned a comfortable bedroom plus a cramped sitting room in what—until the families had been evacuated—had been the army's married quarters.

Jimmy Ross dined alone in his room that night. It was not considered unusual. Senior SIB personnel were a law unto themselves, everyone knew that. In fact, many of the others stayed well clear of these "secret policemen." He got a decent meal of stewed chicken, rice, and steamed pudding with jam. Then he systematically sorted through Cutler's kit and his own. He must get rid of that kit bag. With the name Ross still faintly legible on the side of it, it was incriminating evidence. There were a few other things. He tore from his books the pages on which he'd written his name and flushed them down the toilet. He scraped his name from the back of a shoe brush and tore some Ross name tags from his underclothes.

His worst shock came when he tried on the battle dress from Cutler's suitcase. He'd not calculated on Cutler's having such long arms. Battle dress was the same for all ranks, so he'd reckoned on wearing Cutler's top with his own trousers. But the khaki blouse did not fit him. There was no getting away from it; it looked absurd. He could, of course, continue to wear the corporal's uniform, but there was always the chance that some bright copper would take note of the fact that the dead prisoner from the railway train just happened to be a corporal too. He slept on his problems and woke up rested. It was a wonderful sunny morning. It gave him renewed vigor and renewed hope.

He didn't want to tackle the Bab-el-Hadid barracks alone. A new sentry might well make difficulties for someone in a shabby corporal's uniform. He phoned his office and spoke with Marker. "I've got some things to do in town," he said airily. "Give the Stanhope girl my new pass and have her bring it to me at lunchtime. I'll be in the bar in Groppi's." The famous Groppi was the only restaurant he'd ever heard of in Cairo.

"Very good, sir," said Marker. "I don't think there is a bar there; I'll say the restaurant at about one o'clock. Is that the Groppi Rotunda or Groppi Garden?"

For a moment Ross was floored. "Which do you recommend?"

"Alice will have her car, of course. She could pick you up and take you to Soleiman Pasha; that's the one I always prefer."

"Good, good," said Ross, "Groppi in Soleiman Pasha then." Marker had jumped to the conclusion that Ross intended to use the girl as a guide and driver around the town. Well, that was a good idea. It might prove very convenient.

"Tell her to pick me up from here at twelve noon," said Ross. "Any sign of the brigadier?"

"He's away duck shooting. Back next week, his office says."

"Okay."

"There was one other thing, sir."

"Yes?"

"That fellow died."

"The prisoner?"

"Yes, I forget his name for the moment. But the man you escorted. He died."

"What was it?"

"Heart attack. I don't know the drill for that sort of thing. I suppose there will be a post-mortem and some sort of inquiry. They will probably need you to give evidence."

"Did he die in hospital?" said Ross. He could hear himself breathing too loudly and capped the phone.

"The pathology wallahs will sort all that out," said Marker.

Ross didn't like the sound of it.

"One other thing, sir. Did the prisoner not have any kit?"

"He was arrested on the run," said Ross. "That's why he was in civvies."

"I thought that might be it," said Marker. "I just didn't want to take a chance. You get next of kin kicking up a fuss about personal effects sometimes. Can be a nuisance."

"Yes, of course." Next of kin! There was no worry about his own next of kin; he had none. But what about Cutler? Suppose there was some loose end in Cutler's life that would come home to haunt him? Then he had an idea so obvious that he kicked himself for not thinking of it all along. The army issued everyone with a "housewife": a packet of needles and pins, with a selection of buttons and thread. He must still have his somewhere in his kit. Yes. He got a razor blade and started cutting the crowns from Cutler's uniform blouse.

"If you are my personal assistant, we'd better get to know each other," he said.

Alice Stanhope smiled at him as if he were the first man ever to take an interest in her.

For a moment, Jimmy Ross was disconcerted. She seemed to see right through him. He supposed there were plenty of men making advances to her; she was so lovely. Beautiful, but not in the flashy way that was to be seen all around them in this fashionable eating place. Alice Stanhope was tall, with long blond hair and a clear complexion. Her face was still rather than animated, but her eyes suggested an artful sense of humor and a quick brain. Only a very beautiful woman could have shone in the severe clothes she wore. This, thought Ross, was the sort of outfit a middle-class English mother would consider suitable for a daughter going out into the wicked world: a checked wool suit and pale blue twin set with pearls. On her wrist she wore an expensive gold watch—a twenty-first birthday present, no doubt—but there were no rings on her fingers.

"There is something I've got to tell you," she said, leaning close to him and speaking in a quiet confidential tone. "Your predecessor at the office assigned me to an undercover job."

"Did he?"

She blushed. "Yes, he did."

Ross guessed that she was exaggerating somewhat, but he drank his tea and indicated that she should tell him more about it.

"I am to rent a room in the Hotel Magnifico and stay there undercover."

"Why?" he said, although in his mind he was already approving the suggestion. It would be to his advantage to have her away from the office and would provide an excuse for him to disappear.

"We had an anonymous tip that one of the people in the Magnifico is a German spy."

"You sound doubtful."

She decided to be truthful with him: disarmingly so; it was her way. "I am. He's an elderly Russian. My family and I have known him since before the war. Everyone in Cairo is saying that he's a German spy. These rumors come and go, like fashions in hats. Poor old man, he's quite harmless."

"So why bother?"

"There was a general feeling in the office that we should follow up everything."

"Is that a polite way of saying that no one in the office has any clue to anything that's happening?"

"No," she said, her face saying yes. "The Magnifico is very bohemian. I'm sure I would pick up something valuable there." He wondered what she would classify as bohemian, but before he could ask her, she said, "Did you sew those crowns on yourself?"

"What's wrong with them?" he said defensively. For one terrible moment he thought perhaps he'd sewn Cutler's rank badges on his shoulder straps the wrong way up. He'd sewn the crowns onto his old working uniform. He'd had to use that one so that he could dirty the sleeves a little to hide the places where his stripes had been. But it made him feel out of place among all the "gabardine swine" here in Groppi's.

"Nothing. They're fine. But . . . I'm sure one of the girls in the office would do it more neatly. Or I will, if you like. But why don't you get a new uniform? There's an awfully good tailor just a hundred yards from here in Kasr el Nil. My father had suits made there."

"Yes, that's a good idea."

"He'll do them in two or three days, but you have to bully him."

"You'd better come with me."

"Is it all right then? The undercover job? The Magnifico?"

"I suppose so."

"That's very encouraging," she said bitterly, suddenly forgetting that she was a lowly subordinate.

He smiled. "I'll come with you."

"It might help. Wear the corporal's outfit," she said.

"Don't be bossy," he said. "But yes, I will."

"It's not going to be easy getting a room there. We'll have to give them a sob story."

"We'll think of something," he said. Already there was an intimacy between them. At least he felt there was. Perhaps she had that effect on every man she met.

"Can I get you something else, sir?" said the waiter.

Ross was hungry. Maybe he should hang on here for a few more days before disappearing. Not longer. He certainly didn't want to find himself giving evidence to an inquiry about his own death.

Having finished her shift at the Base Hospital, Peggy West arrived at the hotel in which she lived, thinking only of a hot scented bath. In the hotel lobby she found an army corporal and a tall long-haired civilian girl. The soldier was arguing with Ahmed, a tall Arab with dyed red hair, who was sweeping the tiled floor in that dreamy way that all the hotel servants seemed to assume when working. The soldier seemed to speak no Arabic beyond the half dozen words that every foreigner learns in the first couple of days. He was getting nowhere. Peggy had to sort things out. "You can't have a room here, because this is not a hotel," she explained.

"It says hotel on the sign outside," the soldier protested.

Peggy looked at him. His uniform was the ill-fitting khaki trousers and baggy khaki jacket that the British wore in winter. The corporal was in his middle to late twenties, older than most of the soldiers to be seen in the streets. The colored patches were from some unit she'd not noticed before. The heavy boots, so painstakingly shined, made her guess he was from one of the new transit camps that had been built on the Canal Road. At his feet there rested a crocodile leather suitcase bearing the labels of exclusive hotels: Lotti, Gritti Palace, Bayerischer Hof. It obviously belonged to the girl.

"My cousin desperately needs a place to sleep," he said,

indicating the young woman at his side. "Everywhere's been requisitioned."

"Surely there are lots of places," said Peggy. The girl was very beautiful in the way that rich English girls sometimes were. Her face was composed and detached. She said nothing. It was almost as if she were deaf.

"If she was in the army, it would be simple enough," said the corporal. "But none of these damned clubs and hostels will take civilians. Only the YWCA, and that's full." Peggy looked at him more closely. He was a tough fellow. Despite the faint Scots accent, she decided that he was like an English foxhound, dogs noted for their pace, their nose, and their stamina.

"This place was a hotel once, long ago," said Peggy, feeling that some explanation was due. "Now people live here on a permanent basis. We never have vacant rooms—everyone wants them."

The corporal glanced around the lobby, and Peggy saw it through his eyes. It looked like a hotel. There was the unmanned reception desk and behind it a long mail rack, each pigeonhole bearing a painted room number and a hook. Stuffed under a large brass ornamental scarab there was a pile of uncollected mail, with postage stamps from Britain, South Africa, and Australia. Some of the letters had grown dusty with age. From hooks there hung room keys with the Hotel Magnifico's heavy brass tags. Along the right-hand wall, four tall amphorae were arranged. Above them there was an ancient engraving of a view of Cairo seen from the Citadel. In the corner an imposing mahogany cubicle, with oriental motifs and a frosted glass window, was marked "telephone" in English, Italian, and Arabic. Immediately inside the front door a green baize bulletin board was buried under typewritten notices and posters of all shapes and sizes and colors: dances and concerts, whist drives and jumble sales, tours and lectures, voluntary nursing and language lessons. Cairo had never been more active.

"It says Hotel Magnifico on the sign," said the corporal again.

"I know it does," said Peggy. The late Signor Mario Magnifico—whose daughter Lucia inherited the place—commissioned the sign, after hearing his establishment rightfully called a pension by a client he didn't like.

"Well, can we sit down here for a minute? I need to talk with my cousin," said the corporal. "It's a private matter and very urgent."

There were no seats in sight. Peggy looked around. Where the lobby ended at a staircase, glass-paneled doors gave onto the bar. One door was partly open, and Peggy could see one of the residents—Captain Robin Darymple—holding forth to the usual crowd. Darymple turned in time to see Peggy looking at him. He gave her a wonderful smile that lit up his face. She smiled back. Robin's charm was unassailable. She knew this would not be the right time to take two strangers into the bar. "Perhaps you could sit in the dining room," said Peggy.

Net curtains obscured the oval-shaped little windows in the dark mahogany doors. She swung one open and ushered them through. The dining room was gloomy, only one electric light bulb was lit. There was no one else there.

Through the doors Peggy heard footsteps on the marble as someone came out of the bar, leaving the doors wide open. Darymple's high-pitched voice was now clearly audible. It was the tone he used when telling his stories. "So he said he had spent all night with the carps. Fish? I said. He said, No, dead carps! Crikey, I thought, he means a corpse. I said, And this all happened in Belgravia? And the big fellow with the beard said, No, Bulgaria." There was appreciative laughter from throats down which much drink had been poured. She recognized this as one of Darymple's stories. His skill as a storyteller was renowned throughout the clubs and bars of Cairo.

For the two strangers, Peggy indicated a small table near the window. Again there came the sound of footsteps across the lobby and of the doors swinging closed to hush Darymple's voice. The corporal put down the brown leather suitcase and looked around. It was very still, as only a well-swept, carefully prepared, empty dining room can be. He said, "This will do nicely. May we sit here for half an hour?"

Peggy nodded.

The girl watched her corporal. Only when he seemed to approve it did the girl sit down.

"They'll start coming in for dinner soon," said Peggy. "There are no spare tables, so—"

"We understand," said the corporal. "I suppose it's officers only."

Peggy West was too tired to be provoked into argument. She said, "Tell them Peggy said it was all right. Peggy West."

"Thank you," said the girl. "It's most kind of you." It was the first time she'd spoken. She had a soft upper-class voice. Perhaps, thought Peggy, that explained something about their relationship, the way in which the young corporal was so prickly about the privileges accorded to officers. "My name is Alice Stanhope," said the girl.

The corporal extended a hand and Peggy shook it. "Bert Cutler." He amended it to "Corporal Albert Cutler, if we are being formal." Peggy found the Scots accent hard to detect. Perhaps he'd found it expedient to eliminate it. Or perhaps Peggy had been away from Britain too long. Cutler had a confident handshake, tanned face, pleasant smile, and clear blue eyes. He was an attractive man. It would be easy to fall in love with such a man, thought Peggy, but he would not be easy to keep. English foxhounds were never seen at dog shows, and she'd never heard of one being kept as a pet.

"Peggy West. I live here. Second floor."

"Thank you again, Miss West."

Peggy smiled and left them to themselves. She didn't believe they were cousins. Once back in the lobby she looked behind the desk to see if there was a letter from her husband, Karl, or from her brother in Canada, but there was nothing in the box. She was not surprised; mail took months and months, and it was very uncertain now that everything had to go around the Cape and so many ships were sunk.

She had gone up a few steps when a thought struck her. She retraced her steps and went into the dining room with enough fuss for them to recover themselves if they were embracing. She need not have troubled herself; they were sitting decorously, facing each other solemnly across the small marble-topped table.

"I'm sorry to bother you"—she looked at the girl—"but I suddenly wondered if you could type."

"Type?" The girl looked at her as if humoring a lunatic. "Yes, I can type a bit. At least I could last year."

"You're not looking for a job, by any chance?"

The corporal said, "She's got to find somewhere to stay." He looked at his wristwatch. "I have to get back to my unit tonight."

"Where I work—at the Base Hospital—we need a full-time typist. In fact, someone to sort out the office," said Peggy, looking from one to the other. "We're getting frantic, really frantic." Her voice was hearty. This was the Peggy West who'd been school hockey captain, the Peggy West who bargained remorselessly in the bazaars.

"I have nowhere to sleep," said the girl.

Peggy closed her eyes. Those who knew her recognized such gestures as marks of great emotion. "I'll find her a place to sleep if she'll come work for us." She said it to the corporal. He was the one who made the decisions, and he would not mistake the tones of a solemn promise.

The girl and the corporal looked at each other. She smiled at him. It was a smile of love and reassurance.

"Here? A room here?" said the corporal, suspecting perhaps that Peggy meant to send the girl to some flea-bitten lodgings on the other side of town.

"You'd have to share a bathroom with me and another woman," she said. "The room you'd be using rightfully belongs to an officer at the front. . . . He's been gone into the blue since November, but he could return at any time."

The girl smiled as if she'd achieved something quite remarkable, and the same look was on her face as she turned to the corporal.

Peggy added, "I hope you haven't got too much luggage. There isn't room to swing a cat."

"Just the one case. That's all I have," said the girl, looking down at it. It was small to be a case that contained all one's worldly possessions. The girl smiled sadly, and Peggy felt sorry for her. "I was beginning to think I'd spend the night in the railway station waiting room."

Peggy wondered if she had any notion of what a night in Cairo's main railway station would be like. The girl was like a china doll. It was difficult to guess what sort of person she was behind that shy exterior. Peggy hoped she would get along with the others at the hospital.

"I'll leave you two alone now," Peggy said. "Come up to the second floor. My room is to the left of the staircase. The door has a hand-of-Fatima brass knocker." She smiled. "Don't go wandering farther upstairs. The top floor belongs to a Russian prince. He'll eat you alive if you go into his sanctum."

"Thank you, Peggy," said Alice softly.

When the corporal made no response, Peggy looked again at him. He was staring into space. For just one brief moment she saw within him a different person. Peggy smiled at him but he did not respond. She had the feeling that he wasn't seeing her. Then suddenly his face changed, and he was relaxed and smiling again as if the moment had never been.

"Yes, thank you, Peggy," said Cutler. "Thank you very much."

Peggy West didn't sleep well that night. She went to bed and closed her eyes tightly, but still she worried about what she had done and what she had promised. Suppose Lieutenant Anderson arrived back here without warning and wanted his room? Lieutenant Anderson was not a man to cross. A rough-spoken car commander from Leeds, Andy liked everyone to know that he had been a sergeant until the desert fighting started. Since then he'd won a chestful of medals and a battlefield commission. Andy was a nice friendly fellow—despite his pug's face and scarred cheek—but she dreaded to think what he'd be like if he came back and found his room occupied, his door locked, and his kit stowed away in the storeroom.

At 4:30 A.M. Peggy gave up trying to sleep. She slid out of bed, boiled a kettle, and quietly made herself a pot of tea. At least tea was something freely available here—only sugar and kerosene were in short supply—and tea kept the British going in times of danger. With only the bedside light on, she sat down at the dressing table that she used also as a desk. Waiting for the tea to brew, she pulled a comb through her hair and suddenly saw her mother staring at her with that wide-eyed shock and maternal concern that she'd so often provoked from her. Her mother had loved her, of course, just as her mother had loved her father. But Mother's deepest love was reserved for those damned dogs she kept in her kennels, barking and whining ceaselessly so that it drove her distracted. Her mother would stay up all night with a sick dog, but when Daddy was ill she went and made up her bed in the spare room. Peggy had never forgiven her for that.

Peggy poured herself a cup of tea and put some milk into it. Drinking tea revived her and brought back memories of her childhood in England. But other thoughts intruded. Suppose the girl couldn't type? What if she turned out to be some kind of bad-tempered monster that the other people in the office detested? Suppose she wanted too much money?

And what about that soldier? The look on Cutler's face was that of a man under extreme stress. She had seen such symptoms at the Base Hospital. Of course when he realized she was looking at him, he made every effort to smile and relax, and the tension went away. But that did not alter what she had seen, and what she had seen frightened her.

Until her husband went away, Peggy had never worried about anything at all. Things were different now she'd gone back to living on her own. Her finances were precarious. Would Karl ever return to her? At their first meeting, Solomon had given her a note in Karl's handwriting. Since then the brief notes from Karl had been typewritten, and Solomon harshly dismissed any idea of her talking to her husband on the telephone. She had a nasty feeling that Karl's money might stop any time Solomon decided it should. She didn't trust Solomon. There had been an unmistakable element of blackmail in his request that she keep an eye on the wretched Russian prince upstairs.

Her hospital pay would not go far without Karl's money. Without extra income, her savings would last no more than a month or two in this town. More and more men were arriving every day: British, South Africans, Australians, soldiers and civilians, all with money to spend. Prices were rising steeply. The Magnifico's rents had increased twice in the previous twelve months.

She poured more tea. Now that it had fully brewed, the tea had darkened. She liked it like that: the way Karl always drank it. She wished he'd never gone to take up the job in Iraq; there had been an attempt to overthrow the British rule there last year. Now Solomon said he was in trouble in Baghdad. It was such a long way away. She worried about him.

She was convinced that Karl West was not an uncaring man, but why couldn't he get a job and settle down and make a proper home with her? Last year she'd almost abandoned all hope of seeing him again and asked to go home to England. The British authorities in Egypt had ordered compulsory repatriation of army wives and families. Grief and anger turned to rage when some of the wives of senior officers were exempted from the order. There were places on the ships for other British civilians. At first she'd been tempted, but now she was glad she'd never put her name down. Her prospects had changed when Solomon brought her the good news of Karl. It wasn't the money; now Peggy had something to hope and plan for. Or so she told herself.

She heard the street cleaners calling, and the back door of the kitchen slammed as they dragged the sacks of rubbish outside. Traffic was moving. She didn't open the curtains. She knew that by now the brawny woman across the street would be hanging washing on a clothesline on the roof. She was Italian. Egyptians always laid their washing flat to dry in the sun.

She looked again at her reflection. Everything Mother warned her about had come true, or almost everything. Had her mother still been alive, Peggy would have written her a letter to confirm those old fears of hers. Her mother had always got some grim satisfaction from having her apocalyptic predictions come true. Her mother had said Egypt was no place to have a baby. As unreasonable and irrational as it so obviously was, Peggy had never been able to forgive her mother for that letter. Had the baby lived, everything might have gone differently. Karl loved children. He might have got another job that didn't involve endless traveling.

Peggy combed her hair more carefully and put clips into it. She wasn't yet thirty and she was still very attractive. What was there to worry about?

=6=

Peggy's fears about taking Alice Stanhope to the Base Hospital and getting her a job there abated soon after they arrived the next morning. Alice made every possible effort to fit in.

The senior surgeon, Colonel Hochleitner, who had been landed with the administration problems, had been in Cairo since before the war. He greeted Alice warmly, and liked her, and that was all that really mattered. When Alice was taken into his private office she looked at the chaos of paperwork—and the piles of scribbled notes that had almost buried the typewriter— with that same placid look with which she greeted everything except Corporal Cutler, took off her cardigan, and sat down at the desk. She didn't even complain about the ancient Adler typewriter, which clattered like a steam engine. She was not the fastest typist in the world, but she could spell long words—even some medical words and Latin—without consulting a dictionary, and the typed result was clean and legible.

"Now perhaps the doctors in this bloody hospital can spend more time on the wards and less time plowing through War Office paperwork," said "the Hoch" approvingly.

Peggy was pleased, but her pleasure didn't last long. It was soon inspection time. She hated to walk through ward after ward that had been emptied in expectation of new casualties. The empty beds, their sheets and pillows crisply starched and their blankets boxed expertly, were exactly like the lines of fresh graves and the white headstones under which so many of the casualties ultimately ended their journeys from the battlefront.

She looked at her watch. There was not much time to get ready; then it would be like yesterday, and the day before, and the day before that. The floor of the operating theaters slippery with blood and the mortuary crammed. Tank crewmen burned, mine-clearing sappers with missing legs, and all those dreadful "multiple wounds," soldiers maimed by shell fragments and mortar fire. Gunshot wounds were less common this far back; those men died before getting here.

She nodded her approval and signed the book. She would check the operating theaters, make her usual rounds, and then sit down for a moment before the new arrivals. Lost in her thoughts, Peggy went striding along and did not notice the nurse until she almost blundered into her.

"Nurse Borrows, what are you—?"

"Sister West. Ogburn, the boy with the leg wound, died in the night."

Peggy looked at her. The tears were welling in her eyes. She had kept it bottled up. But now that Peggy had arrived she'd said it, and, having said the terrible words, she lost control. "Pull yourself together, nurse."

"He was fine yesterday at doctor's rounds: pulse, heart, temperature normal. And he was laughing at something on the wireless—"

"How many times have I told you not to write letters for them?"

"Just the one letter for his mother." Her name was Borrows; her screen-struck parents had named her Theda after some exotic Hollywood star. But there was nothing exotic about Nurse Borrows right now. Her eyes were reddened and so was her nose, which she kept wiping on a tiny handkerchief.

"We have visitors to do that for them. Visitors talk to them, help them with jigsaw puzzles, and sort out their problems."

"I didn't neglect my duties, sister. It was my own time. He wanted me to write it. He said he liked my handwriting." Nurse Borrows was a plain mousy little thing but, like so many of the other nurses in this town, where European women were as rare as gold, she had suddenly become Florence Nightingale.

"How long have you worked here?" Peggy didn't wait for a reply. "Haven't you seen men die before? My God, we've lost enough of them in the past week."

"He was just a boy."

"You're a nurse," said Peggy, more gently this time. "Don't you know what a nurse is?"

"I thought I did."

"You're not a woman; you're not a man. You're not a soldier, and you're not a civilian. You're not a layman, and you're not a doctor. You're not a sweetheart or a mother; you are a nurse. That's something special. These men believe in us. They think we can make them well. . . . Yes, I know that's stupid, but that's what patients like to believe, and we can't prevent them."

"He was from Lancashire, not far from me."

"Listen to me, nurse. These patients are not from anywhere. As soon as you start thinking about them like that, this job will tear your heart out. They're patients, just patients. They're just wounds and amputations and sickness; that's all they are."

"He was shot trying to stop the German tanks. They put him in for a medal."

It was as if she wasn't listening to anything she was told. Angrily Peggy said, "I don't care if he was being treated for an advanced case of syphilis, he's a patient. Just a patient. Now get that through your silly little head."

"I loved him."

"Then you are a stupid girl and an incompetent nurse."

The young woman's head jerked up and her eyes blazed. "That's right, sister. I'm a foolish nurse. I care for my patients. I finish each shift sobbing for them all. But you wouldn't understand that. You're an efficient nurse. You never sob. Men don't interest you, we all know that, but some of us are weak. Some of us are women." Peggy had got her attention, all right, but only at the price of wounding her.

"I'm trying to help you," Peggy said.

The nurse had used up all her emotions, and for a moment she was spent. She said, "Don't you ever see them as men who have given everything for us? Don't you ever want to kiss them, and hold them, and tell them they're glorious?"

"Sometimes I do," said Peggy. The admission came to her lips as if she was speaking to herself. She was surprised to hear herself say it, but it was the truth.

Nurse Borrows sniffed loudly and made a superhuman attempt to pull herself together. She stood upright, like a soldier on parade. "I'm sorry, sister. I didn't mean what I said."

"Why don't you take an hour off? Doze for a moment or have a shower. There's nothing to do here until the ambulance convoy arrives."

"I just got so tense I couldn't stand it."

"We all get like that sometimes," said Peggy. She looked around to be sure there were no other weeping nurses. It was not an unusual event. There were many deaths when the casualties were coming fresh from the battlefield. Many arrived here before the shock had taken its full effect, and the arduous journey shortened the life of many serious cases. Most of the army nurses were too young for this sort of job, but there was such a shortage of nursing staff that none of them could be assigned to other duties. That was why the army had added civilians like the Hoch, Peggy, and Alice to the hospital staff.

She went downstairs and across the courtyard to see how Alice was getting on in Administration.

"All right?"

Alice looked up and smiled grimly. "Someone brought me tea. I assume that's a mark of approval."

"Very much so," said Peggy.

"And Blanche has been very helpful."

"Good," said Peggy.

Alice Stanhope did not stop working, but she looked up for a moment to compare Peggy with the AID TO RUSSIA poster that was affixed to the wall behind her. There could be little doubt that someone had selected it and put it there on account of the striking similarity between the Russian nurse depicted in the poster and Peggy West. Peggy shared her high cheekbones and wide mouth with this idealized Slavic beauty. But there was something else too. Peggy West also had the other qualities the artist had depicted: authority, determination, and competence, plus compassion and tenderness. All nurses were supposed to have those qualities to some extent—it went with the job—but Peggy had them in abundance.

"I'll have tea later," said Peggy. "I just wanted to see that you were doing all right."

On her way back to the main building, Peggy met Colonel Hochleitner's stepdaughter, Blanche, and discovered that Alice's arrival had not been greeted with unqualified joy on every side. Blanche was disconcerted at being displaced from her role as the hospital's champion typist. Now she was afraid of losing her position as Hoch's secretary, and that meant a lot to her. She didn't complain, of course. Blanche was a thirty-year-old blond divorcée; she'd learned a lot about the game of life. She smiled and congratulated Peggy on finding such a gem. She made self-deprecatory asides and said how lucky they were to have Alice Stanhope with them. But Peggy knew Blanche too well to take these toothy smiles and schoolgirl tributes at their face value. Blanche would wait her opportunity to talk to her stepfather; she knew exactly how to twist the Hoch around her little finger.

Blanche was not the only one with reservations about Alice. A thin red-haired nurse named Jeannie MacGregor—the daughter of a tobacco farmer in Northern Rhodesia—took Peggy West aside to voice her worries about the newcomer.

"What do we know about her?" Jeannie MacGregor's grandfather had lived in a castle, and through him Jeannie claimed to be a direct descendant of Rob Roy, the famous Scots outlaw. Jeannie's accent and her passion for Sir Walter Scott novels had been acquired during visits to her grandfather.

"I don't understand you," said Peggy West.

"And all her airs and graces, and parking her red sports car right in front."

"That's only for today," said Peggy. Parking cars at the hospital was a never-ending source of argument. "I'll see she knows."

Jeannie nodded, acknowledging her little victory. She was a wartime volunteer. By hard work and intelligence she'd become a skilled theater nurse almost the equal of Peggy West. Having the right instruments ready for the surgeons meant fully understanding the progress of every operation. Perhaps Jeannie should have gone to medical school and become a doctor. In her present job she was becoming an argumentative know-all, upsetting everyone. But good theater nurses were desperately needed, and Peggy treated Jeannie's tantrums with delicate care.

"I saw her at tea break, going through the Hoch's private files," said Jeannie.

"Yes, she's trying to get the office in order. It's a terrible mess. You know Blanche never files anything."

"Before coming to us, this Alice woman was working as a clerk in that big military police building, the one opposite the railway station," said Jeannie and looked at Peggy, smiling triumphantly. "She admitted it."

"Yes, she told me. What about it?"

"Didn't you read what the newspapers said about police spies watching everywhere. Is she a police spy?"

"Oh, Jeannie, I've not had an easy morning. Surely you don't believe all the rubbish the papers print?"

Jeannie would not abandon her theory. "And Hochleitner is a German name, isn't it?" She bit her lip and stared at Peggy.

Peggy West took a deep breath. "Jeannie, you're a senior

nurse. Are you seriously suggesting that Alice is some sort of spy sent here to find out if the Hoch is a Nazi?"

"I know it sounds farfetched," admitted Jeannie. The lowered tone of her voice suggested a retreat from her previous position, but she didn't like the way that Peggy was trying to make her feel foolish. "But there are spies everywhere, you know that."

"I don't know anything of the kind," said Peggy. "All I know is that there are *stories* of spies everywhere! How I wish everyone would calm down and be sensible. We're English, Jeannie; let's try to keep a sense of proportion."

"I'm not English, I'm a Scot," said Jeannie sullenly.

Peggy laughed. "That's no excuse," she told her.

Only with great difficulty did Jeannie MacGregor keep her temper. Her admonition was soft but bitter. "You used to be so sensible about everything."

"I didn't mean to be rude. But you're piling the agony on. Alice is a nice girl . . . and she's a good typist. Things are not so good at the front. Any day now we might be fighting Rommel in the suburbs of Cairo, so I suppose the police have to keep an eye on people. Meanwhile we British all have to help each other."

There was a long silence. Then Jeannie said, "I have instincts about people, and that girl is trouble. I'm always right about these things, sister. You mark my words."

So this was one of Jeannie's "instincts"? Oh, my God, thought Peggy. Her instinct was another treasured thing she'd inherited from her grandfather. "The Hoch has taken her on," said Peggy. "Nothing can be done about it now."

"We'll see about that," said Jeannie spitefully. "That girl is a viper; I can see it in her face. I'll get rid of her. I'll see her off, if it's the last thing I do."

"Oh, go to hell!" said Peggy and turned away. Immediately she regretted it. Had she spent five more minutes with her she might have brought her to a more amiable point of view. Jeannie MacGregor had all the tenacity of her race. If she wanted to make things difficult for Alice, or anyone else, she'd find ways of doing it.

"The dispatch riders are here," someone called from the window. "That usually means the ambulances are right behind them."

"It's too early," said Peggy.

"I heard there will be two convoys," called Jeannie. "I'd better get back to my girls and make sure they're ready." She was more positive now she had work to do.

"Yes," said Peggy with a sigh. Perhaps she could get Nurse MacGregor an exchange posting to one of the new Advanced Surgical Centers, where emergency operations were done as near the battlefield as possible.

She heard the ambulances arriving. It was starting. "Time to earn our pay," said Peggy loudly. She always said that when the ambulances arrived.

=7=

No one claimed to remember when or where or why the little gatherings began, but it had become a custom that, early on Friday evenings, a glass or two of chilled white wine and some tempting snacks were freely available on the top floor to the residents of the Magnifico and any hangers-on.

"Happy days, Piotr," said Peggy West, nodding to the prince as more wine was offered to her by Sammy, his Egyptian servant, dressed in a long black galabiya with elaborate gold facings. "What do you think of your neighbors, Alice?"

"It's so good of you to let me have the room," said Alice, also taking a second glass of wine.

Peggy smiled and looked around. Captain Robin Darymple, in starched khaki shirt and pants, was always among the first to arrive. Talking to him was a sleekly beautiful Egyptian girl, Zeinab el-Shazli, and her brother, Sayed. There were strangers too. Some of them must have started drinking in the afternoon, for there was a loud buzz of talk and laughter.

Peggy smiled across the room at the two Egyptians. She described them briefly to Alice. They were both students at the American University and living on the first floor of the Magnifico. Sayed was a handsome young man. His light-colored healthy skin and clear blue eyes were said in Cairo to be the legacy of Circassian concubines, women renowned for their beauty. Captain Darymple was holding forth on the Japanese attack on Pearl Harbor, using his free hand to bomb his wineglass. America's entry into the war had been the predominant topic of conversation for weeks. Sayed, an Egyptian army reserve officer, was listening to Darymple with a patient look on his face. Peggy pushed past them and, raising her glass to the prince, said, "Thank you, Piotr."

Alice looked at him: this was the man who was said to be Rommel's spy in Cairo.

The prince dwarfed everyone in the room. He was a tall, large-framed man dressed in a black velvet smoking jacket and white trousers. At his neck there was a patterned silk cravat, fastened by a gold pin set with diamonds. Ever since the war started, Piotr Nikoleiovich Tikhmeibrazoff had been calling himself Colonel Piotr. If challenged—as once he had been by Captain Darymple, who lived on the second floor—he calmly pointed to a photo of a smart infantry regiment marching past the Rossisskaya cotton mill during the disturbances in St. Petersburg in January 1913. His father, Prince Nikolei, had owned that regiment, lock, stock, and barrel. When his father was killed in action in 1916, Piotr Nikoleiovich inherited it along with vast acreages of land, farms and villages, the grand town house, and the seaside summer palace in the Crimea. The title of "Colonel—Retired" was a modest enough claim under the circumstances.

Piotr Nikoleiovich had been studying archaeology at Oxford University at the time of his father's death. He remained there during the revolution, which came soon after it. In 1925 he'd visited Russian friends in Cairo and decided to make it his home. Some of the treasures to be seen here in his apartment had been in the twenty-seven packing cases of clothes, furniture, carpets, paintings, icons, and ornaments that his mother had selected and sent from Russia as essential to him while he was at university in England. He liked to talk about his days at Oxford and lately was apt to call himself "a student of world affairs." This was to account for the way he spent most of his mornings reading newspapers and many of his afternoons in the cafés and bazaars, drinking coffee with a large and cosmopolitan collection of leisured cronies.

"Peggy, darling, don't tell me this is our new neighbor. I heard there was a quite ravishing young lady living here." The prince spoke in the astringent and exaggerated accent of long-ago Oxford.

Alice smiled shyly.

"How do you do, my dear. How wonderful that you were able to attend my little gathering." He took Alice's hand and bent over to kiss it.

Peggy had always seen him as a huge and cuddly Saint Bernard, but tonight, as he spoke in that amazing English voice, he reminded her more of an Afghan hound.

"Alice Stanhope," Peggy told him. "I found a job for her at the hospital."

The prince nodded. "That's what I heard." He was a trifle peeved. He called Peggy his "liaison officer" with the day-to-day proceedings of the hotel. She should have told him straightaway. The prince was no longer on good terms with the owner, Lucia Magnifico. She had been up here, making a fuss this afternoon, and left only just before the guests were due. Despite his apparent composure, Peggy knew he was frightened of Lucia and what she might do to get his rooms. He was especially scared when she arrived accompanied by her diminutive Armenian lawyer, poised at her heel like a beady-eyed Chihuahua.

Lucia Magnifico wanted the prince out. She'd already had an architect prepare drawings to convert the top floor into seven separate rooms. Cairo was teeming with staff officers and civilian advisers, American businessmen and Australian purchasing officials: all of them loaded with their government's money. They all wanted a place to stay. She was a woman of the world. Lucia knew that such men didn't want big hotels or official accommodations, with a guard in the lobby to watch their comings and goings. They wanted a small discreet hideout in a fashionable area near the river, a friendly, anonymous, comfortable pied-à-terre like this hotel. Lucia could no longer afford to let the "Russian poseur" occupy the whole top floor, no matter what her foolish father may have promised back in peacetime.

"Life must go on," Lucia had told him with simple directness. "I have to pay my bills." She was a slim woman who delighted in good jewelry and Paris dresses. She exemplified the fact that the Italians living in Cairo were the best-dressed and most sophisticated of the foreign contingents. It was in recognition of this that the Egyptian king surrounded himself with Italian courtiers. Everyone knew the British were ugly, coarse, and ill-dressed. Their soldiers—in huge baggy shorts, threadbare woolen sweaters, and slouch hats—looked like circus clowns. Worst of all, as she'd told the prince that afternoon, they were always pleading poverty.

Having said it, Lucia had looked down at her black silk dress and plucked a hair from it. She frowned. She should never have sat down on his sofa. She'd had enough of his horrid Abyssinian cats, and of his using precious hot water in the middle of the night, and trying to tune to Radio Moscow on his antiquated wireless set, and blowing fuses to black out all the lights in the building.

The prince closed his eyes to repress the memory of this afternoon. He smiled at Peggy and at Alice. He liked having attractive women at his parties, although they held no attraction for him personally. And Peggy was an old friend. The rapport between them was based on the fact that they had both been living in Cairo before the war started. Robin Darymple was treated in the same way, because he held a peacetime commission. They were real residents, permitted to call the prince Piotr; the others were just wartime visitors.

Alice was swept away by a young staff officer who claimed to have met her in Alexandria. As the prince watched her go he turned to Peggy and in a more serious voice said, "Tell me how you met the alluring Alice Stanhope, darling." He offered her a brass bowl of pistachio nuts but didn't bring it very near, knowing she would decline.

"Her father is some kind of political adviser in the Gulf," said Peggy, who had found out very little in their brief and hectic rides on a crowded bus to the Midan Ismail and then an even more crowded streetcar to the hospital. "Her mother got some wretched bug and had to come to Egypt. Mummy lives in Alex." The final part was in a passable imitation of Alice Stanhope's proper English accent.

Piotr gave a tiny smile to acknowledge the joke. "Yes, the mother is a well-known society hostess. The Stanhopes know everyone worth knowing." There was a note of envy in his voice. "Does Alice play bridge?"

"I'll ask her."

"We so need someone," he said plaintively.

"You ask her, then."

"No, you. Don't say for money," he said. "Just for the sheer pleasure of the game."

It was his conceit that he played bridge well. In fact he usually lost. Luckily, he paid up with good grace. Had he not done so, Robin Darymple would have stopped coming. Darymple was a demon gambler and kept accounts in a small black notebook, worrying about whether he was making a profit.

"I think it will all depend on her boyfriend," said Peggy, watching Alice as a group of young men gathered around her. "They see a lot of each other."

"Does he play bridge?" said the prince.

"Are we talking about the corporal?" said Robin Darymple, who had learned in the mess how to listen to two or three conversations at once. He came closer. "A gormless fellow with baggy trousers? I saw him. . . . It would make things damned awkward, spending an evening playing cards with an OR." Darymple made sure he didn't share any social activities with "other ranks," even female ones.

"Why would it?" said Peggy. "I thought the war was being

fought to do away with class distinctions and all that rubbish."

"Do you have soldiers and officers in the same wards at the hospital?" said Piotr, who always liked to stir a dispute.

"Corporals are the worst of all," said Darymple, smiling provocatively. "They can't hold their drink as well as the sergeants, and they lack the fawning subservience of the privates. I would never sit down for a game of bridge with a corporal."

"I hope he plays and beats you hollow," said Peggy. Darymple chortled.

"What's this I hear about you leaving us, Robin?" the prince asked him.

"Ah, that's all very hush-hush, Piotr," said Darymple, and lowered his voice. "I met a old chum in Shepheard's bar last week: Toby Wallingford, RNVR, a very good pal. I thrashed him countless times at school; he says he still has the scars. Now the lucky brute has got himself lined up with some gangster outfit that chases the Hun way out in the blue. They raise a little hell and come back to town to raise hell again."

"It sounds very dangerous, Robin," said Peggy. She knew it was what any woman was expected to say when men were bragging. They were all like that: concerned with their little bits of colored ribbon and their absurd egos. They had to tell you how brave they were, and it had to be done by means of infantile jokes. War seemed to bring out a man's most tiresome side.

The prince said, "We have their measure now, I think. We'll stop them before they get very far. Benghazi is my bet."

"Yes, and I'm just shuffling bits of paper all day. It makes me livid to miss it all. And look at what those Eye-tie frogmen did last month; it's all coming out now. Got right into Alex and blew the bottoms out of H.M.S. *Valiant* and *Queen Elizabeth* too."

"Were they badly damaged?"

"Damned right they were. The dark blue jobs are going through the motions of pretending the ships are in one piece— saluting the quarterdeck, raising the flags, and holding church services every Sunday—but the fact is that both those battleships are resting their hulls on the bottom of the harbor."

"Yes, that's what I'd heard," said the prince.

"I've got to get into the fight soon," said Darymple, reaching over to the bowl of nuts and sifting them to find good ones. "A chap has to have a decent gong if he wants a career in the postwar army. Wally's outfit is my big chance." He put a nut into his mouth and crunched on it.

"Congratulations, old boy," said the prince.

"And I'd go up a rank immediately, that's the drill for anyone accepted by one of those mobs; major."

"Splendid. I wish I was young enough—"

"Combined services: soldiers, sailors, and bloody airmen too, they tell me. My pal Wally is a sailor. But that's the way the war is going. We've got to give them a taste of their own blitz-krieg games. That's the way I see it."

"What will you do with your room?" asked the ever-practical Peggy.

"Steady on, old girl. Don't pick over my carcass yet."

"I've put the new girl—Alice, I mean—into that room Lieu-tenant Anderson said he wanted kept for him. I'm frightened he'll suddenly appear."

"Andy was in the Tobruk show," said the prince.

"Tobruk?" said Darymple. "That was a sticky do." Darym-ple did not admire one-time Sergeant Anderson and the way in which he'd earned a Military Medal, a commission, and then the Military Cross in the course of twelve months' fighting. More than once he'd found reason to give Anderson a blistering rocket. One lunchtime, here in the hotel dining room, he'd admonished the lieutenant for his appalling table manners. And the night before Andy went into the blue, Darymple had summoned the military police here to quell his noisy drunken bottle party. All kinds of riffraff had gone wandering through the Magnifico that night: singing lewdly on the stairs, vomiting in one of the am-phorae, and breaking the chain in the downstairs toilet. Darymple had brought that celebration to a sudden conclusion and bawled Anderson out in front of his pals.

"Yes," said the prince. "He's with armored cars, and they're always at the very front. He was supporting the New Zealanders. They took Ed Duda and linked up with the garrison. Andy did one of his lunatic acts and took his cars forward without waiting for orders. He was one of the first ones to break through the perimeter." Blank-faced, the prince looked at Peggy and at Darymple again. Everyone knew how jealous he was of Anderson.

"How do you know that?" said Darymple petulantly. "None of the official communiqués said who broke through." He reached for a handful of black olives.

"Andy owed me a fiver," explained the prince. "One of his chaps—a delicious young lieutenant—had to bring captured enemy documents back to GHQ Cairo. Andy told him to pop in to see me. He brought me a crate of Italian brandy and a whole Parmesan cheese captured from an Italian headquarters. Lovely cheese; it's on these biscuits you've been eating. And the brandy is not too bad. They live well, even in the desert. The Italians keep a sense of proportion; I've always said so."

This aside was calculated to prove that the prince had not suffered at the hands of Lucia.

"And there was a scribbled note from Andy to say we were quits. It took me about an hour to decipher his writing, but that's what I made it. He's a good fellow, Andy. But I don't think he'll be back in the Magnifico for a bit. He's probably capturing Rommel single-handed by now. His confrere said Andy had been made up to captain—acting, temporary and unpaid—and his divisional commander has put him in for a DSO."

Darymple had been chewing his way through the olives. Now he straightened up to stifle a sigh of exasperation. The prince gave Peggy a little wink. Peggy smiled. Piotr was an unsurpassed troublemaker.

"The flowers on your balcony are lovely, Piotr," Peggy said, to change the subject. "The little orange bush is doing well; the blossom gives off such a perfume. Cairo is so glorious at this time of year."

"Give me an English winter," said Darymple. "This weather is awful: neither one thing nor the other. I looked out of the window this morning and wondered why I wasn't back home hunting."

"Cairo is Cairo," said the prince in that over-stressed English voice. "Listen to its Babel. Breathe in and smell the hot wind off the desert. Where is your soul, Darymple? It's not supposed to be a cut-price version of the English shires."

Peggy looked at him, never sure how much of what he said was a joke. "You said you wanted to talk about something special," she reminded him.

"I don't want everyone to know," said the prince, "just old pals." He looked around and decided that the threesome were not overheard. "My birthday. Wouldn't it be splendid to dress up, go somewhere smart, and have a proper birthday celebration. Just a few old friends?"

"When?" said Peggy.

"You'd give us a Russian meal?" asked Darymple. Before committing himself one way or the other, he wanted to be quite sure that the prince was going to pay.

"Perhaps a Russian dish or two," said the prince, who knew exactly how Darymple's mind worked.

"It's a gorgeous idea," said Peggy. "I'll make a list, and we'll all contribute equally to the cost."

The prince smiled at her, and they both watched Darymple frown. "That's it, then," said the prince. He liked Peggy; she was always quick to understand him. He touched her elbow gently to guide her away. "Perhaps I can ask you to come look at something in the kitchen?" he said. "You're always so clever about parties." He grabbed a bottle from a side table, filled her glass, and then took her away from Darymple and toward his minuscule kitchen.

Once inside, the prince closed the kitchen door and said, "Peggy, darling. I simply must talk to you."

"Whatever is it, Piotr?" Piotr always contrived to look youthful, with his wavy hair and clear skin, but now the last rays of the sun flooded through the kitchen window to strike the side of his face. The pitiless light revealed his age. There were rings under his eyes and loose wrinkly flesh at his collar. His skin was pale, almost white, as if powdered. A lock of his wavy hair had fallen forward over his brow, and his carefully plucked eyebrows lowered as he leaned forward to her. She wondered whether he was on drugs. Cairo was awash with drugs at present, and more and more Europeans were experimenting with them. She saw the results at the hospital.

"Who was that officer grilling you in the lobby the other night? I must know."

"Officer?" She knew what he was talking about but she wanted a minute to think. "In the lobby? Here?" She moved a tray of crackers—each decoratively topped with a sliver of cheese and a piece of anchovy—and made a space to put her glass down.

"Yes. Officer in the lobby," he repeated. "You were showing him your passport."

"Oh, that was nothing. That was an old friend of mine. He wanted my passport number to put me on the embassy list."

"Embassy list? List for what?"

She improvised. "He said he'd get me invited to the embassy parties."

"Are you telling me the truth, Peggy dear?"

"Captain Marker—Billy Marker," she added, inventing a first name for him. "I've known him for ages."

"He had Special Investigation Branch written all over him." And as another thought struck him, he said, "Why would an army captain be putting your name down for the embassy?"

"You'll have to ask him yourself," said Peggy. She hadn't wanted to lie about her encounter with Captain Marker, but one thing would lead to another and she didn't want to start explaining to Piotr about Solomon and the houseboat and Karl's money. It was all private, and she wanted to keep it like that. At least for the time being.

"Captain William Marker," said Prince Piotr, as if committing the name to memory. "I'll make inquiries about him."

"Why?"

"They're trying to kill me, Peggy," he said, in a desperate whisper. He leaned over the sink to look out of the window, as if there might be someone hanging on to it, eavesdropping. Anywhere but Cairo that might have been funny. But in Cairo the chance of someone's hanging precariously from the sill of a top story window to eavesdrop was not to be lightly dismissed.

"Kill you? Piotr, really!" she said reproachfully.

He reached up to get a decorated tin from the shelf. She could see now that he wore a tight corset. She'd suspected it in the past but as he stood on tiptoe it became obvious. He emptied the tin on to the drainboard. It was mostly ancient breadcrumbs and some flour, but there were tiny chips of wood and a broken piece of glass, rounded to suggest it was a sliver from a broken bottle. He sifted through the crumbs and flour with his fingertips until he found some other bits of rubbish: a coarse strand of jute, unidentifiable beadlike blobs, and fragments of cardboard. "These things have come out of the bread," said the prince. "Now that I know what's going on, I've told my man to slice up every loaf carefully and put everything he finds into this tin. I'm keeping it as evidence."

"From your bread?"

"Suppose I'd swallowed that," he said using his fingertips with obvious distaste to separate the splinter of glass from the heap.

"Everyone finds things in the bread from time to time, Piotr. Egypt is like that. No one is trying to kill you."

"I thought you'd be more perceptive, Peggy. You being a nurse." He was sulky, like a small child.

"Who would want to kill you, Piotr? And why?"

"All kinds of people," he said vaguely, as if regretting confiding in her. He pushed the "evidence" back into its tin and replaced it on the shelf. Then he opened the door and without another word went back to his guests.

He was angry, and she wondered if he'd now added her to his list of suspects. She waited a moment to catch her breath, then sipped her drink and spent a moment looking at the flowers and plants on the patio. On the other side of the door she could hear frantic conversation and laughter and the music from the record player. Was she going mad, or were the people around her going mad? Everyone seemed to be obsessed with spies. She didn't arrive at any satisfactory answer. When her drink was finished, she too went back to the party and soon drifted to the door.

Alice Stanhope was sitting on the sofa with an officer on each side of her; she didn't seem to want to be rescued. Peggy looked at the long-case clock; it was still early. Tonight would be a good night to wash her hair, go to bed early, and read a book.

8

To the casual observer, the soldiers seemed to belong here. Their khaki matched the streets and the buildings and the desert that stretched far beyond the horizon. It was the Arabs who were incongruous: the women in black from top to toe, and the men in their ankle-length white galabiyas.

Only the behavior of the crowds showed clearly who was at home. The natives were purposeful. They so obviously lived here. They ran and jumped and shouted and bargained and argued and laughed and cried. The soldiers were mostly young. Wearing their heavy studded boots, they tramped slowly and aimlessly. With nowhere to go, they wandered up the streets and then listlessly wandered down again. They seldom strayed into the quieter areas; they kept to the busy thoroughfares. They got in the way and, blundering into other soldiers, scrambled to stare into shop windows to avoid saluting officers. They huddled defensively in little groups and sat down on the curb to gawk at the intensity of the life around them. Many of them got very drunk; many of them vomited.

For all Cairo's life was in the streets. It was a city turned inside out: empty buildings and crowded streets. Beggars were in astounding variety: men beggars, women beggars, mothers carrying babies, some crippled, some aged and bent, some just learning to walk. Children offered trays of fruit, shoelaces, and flyswatters. There were luridly painted barrows, with arrays of brightly colored foods and drinks. Moving adroitly through the crowds swarmed the pickpockets and smiling guides who whispered of forbidden books, peep shows, and available sisters.

Anyone looking more closely at the khaki-clad figures saw they were not identical. Some wore tartan kilts and some wore turbans. Gurkhas had wicked-looking knives, and the military police had red hats and pistols. The New Zealanders wore wide-brimmed felt hats, and the Australians had a version that was clipped up on one side. It was the hat their fathers had worn when walking through these same streets a war and a generation earlier.

"Well, this is it, sir," Captain Marker told his new boss as they sat down at a table in the flashy little restaurant on Sharia Emad el Dine. "Cleo's Club. Just about every crook and black-marketeer in Cairo visits this place at some time or other."

"They all look very prosperous," Jimmy Ross said. He'd asked Marker to take him to where the successful crooks gathered.

"Of course," said Marker. They ordered drinks and looked at the menu. "That fellow at the end of the bar owns the place. They call him Zooly; he's one of the richest men in this town. If you want a tank or a virgin or your enemy murdered, he'll fix it for you—at a price."

Ross looked at the man. He looked ordinary enough, but he'd know him again. If Ross was going to get a new identity and disappear, he would need some help. A place like this would be where he would find it.

"Roast chicken," Ross told the waiter.

"Same for me," said Marker. "It's probably British army food anyway."

"Can't you arrest him?" said Ross, after the waiter had gone.

"Arresting Egyptians on major charges is a dangerous resort for people like us. They are civilians, and Egypt is still a neutral country."

"So don't our deserters use that loophole?"

"Pose as Arabs, you mean? It's not easy. Everyone over the age of fourteen has to be registered with the Ministry of the Interior and have a *rokhsa*, an employment card. It has finger-prints and a photo."

"Sounds effective," said Ross, abandoning any idea of using an Egyptian passport to escape.

"That's how we police the brothels," Marker said. "Any girl who shelters a deserter has her employment card withdrawn and can't get a job. We also have a photo and description of every prostitute and cabaret hostess in SIB's file. But you don't think he could be one of our own people, do you?"

"Rommel's spy, you mean?"

"That's all the brigadier cares about at present. He'll give you his lecture once he gets back."

Their food arrived and they started eating. At a table not far away, Jimmy Ross noticed two officers consuming a lavish meal. One of them looked like a chap he'd seen at the Magnifico. The other one wore the gold wavy rings of the Royal Navy Volunteer Reserve on the shoulders of his khaki battle-dress blouse. The black triangular patch on his shoulder was, like so many other locally made cloth badges, somewhat crudely stitched. It de-picted a white snake coiled and ready to strike. Under it the letters IDT stood for Independent Desert Teams, Marker told him. Ross had never heard of it.

Lieutenant Commander Toby Wallingford was a tall lean patri-cian figure, with wavy hair that the sun had made golden. He had the bony nose and small perfect mouth that would have led most people to say he was an Englishman even before they heard his drawling voice.

Captain Robin Darymple was sitting opposite him. His sar-torial distinction was in the special dark shade of his khaki. It told those who understood the subtlety of cap-badge snobbery that he was an officer of an elite regiment.

"So you have a free hand?" said Darymple, with unbounded envy. They were both at the coffee and brandy stage of a remarkably good lunch.

"By no means," said Wallingford, who had long ago discovered that officers with a free hand were pestered by friends to do all sorts of things they didn't want to do. "I am responsible to three or four different desk wallahs. That's the worst part of it."

"I thought you said you were the commanding officer."

"But only of my little team," said Wallingford. He stubbed out the butt of his cigarette in the ashtray. "Independent Desert Teams means exactly what it says. We are all separately briefed and quartered, for maximum security."

"And when are you off next?"

"They don't tell us too much, Robbie. With these little shows, you can't afford to have the Hun waiting for you at the other end."

"It sounds damned good, Wally. I'd give anything to be in your shoes." He'd started calling him Wally the way he had at school. But at school they'd not been close friends: more like adversaries.

"I thought you were sent back here because you were sick," said Toby. For a moment or two he said nothing. He was looking at the cigarette pack and the gold lighter he'd arranged on the table. As if with reluctance, he picked up the cigarettes and offered them to Darymple. Darymple declined and Wallingford lit one for himself. He was a compulsive smoker; it was one of the few signs of nervousness he ever revealed.

"Well, that's just it," said Darymple, glad of an opportunity to explain things. "I'll be making my number with the quack next week. Chances are I'll be recategorized, pronounced fit, and sent into the blue."

"Good show!" Wally waved and, without being told, the

waiter brought the brandy bottle and poured another big measure for each of them.

"On the face of it, yes. But with Rommel on the rampage, all officers—without exception—are being dumped into transit camps. I've tried pulling strings but it's not easy."

Wallingford nodded without showing any real concern. "Not so good."

"Instead of going back to my own battalion, I'll just be sent to any mob that needs an officer. My God, Wally, I could wind up serving with some bloody clod-hopping line regiment or yeomanry. I could find myself amid elderly beer-swilling Territorials or a mess full of oiks." He stifled a belch and then smirked to show his embarrassment. They'd both had a lot to eat and a great deal to drink.

"You always exaggerate, Robbie." Wally chuckled at his friend's predicament. He looked at him and nodded. He'd make him sweat. Those school beatings were forgiven but not forgotten, and Robin Darymple had a lot of other sins to answer for. He'd make the little blighter crawl. He sipped his brandy and said nothing. He just looked at the glaring sunlit street outside and at the unfortunate wretches who thronged there, nowhere else to go.

"Could you do something?" said Darymple finally.

"What sort of thing?"

"Make a place for me in your outfit." Now that Darymple had voiced his difficulty, he was affected by it. He was unable to keep the edge of desperation from his voice. "I mentioned it the other day. You said you'd think about it."

"In my outfit? How would you see that working?"

"I'd do anything, Wally."

Wallingford looked at him, pursing his lips as though thinking hard.

"I'd drop a rank," said Darymple in one last frantic plea.

"I'm still thinking about it," said Wallingford. "If there's any way of fitting you in, I'll do it. You can count on me, Robin. You know that." He looked across the bar to catch the waiter's eye.

"I know I can, Wally."

"Looks like the waiters have all disappeared. No matter, they can put it on my account."

"That was a smashing lunch, Wally. Let me chip in."

"No need; I know you're stony broke," said Wallingford. "Yes, it's good. I eat here a lot between our little shows. They know me."

"Is this a club?" said Darymple. He had been studying the women; most of them were young and attractive. "I've never been here before. Some bloody marvelous bints—some of them unattached by the look of it."

"Not for you, Robbie. The sort of unattached bints you see in here would expect to find a solid gold bracelet under the pillow."

"How did you discover this place?"

"I got browned off fighting my way through all those chairborne old bastards sitting on the veranda at Shepheard's," explained Wallingford. "This place is for chaps from the sharp end."

"Really? There seem to be a lot of wogs."

"It's a mixed membership, but they're mostly good types. They're people who can get things done, and that's important in this town."

"Who are they?" Darymple looked around. It was certainly a mixed collection. Despite what Wallingford said about the club being used by fighting troops, there were plenty of rear-echelon people in evidence. There were locals too: prosperous-looking Arabs in expensive suits, with gorgeous women in tow. There were three very pretty girls sitting with some noisy Australians at the long bar. They were drinking heavily, from bottles that were left on the counter for them, and arguing about a card game they'd had the previous night.

"With the cash that passes over that bar each month, Robbie, I could buy up Shepheard's, and Groppi too."

"Where does it come from? Black market, you mean?"

"I don't ask too many questions, old boy. But I'll tell you this: I know a brigadier who spent months trying to get the bloody quartermaster to send him radio-telephone sets. He came in here and found a man who let him have a dozen of them that same afternoon . . . brand new and still in their packing cases."

"A civvy?"

"Yes, a Gyppo."

"Where did an Egyptian get them?"

"Don't ask."

"Good grief, Wally. The brigadier bought them on the black market?"

"If you need something to fight the Hun, get it. That's the way people work these days."

"And you do the same thing?"

"Things are changing, Robbie, and we've got to change too. We can't wait while all those dozy buggers in GHQ refight the Boer War."

"But how did your friend pay for the RT sets?"

"Use your noodle, Robbie. You can always shuffle the paperwork around to make the accounts balance. In fact, if you join us, that is exactly the sort of job I'd need you to do for us."

"An adjutant, you mean?"

"You've had long enough with the Cairo desk wallahs. You must be an expert at shuffling the paperwork by now." He got to his feet, and so did Darymple.

"Well, yes, I suppose I have," said Darymple, not wishing to deny the expertise that might procure for him the job he so wanted.

He followed Wallingford to the cloakroom. The man on duty there had a naval cap ready without even glancing at the ticket. "That's why the food's so bloody good," said Wallingford. "It's all black market grub. We've probably eaten steaks intended for the commander in chief and all his top brass." He said it as though such provenance would add to his enjoyment. He dropped some coins into the tray, and the servant made appropriate noises of appreciation.

Outside in the Sharia Emad el Dine, the doorman had already seen Wallingford coming and was signaling for his driver to bring his car. "Won't you let me chip in for that lunch?" Darymple asked again.

"I thought you were the fellow who was broke and needed a loan," said Wallingford.

"Well, yes," said Darymple, flattered that his friend had remembered the long story he'd told him at their previous meeting.

"Or has your fellow come back and paid up the money you won?"

"No such luck," said Darymple.

"Well, I've fixed up a loan for you, old boy. Five hundred quid on signature. Okay?"

"Wonderful!"

"I'll take you over to my bank. The old boy who runs it owes me a few favors."

"Thank you, Wally."

As they stood outside the restaurant, a long column of men came marching down the street. They were German prisoners of war. Guarding them were weary-looking British infantrymen, with rifles at the slope, and a few red-capped military policemen in their beautifully clean khaki. Mounted Egyptian police, riding at front and back, imperiously held up the traffic to ensure that the column was not delayed. They were going from the railway station to the POW reception center at the Citadel. The British liked to move enemy prisoners through the streets like this; it impressed the natives with British power. And yet the enemy maintained a posture out of keeping with their status as prisoners. Even the torn and stained German uniforms were buttoned carefully, and they marched in step with their heads held high and eyed Cairo with the assurance of conquerors.

The club doorman opened the door of Wallingford's car. It

was an austere military version of a twelve-horsepower family saloon. It was not a grand vehicle, not the sort of thing that generals roared around town in, but any kind of official car was a coveted status symbol. To cap it all, Wallingford had his own driver: a crop-headed fellow with orange-colored South African flashes on his shoulder.

"We're going to see Uncle Mahmoud," said Wallingford, as he settled back in his seat.

"Ja. The Muski," said the driver, naming Cairo's big bazaar.

"And we'll only be a few minutes. I don't want you dashing off to see one of your bints." The driver nodded solemnly to acknowledge the joke. To Darymple, Wallingford said, "Percy has got bints in every street in Cairo. Every shape and size. Is that right, Percy?"

"I am a married man, sir." He spoke without turning his eyes away from the road. His voice was harsh and guttural.

"You're a mad fellow," said Wallingford. "I don't know how you do it. Every shape and size," he said to Darymple. "Every shape and size. And some of them are smashers!"

"Where are we going?" Darymple was looking out at the streets. He had expected to be taken to an orthodox bank. He'd expected to go somewhere on one of the big boulevards, a place with marble and glass and mahogany counters, and he thought Uncle Mahmoud would be a man in a well-cut dark suit.

In fact Toby Wallingford took him to Cairo's noisy, smelly, crowded bazaar which occupies a large part of the medieval quarter named Gamaliyya. They stopped near Feshawi's, a nine-hundred-year-old coffeehouse where middle-class Egyptians went and discussed the problems of the world. Having left the car they pushed through the crowds, past sweet-smelling bags of spices, and through gold and silver merchants hammering out their bangles and brooches. When the narrow dusty alley was at its most noisy and crowded and smelly, Wallingford turned into a narrow entrance almost hidden behind a tall display of antique carpets. The carpets covered the floors and the walls, and a colorful ocean of them was arranged in waves from the ceiling. An agile young Arab leaped forward and started rolling more of them out for display. As each carpet flopped open, he jumped back to throw another in their path.

"We are seeing Mahmoud. In the back," said Wallingford, not pausing in his stride. They went through the display room to a low door. He opened it to reveal a curtained-off little back room that seemed full of smoke. "Mahmoud, you old bastard," Wallingford called. "I've brought a very old friend of mine to see you."

Darymple came to a sudden halt as Wally dragged aside the beaded curtain to reveal the inner room. He considered himself an old Cairo hand, but he'd never been in a place like this before. Blue perfumed smoke billowed to the dark ceiling. Rich carpets colored the walls and floor of this tiny space, into which half a dozen men were crowded. Four of them were dressed in richly decorated galabiyas. They were sitting talking and puffing and passing the mouthpiece of a water pipe from one to another. Two servants moved about behind the sweet-smelling smoke. They were discreetly attending to the preparation of coffee and feeding small blocks of honey-flavored tobacco into the bowl of the water pipe, locally known as a *shisheh*. As if suddenly becoming aware of the tobacco smoke, a servant fanned it up toward the nicotine-colored ceiling.

A backgammon table was moved and two gold chairs were speedily placed on each side of Mahmoud. He was a stout and jovial man with dark glasses of modern design and a white mustache that fitted across his dark face like a strip of adhesive tape. *"Allah ma'ak,"* Allah be with you, he said.

"Allah yittawil omrak," May Allah lengthen your life, replied Wallingford glibly.

The old man bowed. In true Arab style he welcomed them with exuberant compliments and wide movements of his cloaked arms.

Upon a brass-topped side table, tiny cups appeared. The

servant—a man who did little other than continuously make and serve coffee—brought a highly polished long-handled copper pot, a *kanaka*. He held it over the flaming charcoal long enough for it to bubble up and then repeated the action twice more. While the liquid was still frothy he poured it into tiny china cups. The first cup was served to Wallingford, to mark him as the more honored of the guests. Two tiny porcelain plates were produced. Each bore four honey-brown pastries, *kunafa* and *baklava*. Two were filo pastry layered with finely chopped nuts; the others were made of shredded dough. The servant sprinkled them with rose water.

Robin Darymple knew something of the drill. He knew there would be much coffee consumed, and time would pass before they got down to business. It was one of the many things about Arabs he found unbearable. He didn't like being tested and scrutinized, especially by these men. Darymple felt demeaned at finding himself in the role of supplicant. He looked at Wallingford, but he was talking to the thin old man next to him in an animated and amused manner, calling him Tahseen. They obviously knew each other very well. This didn't in itself surprise Darymple. Even at school Wallingford had been something of an outsider. His people had come to collect him one Easter: a weird couple. Wally's father had had a beard and his mother wore too much jewelry. They were flashy. Since then Darymple had always wondered if Wallingford was really as English as he claimed to be.

Offered the mouthpiece of the *shisheh*, Darymple had been about to decline it but decided that such a response might give offense. A servant put a new chunk of tobacco into the bowl and prodded the flames. The smoke had to be drawn through the water; it was chilled and honey-sweet. Such smoking required strongly inhaled breaths, and that increased the effect. It took a bit of getting used to, but Darymple decided it wasn't so bad. In fact, damned good.

Mahmoud's English was slow but fluent. He told a couple of

good stories about losing money on the horse races at the Gezira Sporting Club. Everyone laughed, although not all of them spoke English. They must have recognized Mahmoud's jokes.

Wallingford was not smoking. He said he'd had some trouble with his throat and was under doctor's orders. The bantam Tahseen spoke perfect English. He'd been to school in England and had a son at Lancing. Tahseen's jokes were more English in style.

By the time he'd been there for an hour, Darymple was enjoying himself. He was quite a raconteur himself, and when he stood up and sang a song about an elderly camel from Benghazi, it was greeted with applause.

"We must be off," Wallingford whispered, but Darymple was just getting into his stride. He'd learned that when the water of the water pipe became warm, there was a gesture with the mouthpiece that signaled for the servant to put a new pipe into position. This too won him a round of applause.

"Let's go," said Wallingford again.

"Not yet," said Darymple. "I haven't sung the sandbag song for them."

"I've got work to do," said Wallingford testily. "I've got chaps arriving."

"Don't be such a bloody little swot," said Darymple. "He was always a bloody little swot," he told the others. They looked at Wallingford and nodded sagely.

Wallingford smiled indulgently and said to Mahmoud, "Have you got the five hundred quid for him?"

"It is here. He has only to sign."

"Now listen, Robbie. I've made them give you this loan on the same terms as they do it for the army. You'd better read it all through."

"Where do I sign?" said Darymple. He waved the printed agreement in the air and clowned with it so that the men laughed.

"It's in Arabic on one side, English on the other. Mahmoud's cashier has signed. You must put your name, your address, and your place of employment."

"Place of employment?" Darymple laughed and brandished a silver pen. "I'm in the bloody army, aren't I? What shall I write: GHQ Cairo? Or will Gray Pillars do?" He looked at the others. They smiled.

"Banks prefer a street address. Put Seifeddine Building, Garden City, Cairo. What do you want: Egyptian money, English fivers?"

"Fivers will do the trick, old bean." Darymple signed the papers with a flourish.

Tahseen, who worked for Mahmoud and had worked for his father too, examined the signature and the address. "One copy for you and two copies for the bank," he said, handing Darymple one of the printed sheets. Then he counted out the big white five-pound notes and Darymple seized them happily. "Now I'll sing the sandbag song."

"Save that for next time, Robbie. Always leave them laughing, as they say in show business. It's time we moved on. Where shall I drop you, that little hotel?"

"The Magnifico will be *magnifico,*" said Darymple.

"Percy will be waiting with the car," said Wallingford, to encourage his friend.

"Your Percy is a Hun," said Darymple accusingly. Wallingford took his arm and urged him out into the crowded street.

"Percy is a good sort," said Wallingford calmly. "South Africans are good soldiers. I have half a dozen South Africans."

"Damned Boche. I know a Hun when I see one," said Darymple, his mood darkening suddenly. Then he was propelled forward by the passersby. There were beggars and men selling bootlaces and two children with long sticks who pushed past them, shouting to keep a herd of goats moving through the crowded alley. Darymple was almost knocked off his feet, but Wallingford took his arm and saved him.

"Come along, Robin."

Darymple became quieter as they pushed on through the noise and movement of the crowded bazaar. It was getting dark now, and the electric bulbs made yellow blobs in the tiny shops. The windows were crammed with sweets and spices, beans, brightly colored vegetables, and elaborate gold ornaments. Eventually a minaret of the El Azhar mosque came into view above the heads of the crowd, and Wallingford breathed a sigh of relief.

Percy had parked the car right in front of the main entrance of the most important teaching mosque of the Muslim world. Around him were carts and camels and crates containing chickens. Only with some difficulty, and much sounding of the horn, was Percy able to get the car out into the road. Wallingford heaved Darymple into the back seat. "The Hotel Magnifico," Wallingford told his driver as he climbed into the car.

Robin Darymple slumped over sideways and seemed to be asleep. "Is your friend sick?" asked Percy.

"You know what Mahmoud is like. They kept piling the old hashish into the *shisheh*," said Wallingford. "He's totally stewed. Maybe he isn't used to the stuff. He always was a bit of a berk when I knew him at school."

The driver turned his head and shot a glance at Darymple, who was lying back in his seat, eyes closed and mouth open. "Powell and Mogg will be back any time now," he said.

"Yes," said Wallingford. "Get going. We must unload El Darymple at the Magnifico and turn around fast. There will be lots of work to do when the boys get back." He noticed that the wad of five-pound notes was sticking out of Darymple's pocket. He pushed it well inside and buttoned the pocket. "Did you see the prisoners of war being marched past the club?" Wallingford asked with studied casualness.

"And every one of them perfectly in step," said Percy, as if he'd been expecting just such a question. Wallingford chuckled. Percy liked to have the last word.

* * *

The desert road was narrow. As the sun lowered in the sky the driver switched on the truck's tiny slits of light that were permitted by the blackout regulations. Faintly visible under its coating of dust, the yellow-painted truck bore the stenciled marking of the white coiled snake. It was the same design that Toby Wallingford wore on his shoulder patch: the badge of the Independent Desert Teams.

Two men were sitting side by side in the cab of the truck. "My kid will be five years old on Saturday," said Samuel Powell.

He was a thin man with pinched cheeks and large plaintive eyes. His forage cap was tucked under his shoulder flap. His red hair was cropped short at the back and sides, so that the wavy hair on top of his head sat there like a cheap toupee. His moodiness and glum appearance had encouraged the other men to call him Sandy Powell, after a popular BBC comedian. He was leaning well back in his seat as he held the steering wheel of the AEC Matador. He liked driving it; it provided him with a feeling of power. The Matador was a canvas-sided truck designed for towing six-inch howitzers. On trips across the desert, it was good to know that its heavy-duty tires, winch, and four-wheel drive could drag itself out of almost any kind of sand.

The roof of the cab was canvas. It had been rolled back to let in the air but at their last stop for a cup of tea—at the Halfway House—they'd closed it as tightly as they could.

Next to Powell sat Thomas Mogg. His face and arms bore a coating of brown desert dust. Around his neck was a silk scarf and a pair of sand goggles. He sat inside a cocoon made of a gray army blanket in which he'd spent the previous night. Mogg was a brawny Londoner with a reputation for eating and drinking and being a know-it-all. His hair was dark and he had a neat mustache that made him look extremely handsome until he opened his mouth to reveal a missing tooth. Mogg had been to a grammar school and passed his matriculation exams. He boasted about having been accepted for London University to study geography. He claimed to have volunteered for the peacetime army, giving up college in order to fight Hitler and the Nazis. In fact he'd joined the army because the magistrate had offered it as an alternative to serving a sentence for striking a policeman during an argument outside a pub at closing time.

"Five years old?" said Mogg reflectively. He knew it was the way he was expected to respond. He'd been shown the family snapshots many times. "How long since you saw them?"

"Two years and three months," said Powell. There was no pause for calculation. He kept careful accounting of the time.

"Does your missus manage all right?"

"Last time I heard, she was with her mother. But she's looking round for a place of our own."

"You've got to watch that," said Mogg.

"Why?"

"Birds in a place on their own," said Mogg. "She could get up to anything in a place of her own."

"What are you talking about?" said Powell. He had a quick Welsh temper.

"I didn't mean nothing," said Mogg calmly. He was big and strong. He had nothing to fear from any of the other men, let alone a little fellow like Powell, but he didn't want to provoke him. "But what about the rent and the bills and that?"

"She says when everyone comes back from the war, houses will be hard to get. Now it's easy to find a place."

"Yeah, well, like that," said Mogg vaguely, to show he wasn't really interested in Powell's domestic problems. There was a lot of traffic coming up toward them; it was coming from Cairo. The oncoming side of the road was busy all the time now. Darkness would soon render them invisible to prying Luftwaffe reconnaissance aircraft. Night was a time of movement. Eighteen-ton White transporters had the enormous weights of cruiser tanks swaying gently on their backs. There were long Service Corps convoys. Those dirty old trucks—slow and weighed down by infantry tightly packed into them—had obviously done the journey countless times. Right behind them came a medical convoy that might have come straight from the depot: half a dozen brand new ambulances and a three-ton Bedford operating theater with trailer. There was even a shiny new Church Army canteen. All of it was going westward to the battlefront.

"But we don't get any mail, do we?" said Powell. Sometimes, as now, the Welsh accent was strong. He bit his lip as he caught sight of an oncoming motorcycle, some bloody fool weaving about to demonstrate his riding skill. Powell touched the brake pedal. Blue and white armband: signal corps. Those dispatch riders were all the same. They had to show you how daring they were. As he passed them the rider cut it very fine and accelerated away with a loud burst of sound. "Stupid sod," said Powell without much emotion.

"Well, you must have known what it would be like when you joined us," said Mogg. Mogg hadn't even noticed the closeness of that imbecile on the motorbike. Mogg had never learned to drive. He was like all the rest of them who couldn't drive. They just plonked themselves down in the passenger seat like a sack of potatoes and were completely oblivious to what went on in front of them.

"What do they do with it? Where does it end up?"

"The mail? Just piles up in the army post office, I suppose."

"Along with the letters for the dead and the missing and the POWs," said Powell, thinking about it. "I suppose it does."

"Bloody cold, isn't it? I'll be glad when Cairo comes." Mogg pulled up the collar of his jacket and arranged the blanket around his body. He tried to doze but the road wasn't good enough and he wasn't tired enough.

"Look out, Gestapo," said Powell in a matter-of-fact voice, slowing down to obey the signals of a red-capped military policeman. He was hoping that at the last minute they would wave him on, but it wasn't to be. He stopped with a little squeal of brakes, followed by a hiss of compressed air as he took his foot off the pedal. There were two MPs, with perfectly pressed uniforms and blancoed webbing. Their attire was a way of telling all personnel that from this point eastward, soldiers had to look like soldiers. One of the cops walked around the back of the truck to inspect it. The other one scrutinized their papers very slowly and carefully. "Battlefield salvage?" said the policeman reading from the paper. "What's that supposed to mean?"

"It's signed by the ordnance wallah," said Mogg, craning his neck to look at the manifest as if he'd never seen it before. "It's stuff the boffins want to shufti." On the other side of the cab, Powell got out onto the running board and stood up to inspect the canvas top of the driver's cab. He took the opportunity of watching the other policeman walk to the back of the truck and pluck at the loose canvas to look inside.

"What kind of stuff?" Mogg heard the second policeman trying to open the rear. It was an offense not to have loads secured against casual theft.

"German odds and ends," said Mogg. "Tank periscopes and artillery sights. It's for evaluation at the depot."

"Any small arms?" said the policeman. The second red cap was now writing down the registration number on his sheet.

"Naw, I don't think so," said Mogg. "It's all crated up. Do you want to take a look-see? You'll need a lever or something to open those crates. And I'll want some kind of properly signed paperwork to say it was you lot who did it. Signed by an officer."

The policeman looked at Mogg for a moment before handing back his papers. "Get going," he said. "And take off that stupid scarf, do up your buttons, and get your bloody hair cut. You're not in the blue now, laddie."

Mogg stifled the indignation that almost made him explode. Powell started up the engine and revved it a moment before they pulled away.

"They made a lovely couple," said Powell, when they were well away from the checkpoint and making a good speed.

"Bloody toy soldiers," said Mogg. " 'What did you do in the war, Daddy?' 'I put real soldiers on fizzers for not polishing their boots and washing their faces.' Get your hair cut! Shitheads, that's what they are."

"This road gets longer every time I drive it," said Powell. He looked out across the sand, trying to spot the pyramids that marked the outskirts of Cairo. There were more and more hand-painted signs at the roadside. Pointers indicated the positions of dumps, depots, training battalions, divisional headquarters, field hospitals, and graves registration units. Powell saw no unit names he recognized. It was a turbulent time: Rommel was coming and everything available was being thrown at him. From what he'd heard, half those signs were bogus ones anyway, put there to confuse spies. The whole land was full of spies.

"What's that supposed to mean?" said Mogg suddenly. He imitated the policeman's accent well enough to make Powell jump. "Stupid sod."

"I'm going to talk to the boss about my mail," said Powell. "I've got to know what's happening back home. I want to send my missus some money."

"Old Wally will give you a right rocket if he hears you calling him the boss," said Mogg, and chuckled at the thought of seeing Lieutenant Commander Wallingford's reaction to such a form of address.

"Well, I mean it. I will talk to him," said Powell.

Mogg looked at him and said nothing. Once Sandy Powell got an idea in that Welsh head of his, there was nothing to budge him. "I'm hungry," said Mogg, in an effort to change the subject. "I wonder what's on the stove tonight."

"I can't stand those wog eggs," said Powell, as he began thinking about what he'd have for supper. "I don't think they come from hens."

"No, they're buzzard eggs," said Mogg. "A hen's egg here-abouts is no bigger than a pea."

"Here, boy! Are you serious?" said Powell. He looked away from the road to see Mogg's face.

"'Course I am. Old Ali Baba goes out every morning with his buzzard gun. Don't say you haven't seen him."

"You bloody fool." Powell laughed in relief. "I thought you meant it for a minute."

"Crikey. Look at those bloody pyramids. Spooky looking."

They had made that mysterious transition from the desert to the valley of the Nile. For over four thousand years this place had been celebrated by the pyramids and the Sphinx. The fading light and the dust in the air made the pyramids shimmer with reds and mauves and golden colors. The constantly changing angle of the sun's rays made the shapes flat and unreal. "At the depot there was a sergeant who reckoned they were from another planet."

"The pyramids? Bullshit. They were tombs for kings, Moggy, you know that."

"This bloke reckoned they were enormous cubes of stone, buried deep in the ground. He said if anyone started digging down, they'd find that the pyramids were only little corners of them, sticking up out of the sand."

Powell stole a glance away from the road and tried to imagine how much stone that might mean concealed under the earth. "Bleeding hell!"

"And I'll tell you something else, Sandy. In the time of Jesus Christ people were coming here to see those pyramids, because they were already two thousand five hundred years old."

"Where did you get to know all this stuff?" said Powell. This hint of respect for learning spurred Mogg to provide more.

"And that Sphinx—it's got the head of a woman, the feet of a lion, and the wings of a bird. She asked riddles and bit off the head of all those who didn't give her the right answer."

"Sounds just like my old woman," said Powell, and laughed to show that he didn't mean it.

The sky was like a horrific wound. The sun turned blood red and dribbled away into lacerations slashed through the bruised clouds. Soon it was pitch dark. Only the tiny red and white convoy lights of the vehicles could be seen moving through the darkness. Driving in such conditions was stressful. Out of the night there suddenly came pedestrians and camels and horse-drawn carts. These scares grew more numerous as they neared the suburbs of Cairo. None of the local traffic carried any kind of light. From time to time Powell swerved and shouted abuse.

Mogg said, "You knew there would be no mail, Sandy. You knew that right from the beginning. If you start kicking up a fuss, Wally will bloody castrate you. I mean it. Wally may have a posh voice but he can turn nasty. Very nasty. Last month I saw him floor Percy when he answered him back. Just one wallop," said Mogg in a voice that did not hide a large measure of admiration. "That bloody Percy took it right on the jaw. His eyes closed and down he went: boom. You should have seen it!"

"Percy is a Hun," said Powell sullenly. He detested Percy.

"Yeah, well, Percy speaks languages, don't he? And he's a cold-blooded bugger. I've seen him go crawling right over near the Hun when Wally has got his mind set on some really pricey piece of loot. If Wally ever has to choose between you and Percy, you've had it, chum. Don't make no mistake about that."

"I hate bloody Huns. They started it all, didn't they?"

"In our little show we're all equal, you know that."

"Except for Wally," said Powell.

"Yes, of course, except for Wally. Wally is the boss, like you said."

They drove on for a long time. They were both tired and sick of the desert. "A cube has three sides," said Sandy Powell suddenly.

"What's that?"

"A cube has three sides, you simple-minded bugger."

"What's your drift, Sandy?"

"Those pyramids have four sides but the corner of a cube has only three. . . ."

"What?"

"That bloke in the depot you were on about. Pyramids from another planet: bullshit!"

Mogg laughed. "You take everything literally, Sandy. That's your trouble, my old mate. You've got no poetry in your soul."

Once they got to Doqqi they relaxed. This was Cairo and, for the time being, home. There was a cop directing traffic at the English Bridge. He held up the cars coming the other way and waved them on. "We're right on time," said Powell. "Slowly, now. Look for a flashlight signal."

"There's Wally."

Wallingford was on the roadside at the side of the bridge where it joined Gezira Island. He was waving a small flashlight. Even in the darkness he was easy to spot in his starched white RN shirt.

"Good evening, commander," said Powell.

Wallingford swung up on the running board and leaned into the driver's cab. "Did you get everything?"

"It all went sweetly, sir."

"The machine guns?"

"We paid him with booze, and he was as happy as a sand-boy."

"And no trouble on the road?"

"We gave your tame MP sergeant the money, and he did the rubber stamps and stuff. On the road there were a couple of spot checks, but the red caps seemed happy with the paperwork."

"Have you got your revolvers?"

"You bet," said Mogg. Powell nodded.

"Load them and strap them on. I'm going in there bare-assed. I don't think this one will turn nasty, but you can't always tell."

"Righto."

"And keep an eye on that wog houseboy of his. He's too bloody polite to be real." The two soldiers said nothing. Wallingford was often nervous like this when there was a tricky deal to do. They waited, and Wallingford smiled and said, "Okay. Keep

going, Sandy. You know where the houseboats are. It becomes a
track but the earth is firm; you'll get through okay. I'll walk
ahead to show you where we're going. Park her well up under
the trees near the moorings. Then I'll want you to bring the three
Italian guns onto the boat. Have you got a tire lever or a bayonet
or something to open the crates?"

"Yep," said Powell.

"Yes, sir," Wallingford corrected him. "I want to put on a
show for this blighter. If he buys those Eye-tie guns I'll make sure
you chaps get a little something extra."

"Right, sir. Thank you, sir," said both soldiers.

"And pull yourself together. Button up and try and look like
real soldiers. If he invites you on board, stay off the booze no
matter what he offers you. You'll need all your wits about you."
He jumped down and strode off.

"Who is this bugger he's so nervous about?" Mogg asked
Powell once Wallingford was ahead of them and out of earshot.

"A gun collector," said Powell. "A museum bloke, Wally
says."

Mogg laughed scornfully. "Wally and his bloody yarns. What
will he come up with next? On one of these bloody houseboats?
Museum geezer? That's the bloody limit." He laughed again without putting too much energy into it.

"And what's in the other crate?" asked Solomon. He dropped
down onto the chintz-covered sofa with a happy sigh. He loved
making deals and was never in a hurry to complete one. Lieutenant Wallingford, DSO, RNVR, relaxed and smiling and sitting well
back in the best armchair, was equally happy to take his time.
Only the two soldiers on the upper deck were impatient for the
evening's business to conclude.

The *City of Gold*'s drawing room was cheaply and elabo-
rately furnished in a mix of styles that Wallingford described as
like a chorus girl's country cottage. The curtains were closed and
the light through the heavy lampshades was golden. Wallingford

eyed Solomon with that dispassionate interest that a patient might show for someone with whom he was sharing a dentist's waiting room. And just as two patients in a waiting room might share nothing but the prospect of pain, so did these two men show no hurry to get to the point. "The other crate?" said Wallingford, wide-eyed and supercilious as if seeing it for the first time. "Oh, that. They shouldn't have brought that one in here," he said. "It wouldn't interest you. It's something for me."

Solomon looked at him: this pale-faced English fellow with his long wavy hair. He looked like a girl, thought Masri. How he hated the English. He tried to decide whether this casual dismissal of the third crate was part of Wallingford's artful sales talk. He decided to ignore it. "We haven't talked about numbers," said Solomon. "How many of these pieces are there?"

"There is a whole warehouse of this stuff. Captured last year in the big advance. The Germans didn't bother saving any of the ordnance from Italian armories." He stopped abruptly and sipped his drink. He'd almost added that the German lack of interest was due to the difference in the caliber of their standard small arms, but he didn't want to get into all the complications and failings of Italian ammunition. "We're talking hundreds," added Wallingford.

"Very well," said Solomon, "then let's go back to the Modello Thirty-seven." Two Breda machine guns had been set up on the floor of the houseboat's drawing room. They seemed absurdly big, dwarfing the coffee table and the sofa. "Neither of them is new," said Solomon, and he stroked the barrel of the Modello 37, which stood higher because of the massive tripod upon which the gun was mounted.

"Straight from the factory," insisted Wallingford. They'd already been through this. "Every gun is tested by the army before being crated and shipped. Apart from the test firing, they are new: brand new. I have the dockets; every gun is numbered." Wallingford took another sip of whisky. "It's a beautiful gun. That's why the Italians put them in their tanks and planes.

Muzzle velocity: two thousand six hundred feet per second."

"Yes, better than that other piece of junk," said Solomon, indicating the other machine gun: a Breda Modello 30.

"It all depends on what you like," said Wallingford calmly. "The Modello Thirty fires five hundred rounds per minute, and it's only half the weight."

"And only half the range, and only six point five millimeters," said Solomon. But he picked it up and considered it. "No stopping power, the six point five."

"A gunner can keep a very low profile behind it," said Wallingford. "That's the advantage of the bipod: he lies flat. Also, it's not too heavy: in Abyssinia the Italians were even firing them from the hip."

"And in Abyssinia the dust got into the oil and wore them out in no time," said Solomon. "And there were troubles with vibration and with scattering of the aimed shots."

Wallingford smiled.

Solomon said, "I'll show you a copy of the official Italian report that went to Rome in 1936. Can you read Italian?"

What a serious fellow this one was, thought Wallingford. He wasn't like an Arab, and he wasn't like a European. These Palestinian Jews were sober people. "Don't worry about that," said Wallingford, "I've got paperwork up to here." He touched his eyebrows with the edge of his flattened hand. "Just give me another slug of that rotgut. Is it local?"

Despite himself Solomon grinned at Wallingford's cool nerve. "It's the best scotch in this town, and you know it." He got the bottle from the cupboard and put it on the side table where Wallingford was sitting. Then he sat down, but this time at the end of the sofa: closer to his guest. It was a gesture that revealed Solomon's impatience, and its significance was not lost on Wallingford.

Solomon wanted to be blasé. He'd been determined not to ask him to open the third crate. It was the oldest trick in the world to bring along something you said you didn't want to sell.

And yet he had the feeling that Wallingford was as determined a bluffer as he was himself.

"Neither gun is any good for what I want," said Solomon after a long silence.

Wallingford shrugged. "I don't know what you want them for." He poured himself a tall measure of whisky. "Got any ice?"

Solomon yelled, "Yusef! Ice! And a cold beer."

The servant brought ice in a glass bucket and a light ale in a fine cut-glass tumbler. He remained impassive, and yet he was surprised that Solomon had succumbed. He seldom drank alcohol and had never before touched it during negotiations of any kind.

"Very well. Let's see the other one," said Solomon.

"It's not—"

"Show me!"

Wallingford heaved himself to his feet, went across the room, and stooped down to open the third crate. It was difficult not to admire the beautifully made boxes in which the Italians shipped their guns. He opened the lid and reached into the sawdust and proudly brought out a smaller machine gun with a polished wooden stock and air-cooling holes in the metal jacket of the barrel.

"A Beretta Thirty-eight!" said Solomon. "I knew it, you bastard." He chuckled with satisfaction rather than with merriment and couldn't take his eyes from the machine gun. He held out both hands to take it.

Wallingford didn't pass him the gun. He looked down at it. Mogg and Powell had done it all exactly as he wanted. Good chaps. He'd specified that this gun should be slightly newer and cleaner than the other two. It shone like a jewel. It was a lovely gun. He handed it to Solomon. "Take a look."

The Beretta was quite different from the other two machine guns, which men fired while seated or flat on the ground. This Beretta was a submachine gun, the sort of weapon a man used on his feet. Solomon was a weaponry aficionado: he handled the gun as a mother might nurse a newborn baby. He no longer tried to hide his passion. "This is a Tullio Marengoni design," said Solomon.

Wallingford nodded, although he had in fact never heard of Tullio Marengoni.

"This is a handmade gun. Look at the machining. Look at the wooden stock. It's beautiful. Beautiful."

"Nine millimeter," said Wallingford. "And I'll deliver them anywhere you want them."

"Palestine?"

"Anywhere you want them."

"Could you get me five hundred of them?"

"But of course. More."

Solomon smiled. *"Hallet el-baraka. Hallet el-baraka."* Let blessings truly descend.

Wallingford's cosmopolitan activities left him well equipped to handle such Arabic pleasantries. *"Mabrouk aleik."* The blessing be on *you!* he said.

=9=

"I like them. I think those two are the nicest people staying in the Magnifico," said Alice Stanhope. "I hope they come soon." She looked at her watch. Then she looked at the man she knew as Bert Cutler and smiled. It was a glorious smile, the sort of shy dreamy smile that a woman in love saves for the man she adores. Was it possible that she could fall in love with a man she'd only just met? The answer was yes.

The smile seemed to be lost on him as he used the strainer and carefully poured tea for both of them. Ross was still a corporal. He'd taken advantage of this spell of warm weather to go jacketless, using his own khaki shirt with its corporal's stripes. They were sitting in the back garden of Ashraf's Garden, a tearoom on Sharia Ibrahim Pasha, opposite the entrance to Ezbekiya Gardens. It was crowded; it always was at this time of day. The dozens of office buildings used by the British army were closed during the heat of the afternoon. Everyone found somewhere to doze until teatime, and then they sought cooler places like this to drink hot milky English tea with cakes. The people Alice said she liked so much were Sayed and Zeinab el-Shazli, the two young Egyptians.

"No reason to be any other way," said Ross sardonically. "They're rich and young and beautiful."

"I know you are my superior," said Alice diffidently. "But

there is a lot you don't understand about Egypt . . . about how things are in Egypt."

"So enlighten me." He poured milk into her tea before handing it to her. He hadn't asked her if she wanted milk; that wasn't his style.

She would have preferred lemon in it, but she took the tea from him gratefully. "The Shazlis are caught in the middle. Most Egyptians are penniless fellahin, slaving in the fields on a starvation diet. A rich Egyptian might own a hundred or so feddans of fertile land—"

"Feddan?"

"Just over an acre. An Egyptian with one hundred feddans will have big cars, holidays on the French Riviera, and dozens of servants. His children will be brought up by English nannies and French governesses so they speak French and English fluently and perfectly. Some families here own a thousand feddans of fertile land, which give them untold riches. But the Shazlis are not from such a family. He was just an army officer: socially that's not much. They are probably the children of some middle class merchant who clawed his way out of the gutter. They are not peasants. To speak English and French shows how hard they have worked, not what kind of nannies they had. But people like the Shazlis would never be received in the houses of the rich Egyptians. Never!"

"I see," he said. If only he could take her with him. She totally eclipsed every woman he'd ever met. She was beautiful, yet shy. She was eternally reticent, yet she knew so much. What a wicked twist of fate that he'd met her at a time like this.

"Life is not easy for them," said Alice. "The war has isolated them."

"Isolated them?"

"Before the war such Egyptians clung to the British coat-tails. Now they see that what is good for Britain is not necessarily good for Egypt. Rich Egyptians don't have to worry; they can go abroad and do what they like. But people like the Shazlis are worried and bewildered."

"By what?"

"By a war they do not understand. Worried by the wartime slogans and claims of the British, on the one hand, and of the ranting and raving of all the different Egyptian nationalists."

"You are seeing a lot of the Shazlis?"

"I like to talk to them. I'm trying to brush up my Arabic, and they are very patient."

"Well, top marks, Alice. Your guess about the Shazlis fits in with what Marker dug up from the files. The father is a well-known anti-British agitator."

"That's difficult to believe. They are both so polite and gentle."

"Agitator perhaps isn't the word. He writes Let's-get-rid-of-the-British diatribes in the newspapers and journals."

Alice smiled at him. "Oh, they all do that, Bert. If I was Egyptian I'd probably be writing them too."

"I can believe it," he said feelingly. He'd encountered the firmness of her views. On some subjects, such as British monarchy, she was unyielding in her allegiance. For Egypt's King Farouk she had only contempt. For the Egyptians she had a special sympathy and fondness. He didn't find it difficult to imagine her born again as an Egyptian nationalist. "Are they practicing Muslims?"

"They're certainly not Christians. But they compromise in the way that all Muslims of their age and class have to do."

"For instance?"

"I imagine they pray in the morning and evening. She keeps her head scarf on in class. He probably goes to the mosque on Fridays and avoids sausages in the canteen." She smiled again. It was accepted by all foreigners that eating any kind of Egyptian sausage was suicidal.

"You can be very cynical at times, Alice."

"I didn't mean to be," she said, her regret genuine. "I wonder how I would cope with such a situation. It's almost impossible to combine being a middle class Egyptian with being a devout Muslim."

"And he plays bridge with our bogus Russian prince every week? Is he a good bridge player? Do they play for money?"

"Not very good: average. But you don't have to be good to beat Prince Piotr. They play for tiny stakes: five piasters; nothing."

"Five piasters is a day's wage for local laborers working for the army."

Alice disregarded this rebuke. "Is he a bogus prince? Or a bogus Russian? There were about two million titled Russian aristocrats until the revolution. He seems genuine and moves with the smart set. I asked Mummy more about him. Mummy says he's from a grand old czarist family and has lived here for ages."

"Your mother? I hope—"

"Calm down, Bert. I never tell Mummy anything that could possibly make trouble for you."

He looked at her. He would like to meet her mother. They said she was a typical member of Egypt's stuffy British community. In her waterfront apartment in Alexandria she sat surrounded by the priceless antiques and oriental artifacts that officials like her husband had so easily obtained in the old days. From there she kept in touch with her friends, gossiping and pulling strings and giving advice when no advice was needed. He couldn't imagine Alice ever becoming like that. He said, "Are they really brother and sister?"

She laughed. "You're so suspicious, Bert." She wondered if this man would ever realize that she was desperately in love with him. Everyone who had seen her with him in the last few days seemed to guess. No matter how hard she tried, Alice could not keep it a secret from anyone except him. He gave no sign of noticing her when she was close or of missing her when she was away. Did her voice betray her? Her mother's sudden pleas for

Alice to come back to live with her in Alexandria might be a sign that Mummy had guessed too. "Yes, they are brother and sister. Is that why you are so keen to take a closer look at them?"

"I'm curious about him . . . curious about them both, in fact. There are some damned funny students at that American University."

"It's a mixed bag," said Alice. "That's the idea of a university, isn't it?"

He drank some tea. "Did you say Captain Darymple works in Gray Pillars?" It was the popular name for GHQ Middle East.

"Not for much longer. He's telling everyone he's been selected for one of these cloak-and-dagger shows. He'll be off soon."

"I thought he was unfit."

She looked at him, wondering if he felt he should be away fighting instead of behind a desk in Cairo. There was nothing in his face to tell her. "During the advance last year, Darymple and two of his pals drank water from a poisoned well. One nearly died. Darymple had chronic dysentery. He's more or less cured now and hoping to be passed A-One."

"There must be something wrong with the German poisons," he said.

"What an awful thing to say, Bert." She grinned in spite of that. "Using poison is against the Geneva Treaty, or something. They just make the water bad and undrinkable."

"But Darymple survived. Good for him," he said without emotion. He looked at her, trying to read the concern that he recognized in her face. She was a complicated woman. "Shush! What's that?" Over the bustle of the tearoom they could hear the chanting of a big crowd, a very big crowd. It wasn't like the noise of university students making themselves a nuisance; this was different. The sound was low and almost musical, like the throbbing of some huge steam engine.

"The protests are getting bigger and bigger," said Alice. "Can you hear what they are shouting?"

"It will be the same as yesterday: 'Hail to Rommel! We are Rommel's soldiers! British get out!' "

"Sounds as if they are coming along Sharia Ibrahim Pasha," she said, her head cocked as she tried to locate the noise. The people in the garden—largely British—had quieted. He had chosen a table that was just inside a room that opened out onto the garden. It was dark and cool in here but they could see everything: the umbrellas making circles of shadow and the tea drinkers silhouetted against the sun-bleached garden and the bright green vegetation. "A very big crowd by the sound of it."

The chanting was louder and more purposeful than was usual in such demonstrations. What had been good-natured protests in early 1941 had changed since Rommel and his Panzer army had come to Africa and scored victory after victory. When cotton prices jumped, many landowners began to plant it, which caused continuous rises in the price of bread. This had added a new dimension to the discontent. King Farouk's government was overtly pro-German, and now that Rommel was getting nearer, Egyptian protests were organized, bitter, and determined.

The angry crowds were close now. Ashraf's was a popular gathering place for the British, and the mob knew it. Although the garden wall obscured the street, the demonstrators were screaming to make sure they were heard. "I'll make sure nothing happens to you, Alice," he promised softly. "You'll not be in danger. I don't want you to worry." Her eyes went to him. Was there some flicker of affection in those words?

Even as he said it there was a disturbance at the entrance to the tea gardens. Insults were shouted and then there was a venomous exchange that soon became violent punches, as demonstrators pushed past the doorman. Right there amid the tea drinkers, a melee started and the shouts in the doorway became an angry clamor. After struggling with doorman and waiters, two especially violent men forced their way to the little ornamental well in the middle of the garden and climbed up on it. A waiter was sprawled back against the wall clutching his stomach. Two more figures—skinny teenagers—stumbled through the doorway and picked themselves up to look around. They were wide-eyed and sweating, dressed in torn old short-sleeve shirts and rumpled khaki trousers. For a moment they stood there, surprised at the ease with which they had forced their way into this forbidden British sanctum. For a moment they did nothing but stare. Then they screamed slogans. Their cries were in Arabic. Few of the British properly understood the words, but *Bissama Allah, fi alard Hitler* got some heads shaking. This chant—In heaven Allah, and on earth Hitler—had become a war cry of the militant nationalists and revolutionaries. The intruders did not wait to be ousted. They threw handfuls of leaflets into the air and ran out through the gate with loud whoops of triumph. Gleeful acclamations greeted them as they escaped out to the street. Perhaps there would have been renewed intrusions, but at that moment there came the sound of horses as the mounted police came charging down to clear the street. There was a low roar of fear and then the shrill cries of a mad scramble to get away. The horses clattered past, and more came behind them. In the distance the chanting voices persisted as the crowd continued along the road toward the palace.

No one spoke. The British were stunned by the incident. There was something shocking about the speed with which it had happened. The whole point of coming here for tea was to forget for a few minutes that they were surrounded by millions of dirty and diseased Egyptians. Now the tea drinkers felt threatened; worse, they felt vulnerable.

It was the Egyptian waiters who knew what to do. One of them quickly gathered up the anti-British leaflets, while others came hurrying from the kitchen with big pots of freshly brewed tea. Their big smiles and cheerful solicitude was reassuring, and little by little they restored the atmosphere to something like normal again. Alice looked at Ross and smiled. He didn't smile back.

"So! I find two conspirators! Sitting in the shadows! What

a surprise," said a female voice behind them. "What's it to be
tonight, gunrunning or hashish?"

They looked up wide-eyed, wondering to what extent their
earlier conversation had been overheard. It was Peggy West.

"Hello, Peggy," said Alice. Jimmy Ross got to his feet. Peggy
was looking distressed. Her blue straw hat was dented and her
face flushed.

"I don't want to interrupt a tête-à-tête," she said breathlessly. Despite this declaration she seemed very upset. She put
down her shopping and lingered long enough for Ross to invite
her to sit with them.

Peggy sat down and opened the menu. Her hands were
shaking. She put it aside again without reading it. "There are
thousands more of them coming along Ibrahim Pasha," she said.
"I suppose they'll all demonstrate in Abdin Square again."
Peggy, like all the regulars, knew Ashraf's menu by heart. "That
will stop the number seventeen trams, and there is no other tram
for people going to Gezira or Garden City." She smiled because
those two destinations were ones the British needed. They were
always the first to be canceled; some people said it was done
simply to punish the British.

"Are you all right, Peggy?" Alice asked, not knowing
whether to remark on Peggy's obvious distress. Since seeing
Peggy in her position of undisputed authority at the hospital,
Alice had looked on her as a mentor and something of a surro-
gate for the elder sister Alice never had. Now this was a new side
of Peggy. Who would have guessed that she'd be so upset by a
demonstration in the street?

"Just footsore and weary," said Peggy with a smile. Peggy
had been jostled in the thick of the anti-British crowd. Under her
cheeriness she was very disturbed. For the first time in Cairo
she'd felt frightened by a mob. One of them had spit at her; she'd
never forget his face: wrinkled with age, darkened by the sun,
and tense with spiteful hatred. Only the intervention of a
mounted Cairo policeman, who'd seen her predicament and

come riding at full gallop into the crowd wielding his baton, had saved her from being hurt. Now she understood some of the horror stories she'd heard about riots in the old days. She needed to be with her own kind. She needed reassurance. She needed a cup of tea. But she didn't say any of this. She forced a smile. "I just couldn't walk another step, and I'm getting too old to join in the late-afternoon scrimmage around the trams."

"Have an ice-cream," said Alice, to show Peggy that she was really welcome. "The coffee flavor is delicious."

Peggy shook her head. "Just tea, please." Ross made a sign to the waiter, who had heard Peggy's order. "What will the king do, Corporal Cutler? He's between the devil and the deep blue sea, isn't he?"

"We can't have some pro-German chap running the government," he replied. It wasn't something he was keen to discuss in detail.

"We are waiting for Sayed and Zeinab," explained Alice. "The American University has a holiday too. They said they'd take tea with us, but they are late. Perhaps the demonstration has delayed them. Bert will have to go soon. They have a very short siesta in his office."

"What a shame," said Peggy.

"Or his sergeant will kick his behind," said Alice, and grinned at her secret joke. He smiled ruefully and signaled the waiter and ordered cakes. It was better to order them now, before their guests arrived. The best cakes disappeared quickly because of the flour shortage.

"They are naughty like that: the Shazlis. Being late, I mean," explained Peggy. "The Egyptians have no sense of time. My husband used to say they have rubber watches." She laughed sadly.

"How long have you lived in the Magnifico?" he said.

"I could tell you some stories about that place," said Peggy. But she seemed to reconsider as she looked around the café. "It's weeks and weeks since I was in here," she said. "Last year—

when Greece went down the pan—it became a place for the Greek high-ups to gather. I saw King George's mistress in here one day. She looked miserable, poor soul. She's English, you know. I almost went over and spoke with her, but I lost my nerve at the last minute. At another table, studiously ignoring the poor woman, was half the Greek government: a rude, noisy crowd. I didn't think much of them, to tell you the truth. Before that, this place had been a meeting place for Poles. I wonder what it will be next." Realizing it might sound as if she thought it could become a rendezvous for Rommel's victorious Germans, she smiled nervously and studied the garden to examine the flowers and the climbing plants that covered the walls.

Peggy felt better now that she was here with people she knew. The familiarity comforted her. She fidgeted with the cruet and looked again at the menu, noteworthy for its amazing grammar and misspellings, and at the brass jar of flowers that had wilted in the heat of the day. Now it was afternoon. As the siesta ended and the town cooled, people went back to their offices, while others went to the cafés and tearooms. Ashraf's was regarded as something of a private club for the few remaining British civilian old-timers. The front entrance was small and drab, its Arabic signs unwelcoming to the bulk of the men who passed it going in and out of the Tipperary Club a few doors away.

"I never thanked you properly," Alice told her. "For everything: the room and for the job at the hospital."

"Getting you the room wasn't so easy. But at the hospital I knew the Hoch would jump at the chance. He retired back before the war, but he's the best surgeon we have. He must be over seventy, but the army turned a blind eye to that."

"Everyone is very friendly," said Alice.

Peggy smiled and wondered if Alice knew how much resentment she had stirred up in Blanche and Jeannie MacGregor. "We lost two really good typists when the army sent all the wives away. They didn't want to go, of course. One of them sent a cheeky telegram to the commander in chief. A lot of good it did her. She'd only been married six months. Of course the commander in chief didn't send his own wife away. Everyone resented that."

The tea arrived together with a plate of cakes. They were all English favorites: fruit cake complete with icing and marzipan— left from Christmas, no doubt—slices of seed cake and Swiss roll, lemon-curd tarts, maids of honor, cream éclairs, and a rock cake. Peggy took the pot and poured the tea and said how good it smelled. She was a pretty woman, if not to say beautiful, and appreciative and emphatic about everything she liked. And she liked to make pouring tea into a ceremony. "How many lumps of sugar?"

Alice took the opportunity of looking around at the women in the garden. At first glance they seemed like the well-dressed women seen before the war in smart tearooms in Paris, Vienna, or London. But on closer inspection the women were a mixed collection: Egyptians, Palestinians, Copts, Italians, and Greeks. They were all so alluring, so well groomed, their hair and makeup perfect. They were studied by the predatory staff officers and businessmen who lingered here regularly. Men were in abundance in this town, available women in short supply. Peggy always spoke about her marriage as if it were something past and finished with. Why didn't she open her eyes? Any attractive European woman who couldn't find a husband in this town now was just not trying. And Peggy West was very attractive and clever too.

Alice looked back to see if the Shazlis were coming. Mirrors on the walls of the dark, empty interior rooms reflected the lively activity of the sunlit garden like frantic movie screens.

"The tea is good here," said Jimmy Ross, as if he felt it necessary to explain his presence here with Alice. "And they boil the milk."

He had no sooner said this than Sayed and Zeinab el-Shazli came through the entrance, looking across the garden for them.

All conversation in the café stopped for a moment. They were like two film stars. Zeinab, in her early twenties, had smooth pale skin, large brown eyes, and a perfect figure that her dress of cream-colored silk did not conceal. Her brother Sayed was no less glamorous. He had broad square shoulders and dark shiny hair combed straight back. His skin was a shade darker than his sister's, and he had a toothbrush mustache and very white teeth that lit up his face as he smiled. The only blemish to his perfect face was a slight darkening of the flesh under the eyes, and yet that too was an essential part of his foreign charm. He wore a white shirt with dark tie and dark trousers. He had a gold wristwatch with a leather strap—unsuited to hot weather but very English—and expensive two-tone shoes, which were carefully polished and the laces precisely knotted.

Sayed, hurrying ahead, pulled out a chair for his sister as though she were some regal personage. Then he plucked at his trousers to ease them as he sat down. He gave no explanation or apology for being late. Neither did they express surprise at seeing Peggy there. They ordered mint tea from a waiter who had hurried to be at their side and was waiting patiently. Then they spent a moment waving and smiling to people they knew.

"You have a lot of friends here," said Jimmy Ross.

"Acquaintances," said Sayed. "Some of them are people with whom my father does business."

"What business is that?" said Ross very casually.

"He is a journalist," said Sayed, "but he does other things too." He looked at Peggy and Alice. "No work today?"

"I'm on late shift," said Peggy.

To Alice he said, "Answer in Arabic, Miss Stanhope."

Alice smiled. She had had two lessons with the Shazlis. They were very patient with her mispronunciations.

"Your Arabic is coming along very well," he told her, "but you must practice."

Their tea came. It was in glasses with silver-plated holders, a big bunch of mint leaves in each. Sayed put a lot of sugar into his and stirred it furiously so that the mint leaves pirouetted. He watched it with evident pleasure.

"How are you liking Cairo, Miss Stanhope?" he asked with grave formality. He offered the cakes to the ladies and then to Ross, who took a cream éclair. Peggy wondered why he would make such a point of going to a place where the milk was boiled and then eat a cream cake. But she didn't remark on it.

"Cairo is glorious," Alice replied. "After Alexandria almost anywhere would be."

"What is wrong with Alex?" said Sayed, abbreviating as the British did. That and his challenging tone of voice revealed a youthful taste for debate.

"Nothing. But it is so dull and gray," said Alice. "The buildings and the streets and the sea—so lifeless."

"I've never lived there," said Peggy, wondering if Alice Stanhope's opinion of Alexandria was a verdict on living with Mummy. "But it always seems like a resort out of season when I go there to visit my friends. Isn't your mother afraid of the bombing?"

"Mummy isn't afraid of anything," said Alice.

"Alex always seems much nicer when Cairo starts to warm up," said Sayed. "Have you ever been here in Cairo in summer?"

"No, not yet," said Alice.

"The English find it too hot," he said. "But we are used to it." He drank some tea and wiped his lips delicately. To Ross he said politely, "Where are Rommel's spearheads by now?"

Everyone at the table turned their eyes to Jimmy Ross, who said noncommittally, "We'll hold him. Rommel is no superman."

"I'm glad you think so," said Sayed and produced a sheet of rough gray paper of the very cheapest kind, one of the leaflets that the intruders had scattered. "I'd like to hear your opinion of this, Corporal Cutler." It was a crudely drawn map of the fighting fronts. A large red arrow took Rommel's Afrika Korps to the Suez Canal and beyond. Another such arrow carried the German army fighting in southern Russia down through the

Caucasus. The tips of both arrows joined at the oil-rich region that surmounts the Persian Gulf. The artist had made the meeting point into a jagged explosion. Around it there were dozens of crudely drawn little British soldiers sprawled and dead.

Sayed held the leaflet across the table so that the other man could see it. "It's a bit out of date," said Ross. "The German armies are frozen to a standstill in Russia. And next week's map will show Rommel being knocked back into Tunisia."

Sayed grinned as if to suggest that, were the positions reversed, he would have given an equally evasive reply. "But as a military man, Corporal Cutler, would you not say that, if this was the strategic objective"—he laid his palm uppermost so that his manicured fingernails tapped lightly on the map—"then drawing the Allied armies deeper and deeper into the Western Desert would mean less men to send to Iraq and Persia to oppose a German assault from the Caucasus?"

Ross looked again at the map.

When he was slow to reply, Sayed said, "The Germans have always been experts at grand strategy. Geopolitik is a German word, is it not?"

"I'm not sure I know that word," said Ross. "May I keep your map?"

"Better it is destroyed," said Sayed, taking it back and screwing it up before putting it in his pocket. "You might get into trouble with such subversive literature." He sipped his tea and attacked his lemon-curd tart with a fork. He broke it into segments, tasted the lemon curd from the tip of his fork, and then lost interest in it. That was how he kept so thin, thought Peggy.

"I won't get into trouble," said Ross. "We are fighting a war for freedom to say what we think and to do as we wish."

"Are you? You surprise me, corporal. What freedom do we Egyptians have under your rule? Your soldiers sing obscene songs about our king and queen. Your men regularly smash up our hotels and restaurants, and no compensation is ever paid to the owners. You use our country to have your battles, but Egypt is a neutral country not at war with anyone. Even the English-language newspapers are so fiercely censored they never say anything important."

"What about personal freedom?" said Ross, shifting uncom-fortably.

"What about it indeed? Let's take your own case, corporal. Only officers may go into the best hotels like Shepheard's or the Continental. As a corporal you are barred from such places as the Turf Club, the Trocadero Club, and the Gezira, to name but three. What sort of personal freedom is that for men who are fighting a war for freedom?"

"Why should you care?"

"I don't," said Sayed. "But I do care when your government sends a public school lout here to bully my king and boast of the way he calls him 'boy.' "

"Ambassador Lampson, you mean?"

"You know whom I mean," said Sayed.

"Stop it, Sayed," said Zeinab, smiling and smacking him on the arm playfully. She looked at the others. "We shouldn't have got started on politics. My brother becomes too passionate and upsets people." She was looking at Jimmy Ross.

"No offense intended," said Sayed. "If Corporal Cutler were running things it would all be better, I'm sure."

"Yes, they would certainly allow corporals into Shep-heard's," said Jimmy Ross feelingly.

"But no officers?" said Sayed.

"Certainly no officers," said Ross solemnly. They all laughed, and Peggy noticed the way in which Alice touched her corporal's hand. He was a handsome enough young man, but it was hard to fathom why this upper-class girl was attached to such a lowly soldier. She had only to raise an eyebrow and she would have colonels and brigadiers to do her bidding. Oh, well, thought Peggy, all women seem to look for something different in the men they choose. Perhaps Cutler was an athletic lover, heir to a fortune, or kind to stray animals.

"What did you do in civvy street, Corporal Cutler?" Sayed asked.

"I was a clerk," he said vaguely.

"And now?"

"I'm an infantryman misemployed as an army clerk."

"You are probably too valuable," said Peggy diplomatically. "A lot of soldiers out there in the blue would give anything to be working in Bab-el-Hadid barracks right in the heart of Cairo."

"That's true," said Alice.

"Is that where you work, Bert?" said Sayed. "Just round the corner? What a lucky bloke you are." Sayed had heard so many Australians using the word "bloke" that he wanted to try it out. "Isn't that the military police headquarters? What do you do there?"

"I'm just a clerk. I work for the provost marshal. Filing his papers, mostly. Typing letters and answering the phone."

"The provost marshal," said Sayed. "That's an important job, Bert. Isn't he the man who runs Egypt?"

"Only the military police." He drank some tea as if needing time to consider his words.

"And of course the Special Investigation Branch and some of the intelligence services too," said Sayed. "Give us the low-down. What is happening in the underworld?"

"I'm sworn to secrecy," said Ross. So Sayed knew who worked at the barracks; not many people did.

"You could tell them about the hashish, couldn't you?" said Alice. "The people are locked up." Ross looked at her. She was clever. She was playing her part with all the skills of an actress. And there was nothing against revealing that story, it would be in the papers next week.

"There's not much to tell," he said. "It was a report I typed out. Syrian seamen have been hiding slabs of hashish inside sheep carcasses and tossing them into the water from ships lying off the coast. After dark, men rowed out to recover them."

"How was it discovered?" Sayed asked.

"We pay informers," said Ross. "There is usually someone who will betray such gangs. The trouble is that there are so many of them."

"Your work sounds very exciting," said Zeinab. She was looking at him with new interest.

"I just type out the reports and get them signed and file them away," he said. "It's boring."

"Do you know," said Alice, as if she didn't want the interest to fade, "that black marketeers get one hundred pounds for one heavy-duty tire? One hundred pounds!"

"I must go," said Ross. "I'm all alone in the office this afternoon. Someone has to be there, in case the provost marshal's phone rings." He got up and picked up the bill.

Sayed snatched the bill away from him. "This is on me," he said. "Yesterday the horses ran well for me."

"Thank you," said Ross.

"I hope you didn't take offense, Bert. May I call you Bert?"

"I didn't take offense."

"About the leaflet, I mean. Nothing personal," said Sayed.

Ross put his hand on Alice's shoulder. "You stay with our friends. Keep away from the demonstrations. I will see you tonight?"

"Of course," said Alice.

"She'll be safe with us," said Sayed. "You may have confidence in me. I will look after these ladies."

"Thanks, Sayed."

When Jimmy Ross had left them, Sayed ordered more tea. As he was talking to the waiter, Zeinab leaned close to Alice and said, "He is magnificent, your man!"

She said it with such fervor that Alice was surprised. The surprise must have showed on her face, for Zeinab added, "Did you not see the way his eyes flashed in anger? I like such a man."

It was hard to know whether Sayed heard what his sister had said. Perhaps it was just that he knew the sort of things she was likely to say. He said to Alice, "You will bring him tonight?"

"Where?"

"To Prince Piotr's. Does he play bridge?"

"Yes, I believe so."

"It doesn't matter. It is a party. There is no need to play bridge until very late."

"Is it a party every Friday?" Alice asked.

"Piotr will love to argue with Corporal Cutler. He is bored with arguing with the rest of us, and Captain Darymple is so stupid."

"I say, you mustn't say that," said Peggy West. It was a mild objection, as if she were correcting Sayed's grammar.

"Why must I not say it?" said Sayed with interest. "Is it a military secret?"

"He's going off to the war," said Peggy. "He might get killed."

"You English," said Sayed. "How can you be such outrageous hypocrites?" He made the most of the word "outrageous," rolling it around in his throat as if it were an Arabic word.

Peggy poured more tea. "Why doesn't Corporal Cutler— Bert, that is—why doesn't he apply for a commission?"

"He'd be sent away for training," said Alice, improvising hastily. "He might be posted to East Africa or to the Pacific to fight the Japanese."

"Yes, you're right. It's better the way it is," said Peggy, who understood Alice's fears.

"You have him here," said Zeinab. "That's the important thing." She gave a little grin as if she'd said something wicked.

"You'll bring him?" Sayed asked.

Alice looked inquiringly at Peggy. Peggy said, "Piotr won't mind. The more the merrier, that's Piotr's motto."

Sayed looked at her, pondering the words. "Where does Piotr's money come from?" he asked. Peggy was considered an authority on everything to do with the Magnifico and its residents.

"His family had Suez Canal shares. That's how he got a visa

to live here. But since the war started, he can only have the income in Egyptian pounds; they won't let him change his money. So he's trapped."

Sayed nodded.

"That's what I heard, anyway," said Peggy, feeling perhaps that she'd said too much.

"Zeinab thinks he's a spy . . . a spy for the Russians."

When Peggy looked at her, Zeinab said, "Sayed laughs at me. But that powerful shortwave wireless set in his apartment . . . and having lots of money, and no job."

"For the Russians? I don't imagine he has much to thank Joe Stalin for," said Peggy.

"He has such strange eyes," said Zeinab, as if that was absolute proof of his guilt.

"I think he has a mistress hidden away somewhere," said Sayed. He looked at Alice to see how she reacted to such a notion. Alice could not suppress a grin; one brief meeting with Piotr had been enough to convince her that women played no part in his carnal yearnings.

"I like him very much," said Peggy. "Piotr is generous and easygoing and funny. Look how confident we all are that he will welcome Bert, a stranger. How many people are there like Piotr? If Lucia kicks him out, we will all be impoverished."

Emboldened by Peggy's description of Prince Piotr's hospitality, Alice Stanhope said, "Do you think I could bring someone else too?"

She spoke very softly, so that Sayed had to lean across the table to hear her. "Of course you can," he said. "Does she live in Cairo?"

"He's a he," said Alice. "An American newspaper man. He's a friend of my parents. My mother says he wants to meet 'the real people,' whatever that means. She expects me to entertain him for a couple of days. Where can I take him? It's so difficult if you are a civilian."

"Bring him," said Sayed. "My sister will flirt with him shamelessly."

Zeinab averted her face to hide her embarrassment. "Please don't say such things, Sayed," she whispered.

"We are with friends," said Sayed. "Peggy and Alice know I speak only in fun." To Alice he said, "Bring him. The more the merrier. I must remember that English saying: the more the merrier."

Only a couple of hours later Jimmy Ross was being conducted along one of the most squalid alleys of El Birkeh. The sun had gone down and it was suddenly chilly. He'd put on his old working uniform with its major's crowns. In this environment it seemed like a wise thing to do.

"It's a bloody pigsty," he said as the MP sergeant led him into a narrow doorway past two military policemen and two uniformed Cairo policemen. He picked his way up a flight of stone steps by the light of another policeman's flashlight. It was still daylight outside, but there were no windows giving onto the staircase, and in such places there were no fittings that could possibly be stolen. Even to build stairs of wood was an invitation to thieves, who would strip away anything that could be sold for a piaster or two.

"Wait till you see him," said the red-capped military police sergeant who was leading the way up the stairs. "Talk about stink!"

The room was so small there was not much space in it for the two men to stand. It was a windowless cell, lit by one low-watt electric bulb hanging from the ceiling. The red cap stood in the doorway, relishing the slight movement of air on the landing. Someone said that the dead body of the sergeant major had been left just the way it was found by the MP patrol. But too many people had tramped through this place for there to be much faith placed in that.

Jimmy Ross was aware of the way they were watching him.

He was supposed to be Albert Cutler, the expert detective who knew all about these things. He looked down at the corpse and then at the MP, who was holding a handkerchief to his face. He tried to remember the things they said in movies. "Has the photographer been yet?"

The MP sergeant looked at him. "Yes, sir. He's finished." Yes, silly question; he should have known that.

Ross felt like vomiting but he tried to look unconcerned at the sight of the decomposing corpse. "Have you searched the body?"

"No, sir."

"And you say you found him?" he said to the sergeant. On the way here they'd chatted. He was only twenty-two. He'd been a solicitor's clerk before the war, and the army had made him a military police sergeant. He was an intelligent youngster but far too young for Cairo's streets. "Tell me again."

"An Arab kid came up to us on the street and told us . . . he said there was a soldier feeling ill. We found him like this. No one seems to know anything. And of course I haven't touched anything," he added.

"And the photographers have got all they want?"

"That's what they said. They couldn't wait to get out of here. And the medical officer too. He couldn't fix a time of death; too long ago, he said."

"Yes, so he said on the phone," said Ross. He felt he should show a little expertise. Speaking quietly, he added, "It's tricky when bodies are decomposing in warm climates. And some of the army's medical officers don't know about police work."

"Yes, sir," said the sergeant respectfully.

Ross took hold of himself and looked more closely at the metal cot and the body that was sprawled so that its head and one arm was on the floor. The dead man's face had turned deep purple and was set into an open-mouthed grimace. The hands were swollen so that the fingers had distended into fat sausages. The only decoration was an unframed colored litho of King

Farouk. There was something sardonic in its presence here in this filthy room.

"It's a brothel, you say?"

"Yes, sir, a brothel," said the young sergeant.

Ross leaned very close to the body. The badges showed it to be a sergeant major dressed in the rough khaki uniform that was sometimes needed in a Cairo winter. Steeling himself to the task, Ross reached out and started to empty the dead man's pockets. He hoped the sergeant would go away, but instead he watched the process with grim fascination. Ross tried to seem indifferent to the horror of it. Since being installed in his quarters at the Citadel he had scoured the lending library for "true police" stories. He'd read "Secrets of Scotland Yard" twice. "Look at this, then," he said. The pockets produced plenty of evidence: two paybooks in different names, two cargo manifests that were totally blank except for having signatures and rubber stamps prematurely applied. Then he opened the battle dress, lifted the filthy vest, and examined the chest wound.

"Um," he said, although he felt like screaming. He stood up. "You can take him away, sergeant," he said. His brain reeled as he took a deep breath. What would poor old Cutler have made of it? Suddenly he knew. "I think we're looking for a soldier . . . perhaps a commando or someone with special training."

"A soldier?"

"Look at the wound. Didn't you ever get training in unarmed combat? Knife placed expertly right into the heart. The army is training too many people how to kill quickly and quietly, sergeant. We can't be surprised when they go into business for themselves."

"Johnny Arab is fond of the knife," said the sergeant.

"Ummm. But not like that. In any case, he wasn't killed here."

"How do you know?"

"There's no blood. A wound like that spurts blood. I'd gamble that when this fellow was knifed, his blood hit the ceiling."

Ross looked at the body again as he thought about it. "No, he was killed somewhere else by killers who dumped his body here."

"Why do that? What advantage would that give them?"

Ross bit his lip and thought about it. "They simply wanted to get rid of him. Probably they wanted to clean up the scene of crime. Perhaps he was killed in one of these other brothels. Didn't you tell me that a fancy whorehouse—Lady Fitz—is somewhere near here?"

"Yes. Just along the alley."

"Yes. Tell me, how many British soldiers use these native brothels?"

The sergeant looked at him before deciding how to answer. He was a bit in awe of him. Exaggerated stories about Albert Cutler's skills had preceded Ross's arrival in Cairo. And in the few days he'd been there, Ross, with his corporal's uniform and his limited regard for the army and its ways, had already been labeled a dangerous eccentric by the more conventional lower ranks at Bab-el-Hadid police barracks. The sergeant chose his words carefully. "I see what you are getting at, sir . . . but some squaddies, really short of money, will go anywhere. And of course some people have strange tastes in women and brothels."

"You're right, sergeant. But not this fellow." Having prepared himself for a coup de theatre, Ross bent down, grabbed the tunic and trousers, and heaved the body back onto the cot. Then he carefully turned it over. The young sergeant staggered back at the smell. Ross smiled at him, as though he had smelled bodies far worse than this. He searched the dead man's trouser pockets and took out a bunch of keys. Some of them were recognizably keys from army locks.

"Get the man who runs this place."

The sergeant went out onto the landing and called to his colleague to bring the man downstairs.

"He's not really the man who runs the place. He's his brother-in-law."

"Is that so?" said Ross and laughed scornfully, the way Bogart laughed.

The man they ushered inside was a young Arab, about twenty years old, wearing western clothes: tattered old trousers and a red shirt that had faded to light pink.

Ross looked at him for a moment. "Who brought the body here?"

"Effendi . . ."

Ross grabbed his shirtfront and shook him before throwing him back against the wall. Having hit the wall with a crash, the man was wide-eyed in terror. With an open hand Ross slapped his face hard enough to make him cry out with pain. "Who," said Ross, "brought"—he punched him again but without putting too much force into it—"the body here?"

"I do not speak. . . ."

Ross hit him in the stomach, hard. The red cap was alarmed and tried to intervene. "Wait a minute," he said.

"Stay out of this!" said Ross, so fiercely that the youngster was frightened.

He grabbed the Arab's shirtfront again and pulled him violently so that the fabric, old and frayed, ripped open from neck to waist.

"Okay! Okay!" said the Arab. "Men brought him."

"Who?"

He hesitated, but as Ross brought his fist up to strike him again, he said, "Two men. They work for Mahmoud, the banker."

"That's better," said Ross. To the sergeant he said, "Send someone to take this fool back to the barracks and lock him up. Lock him up solitary. Then arrange for someone to collect the body."

"You were right about this one," said the red cap with profound respect. "I was sure he couldn't speak English; we all were. How did you know?"

"It's the sort of thing a Glasgow detective soon learns," said Ross.

═10═

"Did you hear that it rained in the desert?" said Prince Piotr Nikoleiovich Tikhmeibrazoff to a group of guests. It was another of his weekly gatherings and he was dressed to the nines: a burgundy-colored velvet smoking jacket and a cream-colored silk shirt with matching bow tie. His guests were dressed up too. All the usual crowd were there, plus a couple of outsiders: Alice's young man and Toby Wallingford, DSO, RNVR, who, for the occasion, had put on his dark blue uniform with its gold braid.

Alice's American guest had proved something of a surprise. He was an assertive man named Harry Wechsler, evidence of the wide-ranging influence that Alice's mother wielded. Wechsler's dispatches were featured prominently by the Hearst newspaper chain and used by many other newspapers throughout America. He'd just come back from a brief foray into the desert: "the blue," as he was determined to call it. His hands were red and raw looking, with sand encrusted in the skin. His tanned face had the pale marks around the eyes left by sand goggles. He was in his middle thirties, young in manner and face but almost bald. He affected the informal dress that the British army had adopted. His bush jacket, although stained and battered, was newly laundered and pressed. With it he wore corduroy slacks with suede boots. He sported a red silk neckerchief, and from the top pocket of his jacket protruded pens, pencils, and the stem of a pipe.

"Damned bad form," Darymple had pronounced upon Wechsler's arrival at the party in this attire. "It's a wonder he didn't bring his tommygun."

"He fights with his mouth, old boy," Wallingford had replied. "Never runs out of ammunition."

Peggy West found Harry Wechsler amusing. He proclaimed himself a "compulsive writer." In Cairo for medical treatment, he'd refused to stop working. Over the previous weeks he'd accompanied the U.S. military attaché on many visits to British army installations out in the desert. The way Wechsler told it, the attaché and he were close buddies. Wechsler had opinions about everything. "Sure, college writing courses stifle writers. But they don't stifle enough of them." He had a loud laugh and a tough charm that came from being self-sufficient. To this was added the confidence that came from knowing he was syndicated to several million readers.

Peggy had circulated to speak with as many people as she could. This afternoon she'd gone to a hairdresser for the first time in months. She'd chosen her dress and her makeup with special care. She looked enchanting. She'd remained faithful to Karl, but the angry words of Nurse Borrows had shaken her: Men don't interest you, we all know that. Is that what the other nurses really thought? And if that's what they thought, were they right? There were so many interesting men in Cairo. Here tonight there was the suave and gentlemanly Darymple, so precise and proper, his uniform made by a London tailor and his handkerchief tucked into his sleeve. His friend Wallingford was lounging on the sofa, languid and self-assured, like World War I poets she'd seen in old photos. There was Alice's corporal, a wary fellow, tough, bony-faced, and athletic. And Sayed was like the handsome Valentino, who'd made the ladies swoon in old silent films. Even Prince Piotr had reacted to the current climate by smartening himself up with clothes from his extensive prewar wardrobe.

It was Alice Stanhope who replied to Piotr's question. "Rain in the desert. Yes, Mummy heard that too, but where?" Alice was wearing an expensive high-fronted dress of the sort that over-protective mothers choose for pretty young daughters. Despite its austere design she was looking radiantly attractive, as she always did when Jimmy Ross was with her. Peggy had said as much, and tonight Alice was determined not to let her feelings for him show so much.

"An absolute deluge. Men were drowned." His manservant held still while Piotr helped himself to a glass of wine from a brass tray.

"But where? No one seems to know where," Alice asked the world in general.

Harry Wechsler smiled. He knew. "It rained all along the Via Balbia, from Tobruk to Halfaya Pass. Mid-November, before I arrived here. A little village named Gambut got it worst. I flew over the spot. It washed trucks and men right over the edge of the plateau. The rain came after dark and put paid to a German offensive. I did a story about it."

"The first rain there for sixty years, I heard," said Toby Wallingford from the sofa.

"An act of God," said Piotr solemnly, and drank some wine. The presence of Toby Wallingford disconcerted him. He'd never met him before, but that beautiful face and long wavy blond hair reminded him of a boy he'd fallen for at college long ago. Piotr's desires were never extinguished, just simmering. "Yes," he said reflectively while stealing a look at Wallingford, "that rain put paid to the German plans."

"Someone told me that the king of Italy tells the British about the Axis battle plans," said Alice diffidently. She offered this story for Piotr to comment on. He liked to give the impression that his birth into the aristocracy gave him some mysterious entrée into the affairs of royalty everywhere.

But it was Wechsler who replied. "I was in Rome. I got myself out of there just three weeks before Pearl. You can take

it from me, the Italian king hates Mussolini and would do anything to see the British win."

"Exactly," said Piotr with great satisfaction. He cherished
this rumor because, on the previous day, his mention of it had
made Lucia Magnifico almost speechless with rage. Lucia de-
spised the Italian monarchy. With Rommel in the ascendant, she
had expressed her hope that Mussolini would soon enter Cairo
at the head of a conquering army.

"And here we are in Cairo," said Robin Darymple mischiev-
ously, "with an Egyptian king who'd like to see the Axis win.
What an upside-down world, eh?"

Sayed would not let such a remark go unchallenged. "You
must not say such things, Captain Darymple."

"No offense, old boy, but I thought everyone knew that
Fatty Farouk and all his Eye-tie cronies in the Abdin Palace are
sending radio messages to our enemies in Rome every night."
Darymple looked around, waiting for a reaction.

"I don't believe that," said Sayed.

Harry Wechsler was watching the exchange. He said, "Well,
if King Farouk does hate the British, it wouldn't come as a shock,
would it? I mean it would hardly be a scoop. You British treat
him with studied contempt, even in public matters."

"Steady on," said Darymple mildly. "The Egyptians have
never had so much money in all their lives, and everyone here is
on the fiddle. Don't tell me the king and all his royal bastards are
not thieving away as hard as they can."

"That is a detestable way to speak of our king," said Sayed.

Darymple gave a brief laugh. "Keep your hair on, Sayed.
Everyone's got his hand in the pocket of the British army. That's
what keeps Cairo going, isn't it?"

Sayed, who had got to his feet in outrage, decided not to
storm out of the room. "You say these things just to make me
angry," he said. He rearranged the cushions as if that had been
the reason for him to stand up. Then he sat down again.

Darymple gave Wechsler a brief smile. "I say these things

because they are true, Sayed, old sport. Calm down and have another drink." He lifted his glass to Piotr. "It's the real thing tonight, Piotr. Quite a change from the usual battery acid."

"I'm glad you are enjoying it, Captain Darymple. I am reluctant to serve you my best scotch whisky lest you think it stolen from your military supplies."

"Touché," said Darymple, while watching Sayed, who was still visibly agitated. He was pulling at the tassels on one of the cushions. His sister saw what he was doing and tried to catch his eye and stop him, but he was not looking her way.

To calm him, Darymple said, "It's not the British army who hate your king; it's all those half-witted pen-pushers in the British embassy. The army wants a quiet life. I can tell you that without fear of contradiction. No one, from the commander in chief down to the lowest squaddie, wants any trouble back here in the streets of Cairo. It's obvious, I would have thought. We're not trying to stir up trouble, we've got enough trouble with Rommel and his pals just down the road in the desert."

"You sure have," said Wechsler.

Sayed looked at Darymple. For a moment he seemed about to reply; then he just nodded and let it go.

Darymple said, "Same goes for the Cairo police, let me tell you. We are all sick and tired of those embassy wallahs kicking the king's arse. Why can't those Foreign Office buggers let things be, so we can all get on with the war?"

Toby Wallingford said, "It's simply a matter of politics. The embassy people are frightened of what will happen if they let these anti-British Gyppos continue running the show. We should have taken the wog government over, when war started, and run Egypt our way."

"Perhaps. But there's no need to rub poor old Fatty's face in it, is there?" said Darymple, turning to where his friend was occupying the whole sofa, head propped on hand and one stockinged foot disappearing in the cushions. "I mean, Lampson or one of his little men could just have a private word in the king's earhole, right?"

Wallingford said mockingly, "Is that the official verdict at GHQ, Robbie, or your own brilliant analysis?"

Darymple flushed bright red. He knew Wally was trying to make a fool of him in front of everyone.

"So you've been in the blue, Mr. Wechsler?" Wallingford said in his most supercilious manner. "Did it get a bit noisy for you out there?" It was a clear implication that Wechsler had run away from Rommel's offensive.

"No point in staying there writing stories that your British censors cut to ribbons, commander."

"What did you write that upset them?" said Darymple.

"I wrote the truth instead of a lot of dumb Keep-the-home-fires-burning-rah-rah-rah! That's what upsets them."

"What is the truth?" said Darymple mildly. "I'd love to hear a little of that after a day at GHQ."

"The truth is, captain, that Rommel is running rings around a lot of incompetent British generals who don't know their ass from their elbow. The truth is that things will stay that way while your commanders sit in their dugouts fifty miles behind the lines, singing 'Rule Britannia,' saying everything will come out all right in the end, and sending their laundry back to Cairo. And the truth is that the British combat rank and file are sick of it and getting damned cynical."

"Perhaps that's because you keep telling them about it," said Darymple.

"Maybe it is. I come from a place where citizens are entitled to read the truth, even if they are wearing khaki without gold braid on it."

"I thought we were allies," said Darymple.

"Look, buddy, Uncle Sam isn't fighting this war in order to save the British empire for you to suck dry. In the Pacific, we Yanks are paying the price for your colonial tyranny. It's time you Brits started fighting your own war. Even right here in the desert, the Australians, New Zealanders, and South Africans are suffering the most casualties while the British doze in the back areas and sit in GHQ worrying about their next promotion. That's the truth and there's no getting away from it, censor or no censor."

Darymple saw the mention of GHQ as a direct attack on him. Even the languid Wallingford was moved to react to Wechsler's spirited assault. "It's not the whole truth," he said. "The empire has always recruited fighting regiments. The British furnish the ordnance depots and supply lines and services. It's unavoidable that the Aussies and Dominion regiments suffer a higher proportion of battle casualties."

"So stir some of those Brits out of those goddamned 'ordnance depots and supply lines and services,' old buddy," said Wechsler, with heavy sarcasm. "Scour these Cairo offices for khaki-clad bums. Give those goldbricks guns and get them up to the sharp end. Then maybe you'll halt Rommel—you could even start winning the war."

Darymple was flustered by Wechsler's harsh words. He got to his feet. Darymple realized he'd started it all with his indiscretions. It was always bad form to get into this sort of political argument. Also, it would be a stupid misjudgment to have a row with the American, and perhaps upset old Piotr, who served such good booze. More importantly, he didn't want to appear ruffled in the presence of young Wallingford, who was going to get him into his Desert Teams setup.

Piotr poured oil upon the troubled waters. He offered up a box of cigars he'd been hoarding and said, "So what story are you working on now?"

"I picked up some kind of bug. I had to be checked out regularly at the hospital, so I decided to do a story about the U.S. embassy here in Cairo. With my pills and medicines in my pocket, I've been sticking close to our military attaché. You Brits sure give Yanks the red-carpet treatment: I saw more in three days with him than in the previous month. We flew everywhere;

that's war à la mode. Even the British brass hats move their asses when he comes into view. I guess someone on high has told them that Uncle Sam calls the shots."

"Calls the shots?"

"Haven't you guys heard of the Lend-Lease Act? You folks ran out of money last year. Every gun, tank, and bomb, every last round you fire, is a gift from Uncle Sam."

He looked around to see the reaction, but Darymple and Wallingford were talking together. Only the corporal was listening attentively. Calmly Piotr drank wine and said, "So what's the next story?"

"I finished all the pills. Looks like I've got to go into the blue and find Rommel for you."

"No more Cairo stories?"

"I don't sit in bed taking aspirins. I get around. I've just filed a great story, but the censors are giving me trouble with it."

"You can tell us," said Piotr.

"Why not?" said Wechsler, who liked an audience. "Listen, guys," he said, tapping Darymple's arm and getting Wallingford's attention too. "This is a story that will be in the history books when names like Rommel and Auchinleck are long forgotten."

"Do tell," said Piotr, on cue.

"The creation of the state of Israel," said Wechsler. Several heads turned, and conversations stopped suddenly. "The Jews in Palestine are training and arming and otherwise equipping an army to take its rightful place in the world. Many of those guys have escaped from the Nazis in Europe. They'll fight for what is theirs. That's the story."

"Is this a fancy way to sell a yarn about gunrunning?" said Wallingford, his voice plummy and mocking.

Wechsler grinned. "Yeah, that's part of it. An army has got to have guns, and right now there are guns lying around in the desert for anyone to pick up."

"I can see why you had problems with the censor," said Piotr.

"I never filed a story that revealed any kind of military secret," said Wechsler.

Darymple decided to get away from this conversation. These were disturbing issues he didn't want to think about, let alone discuss. As he went across the room he heard Wallingford give a howl of laughter at something Piotr had added when he was out of earshot. Darymple wondered if his sudden departure was the subject of the joke, but he didn't look back to see if they were looking at him.

It was all right for Wally, thought Darymple; he didn't work at GHQ among all the big brass. Wallingford didn't care what outrageous things Wechsler said. Wally frequently said things about the generals at GHQ that shocked and offended Darymple. Wallingford was pouring on the charm tonight. He must have decided that Prince Piotr would be useful to him. At school Wally had always been like that: crawling to anyone in authority. He was an awful little swine. One day Darymple would tell him some home truths, but not now.

Darymple went to the bathroom and washed his hands. It was his way of escaping from the conversation. By the time he got back he hoped they would have changed the subject.

Darymple spent a long time washing and drying his hands. Even then he didn't return to the party. He stood there admiring Piotr's amazing bathroom. There was a huge marble tub with silver taps, a couple of lovely old mirrors in heavy baroque frames, and heavy pink damask wall hangings. The floor was strewn with silk carpets. On a side table there was a set of silver-backed hairbrushes and an array of oils and lotions. It was the bathroom of a sinister old deviant, Darymple decided, not for the first time.

When Darymple got back to the main room, the corporal was playing Gershwin on Piotr's old Bechstein. He'd gone to the piano as a way of escaping the exchanges that had so disturbed

Darymple. He played a few chords that became "Willow Weep for Me." Even Darymple had to admit that the corporal could play the piano. If one had to have an other rank present, having him at the keyboard made his presence less of a constraint. Suddenly Jimmy Ross looked up at Darymple and winked. Darymple's face stiffened as he forced a brief smile and moved away hurriedly. That was exactly the sort of embarrassing exchange that was bound to come when ranks mixed in social gatherings.

Alice had discovered that Peggy West had been a talented amateur soprano. Now that they suddenly had a wonderful pianist, she was determined to get her to sing. Peggy was reluctant but Alice Stanhope was determined. She knew Peggy needed cheering up.

"It's a lovely song but it's too difficult for me," said Peggy. She said it mechanically, as if her mind was somewhere else.

Peggy West had not been herself since getting caught up in the afternoon's big political demonstration. Nothing like that had ever happened to her before. She had lived here for years and got along well with many Egyptian friends, both men and women. Today, however, had been different. The crowd had closed in around her, and she'd found it terrifying. It had been stifling and claustrophobic. They'd been shouting very loudly, so that she was deafened, and she'd been aware of the sweat on their faces and the foul smell of their bodies. Some of them had pushed her from one to the other, grinning, spitting, and shouting their anti-British slogans all the while.

Once home she had got into the bath and stayed there a long time. Tonight she was looking truly radiant. It was part of her attempt to cheer herself up, but it hadn't completely done so. The irreparable damage was that done to Peggy's ego, or to her soul. Until this afternoon she'd known herself to be an educated liberal who viewed all the inhabitants of this world as equals. She'd been proud of the relationships she'd been able to develop with Egyptian friends at work and everywhere else. Everyone always said that Peggy West understood the Egyptians and loved them. Now she knew it was not true. She'd loathed those demonstrators with all her heart. At that moment, with those people crushing her half to death, she would have given anything to be home in England again. And this feeling had not completely left her. This was a foreign land, and she didn't want to die here.

Standing at the piano, watching the hands on the keys, she kept telling herself that the Egyptian demonstrators had been relatively good-natured. Their pushes had not been violent and had not seriously hurt her. She told herself that their strained faces had not shown real violence; they were just the faces of men shouting. But Peggy wanted to go home.

Jimmy Ross changed key and said, "We'll find something for you." He began playing "A Nightingale Sang in Berkeley Square."

She saw that people were looking at her. "Do sing, Peggy," said Alice. "It would be lovely." There were affirmative sounds from the other guests.

"I promised Piotr I'd make coffee. His servant can't make it European style."

"I'll do that, Peggy. You sing."

Peggy still wasn't sure. "Use the big blue jug: three measures of coffee and a pint of boiling water."

"Don't fuss: sing."

Peggy let the melody go around in her head. She had sung this one at the Christmas concert to benefit the Empire Services Club, sung it so well she'd been pressed to do an encore.

"Can you do it in E flat?" said Peggy.

Obligingly he modulated to the required key and gave her a few bars of introduction. She smiled at him to say she was ready to start.

" 'I may be right; I may be wrong,' " sang Peggy. It was a firm clear voice. Once she started singing, her gloomy mood lifted a little.

Alice could hear the music while she waited for the kettle to boil. Harry Wechsler had followed her into the kitchen. He'd become keyed up by his earlier arguments, and when the music started he'd come into the kitchen to find a new audience. Now he was in full swing.

"When this European war broke out in 'thirty-nine, I was covering the Japanese army in what everyone said would be the final push along the Yangtze. My agency sent me to Berlin. What happens? The Battle of Britain gives our London man all the front pages. When I decide the big story is Rommel, the German propaganda ministry take weeks to accredit me to Rommel's HQ. While I'm kicking my heels, Hitler invades Russia. By that time I'm on my way to Rome. Still in Rome, waiting for a plane to Tripoli, what happens? The Japs bomb Pearl. Can you beat it? I would have done better to stay with the Japs on the Yangtze. That's the story of my life, honey." She pushed past him to get to the stove. He drank some wine.

Over her shoulder Alice said mockingly, "And then, when finally the Cairo brass hats let you go and take a look at the battlefront, you get a virus and end up back here again."

He put an arm around her waist. "That's it. What do you think I do wrong?"

"You try too hard, Mr. Wechsler," she said, slipping away from his attempted embrace to warm the coffee jug.

He took the rejection with good grace. "My name is Harry! Maybe you're right. All I can be sure about is that with the Japs fighting American boys, Mr. and Mrs. America are not going to be too concerned about the British letting the Krauts snatch back a few desert villages somewhere in Africa."

"Does that mean you'll try and get to the Pacific?"

"No." Wechsler bent over to sniff at the flowers. "Like I said, there is a big story here: Arab nationalism, British colonialism, the Jewish homeland, and Nazi expansionism. Everybody fighting everybody. I'd say this story could run and run."

"I hope not, Mr. Wechsler."

"It's principally a matter of finding the right angle. Say, none of these flowers have any smell."

"I know."

"But they all have thorns."

"Don't complain that the rosebush has thorns; rejoice that the thornbush bears roses."

"Say, that's cute. Did you just make that up?"

"It's from the Koran," said Alice.

"Is that right? I like it. I'll try and work it into my next story." It was very unlikely that he'd find a way of doing this, but he'd found that people liked him to say such things.

It was while Alice was in the kitchen with Harry Wechsler that Piotr's servant answered the door to a soldier bearing a message for "Corporal Cutler." He was wanted downstairs in the hotel lobby. It was an emergency and he must hurry. "Oh, dear," said Piotr.

When the song ended to polite applause, the prince conveyed the message to him. "Duty calls, corporal. A sergeant has come to take you away from us. I do hope you'll come back and see us next week. I'm sorry about the piano; it's so difficult getting it tuned nowadays."

"Thank you," said Jimmy Ross. Such a sudden summons alarmed him, but he tried not to show it. "It was wonderful to play a really good piano again."

"What can you have done?" said Peggy anxiously. She knew there was seldom anything desirable awaiting corporals who were rounded up and summoned back to barracks.

"Tell Alice not to worry. I'll soon sort it out," he told Peggy. He told himself that it couldn't be really serious or they would have come up here and arrested him. On the other hand, they could wait downstairs in the confident knowledge that there was no other path of escape.

"Did you leave the typewriter ribbons unguarded?" called Darymple mockingly. "Well, don't worry, corporal. I'll look after Alice for you."

Ross smiled. He looked around and couldn't see Alice anywhere. But they were all watching him, so he waved and took his leave.

He was down two flights of stairs when Peggy noticed that he'd left his silver pencil on the piano. She could hear his metal-studded boots on the stairs as she hurried after him.

But Ross was moving fast and he was already greeting a MP sergeant as Peggy got to the top of the final flight. The sergeant was standing in the lobby with an officer's army battle-dress blouse draped over his arm.

"What is it, sergeant?"

"It's not too good, sir," said the sergeant. "The captain is waiting in the car outside. He's got all the latest gen. He'll explain." Still talking, they pushed their way through the entrance doors.

"Bert!" called Peggy. But by the time she was downstairs and out into the street she saw him a hundred yards away. He was scrambling hurriedly into the front seat of an Austin utility. The sergeant jumped into the back, still clutching the army jacket, just as the driver let in the clutch and pulled away into the traffic.

Peggy stood there for a moment in the evening gloom. Poor Bert Cutler, she thought, what were they going to do to him? The driver looked just like that Captain Marker who'd searched Solomon's houseboat and brought her back here to check on her identity papers. But it was almost dark; she was probably mistaken.

≡11≡

"The balloon's gone up," said Lionel Marker as he pressed the accelerator of the Austin pickup and pulled away into the traffic. Marker liked driving in these crowded streets. It had become a game with him.

Jimmy Ross grunted and took a tight hold on his seat. He'd heard about Marker's driving.

"Nothing coming through on the teleprinter as yet, sir. It sounds like the king was told to change the government, turned nasty, and was kicked off the throne. The brigadier's flown back to be here. He said there was a colossal flap at GHQ. He'll be outside the palace. Wants to talk to you there, he says."

"I brought your jacket, sir," said the sergeant from the back. "It came from the tailor this evening." He passed forward the new battle-dress blouse with major's crowns on the shoulder straps.

"Yes, I'd better wear it," said Ross with a sigh of relief. So he'd meet the brigadier. It was as well that he wasn't going to face him wearing the corporal's uniform and try to explain that he needed it for some nonexistent investigation. Awkwardly he took the jacket, twisted around as he put his arms through the sleeves, and then buttoned it up. His sergeant passed him his webbing belt with a revolver in the holster.

"It's a stand-to," said the sergeant. "Officers with side arms,

I expect." Sergeant Ponsonby was assigned as assistant and clerk to the major. He looked like an artful old devil but very efficient.

"Thank you, sergeant."

"I knew this would happen," said Marker, "I knew it. Lampson is determined to put the Wafd party back in power." The streets were crowded. A donkey came wandering out from a side alley. It brayed its anger as Marker narrowly missed hitting it. "I predicted it."

Ross held his breath for a moment. Three old men grabbed the donkey and shouted something after them. Their vehement curses were lost in the swirl of exhaust smoke. "Did you?" said Ross with studied calm. "Then I wish you would explain it to me in words of one syllable."

Marker took a deep breath. "Well, that arsehole Lampson is the troublemaker. The Foreign Office people in London have never understood what's going on here. Those people still live in the age of send-in-a-gunboat. They won't listen to the commander in chief, and they can't get it through their thick skulls that the army have enough on their plate trying to stop Rommel without coping with the consequences of their chronic diplomatic failures. We can't hold down a few million excited Egyptians with our little garrison and fight a war as well."

So that's why Marker was upset. Well, that was all right; at least the death of Major Cutler had not been uncovered. Marker just wanted to vent his anger about the strange activities of the British embassy people. That was a tirade Ross could understand—and join, if need be.

"Have you got any cigarettes, sir?"

Ross took out a pack and passed him one. He had read up on Egypt over the last few days and picked Alice's brains as well. "But what's the problem? Lampson wants the Wafd back in power, and the Wafd is popular—they're the Nationalists, the biggest political party in the land."

"Well, the Wafd won't be so bloody popular after it's been

put back into power by means of British bayonets," said Marker, getting a lighter from his pocket.

"I don't get it," said Ross. In response to awkward questions, Ross had found the best course was to say that in Scotland he'd been a police detective, and there police work had always meant staying out of politics. But, as Alice had told him, here in Egypt politics permeated everything the department did. There was no way of avoiding it. According to Alice, Marker had an instinct for local politics. He always knew the score and seemed to get the political line right. She said even the brigadier, surrounded as he was with all the GHQ experts, would sometimes invite Marker's interpretations of what was happening.

Marker deftly lit his cigarette, using only one hand. "Official British policy in Egypt has always been to drive a wedge between the king and any big political movement. That's the whole theory behind British power here."

"So what will the king do now?"

"Lampson is a mad, vindictive sod. Giving orders to a king has turned his head. Now that he's kicked Farouk off the throne, Lampson will start to play emperor. I think we should prepare for the worst."

"Riots?"

"I just hope someone is watching the Egyptian army. They've got heavy weapons."

"Jesus! Will it come to that?"

"Why not? No matter what the soldiers privately think about their king, the Gyppo army will regard our booting him out as a stain on their honor. You know what all those hotheads are like: Long live Rommel and all that shit."

"And the king got the army their big pay hike. That was smart."

Marker shot him a glance of appreciation. His new major had done some homework. "King Farouk is not a fool," said Marker. "Fatty is as cunning as a wagon load of monkeys. That's where Lampson always gets it wrong."

By now they were turning into Midan Abdin, the vast square that fronts Abdin Palace. Some soldiers and policemen were standing in groups, talking. Apart from three British armored cars, parked unobtrusively away from the palace forecourt with their lights extinguished, it all seemed very quiet. The only thing that made the scene in any way unusual was that lights were shining from all the windows of the palace. Through one window, some servants could be seen moving furniture around.

The police must have blocked off all the entrances to the square, but even so there were a couple of Arabs peddling trinkets. They could always wriggle through: even in GHQ, with armed military police on every door, they'd find Arabs in the upstairs corridors, selling their wares. What a thankless task for a security officer.

The three men looked around for their brigadier but without success. They drove on to the corner of Sharia el Bustan. There were two khaki-colored staff cars with British Troops in Egypt markings and a Bedford truck with British infantrymen sitting unnaturally silent in its dark interior. The truck was parked right across the streetcar tracks at the place where they turn the corner.

In Abdin Square, near the tall railings, half a dozen British officers stood in twos, talking together. All wore revolvers. At the palace gates, near the regular Egyptian army sentries, there were some Egyptian policemen in their black wool winter uniforms.

"Look," said Marker. "That gangly-looking lieutenant is named Spaulding. He works in the brigadier's office at GHQ. Ex-university don or something of that kind, they tell me. He's too damned keen. Watch out for him: he's a sycophantic little crawler, and the brigadier thinks the sun shines from his arsehole." The subject of Marker's description was standing near a staff car bearing the brigadier's markings. They drove over to him.

Ross got out of the car and said, as casually as possible, "What a glorious evening. Now what's it all about, Mr. Spaulding?"

The lieutenant was wearing a steel helmet and had a pistol in a canvas holster at his hip. There was an air of keenness about him. Some men took naturally to the military life, thought Ross. Perhaps it wasn't too different from the monastic world of the university.

Lieutenant Spaulding saluted with all the energy and precision of a Guards sergeant and said, "Yes, sir, a truly memorable evening, sir. Are you up to date on the palace situation, sir?" Spaulding meant was his major up to date on what he and the rest of GHQ thought about the palace situation.

"No, I'm damned if I am," said Ross. It was wonderful being a major. He was saying the same sort of things he'd said while a corporal, but now he was taken seriously by those around him.

Perhaps the lieutenant was suddenly affected by the beauty of the night—the air cool and silky, the purple sky pricked by countless stars—for he smiled and in a more normal voice said, "Ambassador Lampson gave the king an ultimatum. It expired at eighteen hundred hours. The king's in there now, with a crowd of politicians. He's decided to abdicate, but no one is quite sure who will take over."

"What sort of ultimatum?" Ross looked at Spaulding; there was nothing wrong with the lieutenant's uniform, it was of good quality and fitted well, but Spaulding was one of those men who, despite his obvious efforts, would never look like a soldier.

"The king has been told to invite the Wafd to form a government. London have had enough of this crowd."

"And if the king refuses?"

Spaulding gave a dry donnish smile. "That's what I'm telling you: he's already refused. The ultimatum expired at six P.M."

"So, what now?"

"Lampson has demanded an audience and he's due back at any minute. As I understand it, he'll have General Stone or someone else from BTE with him. They're going to force the king to sign the abdication."

"And then?"

"They want the army to escort him to the airport straightaway. The RAF brought a plane in and have it standing by. I'm not sure where he'll be flown to. Somewhere in the Sudan, perhaps."

"What a shambles," said Ross. "Are they our people?" He nodded in the direction of the Bedford and the men inside.

"No. None of our people are here except us. The brigadier said our people should be kept out of this: it's too public. I kidnapped a platoon of red caps from the barracks to do the dirty work. Motorcycle outriders and all the trimmings. We'll do it right. I'm keeping them out of sight in Sharia el Bustan until the time comes." He took off his steel helmet and wiped his brow with a handkerchief. Spaulding wished he'd not brought the helmet but, having nowhere to put it, there was little alternative but to keep wearing it.

"Good," said Ross without enthusiasm. "Sounds as if it's going to be a long night."

"You never said a truer word, Major Cutler," said a low plummy voice. It was the intelligence brigadier from GHQ. He'd been going around inspecting the military police detachment that Spaulding had hidden away in the next street. So this was the man Ross had heard about; he looked an avuncular figure. He was a big bearlike man whose long service in the tropics seemed to have thinned his blood. Even on this unusually mild evening he was wearing an overcoat buttoned to the neck over a thick wool scarf. He returned the salutes of his two officers with a wave of his leather-covered swagger stick. "At last we meet, Major Cutler. Well, this is what the bloody civilians get us into. Don't forget it." He looked at his wristwatch.

"No, sir."

"And that bloody man Lampson doesn't even speak Arabic. I can't think why Winston keeps him here." He looked at his watch again. "What time is Lampson due back?" he asked Spaulding.

"At twenty-one hundred hours, sir."

"It's almost that now," said the brigadier petulantly. "Everyone at GHQ is damned jumpy today. The map room is running short on pins." He grinned to show it was a joke. "If they don't stop Rommel soon, he'll be sitting on the veranda of Shepheard's Hotel finishing up the last of the Stella beer."

Just about everyone in Cairo was making the same joke. Ross was not quite sure how to react to a brigadier in one of these you-and-me-back-to-back-fighting-all-the-world moods. Was he expected to say yes or no? Ross nodded and cleared his throat.

"Looks like the Auk will sack Ritchie," said the brigadier, wanting to show the lower ranks the sort of high-level discussions he was a party to.

"Will we be able to hold them?" said Ross.

"At Gazala? I hope so. Ritchie should be fired, really. No one has faith in him any more."

Ross looked at Spaulding, but artfully Spaulding was looking at him for a reply. Ross said, "Will it improve morale to sack the army commander?"

The brigadier looked at him and smiled. This new major was sharp; some of these civvies were bright. "That's exactly what the old man will be thinking, eh?"

"Yes, sir."

"And here they come. At least the wretched man is on time."

Into the square came Lampson's car, accompanied by a car filled with embassy people. Then came four armored cars and three trucks that were weighted down with infantry in full battle order, complete with rifles.

The palace gates were closed and locked. The little procession came to a halt there. The Egyptian sentries were standing well back from the railings. A British officer went forward and grabbed the gates. He rattled them vigorously but found them locked. He went back to the car for instructions and evidently got them, for he was immediately on his way again. Using his Webley revolver, he shot the lock off the gates. The shots echoed across the empty square. There was a squeak of metal as he opened the gates wide. The first car through was an armored car. The driver took the turn too steeply, and there was a loud screech as the armor tore a piece of metal off the gate.

Lampson's car followed, stopped, and the men inside alighted. Walking past the armored car, Lampson led the way along the drive to the front doors of the palace. The door opened as he got there, and he went inside. The armored cars and the trucks remained near the railings. No one got out.

The brigadier watched in silence until Lampson disappeared inside. "History is being made tonight, gentlemen." After leaving a few moments for this ponderous pronouncement to take effect, the brigadier went off to confer with someone in one of the armored cars.

Lieutenant Spaulding said, "The most bizarre thing is that Sir Walter Monckton is here in Cairo. He's the man who drafted the abdication signed by the Duke of Windsor. Now they have him drafting the abdication for Farouk."

"Why is he here?" said Ross.

"Entirely coincidence. He's been polishing a seat in one of these offices where the real war is being fought. Director General of British Propaganda and Information Services is, I believe, his full title."

"Do I hear a note of cynicism in your voice, Mr. Spaulding?"

"Not at all, sir. They also serve who only stand and propagate."

Ross smiled; you got better jokes as a major, as well as better food and lodging.

The brigadier came back with good news. "Lampson seems to have pulled it off. No abdication. The king has agreed to put the Wafd party back into power. We can all go and get a night's sleep after all. Except the provost people, of course. All leaves and passes are canceled: all troops are recalled to barracks. They'll double up the street patrols and crack down on all the usual whorehouses. With average luck, it will all pass off peacefully tonight. What tomorrow brings is anyone's guess."

He reached out with his swagger stick to tap Ross's shoulder and waved the stick in the air to indicate that he should follow him as he walked away. Marker had said he was a man much given to signaling. Rumor said he'd started his military career as subaltern of a signals platoon in the days of semaphore flags.

"A word in your private ear, Major Cutler."

"Yes, sir?"

"I know you have your own way of doing things. Cloak and dagger . . . dressing up in false beards and climbing up the minarets."

"Only when absolutely necessary," said Ross.

The brigadier continued as if not hearing him. "Yes! Just what that fellow Lawrence of Arabia did back in the last show. Splendid! Buried in Westminster Abbey, they tell me. Or Saint Paul's or somewhere. But there are one or two aspects of your present task that I should like you to bear very much in mind."

"Yes, sir?"

"London, sometimes even Winston himself, has been giving the old man a bad time lately. Winston is getting rather fed up with being forced to make so many of those backs-to-the-wall speeches he does so well. He seems to be looking for a theme more spirited: a few significant battlefield victories, naval battles won. Something more suited to that slightly overwrought prose style of his." The brigadier laughed to indicate that his criticism of the prime minister was limited to that great man's literary efforts.

Ross said nothing. He tried to guess what was coming, but so far this evening the brigadier had proved a man of constant surprises.

"Fact is, Cutler, old chap, I'm getting a serious hurry-up on this one. I know you can't work miracles but"—he lowered his voice to emphasize confidentiality—"London have some sort of mumbo-jumbo earhole so they know verbatim what our pal Rommel receives in the way of secret signals from Berlin. Ver-bloody-batim!"

The brigadier paused long enough for Ross to peer at him, trying to see what might be coming next. When he was quite sure of his major's whole attention, the brigadier went on.

"I'm sorry not to have seen you before this, but I knew you'd go through your predecessor's confidential files. So you'll know that Rommel is getting to hear of every disposition the old man makes, even before the dust settles. Every tank squadron, every infantry battalion, every last detail down to the mobile bath and delousing units." He paused and nodded to himself.

Ross said nothing. Marker had told him not to interrupt the old man's speeches. He liked to say everything two or three times; it was the army method.

"Yes," said the brigadier, "Rommel is being told every last detail of our chain of command and deployment. And whoever is telling him is getting it right. It must be coming from Cairo: some of it is stuff London don't know. If we don't crack this one soon I'm going to have my head in a sling: know what I mean?"

"Yes, sir." It was exactly the brief he'd read in the files. And exactly what Marker had told him the brigadier would say.

"Good man. Gyppo army chaps, eh?"

"I beg your pardon, sir?"

"Egyptian army. That's where it's all coming from. That's obvious, I should think."

"I'm not yet sure on that one, sir."

"You're the detective, Cutler. I'm just a soldier. But surely you can see that it has to be someone who knows his way through British army paperwork. It's not one of our people. In GHQ we've sifted through every last man with access to this sort of material and come up with nothing. It's got to be someone outside. There's too much of it for it to be collected by a single spy; it's a network. Who else but those Gyppo army types? We know they want Rommel to win; we've heard them say so often enough."

"I'll keep at it, sir."

"I understand you have one of those Gyppo army firebrands in your sights?"

Sayed, of course. Ross wondered what else had got back to the old man on his duck shoot. "Yes, sir, I do. But if we move too soon he'll bolt and we'll be back to square one."

The brigadier slashed the air with his stick. "No need for every last jot and tittle of evidence, major. You won't be standing in the Old Bailey, facing a cross-examination from some nasty little KC for the defense. If you point the finger at who you think this bugger is, we'll spirit him away and that's the end of it."

"I know, sir."

"That's the way things are done here."

"Yes, sir."

The brigadier didn't want to leave it like that. He felt he hadn't made his subordinate understand how things were here. "King Farouk has decided what's best for him. Tomorrow the old government will be kicked out and the Wafd will be sworn in. The new boys will go after the old lot with a ferocity that knows no bounds. Some of them will wake up in clink, and some of them will end up feeding the fishes in the Sweet Water Canal. By the end of next week, all the bribes will be paid into new bank accounts, and Egypt will settle down to stable government while we get on with the war." Another fierce slash with the stick. "Still, all this sudden upheaval might provide you with a chance to nab the fellows we're looking for. If we have to pay a big fat back-hander to someone to make them do their duty, so be it."

"Yes, sir."

"You know what I mean?"

Ross suspected that the brigadier wanted him to pay for false witness but he wasn't sure. "The corruption here is one of the things that makes my job difficult."

"Nonsense, Cutler. You mustn't think of it like that. It's as misleading to look at Egyptian corruption through the eyes of an Englishman as it is to look at English drunkenness through the eyes of an Egyptian Muslim."

"I'll remember that, sir." He decided not to tell the brigadier that he was Scottish, not English. Such corrections, no matter how gently offered, always made Englishmen excited.

The brigadier sniffed and tackled him head on. "You don't think it is the Gyppos, do you."

"I'm keeping an open mind, sir."

"It's got to be a network, major. Admit that."

Ross had spent hours going through every last file in the office. "That wouldn't reduce it to the Egyptian army, sir. There are many espionage networks in this town. The Italians, the Vichy French, the Greeks, and the Jews from Palestine all have tightly knit nationalist communities, here in Cairo and in Alex. Some big, some small. Some official, some less so. Such people all gather information and coordinate it. You might almost say they all have networks."

The brigadier had been certain that his theory about the Egyptian army was unassailable. Now these alternative suspects made him less certain. He blinked as if hit, but he soon recovered from his dismay. "And are you following all these blighters up?"

"Yes, I am, sir."

"Cheer up, Cutler. You couldn't wish for a more understanding and unconventional commander than me, eh?"

So that's how the brigadier saw himself. "No, sir. Indeed I couldn't."

"Ah, look at that! Lampson and his merry men are coming out of the palace. What it must be to walk with kings and keep such a very common touch!"

≡12≡

Bab-el-Hadid barracks was a curious-looking three-story structure, built to look like a small crusader castle, complete with castellated ramparts and a square-shaped tower. Facing across the gardens and open spaces to Cairo's main railway station, it was seen by hundreds of people who arrived and departed every day. Yet few people, except those from the army's Special Investigation Branch, Field Security staff, military policemen, and prisoners, ever saw inside this outlandish place on Sharia Malika Nazli.

The office where Jimmy Ross now reigned was a large high-ceilinged room with an electric fan and two good-sized windows. One of them gave a view across the square to the railway station. From the other one you could see roofs of the Bulaq, a squalid neighborhood where Europeans seldom went. The view downward was a parade ground, with sandbagged emplacements in front of the guardhouse. At ground level there was a row of cells, their doors all newly reinforced since the previous June, when five handcuffed Australian soldier prisoners ingeniously removed the screws from their cell doors and escaped in a refuse truck. At present the courtyard was empty except for a big Humber saloon car with balloon tires and two Austin Tillys: utility pickups with canvas tops. One of them was assigned to Major Cutler, and Jimmy Ross delighted in the luxury of using it.

He told himself over and over again that he should make a run for it, but he was enjoying himself so much he couldn't tear himself away. He treasured every minute he spent with Alice; she'd made him discover things about himself he'd never before known. Was that a symptom of falling in love? But it wasn't only his infatuation with Alice Stanhope that kept him coming back here every day instead of bolting. At least he tried to convince himself it wasn't that. Perhaps it was the actor in him. Or the infantile delight he got from deceiving them all. Or the pleasure that came from being the boss after a lifetime of being a nobody. Whatever the reason he kept extending the deception, continuing and refining his role. Only an actor could understand the challenge. Success would come not so much from providing an authentic Albert Cutler as from a skillful creation of the person they all expected Cutler to be.

He sat back in his chair and put on a slight frown, as Captain Marker gave him his daily briefing. It was Jimmy Ross's great good fortune that his immediate superior, the brigadier, had his office in the monolithic GHQ "Muddle East" building in Garden City on the other side of town. He was left to run things the way he liked. It was nice to wonder what would happen if he did the impossible and found Rommel's spy. Sometimes, losing himself in his impersonation, he had the feeling he was on the way to doing so.

"And what do you make of it, Captain Marker?" he said as Marker's briefing came to an end.

It was Marker's daily task to go through all the new paperwork, sifting from such diverse sources as the embassy to the meanest Arab informant. This had been a long morning for him. Since the British brought their armored cars to browbeat the king in his palace, the atmosphere in Cairo had been threatening. The city was alive with rumors and stories. The regular police informants were lining up to report endless variations on a plot to overthrow the British occupying forces.

Marker added a few extras: "There have been demonstrations, ragged and unorganized. The Amr mosque was adorned with anti-British slogans and streamers. A few mobs are still roaming around looking for trouble. All army units are on the alert, and we've warned all Europeans to stay off the streets except for essential journeys."

"Spaulding phoned and said they'd closed the Royal Automobile Club," Ross said. "He was going there for lunch, I suppose."

"And arrested its president, Prince Omar Faruq. The new government says the club had become a haunt for some dangerous political groups."

"Spaulding said the king liked it."

"Yes, he'll be furious that it's been closed down." Marker blew his nose.

"You're getting a cold."

"It's the dust."

"If most of the noise and excitement in the streets is just support for the king, we can cope with that." Jimmy Ross tried to make it sound magisterial.

"Support for the king is often a crafty way of saying, Kick out the British," said Marker.

"I suppose it's better they let off steam where we can see it happening. But can't we keep the new government from arresting these politicians and trade union officials? That sounds as if it could trigger real trouble," said Ross. "Who are they giving the jobs to?"

"Kith and kin. Brothers, sons, close friends, and people who will split the take. They want to get their hands on some quick money. The Wafd have got to make up for five lean years in opposition."

"Well, that's all part of the game, I suppose."

"These people play rough," said Marker. "There have been a lot of fatal accidents already."

"What are the embassy people saying this morning?" asked Ross.

"The usual tripe: 'The Wafd party has been Britain's most reliable ally since 1936. . . .' "

"So we let them do what they like?" said Ross.

"It's their country."

"Don't be too blasé about it, Captain Marker. And why the priority alert for this bugger Abdel-Hamid Sherif?"

"The Wafd are trying to sack the army's chief of staff. They want to politicize the armed forces. That could become a real thorn in our side. Lampson and the embassy people don't know how to deal with it."

"Umm," said Ross, recalling a report he'd just finished reading. "And I suppose the Wafd will try to do the same thing with al Azhar appointments. They'll try to politicize everything in sight, but the students will fight that." Marker raised his eyebrows. Ross decided he was doing all right. "But you haven't answered my question. What about Abdel-Hamid Sherif?"

"He's confronting us. He's putting together a political petition about fascistic British interference in Egyptian democracy. He's threatening to send a copy to all the neutral embassies here in Cairo."

"It's a clever move. You'd better find out more. The brigadier is bound to ask me about that one."

"Thank you, major."

"I'm sorry, Lionel, but someone has to do it, and the brigadier is chasing me about this Rommel's spy business. Add Abdel-Hamid Sherif to your list and keep me up to date on it. What do you think will happen next?"

Captain Marker sighed. "Everything Lampson says he wants to prevent. The Wafd party will lose the support of the *effendiyya*, the students and the young army officers. The bourgeoisie will become even more anti-Wafdist. Farouk, on the other hand, is beginning to enjoy a popularity he never dreamed of."

"Anything else?"

"I'm afraid you've missed Burns Night," said Marker, putting a sheet of paper before him. Seeing the puzzled look, he added, "The men of Scottish extraction. You asked for a list of men born north of the border."

"Ah, yes," said Ross. Fearful of bumping into some old friend or colleague of Albert Cutler, he had asked one of the clerks to compile a list based on their files. So Marker knew about that; it was not easy to keep anything from Marker. He looked down it anxiously. There were only two men from Glasgow, and neither had been on the police force. "Too bad," said Ross, pushing the list aside and feigning disappointment. "No matter. We'll try again when it gets near Saint Andrew's Day. Well, I won't keep you, Mr. Marker, I know you are keen to start tracking down Abdel-Hamid Sherif." Ross gave him a little smile. He liked Marker.

"Exactly," said Marker. The feeling was mutual. Marker had not enjoyed a close relationship with his previous boss. He liked this new fellow and his unorthodox methods. He'd still not got over the surprise he'd had at hearing about Major Cutler's amazing performance in beating up the Arab in the brothel. It was not what you'd expect from him, somehow. Still, Marker's law practice in England had taught him not to sum people up too quickly. He had a feeling that Major Albert Cutler was a complex personality. Looking at him, Marker could see elements of hesitation . . . of reticence . . . almost of apprehension. But what would a tough fellow like that worry about?

Marker picked up his notes. "See you later, major. I would go armed for the next few days, by the way."

Ross smiled at him.

As Marker left, Major Cutler's sergeant clerk brought in a cup of tea and said, "The brigadier will phone you at eleven thirty, sir." Sergeant Ponsonby was over forty: a thin inscrutable Yorkshireman, his short-sleeved shirt revealing tattoos right down to his wrists.

"How long have you been in the Middle East, Sergeant Ponsonby?"

"Since April fifteenth, 1936, sir."

"My God! Never been home?"

"No, sir. No family, no one to visit."

"Which regiment was that?"

"Ah, the infantry all go home eventually. I came out with the Engineers. Sappers don't get sent back to Blighty like the battalions do."

"Do you know what the brigadier wants of me, sergeant?"

"No, sir. Urgent and important. That's all his office said. The brigadier will be off for two or three days after that."

Two or three days usually meant the brigadier was departing on a duck shoot. The embassy and GHQ staged duck shoots every week. Once someone from the Field Security office at the docks had poked his nose into the diplomatic consignment from London and discovered ten thousand cartridges.

"It's a damned strange war, sergeant."

Sergeant Ponsonby looked at him and nodded. Ponsonby had seen his fair share of fighting. He'd earned his third stripe clearing minefields under fire. He'd fought the Italians in Ethiopia and the Germans in Greece. The SIB had claimed him because Ponsonby had learned a reasonable amount of Arabic, together with Hindi and some other Indian languages. "You take the rough with the smooth, sir," said the sergeant. "Cairo has always been a cushy number."

"Yes. Thank you, sergeant. Did you read this one?" Ross tapped his fingers on a report about the death of the thirty-three-year-old Ordnance Corps sergeant major.

"I did, sir."

Ross was cautious in his dealings with the sergeant in a way he was not cautious with the others. Ponsonby had all the cunning and instinct of the old soldier. If Ross set a foot wrong, Ponsonby would spot it before any of the others. "Wonderful, isn't it? The most squalid brothel in El Birkeh, and it's only a few steps from Shepheard's Hotel."

The sergeant looked at him. Everyone in the building had by now heard of their major's remarkable tough-guy act, interrogating the manager of the brothel. "Death was caused by knife wounds," said Ponsonby, who was keen to get the file closed and put away. "Poor sod."

"You and I, sergeant, have had to make do with only one paybook apiece. This sergeant major had two of them. And a whole lot of other critically important army paperwork." He opened the file to refresh his memory. This sergeant major had been a chief clerk, issuing what the army quaintly called "war-like stores" in the Command Ordnance Depot and Workshops at Abbasiya. Lately the depot had been losing too much to thefts. Not just boots and tires but guns, signaling equipment, and explosives, the sort of thing the dead man had been handling. Ross looked at Sergeant Ponsonby. "What happened to the paybooks I left in the drawer, sergeant?"

"Gone, sir."

"I know that. I can see that. Gone where?" Ross had planned to keep the blank paybooks for himself. They'd be useful when he changed identity. He remembered an E. Phillips Oppenheim story in which the spy had changed his identity three times in close succession. His pursuers had detected the first two changes but he'd got away under the third identity. It sounded like a good method.

"Evidence for the inquiry, sir. I knew you'd want it all sent on to them."

"I see." The genuine blank army paybooks were probably worth a fortune on the black market. He suspected Ponsonby of taking them for himself, but it would be dangerous to challenge him. It was particularly disconcerting that the paybooks had been in a folder under a wad of other papers in his desk drawer. It indicated that Ponsonby sifted through everything on a regular basis and was not afraid of letting him know it. Suddenly Jimmy Ross started to worry about the army servants—and the Arab cleaners—who went into his rooms at the Citadel. Had they gone through his kit? What did they know about him?

He looked at the sergeant. So Ponsonby took the rough with

the smooth? Many of the old-timers were like Ponsonby. They took life as it came, not resenting the luxuries that were enjoyed by the rear echelons while the men at the front risked their lives in constant discomfort. Perhaps that was the way to deal with all the problems of life: to take every day as it came. He looked at the clock on the wall. So the brigadier would call at eleven thirty. All the brass did it like that: they made appointments so there was no chance of your being elsewhere. Ross hated such commands; he hated being at someone's beck and call.

"You saw the answers to your supplementary questions, sir? And my report?" Ponsonby asked. He leaned over and touched the typewritten sheets that had come from the army pathologist who did the post-mortem.

"Yes, I saw it," said Ross. "Traces of mutton fat in his mouth but none in his stomach. More to the point: no traces of semen anywhere on the body, and none on the underclothing or outer clothing. So why was he visiting a brothel?"

"You can't ever be sure why any man visits a whorehouse," said Ponsonby. Ross glanced at him. So Ponsonby was being philosophical today.

"Wouldn't a brothel make a convenient place for a secret meeting?" suggested Ross, as a teacher might elicit a reply from a small child. "Not much chance of being spotted."

Ponsonby had already admitted that Ross was right about this, but if his boss wanted reassurance, so be it. "And our MPs, being mostly lance corporals, are not so keen to challenge a sergeant major who knows his way around," said Ponsonby reflectively. Then, as if suddenly deciding to reveal a secret, Ponsonby said, "I am somewhat familiar with the location in which the body was found."

Ross looked up. "Go on," he said.

Ponsonby's words had been chosen to indicate to his master that he'd been to El Birkeh only in the course of duty, but now he reverted to his normal syntax again. "It's a filthy Arab hovel. Not many soldiers would go into a lice-infested rathole like that, let alone"—he hesitated—"have a meeting there."

"Look, sergeant. I know all about where the body was found. I examined the body before we moved it: where do you think I got the paybooks? And we already have an eyewitness to these two men being regular visitors to Lady Fitz. So let's stop all this nonsense, shall we?" It seemed as if the whole damned army had a soft spot for Lady Fitz. She'd become a sort of legend among the fighting men, like Lili Marlene and Rommel. Even men who would never think of visiting a brothel would speak in her support.

"But we don't have an eyewitness who saw them on what we think was the night of the killing."

"Of course you're right, sergeant." He didn't have to be reminded of that fact. "Yesterday I went to visit Lady Fitz, as she's actually calling herself nowadays. She didn't try too hard to persuade me it wasn't done there. She sat there with a gin and tonic in her hand, looked me right in the eye, and told me she doesn't know what her clients do upstairs. There have been murders in some of the most exclusive hotels in London and Paris, she said." Ross fumed at the memory of her haughty manner.

"And is that true?" said Ponsonby.

"Of course it's true. The old cow! I'd like to throw her into the native cells for a week and close that whorehouse so it stays closed, but Mr. Marker says she has too many friends in high places."

"Yes, sir, she certainly does," said Ponsonby, with an emphasis calculated to deter his master from any such rash course of action.

"But did you get anything more out of number twenty-three?" He turned over page after page of Ponsonby's horrendously inexpert typewriting. The Cairo informants were all known by numbers. It had started as a way for the British to cope with Arab names, but as the city became more dangerous it also afforded protection to the informants. Number twenty-three reported regularly. Because she was a prostitute they didn't have to set up clandestine meetings. She came to the police barracks just as all the other girls did at some time or another. She was a Turkish girl who could successfully pass herself off as French, except to French clients.

Ponsonby nodded. "Number twenty-three said that Lady Fitz suddenly decided to have just that one room redecorated. It didn't need redecorating. It probably was marked with blood, as you guessed. Number twenty-three affirmed that the sergeant major was always there with another soldier. It's all typed there," said Ponsonby, proudly pointing to the laboriously typed report of the interview.

"I know. I read it. She said he was there with a German." He paused. "You say with a South African. Did you pursue that with her?"

"South African badges. She described his uniform."

"I'm not talking about bloody badges," said Ross, boiling over. "Why did number twenty-three say the man was a German?"

Ponsonby was unmoved by his master's sudden burst of temper. "Because he sometimes spoke German with Lady Fitz."

"That bloody woman!"

"Does it matter if he spoke German? Or where he did the killing? He's not likely to go back there again after that stunt, is he?"

Ross closed the folder. "I want someone to give me the exact dimensions of that dagger wound and see if someone can discover what the murder weapon might have been. It's not the right shape and size to have been a bayonet, or an army issue folding knife." He handed the folder to Ponsonby for filing. "I'd like to know if it's the sort of blade an Arab peasant might carry. I have a feeling there is something big behind this one, Ponsonby. We have a killer who speaks fluent German. And if you look at our file on number twenty-three, you'll see her second husband was a German. She knows a German when she sees one. And this fellow, whoever he is, has enough influence to have Mahmoud the banker send his men to move the body. It's an all-star cast."

"I'll get someone onto that, sir," said Ponsonby. He'd taken the file but he held it in front of him. "But meanwhile workshops are waiting for us to reply."

"What's the hurry?" said Ross.

"They'll want to know what the incident report will say. I can phone them if you like. His unit will want to do the paperwork: next of kin and so on."

"What's stopping them?"

"They'll want to know what we are going to say."

"Am I being particularly dense this morning, sergeant?"

"His unit will want to say he died on active service. They'll want to tell his next of kin that he was a brave man who gave his life for his country, was loved by everyone . . . you know how they write them, sir."

So Ponsonby was a dedicated cynic. "Well?"

"If they do all that and then sometime later we let on that he was stabbed in a whorehouse . . ."

"Oh, I see." Ross sighed. He'd never get used to the army's way of doing things. It was as well that he had Ponsonby to guide him along the not very straight but exceedingly narrow path of army procedures. "I'll think about it."

"Today, sir?"

"Maybe. Why?"

"He's downstairs in our mortuary, sir, and the refrigeration has been giving a lot of trouble. They are trying to mend it again now, but the system is very old. He's getting very pongy."

"Oh, my God! Release the body and get him buried. They can say he died in action, as far as I'm concerned."

"Very good, sir. Died in action. I'll tell them to say that."

"And take that smirk off your face, Ponsonby."

"Yes, sir. Shall I release the prisoner too?"

"The brothel keeper? Yes, I suppose so. Has the poor sod been in solitary all this time?"

"Yes, sir."

"Kick his arse and send him home. Oh, and Ponsonby: what's the latest on that poor fellow who died on the train?"

"Didn't you see that, sir? I left it on your desk."

"See what?" Ross felt anxiety well up in him so that he felt physically ill.

"Tell a lie, I gave it to Mr. Marker. I'm really sorry, sir. They said I should tell you straightaway. It's my fault."

"Ponsonby! What are you talking about?"

Ponsonby mistook his anxiety for anger. "Well, I can remember it well enough: natural causes. The prisoner died of natural causes, so there will be no further inquiry. I don't know what I did with the papers, but I'll find them." He went out muttering lamentations.

No sooner had Ponsonby departed to his outer office than he reappeared.

"A call on the outside line, sir," he said, his head around the corner of the doorway.

"Who?"

"It's Miss Stanhope, sir."

"Hello," said Ross, picking up the phone. His heart was beating frantically and he tried to sound calm.

"Bert?"

"Yes."

"It's Alice Stanhope."

"Yes, go on."

"There's something very strange happening here this morning. At the Magnifico, I mean. We must talk. Can you meet me somewhere?"

"Are you there now?" He looked at his watch again. There was not much time, and the brigadier, for all his good points, was not the sort of man who would recognize that any duty could be more important than being at the phone when he called.

"I'm phoning from that perfume shop at the Bulaq Bridge." She couldn't very well say it was the shop of an informer who reported regularly to the SIB of what went on in the Bulaq, one of Cairo's most lawless districts. "I didn't go to the hospital this morning. I haven't got the car."

"Stay where you are. I'll come see you there. Tell our friend that I'll want to put my van into the lockup there." Leaving any vehicle in the streets of the Bulaq would make it vulnerable to some of the most expert thieves in the world.

The perfume shop had a narrow front. Its door opened into a tiny room with a long sofa and a fly-specked mirror on the wall. Arrayed on mirrored shelves that stretched around the room were bottles of a variety of shapes: globes, cylinders, pianos, guitars, motorcars, yachts, knots, and flowers. The mirrors multiplied their profusion. The perfumes—brightly colored liquids of acid green, sulfurous yellow, and fleshy pink—glowed in straight-sided flagons in a closed and locked cage-front cupboard.

"Have you chosen your perfume yet?" Jimmy Ross asked her as he came in and sat down on the green velvet sofa.

She smiled at his feeble joke, but before she could reply, the proprietor came in with two coffee cups on a tray. He was a stout Arab with a pockmarked face and expensive-looking horn-rim spectacles. He wore green linen trousers and a shirt that buttoned to a high collar. He poured strong coffee from a long-handled brass pot.

"I bring you sweet pastries with honey."

"No, thanks, Vittorio."

"Just a sample of my wife's cooking, *khawagga* Bert." So saying, he produced a plate of pastries out of nowhere and put them on the table with a flourish of his huge hands. Vittorio had adopted many Italianate gestures along with his newly acquired Italian name after living for a few years in Benghazi. Now he'd become a police informer as a way of proving that he was not an agent of the Italian enemies. "Now I leave you alone."

"Good," said Ross, and got up and went to the door to be

sure it was closed. "I wish he wouldn't call me *khawagga* Bert. What the hell does it mean anyway?"

"Bert in a western hat," explained Alice. "In other words, a respected foreigner."

Ross smiled despite trying not to. "How the hell did he find out my first name?"

"It's just politeness. Like effendi," she added, not wanting to get poor old Vittorio into trouble.

"You heard what happened?"

"Have the Japanese taken Singapore?"

"No. I meant about Lampson and the king."

"Oh, that. Everything is going wrong for us, isn't it?"

"Alice. You said you had to see me. What is it?" She could see he was not in the best of moods. She wondered if the brigadier was being difficult; her mother said the brigadier was unpredictable. Her mother was always asking questions about what she did at work for him.

Alice said, "It's Sayed . . . Sayed el-Shazli. He's up to something, I'm sure. He didn't go to the university this morning. His sister went alone. Sayed put on a uniform."

"Uniform?"

"Khaki shirt and trousers."

"Well, that's not a uniform."

"I know I'm right, Bert. When you see the way he's wearing it, you'll see that it's an army uniform. And he has a forage cap under the shoulder strap. Also there is a big Bedford truck with Egyptian army unit markings, parked behind the Magnifico. It must be for Sayed."

"Army markings? Which unit?"

"Signals." She had the answer ready.

He tapped the table and then started across the room. Finally he said, "You're probably right. Where is he now?"

"He's at the Magnifico. He'll go to prayers first. I haven't got the car today. May I take your Tilly?"

He had driven here in his Austin utility van. If Sayed el-

Shazli was using a Bedford truck, she'd need some sort of vehicle
to keep an eye on him. "Okay."

"Thanks, Bert."

She waited for him to congratulate her and tell her how
pleased he was, but he was too preoccupied to be aware of her
existence. Finally she prompted him. "You said he was a member
of the Free Officers Association. You said when the time came,
the conspirators would summon Sayed from his studies so he
could be the spokesman in their negotiations with the Germans."

He looked at her. She was a captivating young woman.
When she was with him he found it difficult to take his eyes off
her. Yes, he had said all that. Marker had said it to him. But he
hadn't expected her to remember it so exactly. He wondered
what other things he'd said that she would bring up at some
inconvenient time in the future. "But is this it? I mean, has the
time come?" He looked at his watch. He must get back to the
office in time for the brigadier's phone call.

She said, "Lampson's confrontation with the king has an-
gered all the Egyptians, Bert. Even the ones who wanted to hang
the king are angry about the way he was treated."

"You're wonderful, Alice." He reached out and touched her
arm. If only he was a free man. But he wasn't a free man and the
brigadier would be phoning soon.

"Try the coffee. It's delicious."

"I don't feel like it," he said.

She could see he was troubled and wondered if she had done
something to annoy him. He kept looking at his watch as if being
with her was consuming too much time.

"Here's the distributor arm for the Tilly. Make sure you
remove it every time you leave it unattended. It looks bad if we
have vehicles stolen."

"Yes, Bert."

For a moment she thought he was about to kiss her but then
the moment passed, and he just smiled and said, "And be careful.
The Arabs are all damned twitchy these days, what with this

business with the king and Rommel's advance. Marker thinks it will go on for some time."

Deprived of his Austin van, Ross walked back to Bab-el-Hadid barracks. The center of the city was a geometric pattern of long wide boulevards that intersected here and there to make an impressive *étoile* in the Parisian style. But immediately outside that grid, Cairo became a zigzagging maze of medieval alleys, the oldest surviving city in the world.

The Bulaq was a region like this, and it was through that district that Ross walked to get directly back to the police barracks. Soon after leaving the shops near Bulaq Bridge, he turned into the back streets and alleys. The stench became sickening, but he didn't turn back. Perhaps he'd never been in the most distressed parts of the city before, or perhaps it was the time of day or the mood he was in, but the walk back through the Bulaq shocked him.

The horror of it was with him for many days and nights afterward. The cripples and beggars, the diseased children and the starving women, their skin tight on their bony frames, did not pester him. In these back alleys no stranger was likely to have anything to give. He passed children squatting amid dung and human excrement, their bodies defiled with open sores upon which hordes of flies fought and feasted.

He glanced inside doorways to see faces wide-eyed and blank with defeat. Even the cats and dogs that came sneaking past him were not like other animals he'd seen. Here were houses without doors, windows without glass, and floors that were just dirt. Steps to the flat roofs of these mud huts were made of stone and mud because anything constructed of wood would be stolen immediately. Not one single usable item was to be found on the heaps of garbage that were strewn with dead rats.

He was pleased when he found himself emerge into Bulaqiya Street. Even the grimy old Bab-el-Hadid barrack block was a relief after the grim back streets through which he'd come. He looked at the clock. It was eleven twenty-five. The sentry on the gate saluted him.

He climbed the stairs, went into his room, sat down, closed his eyes, and sighed deeply. He opened his eyes. A cup of tea, into which a big spoonful of condensed milk had been stirred to make it pale and sweet, appeared before him magically. It seemed to have little effect that he'd told Ponsonby, and everyone else in the office, that he didn't care for this disgusting mixture. They all believed he would develop a taste for it.

The phone call came at eleven forty-five.

"Major Cutler?"

"Yes, sir?"

"I'm sure there's no need for me to tell you how important it is that your departmental staff are not endangered in any way."

"No, sir. Of course not." He wondered what the devil the old man was trying to tell him this time. The brigadier was not usually quite as obscure as this.

"Especially civilians."

"Yes, sir."

"Army personnel are paid to take risks; that's what soldiers do for a living."

"Yes, of course."

"Do you understand me, Major Cutler?"

"I'm not quite sure I do, sir."

"I know the mother. A wonderful woman: cultured, educated, elegant, and charming, with a brilliant mind."

"Who is that, sir?"

"She studied for the bar and then—What did you say? Who? Mrs. Angela Stanhope. Wake up, Cutler. It's nearly noon."

"Mrs. Angela Stanhope?"

"You can't wonder that she shows some anxiety for her daughter. She's been on the phone half a dozen times this week already. She's got the idea that her daughter is being used on some sort of undercover work. I reassured her on that point."

Jimmy Ross said nothing. Didn't he have enough problems without the brigadier hanging this one on him? Not for the first time Ross decided that he hated the army.

"I told her there was no question of your employing her daughter on any sort of work that could ever be dangerous. I just wanted to make sure you know that I've given her my solemn word."

"Yes, sir."

"So make sure the young lady is well looked after."

"Yes, sir."

"Because if anything happened to the girl—frightened, even—the mother would raise the very devil."

"Yes, sir."

"From the way you say 'yes, sir' I can tell you have no idea of the sort of hell that Angela can raise, should she put her mind to it. Dammit, Cutler, the Stanhopes know half the cabinet by their first names, and the other half are their relatives. If anything happened to that daughter of theirs, I wouldn't be surprised if Angela didn't put a call through to Winston personally. You and I would be roasted on a spit."

Jimmy Ross swallowed. He looked at his watch and wondered where Alice Stanhope was right now. The brigadier was in a highly emotional state. He tried to remember some film or play that would help him in this predicament, but he couldn't. The nearest thing to this was dealing with anxious actors about the size of their names in the advertisements. He'd found the wisest policy in such situations was to lie categorically. "You can reassure Mrs. Stanhope that her daughter is solely engaged on secretarial duties. The question of danger does not and could not arise."

The brigadier was not immediately calmed. "She was appalled to hear that her daughter had been working in Bab-el-Hadid barracks. She'd never heard of the place until her daughter told her she was working there. The mother was in Cairo the other day and went to look at it. She drove past in her car. Horrified. She was horrified, Cutler."

"Yes, sir."

"You can understand why?"

"I can indeed, sir."

"It's a grim-looking place, you must admit."

"Indeed I do, sir."

"And she discovered that we hold military criminals in custody there. She said she didn't want her daughter working in a prison."

"Yes, sir."

"They are a fine old family, Cutler." The brigadier was more composed now.

"I'm sure they are, sir."

"Well. . . . Yes, I'm pleased to hear that you have everything under control at your end. Any development on that other business?"

"One or two leads, sir."

"Oh, good. Well, I'm pushing off for a couple of days. There are some embassy blighters I have to see, and the duck shoot is the only opportunity I get of sitting them down and making them listen to our point of view."

"Good luck, sir."

"What's that? Oh, I see. Yes. Thank you, Major Cutler. That's most kind of you. Goodbye."

"Goodbye, sir."

Ross put down his phone and held both hands on it as if to keep the brigadier from calling back. Then he emitted a long deep sigh. "Ponsonby!"

"Yes, major."

"I'm ready for another large cup of that filthy tea you brew out there."

"I thought you might be, sir. I have one here, nicely drawn and all ready to pour out."

Ponsonby was right. There were times when a large cup of scalding-hot sweet tea, tasting of condensed milk, was the only alternative to jumping off the balcony.

=13=

Alice Stanhope had learned to drive her father's four-liter Brough Superior when she was fifteen years old. Handling the Austin utility van on this desert road gave her no problems. The difficulty was in keeping the Bedford truck in view without letting Sayed or his Arab driver know they were being followed. Surely he was bound to spot her now when they were trailing behind a long convoy of army trucks, going agonizingly slowly along a flat stretch of desert road.

"I'm so glad you're with me, Peggy," said Alice, not for the first time. It was Peggy who'd first pointed out that Sayed was behaving strangely and said he should be watched. She should have told Bert about Peggy's involvement, but today he had been so touchy she decided against it. Anyway, she had no second thoughts about recruiting Peggy for this escapade. Peggy was as British as anyone could be.

"I couldn't have let you come alone," said Peggy West. "It's dangerous for a woman. Even the two of us—"

"You don't believe all that tosh, surely, Peggy? White slave traffic . . . all those stories were invented to keep women at home and subjected."

"I hope you're right."

"I am."

Peggy West looked at her companion. Alice Stanhope

wasn't the subdued creature she sometimes liked to pretend to be. Escaping from that mother of hers had required pluck and determination. Since leaving home she'd tasted freedom and she was flourishing on it.

"Where do you think he's going?" Alice said. Neither of the women had considered it possible that Sayed would drive out of town. They were expecting him to go to some clandestine meeting in the city. Now, as time went on and he continued on the desert road, they were not sure what to do.

"I don't know this road," said Peggy. They passed a huge sign, DANGER—BEWARE SOFT VERGES. Some joker had painted VIRGINS over it.

"We'll have to watch the fuel gauge. The army might not want to supply us." And then Alice said again, "I'm glad you're with me." She didn't want Peggy to think that her dismissal of the dangers meant she didn't need a companion.

"I'm sure Sayed is up to something." Peggy felt uneasy. If Sayed was going to meet his Arab friends, they would make short work of two Englishwomen who'd been following him.

Alice said nothing. She tapped the glass of the fuel gauge, hoping it would spring to full. It didn't. She sighed.

They had adjusted their speed to the army convoy and were going very slowly now. "It's so beautiful at this time of year," said Peggy. "It's no good trying to describe it to people who haven't been here. My friends in England are determined to believe that Egypt is nothing but undulating sand dunes. How can you describe a landscape like this? Look at the colors of the rocks, the strange dusty light, the wildflowers."

"Don't get too carried away," said Alice. "It's not a jaunt, Peggy." Up ahead the soldiers in the truck had noticed that there were women behind them. They were leaning far out over the tailgate, smiling and waving. Alice and Peggy were both wearing the khaki twill skirts and brown shirts that all the hospital staff were given. They didn't look convincingly like members of the armed services, but at least they didn't attract the sort of attention that women in civilian clothes would get on the road out here.

Peggy said, "It's probably the Free Officers, this revolutionary party the army officers belong to. But it's hard to believe that Sayed would do anything to harm us, isn't it?"

"He's acting so suspiciously, Peggy. Why should he suddenly put on that uniform and get a Bedford army lorry and come out here?"

"We'll be stuck behind this convoy forever," said Peggy. "He's sure to spot us sooner or later." The road was very narrow. What had been wide enough for horses and camels could not take two lines of motor traffic. The vehicles ahead had slowed to walking pace. All the drivers were carefully avoiding the soft road edges that would bog them down for hours. Military policemen on motorcycles were roaring up and down the road, fussing about and shouting warnings to the drivers. Finally, after a few fits and starts, the whole convoy came to a complete stop. Sayed's truck was up ahead. One of the helmeted motorcyclists jumped from his bike and began waving. In response, Sayed's truck pulled out onto the off side of the road and kept going. The MP waved Alice onward too, in the imperious manner that traffic cops cultivate.

Alice pulled out. Now there were no vehicles between her Tilly and Sayed's Bedford as they crawled past the long line of army vehicles. Alice left as much space as she could and prayed that Sayed would not spot her in his driving mirror.

"Damn!" she said. "Sayed will surely see us now."

But there was no sign that the occupants of the Bedford had noticed anything unusual. Because Alice was going too slowly, the traffic cop became impatient. He directed her back into the line of parked vehicles while three oncoming trucks came through. Alice sighed. From being anxious about being too close to Sayed's truck she now fretted that she would lose him. Only when the oncoming traffic had passed was Alice able to pull out and continue driving.

Up ahead, the cause of the holdup could be seen. There was another army convoy coming up the other way. Its trucks were drawn up and facing them. Alongside their vehicles, dozens of men were sitting by the roadside brewing tea over sand-filled cans aflame with petrol.

It was a relief to get clear of the convoy and put her foot down on the open road. Sayed perhaps felt the same way. By the time she got clear of the traffic holdup, there was no sign of the Bedford on the road ahead. The only traffic in sight was a file of camels laboring under blocks of limestone and goaded by a dozen small boys with sticks.

"Could he have turned off?" said Peggy.

"I don't think so. These rough little side tracks don't go anywhere; they lead just to single villages and wells."

"There they are!" said Peggy, seeing the Bedford far ahead. The driver was slowing to find an intersection.

"And they *are* turning off the road! They'll see us if we follow them, Peggy. What shall I do now?"

An irrigation ditch marked by tall reeds followed the road. On the other side was a footpath, some dusty vegetation, and every now and then a few trees. They could see the Bedford as it bumped along a narrow side track that followed another irrigation ditch. It was heading toward a cluster of trees and mud huts. Beyond that the land sloped away gently, and then there were distant hillocks.

The sort of visibility the landscape provided would make it impossible to follow the Bedford without the Tilly being spotted. "What shall I do?" asked Alice again as they got closer to the intersection. When Peggy didn't reply, Alice said, "I'll park at the turnoff, where the trees are. You stay in the car, Peggy. I'll go up the track on foot and see what's up there."

"You can't go alone."

"Don't be silly, of course I can." Alice slowed. The path Sayed had taken was just an unmarked camel track: loose gravel strewn with rocks. Alice drove past the turnoff to get to a nearby group of stunted palm trees. She found a shady patch of sand in which to park.

"I'll go with you," said Peggy bravely. She didn't fancy intruding into an Arab village, and Alice could hear that in her voice.

"Better you stay with the Tilly," said Alice. "You know how Arabs always appear out of nowhere. They'll have the wheels off it and strip it clean in five minutes, if we leave it unattended."

"I suppose you're right, but do be careful. Do you have a gun?"

"A gun?" Alice laughed. "What would I be doing with a gun?"

"What would you be doing following Sayed in a British army vehicle you've borrowed?" said Peggy.

Alice looked at Peggy. She wondered how much Peggy guessed, but this wasn't the time to ask her. Alice smiled and looked again along the track that Sayed had taken. There was some sort of village there. She couldn't see the Bedford.

Alice got out. Here, where she'd parked, had once been some sort of roadside army structure. There was a sign in Arabic and some metal drums. A splintered wooden stub embedded in a concrete-filled drum was all that was left of some military signpost.

"If anyone wants to know what you're doing here, tell them we've broken down. Tell them we're waiting for a mechanic to fix it."

"Don't be long, Alice. I don't like being here on my own."

"No one's going to harm you, Peggy. There's a big spanner under the seat. If anyone pokes their head inside, you can bounce it off their skull."

Peggy smiled grimly. She hadn't counted on the drive into the desert becoming this sort of escapade. Work in the operating theaters had become nonstop over the last week or so. She needed a rest, not an adventure. "I'll be all right," she said.

"Of course you will." From her large leather bag Alice

brought out an army forage cap. She positioned it carefully on her head and fixed it with bobby pins. She took a quick look at herself in the car mirror and then turned and smiled at Peggy. "It's a good thing I brought my flat-heel shoes. Won't be long."

"Take care, Alice." Peggy could not see that wearing an army hat was any sort of protection, but Alice clearly thought it would be. Peggy smiled back at her and then looked around anxiously. In that miraculous way in which people seemingly appear out of nowhere, a handful of Arabs were now squatting at the place where the irrigation ditch entered a culvert. The men were looking at the utility van and at the two women. Their faces wore that blank expression that Arabs so often adopted in the presence of their occupying armies.

Alice slammed the car door and didn't look at the men. She put the strap of her bag over her shoulder and walked past them with a purposeful stride, following the rough rocky path toward the village where the Bedford had disappeared. She kicked the earth, making as much noise as possible as she walked. The banks of such irrigation canals usually abound with snakes, and her low-cut walking shoes would provide her with little protection against bites. She halted for a moment to catch her breath; there was still a long way to go. There was a rustle in the weeds, but she persuaded herself it could not be a snake: a frog or a toad, perhaps. She kept walking.

The cluster of mud huts proved farther away from the road than she had estimated, and the sun was high by now. She looked back, but the utility van was hidden from view behind the scrubby trees. There was no traffic on the main road; the convoys had stopped as they always did about midday. She wiped her sweaty face with her handkerchief. From the fields on each side wafted the acrid smell of dung. Clouds of flies buzzed around her with an amazing persistence. As she waved her hand to discourage them she felt them strike against her palm. She looked around. Here and there she could now see a few people. They were bent low, attending some sort of stunted crop, its dusty brown leaves making it almost indistinguishable from the sandy earth in which it grew.

She started plodding forward again, slower this time, and was breathless with exertion by the time she reached the mud huts. Her mouth was dry and her heart was beating fast. Her shirt was damp with perspiration. When she got to the village she went down a narrow street to find the square that was the center of most such places. At the corner, before stepping out into the sunlight, she paused to look around. The huts were built around an open space. Men were loading heavy sacks onto a bullock cart. Other men squatted nearby, watching them. Two black-garbed women were crouched on the ground sorting through a pile of beans. Alice saw no sign of the Bedford truck.

She began to wish she'd let Peggy come with her and risked what happened to the van. The people had seen her, but they did not look at her directly. They studied her with furtive and unfriendly glances. Summoning up her courage, she walked across the central space. The sun was hot, and hotter still as it rebounded from the dusty ground. She greeted the men loading the cart. *"Assalamu aleikum!"* Peace be upon you.

The men pretended not to hear her. They continued carrying sacks from one of the huts and did not look in her direction. It was as if she did not exist.

She walked away from them and followed the high mud-colored wall that ran along the edge of the row of huts. Where the wall ended there were some palms, some animals, and a group of women with buckets of water. Here was the well, the true center of the village and the reason for its existence. Here too was the *mastabah,* the low seat where the village elders met.

Unless the big Bedford truck had disappeared completely, it had to be behind the high wall. Alice walked to the well, to see how far the high wall stretched. The women stopped chattering as she got closer to them. She turned the corner and saw that the wall continued for a hundred yards or more.

She was not surprised; she'd lived in this part of the world long enough to know that such large properties were often hidden in dirty little villages. Set into this side of the walled enclosure were large wooden doors guarded by two somnolent Arabs, who scrambled to their feet as they caught sight of her. Alice stopped.

"Please keep walking, madam," said a voice from behind her.

She whipped around and found a pale-skinned man with a square-ended mustache and dark frizzed hair graying at the temples. He was dressed in western style; in fact, dressed in the same sort of anonymous combination of khaki shirt and pants that she herself wore. She recognized him as the man who'd been driving Sayed's truck.

He smiled. "You are looking for my master?" The gesture he made was welcoming, but there was a coldness in his manner and tone. He indicated the doors with his outstretched arm. "Please be welcome."

With much clatter, the guards opened up the tall wooden doors to reveal an extensive yard. Dominating it was a grand house with shuttered windows and imposing entrance. The yard was not bare. Everywhere enormous decorated pots overflowed with roses and carnations. Six tall palms sliced across the façade of the house, and in the yard's center there was an ancient well decorated with brightly patterned tiles. There were vehicles there too: not only the Bedford but also a Lancia saloon and a big Canadian Buick.

"Do not be afraid," said the khaki-clad man. "My master is expecting you."

"Is he?"

Suddenly two figures appeared at the entrance to the house as if ready to welcome her. She went up the steps. One of the welcomers was some sort of majordomo. He bowed. *"Allah yaateeki el-sihha. Meet ahlan wa sahlan."* May Allah grant you good health. Welcome a hundred times.

"Moutta shakkera. Allah yebarek feek," said Alice uncertainly. Thank you. May Allah bless you.

In the shadows, Sayed el-Shazli watched the exchange with pleasure. As she pronounced her careful Arabic, he smiled, as a music teacher might smile at a favored pupil playing the piano. "Miss Stanhope," he said, stepping into the light and bowing formally to her. "Welcome."

It was gloomy inside the large anteroom. Rays of sunlight picked out patterns on the richly colored carpets that covered the floor. Waiting patiently inside, she saw a short thickset bearded man. He was wearing a white western-style suit and red tarboosh. His nose was large and he wore gold-rimmed spectacles. Upon his hands glinted gold rings with large shiny gems, and around his neck there hung a heavy gold chain.

Alice was trying to decide how to account for being here, but Sayed did not accuse her of following him. She was a guest, and the Arab culture does not permit criticism of a guest. Perhaps that would come later.

"Ahmed Pasha, our host, invites you to drink tea," said Sayed.

The old man named Ahmed readily accepted the title of Pasha, which signifies a man of wealth and social status. He waved a hand languidly to indicate a bench carved with leaves and roses. The bench was almost hidden under richly embroidered cushions inset with pieces of shiny metal that reflected the light from the door.

"Thank you," she said. To refuse food is an insult in this part of the world. She was grateful for this formality, grateful for any chance to defer her explanations.

She sat down with them. Through the opening in the curtained doorway she could see sunlight biting hard into the dusty brown yard, the bedraggled palms, and the sleekly polished cars. Overhead a piece of fabric, its rope tugged by some unseen hand, swung steadily backward and forward but produced little movement of air. A black servant entered silently. He put down a brass tray set with tiny cups. The bearded man reached out, opened the pot's lid, and stirred the tea. There arose a steamy mist that filled the air with the smell of mint.

She took the tea and sipped it slowly. Her throat was parched, and the sweet aromatic tea soothed and refreshed her. She smiled her thanks. "You wonder why I am here," she offered.

"You are here because Allah guided your steps," said Sayed. "Everything is predestined; it is our belief. Allah led you here. Allah, master of the world, I place my fate in your hands. We are creatures of your will."

Their host nodded thoughtfully.

"This is the village where my father, and his father too, was born," said Sayed. "I come here to consult Ahmed Pasha whenever I need guidance."

Alice nodded.

"You may remain," Ahmed told her. Sayed bowed to indicate his happy compliance with this decision. "Let us begin."

Ahmed clapped his hands and servants appeared. One had a brass pot that he placed at the old man's feet. Another servant brought a *mangal,* a pan of burning charcoal. He placed it on a wrought-iron stand in front of his master. Alongside it he placed a tray arrayed with a selection of spices, leaves, pods, and small pieces of wood. Some children came in carrying small drums. They settled down in a far corner and played soft complicated rhythms.

Without hurry, Ahmed fed the fire so that sudden puffs of sweet-smelling smoke arose. He used a plaited leaf to fan the fire so that flames lit up the gloomy interior of the room. Bending low, as if about to blow upon the embers, he murmured some sort of incantation.

Alice glanced at Sayed and thought she saw on his face a look of extreme anxiety. And yet he seemed totally oblivious of her presence. Now she knew for sure that the old man was a wizard, and that she was being allowed to see Sayed consult his magic powers. Hearing the soft reedy notes of a flute, she looked around for a flute player but there wasn't one in sight.

The three of them sat for uncounted minutes while the fire burned so that perfumed smoke filled the room. The scorching heat of the day and the smoke that parched her throat made her suddenly feel faint. The old man turned to her and said something in rapid Arabic. She could not understand him. She looked at Sayed; the room wobbled.

"Give him your hand," said Sayed solemnly.

She extended her hand, and the old man held her fingertips and looked at her palm. Then, in a movement she could not follow, he dabbed the fingers of his other hand into the brass pot and then tapped her palm very gently. She looked down to see that he was making marks on her hand with reddish-brown pigment from the pot.

"It is written," said the old man.

The music seemed louder and more insistent. She closed her eyes. Waves of nausea swept over her so strongly that she felt she was going to vomit. Only with difficulty did she retain her balance and try to remain outwardly calm.

When she half opened her eyes, the rings on the old man's fingers flashed in the light. He touched her hand again. Then he bent low to look more closely at the marks on her palm, reading, muttering, and murmuring his findings.

"The moon will bring a propitious day for your hopes and aspirations," said the old man solemnly. "You will follow the stars westward and find the outcome you desire."

"Where?" said Sayed, his strangled voice revealing his concern. "Where?"

"The moon," said the old man.

For a moment Alice had believed she was feeling better, but the faintness and nausea returned so she felt she must rest her head. She tried to draw her hand back from the grip of the old man, but he would not release it. "I must . . ." Her throat was parched. She turned to get more tea from the big brass tray, but as she reached for it she began to lose her balance. The room went out of focus. As if in slow motion she toppled until, unable to save herself, she crashed upon the tray, sending the dishes and cups and pot flying in all directions. The tea was no longer hot enough to scald her. It was tepid and sweet, and she smelled the sickly perfume of mint as warm tea splashed upon her outstretched arms and her face. All she could think of was her embarrassment. She wanted to apologize for making such a mess on the lovely carpet. She was trying to think of some way of telling them how ashamed she was as the room grew smaller and dim. She realized she was losing consciousness, and she was determined to resist it. The music had not faltered: it continued its curious dissonant patterns. She tried to shout but no sound came. Slowly, she sank down into darkness.

She recovered consciousness with a jolt. Peggy West was holding a bottle of smelling salts under her nose. It was a powerful acrid smell, and Alice pushed it away.

She was sitting in the passenger seat of the utility van. For a moment she thought the whole thing had been a dream. Then she saw that the van was now parked near the well in the courtyard of the big house. The shiny Buick and Sayed's Bedford army truck were there too. So was the Lancia.

As she adjusted her eyes to the glaring light, she saw Sayed and the old man, Ahmed. They were standing by the well. A British military policeman was talking with them. Was he, she wondered, arresting the two Egyptians? Had Peggy West arrived just in time? Even as she was trying to figure out the answers, the MP stepped back and gave Sayed a smart salute.

"I had to come here," Peggy said apologetically.

"I don't know what happened to me," said Alice.

"You walked in the sun. It's never wise to do that at midday, even in winter."

"You brought the policeman?" Alice was bewildered.

"He nearly arrested me," said Peggy. "I had no papers for

the van. He simply wouldn't believe that you had walked up here to the village in the heat of midday. Why didn't she drive? he asked. What could I say?"

The MP gave the two women a perfunctory wave and then got on his motorcycle. He straddled it for a moment, adjusting the chin strap of his helmet. Then he pulled his goggles down over his eyes and kick-started his engine.

The big wooden doors in the high surrounding wall opened as if by magic, and the motorcyclist accelerated, swung around in a tight circle, and disappeared in a cloud of dust.

The Arab sentinels at the gate watched the motorcyclist with great interest. When he'd gone they chattered excitedly.

Sayed came over to the women. No wonder the MP had saluted him. Sayed looked every inch the British officer. He had no Egyptian army badges, just two pips on each shoulder strap. His complexion was no darker than what many of the British had acquired out in the desert sun.

He smiled a flashing white smile. Was it a smile of triumph, or was this just the same friendly Sayed that she knew from the Hotel Magnifico?

"Are you all right, Miss Stanhope?" Sayed asked. He seemed genuine in his concern for her.

"I'm sorry," said Alice. "I've caused you so much trouble."

"Hush. Here, drink some more water. It is good water." He handed her the glass, and she sipped some and felt better for it. "Peggy thought you'd be better out here in the open air."

"I fainted."

"Are you fit enough to return to town?"

"Of course," said Alice.

"Can you drive the van, Miss West?" It was Miss West when he spoke to her; Sayed was always respectful.

"We'll be all right, Sayed."

He smiled. "This is my father's village," he said again. "They are good people here."

* * *

"You're safe," said Jimmy Ross feelingly, "and that's the only important thing."

"I completely messed it up," said Alice Stanhope. She felt like weeping, but she decided that such a display of emotion would spoil her chances with him forever.

"I should never have sent you," he said.

"It was my idea."

"I should never have sent you."

When he repeated the same words she looked up at him with a sudden thought. "Has Mummy been interfering again?"

"It's nothing to do with your mother, Alice. It was my stupid decision."

She sat in silence for a minute or two. "Was it all a stunt, Bert?"

He answered without hesitation. "I don't think so."

"But the magician: the chanting and the magic spells. You don't believe in magic?"

"But Sayed does."

"I suppose he does. Do you know who the magician is?"

Ross smiled. "Yes, Sayed's father. That was Sayed's house you were in."

"Good Lord! Is he a part of it?"

"Ahmed Pasha?" said Ross. "Sure to be. He's so anti-British he'd help Satan himself occupy Cairo, given the chance."

"I can hardly believe it."

"That damned house out there is a center for intrigue and treason. My predecessor tried and tried to get someone inside, but it's no use. The old swine vets every servant carefully."

"But what was it all about? What was Sayed doing there with his father?"

"They were helping Abdel-Hamid Sherif. He's an Egyptian army captain. Marker is chasing everywhere after him. He's been collecting signatures from all the opposition leaders. It's a sort of declaration that says Britain is fighting fascism in Europe while actively supporting it in Egypt. They plan to send a copy to all the ambassadors in Cairo: American, Canadian, French, Dutch, Norwegian—anyway, you see what damage it will do. It's certain to get into the newspapers."

"Helping him how? What is Sayed doing?"

"I should think that was obvious: he's helping this fellow Abdel-Hamid Sherif."

"I don't understand," said Alice.

"Helping him to get away. Sayed's driver. You said he was thinnish, about six feet tall, with pale skin, black mustache, and black frizzy hair graying at the temples? That was Abdel-Hamid Sherif."

"You can't be serious."

"Why not?"

"He was driving the Bedford. He was so ordinary."

"You can become ordinary when you have a price on your head and an army of police and informers trying to catch you."

"You say it as if you are sorry for him."

She'd caught him off guard. "It's my duty to catch fugitives."

"Are you going to raid the house?"

"It's too late now. Once clear of the city, a fellow like that can dress in rags and just disappear into thin air. By this time they'll probably have taken him to Suez and put him aboard a ship . . . a neutral ship that they know we'll not want to stop and search."

"I'm sorry, Bert."

"It's not a complete disaster, but Sayed will know that we are on to him. Perhaps he'll move out of the Magnifico. In any case, you stay there for the time being. You didn't tell Peggy West about . . . about me, about what we do in the office here?"

"No, of course not."

"She'll guess."

"She's British, Bert. She'll not tell anyone, will she?"

He looked at her. He wondered whether to tell her that

Peggy West was in regular communication with what he strongly suspected was an illegal Jewish spy network. For the time being it was better that she didn't know: Peggy might detect a change in her. "No, of course not. Let's go and get something to eat, shall we?"

"There's one other thing, Bert. The other night, after you left Prince Piotr's cocktail party, one of the people there bought wine in the downstairs bar, using this." She pushed an Egyptian bank note across the tabletop to him. It was disfigured by a pattern of tiny dark-brown spots.

He picked it up and looked at it for a moment and then said, "Damned good work, Alice. The blood is spotted just like the paybook we took off the body of the ordnance sergeant major."

"Yes, I remembered the paybook. I try to keep up with what's happening."

"Who passed the money?"

"The naval officer. You saw him. A thin man with wavy hair. His name is Wallingford. He's a great friend of Darymple; they were at school together."

"Damn good work, Alice."

"You won't take me off the job, will you? No matter what Mummy says?"

"No, I won't, no matter what Mummy says." Her hand was still on the bank note. He reached out and touched her hand. It was the first time he'd ever made such an intimate gesture. For what seemed like a long time they sat there, his fingers resting lightly upon the back of her hand. She didn't move; she tried to read his face but he was not a man who revealed his feelings even in normal circumstances.

The circumstances were anything but normal. He was frightened of getting more involved with her. He must get ready to disappear as this artful man Sherif had done.

=14=

Harry Wechsler had been thinking about Alice Stanhope right up until the time of departure. And now, as the car bumped through the busy Cairo streets, he went back to thinking about her. He'd been thinking about little else since meeting her at the party. She was beautiful in a withdrawn and reticent way that haunted his memory. And she was highly intelligent and educated too, without showing any need to challenge him or make him feel like a dope, the way so many of his female colleagues seemed to want to do. And of course there was the potent fact that Alice Stanhope had shown no interest in Harry whatsoever.

Among newspapermen, most of whom worshiped more frequently at the shrine of Bacchus than Aphrodite, Harry Wechsler was regarded as something of a ladies' man. Ever since his second wife left him back in 1938, Harry Wechsler's love affairs had been intense and emotional but of fleeting duration. Meeting Alice Stanhope had had a strange effect upon him. It made him think it was still possible for him to fall in love.

"A penny for 'em," offered the driver. His name was Chips O'Grady. He was a small furtive figure who held the wheel with whitened knuckles and had to have a thick foam rubber cushion under his behind to give him a good view over the wheel. He was wearing a British army bush shirt and shorts. Anyone who thought that one bush shirt was much like another had only to

compare the one Chips was wearing with that of Harry
Wechsler, sitting beside him. Harry Wechsler's bush shirt was
one of a dozen he'd had made for him by a shirtmaker in Rome.
It was a subtle shade of olive green, the stitching was precise,
and the buttons were made from horn.

"Packing. Just going over things in my mind. Thinking back
to be sure I've not forgotten anything," said Harry Wechsler,
who shared his opinions with everyone but his thoughts with no
one. Perhaps it was just as well that he was going into the blue
again. All his life he'd mocked and derided men who talked about
the magic fascination of the desert. But, without admitting it to
anyone, he was finding the prospect of going back a welcome
one.

He settled down for the long journey. His driver, Chips, was
an Irishman, a notorious drunkard who'd worked for—and been
fired by—almost every news agency in the Middle East. Harry
Wechsler had stumbled on Chips in Tommy's Bar, one of Cairo's
best-known drinking places. Chips had been out of work for
almost a month, and the manager at Tommy's Bar, like his many
other creditors, was pressing for payment. It seemed as if fate
had arranged their meeting. Harry hired him immediately as his
assistant. Chips already had a press card and accreditation,
although it was over a year since anything he'd filed had actually
got into print. Chips could drive, type, speak enough French,
Italian, and German to get by and enough Arabic to handle the
sort of transactions a newspaperman was likely to enter into.
Chips knew that working for Harry Wechsler was probably his
final chance to get his life back on the rails. All he had to do was
keep away from the hard drink.

"You know the way?" said Harry, whose career had persuaded him that it was better to voice the obvious frequently
than face the consequences of things going wrong silently.

"Do I know the way!" said Chips feelingly. He'd learned to
recognize every inch of this road since the fighting started in the

summer of 1940. There was only one main road to the Western Desert. This was the highway to the war.

It was half past five in the afternoon as they crossed the Nile. The sun shone upon the domes of the mosques, which Allah decreed must be of gold. Sundown: time for prayer. From all the tall minarets across the city came the call of the muezzin.

The heavy Ford car rattled onto the island of Gezira and over English Bridge to Doqqi and followed the road alongside the river. They passed the university before turning west. At Giza they looked—for everyone looked, no matter how jaded a spirit—for the place where the great pyramids of Khufu and Khafre cut notches from what was now a pink sky.

The Khafre pyramid looks bigger than its neighbor, but this, like so much else in Egypt, is a deception. The Khafre pyramid stands on higher ground.

"It's good to be out of that fleapit," said Chips. So far, he'd kept off the drink just as he'd promised Harry he would. One pint of beer a day was all he allowed himself, and a pint of local Stella beer was too thin to have much effect on anyone. To some extent, Chips's abstemious regime had been made easier by his dedication to the preparation of the car. Harry Wechsler's agency had footed the bill, and with that sort of blank check Chips had come back with something exceptional. It was a secondhand Canadian-built Ford station wagon with a V-8 engine. By discreet payments to the right people, Chips had had it completely rebuilt in the army workshops. Now it had army sand-color paint, desert tires, roof hatches, and a reinforced chassis just like the station wagons the army used in the desert.

"It's a good goer," said Chips as they left Cairo behind. He had taken a personal pride in the car and said such things from time to time, as if a few such words frequently repeated would encourage the Ford to keep going. "Sweet. Sweet."

Harry nodded. He didn't like driving, and Chips was a good driver as long as he was sober. Harry looked at his diminutive companion, with his drawn face, red ears, pointed nose, and thin lips. The photo on his press card showed a man looking at the camera with amused contempt. Rodentlike was the first description that sprang to mind, and his stealthy movements encouraged that idea. And yet so far Harry had found Chips to be a decent, hard-working fellow. He wondered to what extent the prejudice arising from a man's appearance disabled and dogged him throughout his life.

There were a few scattered dwellings and some fields of beans, and then the land of the Nile ended and abruptly the landscape became sandy and bare. When they reached the place where the route goes north, Chips waved to the poor devil on duty. The corporal was grateful for any sign of compassion from a human race that seemingly loathed military policemen with a terrible vindictiveness. More than once he'd had to jump aside to escape the wheels of heavy trucks. He waved back. There was always a military policeman detachment at the junction. Perhaps they thought some dozy drivers might keep going and wind up somewhere out there in the Libyan Desert, on the edge of the mighty Qattara Depression, the loneliest place in the world.

They made good speed on the open road. It was the right time of day to travel. In the gloom they saw corrugated-metal Nissen huts and the lines of carefully whitewashed rocks that are the mark of British military presence anywhere in the world. "That's the airfield at Amiriya," said Chips, pointing at it. "Looks like they have a flap on."

Harry looked at where the floodlights illuminated a fighter plane having its engine revved up.

"Look at that," said Chips. "The RAF have started painting those big shark's mouths on their fighters. There might be an American story for you there."

"How?" Harry was always looking for stories with some sort of U.S. connection.

"Those planes are American: Curtiss Tomahawks. The big mouth and teeth would make a great photo."

"No, no. By the time we get back the RAF brass will have

ordered them painted back to camouflage again. You know what stuff shirts they are."

"They've been painted like that since September last year."

"Watch the road, Chips."

"I could drive this one blindfold," said Chips.

"Curtiss Tomahawks?"

"He's come from One-twelve squadron at Gambut, unless all the squadrons are copying the same paint job."

"I know Gambut. I flew there last month."

"We'll pass it on this road."

"Okay, that might be a story. Can you handle a camera?"

"What kind of camera?"

"Speed Graphic."

"I can manage, but I'll need a meter."

"I'll give you a lesson or two."

"Why don't you see if you can pick up a Leica . . . they use that roll film. It's easier for the sort of stuff you want. And near the fighting there are always good cameras to be had, if you've got the cash . . . they take them off the German prisoners."

"What sort of shots do I want?" said Harry.

"Candids. Human interest. People. A Speed Graphic is bulky, and changing those damn slides is too slow for that kind of coverage."

Chips was right; he was no dummy. "Keep your eyes open for a Leica, then."

"Okay, boss." Just a few miles along the road Chips pointed out another airfield. "Dekheila. Looks like they have planes on the circuit to land."

"Bombers, I hope. I'm telling you, Chips, your people will have to bomb the shit out of Tripoli if they're to stand any chance of bringing Rommel to a halt. A few more shiploads of those up-gunned tanks he's using, and he'll come through Egypt like a hot knife through butter."

"Easy does it, boss," said Chips. He'd discovered that he was expected to play the Limey sparring partner in this sort of exchange. "We've given the Hun a headache, made him come to a stop, and knocked out half his tank force. And the RAF is really beginning to get his measure now. Admit it, Harry!"

"The trouble is that last year your British propaganda flacks were handing out a lot of garbage about how strong the British army is. Now that Rommel is pushing them back again, everyone is looking pretty damn silly."

"You're right, Harry." Chips always let him win the arguments. Then to himself he said aloud, "Mustn't go wrong at the next turnoff." It was cloudy, and the moon switched on and off like a flashlight.

At Alexandria the road skirted the town, and Chips kept his foot down as they found and followed the coast road. As the moonlight became brighter its beauty became evident.

"What do they call this place?"

"El Alamein: there's no decent place here to eat or sleep. Too near Cairo to be of much use as a stopover."

"It's pretty." For the first time Chips saw that Harry was right. On one side of the road there were fig plantations, still in good shape despite the war. On the other side of the road, the pure white sand made the sea look dark and deep. The waves came rolling in to break into a vast lace overlay, so that the sea seemed to disappear against the white sand. The moonlit scene was so inviting that Harry felt like stopping the car and taking a swim, but he resisted the temptation. There was work to be done.

At the place where the fig plantations ended, the road deteriorated into a maze of potholes and corrugations. "You know something, Chips? That was really smart of you British to build a railroad along the coast. And monumentally dumb of the Italians not to do the same along their coastline."

"The British didn't do it," said Chips. "The Arabs built it in the nineteenth century."

"Is that so? Well, it's come in useful for the war. The railroads can move all the heavy stuff and leave the highway free.

Rommel hasn't cottoned on to that yet. Maybe Rommel's not so bright after all."

"I hope not."

"The British have got enough on their plate with a dumb German general down the road, Chips, without having to contend with a smart one."

Chips nodded. Harry Wechsler liked to have the last word. He was like a film star, thought Chips, who during his time as a newspaperman had met many of them. Harry gave a great deal of attention to his clothes, his appearance, and his comfort. And he had that childish need for approval and admiration that is so often the driving force behind success in public life. Harry Wechsler could have managed this trip quite easily on his own, but he seemed to need a companion, a sounding board, or maybe an audience. Whatever it was Harry Wechsler needed, as long as the pay was adequate, Chips O'Grady was happy to provide it.

The paved road followed the coast and the railway line. Now and again they passed supply dumps that stretched for miles. Sometimes signs pointed to a hospital or a repair workshop. Some of the signs were bogus ones, put there to deceive. Then evidence of human activity grew less. For miles at a time they saw no traffic on the road. The desert stretched away to the south of them, but it was not the rolling sand dunes depicted in the movies: it was hard sun-baked earth and ocher-colored rock. El Daba came up. Chips pointed it out and told Harry that it was celebrated in a British soldiers' song. What did the soldiers sing? Some obscenities about Farouk seated on a camel, eating bacon sandwiches and the wind blowing up his backside. Chips could not recall the exact words but El Daba always brought the song to mind because, in keeping with the chorus, El Daba did seem to have a permanent sandstorm blowing across it. Maybe that was why the British had chosen it as a place to establish a transit camp for war correspondents.

The entrance was in a corrugated-steel Nissen hut that had been erected on a concrete base, a luxury building by desert standards. The guard was a soldier sitting on an oil drum smoking a cigarette. He waved them in. ALL VISITORS MUST REPORT TO THE DUTY OFFICER said a sign on the door. The only other vehicle in the compound where they parked was a big AEC Matador, a canvas-sided truck complete with jerry cans marked WATER and PETROL, bedding rolls, and bundled netting for camouflage.

Inside the hut they found an office where the sergeant in charge of the transit accommodation was playing darts and drinking tea with a clerk.

"That's okay. The duty officer will have to look at your accreditation and then we'll sort you out," said the sergeant. "If you want a meal, my lads will take care of you." He put his darts down on the desk and phoned the duty officer. This was an elderly warrant officer, who had to be found in his billet and who, despite the early evening hour, arrived in a camel-hair dressing gown and smelled of whisky.

The paperwork done and their car filled with petrol, they went in to eat. The room contained a stove, a counter, and some chairs and tables. "Spam and egg and peas."

"Sounds delicious," said Harry.

Harry had made sure that the back of his Ford was crammed with supplies. There was tea and coffee, canned bacon rashers, canned beans, and a sack of rice. But such things were better kept for emergencies or for trading for favors with front-line units. So it was Spam, egg, and peas.

The processed ham was fried and the egg was of the reconstituted powdered variety that a skillful cook can make into a semblance of scrambled fresh egg. This cook was not so skilled. The peas were canned and came in a thick greenish-yellow blob. There was hot tea too, of course. "No wonder your British army depends on tea," said Harry, watching as the meal was being prepared for them.

The only other visitors in sight were two men dressed in the heavy khaki battle dress that was needed on winter nights in the desert. They were both clean and tidy, with tanned faces and war correspondent badges on their shoulder straps. The younger one was a muscular fellow in his middle twenties. He had the sort of square-ended mustache that many of the British officers affected out here: squared and trimmed short almost to the skin. At his side he had two cameras in leather cases and a bigger case that probably contained lenses, film, and accessories. The second man was older: thin, dyspeptic, and unwelcoming. He had wavy hair colored red, the shade that ladies' hairdressers call titian.

They were drinking tea from tin mugs. The younger one was finishing his meal by eating slices of heavy brown fruit cake that, judging by its shape and texture, had come from a can. His chewing revealed that one of his front teeth was missing: it gave him the look of a street urchin.

Harry sat down at their table, offered them cigarettes, and gave them one of his big smiles. "Harry Wechsler," he said by way of introduction. "And this is Chips O'Grady. We're heading west."

"Mogg," said the younger of the two men. "Tommy Mogg." The other man—who'd been lost in his own thoughts—looked at his partner in disapproval and did not introduce himself.

Chips went to the counter and waited while the soldier put the food onto plates and poured out tea.

Harry spread a map across the table and asked the two men questions about the places he stabbed a finger at. "Siwa Oasis. What kind of a place is that?"

The two men—photographer and writer—had been to Siwa Oasis. They said it was two days' journey southward into the Sahara.

"What's to see at Siwa?" said Harry as Chips put the food down in front of him. "Thanks, Chips."

Chips paid no attention to the others. He sat down with his food and started eating.

"I'm just asking these guys: what's with this Siwa Oasis?" said Harry and began picking at the Spam and egg.

Tommy Mogg, the younger man, answered. It was typically

so, thought Harry. The photographer was strong enough to lug his gear around and always more friendly to other correspondents. The writers, older, more experienced, and suspicious, were always fearful that they were giving away their stock in trade. "The story we heard was that it's the base for the Long Range Desert Group."

"Who are they?" said Harry.

The younger man looked at his partner. "One of these 'private armies' who make long trips into the desert far south of where the Eye-ties have any front-line units."

"Did you get pictures?"

"We got bugger all. Just a few wogs. I got some pictures of the palm trees and a wrecked tank."

"What did the army say?"

"We went without a conducting officer."

Harry laughed. "This man's army doesn't like any display of initiative, especially from newspapermen. They probably made sure the cupboard was bare."

"Perhaps."

"Are you staying here?" said Harry. They nodded. "What's it like?"

"It's okay," said the younger man. "Tents. Showers. Hot water. Booze. It's okay."

"Tents?"

Seeing the look on his face, the photographer grinned. "You're lucky to get a tent. Until last month you were expected to tuck up in your own bedroll and go to sleep under the stars."

"I think we'll keep going." Harry pushed away his uneaten meal and lit a cigarette. "Spam, is that all you ever eat in the desert?"

"You'll get used to it," said the photographer. "The Arabs don't eat pork, see. So they don't pinch it." So saying, he reached across, speared Harry's Spam on his fork, and put it on his own plate.

Chips O'Grady contributed little to the conversation. He let

Harry Wechsler talk to the two men. Harry liked talking to strangers. He called it research. Chips ate his Spam and used a piece of bread to wipe the final traces of egg from his plate, but even Chips left the peas. Then he went back for more tea and got slices of the fruit cake for himself and Harry. He understood why Harry Wechsler took it for granted that Chips would wait on him, like some sort of body servant, but it made him feel a fool. In this country, servants were natives. He wished he could find some way of getting that simple fact into Harry's brain.

Harry Wechsler put his feet up on a dining chair, smoked his cigarette, and studied the map. "No, we'll press on along the coast," he said. "We got all the pictures of Arabs we need for the time being."

The photographer smiled politely and said good night. The two men had an early start in the morning.

Once they were back in the Ford, Harry Wechsler changed his mind. "How long would it take us to mosey down to this Siwa Oasis, Chips? Ever been there?"

"I've been there. That was back before the fighting started. It was as near to the Italian frontier as you could get. It's right on the wire." He looked at his watch. "It's a long drive. I wouldn't want to try any of the unmarked camel tracks. They start off looking very nice at this end, but you get fifty miles into the desert and they peter out."

"So?"

"We should head south after we get to Mersa Matruh. That's a better way."

"Can you do it?"

"Not in one go. Not unless you spelled me on the driving. Even then we couldn't do it overnight. It's the best part of two hundred miles after we turn south."

"Those guys," said Harry. "I wouldn't trust those guys an inch."

"The newspaper people? They were all right."

"All right? Are you kidding? I think they found a story down there in the desert. Something they don't want us to get on to."

Chips was surprised by this idea. "Why do you think that?"

"I have this unfailing instinct about people, Chips. My mother was the same way. Those guys were trying to put us off. You saw the way the older one clammed up?"

"I don't think so, Harry. They were just tired."

"I can tell tired from cunning. I've been in this game a long time. I got where I am by knowing what makes people tick. There's a story down in that oasis or I'm a Chinaman."

"There'll be nowhere to sleep," Chips warned him, having concluded that comfort figured largely in all of Harry Wechsler's decisions.

"Get lost! Do you think I'm some kind of cream puff?"

"Whatever you say."

"We'll see which of us will be yelling for Mom."

"I didn't mean anything, Harry. I just thought I should tell you we might have to spend the night in the car." He stole a glance at his chief.

"Okay, okay."

"You don't want to see if we can get an army okay for the trip down there?"

"And waste time prizing more of these 'officers of the day' out of their boudoirs?"

Chips nodded. He knew he was going to hear a lot more about the warrant officer who had arrived in his camel-hair dressing gown. He'd seen the incredulous look on Harry's face.

"Why would we need their okay?"

Chips was going to tell him all kinds of reasons, from the possibility of stumbling into newly laid minefields to the chance of being shot up by friendly fighter planes. But he decided that this was not the moment.

"We've got cans and cans of gas." Harry looked at his watch. "Two hours each at the wheel: starting now. Right?"

"Even so, I'm not sure we can get to Siwa by morning, Harry."

"Give it a try, buddy. You're not with one of your dozy Limey news outfits now. Give it the good old American try."

"Sure, Harry, sure."

The drive down to Siwa was nothing less than spectacular. The track leads across the hard sand of the so-called Libyan Plateau. In the moonlight it was white and crisp for as far as they could see. At first they were leaving a long gray plume of dust behind them, so Chips drove off the usual route. Keeping a hundred yards or so to one side of it, he found his own way across the desert. There he put his foot down and, despite the weight of the tents and supplies that Harry had insisted were necessary, the station wagon kept up a steady fifty or more miles an hour. Now and again they saw army trucks keeping to the prescribed route and trailing clouds of white dust.

Only once did Harry show any sign of having second thoughts about this long detour, hundreds of miles into the Sahara. Even then he wanted only a little reassurance. "Would they have gone to such trouble to say there was nothing there, if there was really nothing?"

"I don't know, Harry."

"Ask yourself," said Harry testily.

"You mean if Harry Wechsler had been down to Siwa and found nothing, he would have gone around telling everyone to go there?"

"Don't be a smart-ass," said Harry irritably. Then he thought about it and laughed. "Maybe I would at that," he said, and laughed again.

Siwa is a major oasis, deep in the desert and on the northern edge of the ever-moving Great Sand Sea. Anyone continuing south from here must face hundreds and hundreds of miles of uncertain, shifting sand and many days without water.

At Siwa, rocky valleys form a shallow depression and provide access to the little lakes that are the waters of the oasis. The famous pink rocks give shelter to groups of date palms, which the tribes say grow the most delicious dates known anywhere in the whole Sahara region.

Harry Wechsler and Chips O'Grady were completely exhausted when they arrived, early in the morning. There was no one in sight. They drove past the seemingly empty mud-hut villages and parked before some concrete buildings where peeling notices in English and Arabic read KEEP OUT. ARMY PROPERTY. DANGER. A smaller notice in red and white said, *You are now in a malaria region. Take precautions!*

Dutifully Harry reached for his smart canvas satchel, found his quinine tablets, and took two. He swallowed them without water, gulping noisily as he did it. "Take your tablets, Chips."

"I'm okay. Mosquitoes don't seem to like the flavor of my blood."

"Maybe that was because your blood was largely alcohol. Now maybe they'll find a taste for it."

"I'll be okay, Harry."

"If you're thinking of managing without your salary, okay. But just as long as you're working for me, you do things my way. That means you stay off the booze and take your malaria tablets and your salt tablets every day." He shook out two more tablets for him.

Chips threw two tablets into the back of his throat, swallowed, and smiled. He wondered how long he would be able to endure Harry Wechsler without the consolation of a little whisky now and again.

"What kind of place is this?" Harry pointed to the ancient single-story huts.

"Gyppo army. This was one of their bases when they manned the frontier. Not here any more."

"I guess we've got to be very near the old frontier here. The wire, you call it: right?"

"We're right on it." He pointed to a space between two

outcrops. "If we follow the old track that leads west, we'll come to the wire."

"Can we get through?"

"We can give it the old American try."

"Attaboy!"

As they drove west they saw evidence of the dangers that the Great Sand Sea offered. Not more than fifty yards off the marked path, two big ten-ton trucks had been abandoned. The sand was almost covering their wheels and there was no chance that any sort of machinery could winch them out now. Not many people, on foot, camel, or motor, risked the journey southward. The local tribes—the Siwans and Senussis—were convinced that it was a region of evil from which few travelers returned.

And yet men of the Long Range Desert Group dared the shifting sands. They made journeys so far into the distance they had to be refueled by rendezvous with aircraft. That was a story that Harry Wechsler would like to tell, but the British were secretive. They were determined that the enemy not discover anything about how and when and where the LRDG patrols operated.

"There's the wire!" said Chips. He stopped the car and turned off the ignition. As the engine was silenced, the whine of the wind was suddenly very loud.

"Chips, old pal, that's quite a sight!"

The border defenses, which Mussolini had decreed should run along the frontier between his African empire and Egypt, was nothing less than a river of barbed wire. It was supported on steel stakes, each one bedded in concrete, to make a barrier extending about three meters. Intricate and forbidding, it flowed uninterrupted for four hundred miles or more across the rolling sands. Harry got out of the car and began framing the scene from different positions using the L-shapes of stretched thumbs and forefingers. "Get the camera, Chips."

When Harry had got one general photographic view, Chips drove along the edge of the barrier until Harry had chosen a sandy mound from which to get better photographs. Then there was a photo with the Ford station wagon in the foreground, and two pictures of Harry with a foot on the running board. As they were standing there in the early morning sun, they heard aircraft. There were three of them, twin-engined bombers, very high and heading due east. Harry tried to get a picture of the planes in the sky, but he was too late and they were too far away.

"Oh, well. They would have been just fly specks, I suppose. We would need a really big telephoto to get anything worth using. Maybe you're right about me having a Leica. We'll chase that one up." He pointed to the wire barrier. "Are there any gaps in this stuff?"

"Let's find out," said Chips. He was very tired. All he wanted was to sleep, but Harry Wechsler seemed to go on forever. "What gives you all that energy?" he asked, once they were back in the car and crawling forward, looking for a way across the frontier.

"Money," said Harry without hesitation. "Do you know how many readers I have?"

"Yes, you told me."

"Is that a gap in the wire?"

He was pointing to a place where the sand had drifted to cover the tops of the steel stakes. "Drive over the sandy place there," said Harry.

"You know what will happen if a tire runs onto one of those buried steel stakes?"

"Yeah. You'll have to change the wheel."

"We could lose the sump."

"We could lose the war. Get going."

Chips didn't like it. The Ford was a heavy vehicle. The reinforced chassis and all the luggage made it heavier still. Apart from the danger from the steel stakes, there was the chance of getting stuck in a patch of soft sand. But Chips did as he was told, and when they reached the other side Harry was pleased with himself. "We're in Libya. We did it! Where do we go from here?" He looked around him. He'd never felt so far from civilization in all his life.

There was a track across the desert that Chips said must lead to Al Jaghbub, the corresponding oasis on the Italian side of the Libyan border. Harry produced his compass and then went well away from the car to be sure the metal had no effect upon the needle. Once he'd taken a compass reading and compared the maps, they started to crawl forward, looking for trail markings. Once they'd left Siwa out of sight behind them, they were in the open desert. There were no signs of birds, or rats, or snakes: every living thing seemed to be hiding from the sun.

About half an hour later they saw a blur on the horizon. "It could be a mirage," Chips warned. But it was exactly in the right place, and soon the blur became the palms that marked Al Jaghbub. "We could brew up some tea and get a sleep while the sun is up."

"Tea and sleep: that's all you guys think about," said Harry, but Chips had got to know him well enough to discern agreement in his voice. The village of Al Jaghbub shelters under the cliffs of a depression. And nearby there was a lake deep and wide enough for a swim.

Chips brewed tea in the traditional way of the desert army. He filled a can with sand, poured some petrol in it, and set it alight. Over it he boiled a kettle of water. The tea tasted good. Even Harry had to admit it.

They dropped into the water with a whoop of delight. Water acquires its true significance in the desert environment. Dipping his head below the surface Harry found it to have a strange texture, and it tasted of salt and sulfur. Back home such a swimming hole would have been a place to avoid, but in this dusty, dirty, gritty world, to be immersed in cool water was a luxury beyond compare. Neither of the men spoke. They floated in the buoyant water and flapped their arms gently enough to stay afloat with head above water.

While they were in the pool there came the sudden loud noise of an aircraft. They looked up. It was a light plane, flying so low that it seemed as if it must crash into the cliff side. It turned and came back again but this time it banked steeply, sideslipped, and disappeared behind the trees.

It was a secluded place, and for a time it was as if they had the whole world to themselves. After they had bathed they found a patch of shade and sat around drying themselves. The salt was sticky on the skin and stiff in the hair. An Arab boy found them and sold them a pile of fresh dates, which they ate. "Ever go to a ball game, Chips?"

"No, never."

Harry sighed and sank back in the sand and went to sleep. . . .

He awoke when a boot kicked him hard in the shoulder. He looked up to find half a dozen men had arrived at the water hole. "Stretch your hands out! Roll over!" The voice was harsh, with a regional English accent that Harry found difficult to comprehend.

Harry hesitated. Half asleep and not understanding what he was expected to do, he grabbed his shoe, in which he'd put his glasses and wristwatch for safekeeping. He was kicked again, spitefully enough to make him call out with the pain.

"You heard me, you bastard! Roll over!" It was a man wearing khaki shorts and bush shirt with sergeant's stripes, although without his glasses Harry Wechsler was mostly aware of his heavy army boots and woolen stockings. The sergeant reached down and snatched Harry's shoes away from him and examined them carefully.

Chips seemed to understand what it was that these aggressive newcomers wanted. He reached out his arms, with open palms, and rolled over, well clear of the place where he'd been sleeping. They wanted to be quite sure the sleeping men did not have guns tucked down beside them in the sand. As another kick was aimed at him, Harry rolled over too.

The sergeant trailed the heel of his boot through the sand, to be sure there was nothing buried there, and then kicked the surface, but he found nothing. "We locked everything in the Ford," said Harry. "Give me my glasses."

The sergeant passed his shoes to him, and Harry put his glasses on. Now he could see that the sergeant was a weather-beaten man about forty years old. His exposed arms, right to the wrist, were covered with an intricate pattern of tattooing. His open-necked shirt revealed more tattoos that went right up to his neck. On his shirt some campaign ribbons marked him as a long-service soldier. Standing well back, guns in evidence, there were a dozen or more soldiers—young lance corporals—all wearing the clean and well-pressed uniforms that, military po-licemen are taught, are a necessary sign of their trade. "So you say that's your Ford?"

"Where's your officer?" said Harry. "I'm a U.S. citizen in a neutral country. I don't have to put up with British army bull-shit."

Chips made a frantic sign with his hand, trying to make his boss see reason. He knew that the sort of men who became military police sergeants did not readily endure such rebukes in front of their inferiors.

The sergeant saw the gesture. "Get up. And put on your shorts and your shoes." He tossed Harry's other shoe into the sand and then looked at Chips. "And you, chum! I don't want any trouble with either of you. Get it?"

"I'm an American; we're both civilians," said Harry.

"And you're both under arrest," said the sergeant.

"What for?" said Chips.

"Talk to my officer about it," said the sergeant. "He's in charge."

Jimmy Ross preferred to stay in Cairo. He felt safer in the bustle of the town, and he wanted to be in regular contact with the office so that he would be prewarned of any development that would affect him. It did not improve his temper when, after suffering the discomfort of the journey out to the oasis and finding nothing but old guns and a couple of war correspondents, the brigadier came swooping in unexpectedly in a light plane. The brigadier was in a hurry, and so they stood having their conversation in the shadow of the plane's wing.

"I don't want you to think that I'm breathing down your neck, Major Cutler."

"No, sir." He looked at the brigadier and then at Lieutenant Spaulding at his side. He hadn't seen Spaulding since the fiasco at the Abdin Palace. Did Spaulding go along on the brigadier's duck shoots and all the other outings to which the brass devoted so much time? Spaulding smiled, almost as if guessing what was in the other man's mind.

The brigadier looked at one and then at the other: there was not much love lost between these two men; they had hated each other on sight. They were a couple of prima donnas, thought the brigadier. Spaulding played soldier but wouldn't give up being an Oxford don. Cutler: too damned distant. Perhaps he was convinced that his time in the police service made him the only professional among them. No matter; in wartime the army had to use what it could get. "Two captives, I hear?"

"Not exactly, sir. Two men arrived here a couple of days ago but were frightened away. The chaps arrested today are bona fide war correspondents."

"Are you quite sure?"

"Yes, sir. I know one of them by sight and am staying away from him for that reason."

"Quite so. Good security. Are you feeling well, Major Cutler? I hear you're in that damned office all day and all night, reading through every file and report they have there. Don't overdo it. I don't want you going down sick."

"I'm perfectly fit, sir. With respect, sir, what I need is time to get on with the really important investigation."

"Rommel's spy, you mean? Yes, that's the big one, but in the army we have to obey orders, no matter how illogical they sometimes seem."

"I must take the rough with the smooth," said Cutler. "My sergeant told me that."

The brigadier was not pleased with this reply; in the prewar army such a response would have been punished as open rebellion, but this was wartime and this specialist was a special case. And the brigadier was astute enough to see that an obsession with tracking down the spy might eventually bring immense benefit. The brigadier, having had a sound night's sleep and an excellent breakfast, and with the feeling of well-being that comes from being given the exclusive use of an airplane, said, "Yes, yes, yes. As I said, the chief sent a plane for me. There's a big pow-wow at Corps. I'm bound to face a quizzing about this little discovery here, so I dropped in to see exactly what has been found."

Jimmy Ross, who'd been awake all night bumping around in a truck, said, "Eight hundred and fifty Beretta submachine guns and about a million rounds of ammunition." He was repeating what he'd already told Lieutenant Spaulding on the telephone that morning. Spaulding's face registered surprise as if hearing it for the first time.

"Here's one of them," said Spaulding. He had wandered off and picked up one of the Italian guns from a wooden packing case. Now he was brandishing it, stroking its machined metal parts and waiting for his chance to explain it.

It was curious that Spaulding was so fascinated by guns, thought Ross. It wasn't something one associated with academics.

"Yes," said the brigadier. He craned his head while keeping his distance. Politely he inspected the gun that Spaulding was holding out to him like a baby being offered to the Pope for a benediction. "What's the verdict, Major Cutler?"

It was Spaulding who answered. "Enough for five paratroop *Kompanien* of one hundred forty-four men each."

"I wanted Major Cutler's opinion," said the brigadier mildly, although inwardly he was angry that Spaulding should jump in with his answer so pat. It made him look a fool.

Ross looked from one to the other of the two men. "They're Italian guns. Do the Italians have parachute formations?"

The brigadier didn't smile, but he was amused at this reply. The major was probably right: there were no Italian paratroops as far as anyone knew. The brigadier decided to keep that foxy response up his sleeve, to counter any sticky questioning at headquarters.

"No one would be asking them for their passports," said Spaulding in his dry donnish manner. "Germans, Italians: what's the difference? And anyway, it's as good as the German equivalent—the MP Thirty-eight. They might well have some logistic reason, like ammunition supply."

"I'm not an expert on firearms," said Ross.

The brigadier said, "If the Hun dropped in and seized this oasis, plus the Siwa one across the wire, he'd be a thorn in our flesh, wouldn't he?"

"He'd have to be fed and supplied," said Ross. He knew little or nothing about weapons, strategy, or tactics.

"Water is the main problem for a besieged garrison," said Spaulding authoritatively. "Men can go a very long time without food."

Ross was tempted to add: but not without ammunition. But getting into a wrangle with Spaulding—even a good-natured wrangle—was not a good idea. He was in enough trouble already, without making more. And according to Lionel Marker, the brigadier was in awe of Spaulding's academic qualifications and listened to his theories on everything from astronomy to Zionism.

Spaulding interpreted the silence as a sign that both men wanted to learn more of his theory. "I don't know if you've been reading the intelligence summaries about the Hun paratroop forces, but he's likely to take over a few places like this without anyone catching a sniff of what's happening. Then suddenly we have to contend with a German box sitting out here in our rear, preying on our supply lines."

The brigadier was not immune to the pleasure that comes from watching subordinates vying to impress. "What do you say to that, Cutler?"

"I've certainly read a great many intelligence summaries lately. Too many. The Crete invasion has given a lot of people an obsession about German paratroops. My people think these guns are just part of a consignment from one of the old Italian dumps."

"Dangerous toys, Cutler," said the brigadier, who was rehearsing the sort of discussion that he'd face at the powwow. "If the Hun has left this sort of thing round here, plus explosives and ammunition and so on, he could drop his men in and be ready to go in an hour or so."

"From the intelligence summary I read," said Ross doggedly, "a three-engined Junkers transport plane holds only twelve fully equipped paratroops. To bring five infantry companies in here, they would need about seventy of those big planes. That's a lot of noise and commotion for a clandestine operation. And they would need a lot of luck to fill the sky with planes and still avoid our radar and fighter defenses."

"Even so," said the brigadier. He didn't want to entirely abandon this threat to the oasis. Writing it off as briefly as Cutler had done would mean his time in the conference limelight would be severely limited. He decided to handle it the way it would do most good: a little danger but not more than his men could deal with. "I think we must leave the Beretta guns here and put a guard on the place: twenty-four-hour watch. The usual sort of thing. Sort out some reliable chaps, Cutler."

"There is another dimension, sir," said Spaulding. "Siwa Oasis was a base for the Egyptian army at one time."

"Yes, that's right," said the brigadier. He grabbed at his face and massaged it. It was a sign that he didn't follow what Spaulding was trying to tell him, and Spaulding was quick to recognize such signs.

"Could this be a dump for the use of our Egyptian army friends?" said Spaulding, who, having had his entire kit stolen at the quayside on the day he arrived, found it hard to look charitably at anything the Egyptians said or did.

"Um," said the brigadier. "They've been decidedly unfriendly of late. What do you think, Cutler?"

"It's quite possible, sir. There is of course a very disgruntled element in the middle ranks of the Egyptian army. Our most recent information is that the usual dozen or so conspirators are threatening to contact Rommel with as much intelligence material as they can lay their hands on. But mustering a fighting unit of Egyptian volunteers, arming and equipping them so that they could assist Rommel. . . . It's a tall order."

"Yes, usually they're more vocal than active," said the brigadier.

"They don't go round shooting at British soldiers," said Ross, "and I hope they don't start doing so."

"Of course, of course." He looked at his watch. "Is my pilot here?"

"He's waiting, sir," said Spaulding.

The brigadier spent a moment staring at the toes of his high boots and thinking. "We're all of one mind, chaps. The message is: Don't provoke the locals or we'll have a civil war on our hands. Eh? What?" He wasn't asking them, he was telling them. "There's just one other thing, Cutler."

"Yes, sir?"

"I don't like the idea of these damned machine guns sitting round here, waiting for their owners to arrive. We'd better get some boffins from Ordnance to come down and take the firing pins out, or whatever you do to make guns inoperable."

"Better than that," said Spaulding, "make them so the rounds explode in the breach after a couple of shots are fired. That way we write off a few extra Huns for nothing."

"Good idea, Spaulding. Get on to that one, Cutler."

"Yes, sir." He didn't know if Spaulding's artful modification was a practical possibility, but he didn't want to delay their departure.

The brigadier turned to the plane. Spaulding called to the pilot, and opened the door, and made sure the brigadier's booted foot was firmly positioned on the step. Then he steadied the brigadier's arm to help him clamber up into the cabin.

Ross watched impassively. Then Lieutenant Spaulding climbed into the plane, still clinging to his Beretta machine pistol. "I'll keep this, Major Cutler. Someone from headquarters might want to see it."

"Yes, Mr. Spaulding," said Ross. At the prospect of being alone again, he felt better. There were times when he thought he could continue his impersonation forever. On the other hand, it was tempting to believe that his best way of escape was to get nearer to the fighting. How many other men had solved their personal problems by assuming the identities of fallen comrades? The essence of the dilemma was whether it was better to carry the identity papers of a real person or of a fictitious one. Real identities got paid and were a part of the legitimate organization, but real identities could be proved false very easily.

He saluted, and the brigadier waved imperiously. Ross stood and watched the plane trundle out to the end of the hardened sand strip. The pilot revved the engine and, flaps down, it roared along into the wind and teetered unsteadily into the warm air. There hadn't been room in the plane for all the brigadier's kit and his servant too. Poor Spaulding. He'd probably find himself polishing the brigadier's boots. It was a comforting thought.

Two and a half hours later the Ford station wagon containing Harry Wechsler and Chips O'Grady could have been seen driving along the desert track that leads from the oasis of Al Jaghbub, alongside the old frontier wire, to the coast. The going was not as good as it had been on the Egyptian side of the frontier, and every now and again Chips slowed down to make sure he was keeping to the marked track. Several times Harry Wechsler got out and went ahead to find markers that had been buried by the drifting sand.

It was only when they were a long way north that Harry brought up the subject of the long and hostile interrogation they'd been given by a British captain named Marker before getting a grudging permission to go.

"We never saw that goddamned major," complained Harry. "He kept well out of the way, didn't he? At first they kept threatening us with what the major would say. Then suddenly he was not available."

"Yes, funny, that," said Chips.

"Nothing funny about it," said Harry. "That son of a bitch knew I would make it damned hot for him. I still might."

"I wouldn't do that, Harry. Those security people are a law to themselves. You start stirring the shit for those buggers, and you'll suddenly find your accreditation withdrawn."

"They couldn't do that," said Harry angrily.

"I wouldn't bet on it," said Chips.

"How?"

"They just say you're a security risk, and suddenly your newspaper agency will disown you. I've seen it happen. Newspapers make sure they don't upset the army, or maybe they'll lose out on all their other reporters. You can see the sense of that."

"I can see the sense of it," growled Harry. "So can the Gestapo."

"They're fighting a war, Harry. They're playing for keeps. You take the gloves off, and they'll hit you with an iron bar."

"They wouldn't even give me the guy's name."

"Security, Harry. They always have the drop on us. No one's going to take our side if it comes to a showdown."

"I guess you're right," said Harry.

"I am," said Chips.

"It was something about machine guns: Berettas. Did you hear what the little guy was saying outside the door?"

"I heard. The whole landscape is littered with small arms. If the Gyppos start collecting them together, they could make a lot of trouble."

"I guess so."

"No story in Siwa," said Chips reflectively.

"That's what I was thinking," said Harry. "You know something? I'd say those guys we saw at supper last night were in some kind of racket."

"You didn't say that to the security people?"

"Of course not," said Harry.

"No, of course not. If you'd mentioned those two we'd be in close arrest for conspiracy or something before the fact. Or something."

"Those guys weren't press reporters," said Harry.

"Did you only just figure that one out?"

"You knew all along?"

"No, but afterward—once I started thinking about them—I knew they weren't newspapermen."

"How could you be so sure?"

"Look, Harry," said Chips. "Perhaps I don't know every last one of the press reporters in this part of the world. There are probably a few phonies and a couple of stringers and a roomful of freeloaders I've never met. But one thing I am damn sure about: all those guys know *me*, know my name. When I say my name is Chips O'Grady to a newspaperman, they know me. Right?"

"I see," said Harry.

"I mean, they don't stare into space and yawn. They gawk at me and say to themselves, So that's the drunken bastard I've heard all the stories about."

"So who were those sons of guns?"

"Crooks of some kind. Deserters, probably."

"And something to do with the Berettas?"

"Just back from Siwa Oasis and trying to persuade us not to go that way. It would be quite a coincidence if they were not," said Chips.

"Gunrunners. I wish I'd taken a closer look at them and that truck of theirs. We missed a story," said Harry.

"I should have asked them about buying a Leica," said Chips.

=15=

This was a different world. In this strip of desert where the war was being fought, the men were different. Their clothes were different, their speech was different, the looks on their faces and the way they moved, all these things were different from the way it was in the rear areas.

Wartime Cairo was infested with criminal gangs, so that the authorities were overwhelmed. For Toby Wallingford and his band of deserters, wholesale theft had become their normal way of life. And yet, perversely, most of them preferred being here. They were seldom heard to say so. All of them persistently told each other that Wally must be mad to bring them up to the sharp end while they could have been getting rich stealing army supplies and spending their money on nightclubs, booze, and women.

The front-line area was a soldier's world where Arabs and locals of any kind were only occasionally seen. And yet the appearance of the fighting soldiers was in no way martial; they looked more like vagabonds. Their clothing was stained and torn, their faces weatherbeaten, and their eyes always moving. And, like vagabonds, everyone seemed to be wearing every garment he possessed. Even in the heat of noon, men and officers alike were bundled up in overcoats worn over jackets and sweaters. Wearing such things was the most convenient way of carrying them.

Wallingford's two trucks were marked with the insignia of the Independent Desert Teams. Wallingford had invented that secret unit, and yet it was no more exotic than many of the official ones, like Popski's Private Army. As they drove past a sentry, he looked at them with no more than casual interest. They were entering one of the "boxes" that the generals had decreed as part of the new defensive strategy. Behind barbed wire and trench-line forts, artillery and infantry and, in this case, armored cars waited for Rommel's next move. Vast minefields had been laid to connect these boxes and thus form a long defensive front.

In this box there were armored cars and tents and a few ramshackle huts that had been built by an Italian desert survey team, long before the war. From a distance there was little to see, for this army had been in the desert long enough to learn that digging in could be the difference between life and death. The armored cars and other vehicles were sitting in dug-out depressions in the hard sand, and tents had been erected in the lee of them. Here and there, shelters had been improvised from such things as captured Italian groundsheets, pieces of corrugated iron, and wooden crates. Everything was covered in camouflage netting, the shadows of which made hard patterns on the sandy earth.

"Watch your pockets! It's Wally the sailor!" shouted an officer in a leather jerkin and battered peaked cap.

Wallingford waved and stopped the truck. "Hello, Piggy," he said. He navigated his way around from school chum to school chum. It wasn't difficult; there were plenty of them.

"Where are you off to this time?" Lieutenant Piggy Copeland had a pleasing smile, a sunburned nose and forehead, and a grotesque haircut that had left him bald in places while several large tufts of hair stuck out at the back of his head.

"It's beginning to warm up, isn't it? We're pushing on along the track as soon as it's dark," said Wallingford. He jumped down from his seat and, in a schoolboy gesture, stooped and grabbed a handful of soft sand.

"And you want something to eat? How many of you?" The sweat dripped from Piggy's face. He wiped the perspiration from his brow with a side of his hand.

"Me and fifteen ORs." Wallingford let the sand trickle through his fingers.

Piggy said nothing. He'd seen other men arrive and want to touch the desert sand. But men who lived here and fought here didn't do that. Piggy had had enough sand to last him the rest of his life.

Piggy walked around and looked at the two lorries with their Snake badge stenciled on the tailgates. Like most other young officers, he would have liked a chance to serve in one of these swashbuckling little outfits that were springing up everywhere. He envied Wallingford his good luck. "Send your rankers over to the mess tent. There'll be plenty left from lunch. We're damned short of drinking water, as always, but there's tons of food."

"Did you hear that, sergeant?" Wallingford asked Percy. "Get the mechanics to check the wagons and have them both filled up. Get the jerry cans filled too. The rest of the men can get something to eat and maybe steal some shut-eye. If you need me, just shout. I won't wander far away."

"Yes, sir!" Percy delivered a stiff and perfect salute, which Wallingford returned with a flick of his fingers. The two men exchanged looks. Percy knew how dangerous it was for Wallingford's gang of deserters to mix with real soldiers. It would take only one foolish outburst to reveal what they really were. But with Percy overseeing events, such a disaster was less likely. The prewar year that Percy had spent in England, writing a university thesis, had given him a sound insight into the English, the sort of insight only outsiders knew.

"And get some netting over our vehicles," called Wallingford. "You're at the sharp end now."

Wallingford watched Percy muster his men and move off. Then he turned to his old school friend and smiled. The jeopardy of this little adventure gave him a tingle of pleasure; if only Piggy knew his secrets! That would make him sit up.

"Where are you heading, Wally?"

"You know I can't tell you that, Piggy."

"Some kind of raid?"

Wallingford gave a hoarse snort. "With fifteen other ranks and me? What a thought."

"Virtually no one west of here but Huns," Piggy warned. "There are miles and miles of minefields on our left. They stretch all the way to where the Free French are holding Bir Hacheim. I've never been that far south. An Indian outfit has moved up and taken position on our right—Sikhs; bloody good night-fighting infantry, Wally. But the night before last they sent a patrol out, hoping to get a prisoner, and only one Sikh came back."

"Sounds bad," said Wally.

"When the Hun is so determined not to be observed, it usually means he's up to something."

"I brought you a case of Johnnie Walker, Piggy. That should help you forget your troubles. You said the CO liked Johnnie Walker."

"I'm afraid we lost the old man," said Piggy. "Two weeks back. His driver ran into an old unmarked minefield. What with the mines the Eye-ties and then the Hun have put down, plus what we put down when we first came this way, its nigh on impossible to keep track of where they are. You'd better have a good look at the map before you go. Even then you might run into trouble. Have you got a mine detector?"

"You're a cheerful sod, Piggy. Just like when we were at school."

"Yes, that's why I've stayed alive," said Piggy.

"So who's got the CO's hat?"

"The adjutant took over until he got a septic tooth. Then Captain Anderson became senior."

"That farmer's boy?"

"Steady on, Wally." He paused. "Of course, no one knows if Andy will be confirmed."

"He was a sergeant only last year, didn't you say?"

"Things move fast out here, Wally. You should know that, with lieutenant commander's rings on your shoulders. Hello, here's Andy coming now. No more farmer's-boy jokes, Wally. Andy has become damned touchy just lately."

"I'll not upset him," said Wally, amused by his friend's anxiety. "I need his help, don't I?"

A tall officer had emerged from the low profile of a tent. He was brandishing a walking cane, which he needed since banging his knee getting out of a burning car. Wallingford remembered him from his previous trip and didn't like him.

Captain Andy Anderson sauntered over to them. He wasn't friendly. He'd been in the tent with the wireless man, trying to pick up the BBC news bulletin. Reception was always poor in daytime, and he'd heard little but static and crackle. Now his puglike face was set in a scowl as he said, "So you're back again, Wallingford. Where did you anchor your ship? Off to win the bloody war, are you?" He did nothing to modify his rough Yorkshire accent. He smoothed his hair with the flat of his hand. His haircut, although not as bad as Piggy's, was chopped like stairs at the back of his head, where the barber had been unable to trim it properly.

To save his friend from having to respond to Andy's rudeness, Piggy changed the subject. He'd seen Wallingford studying their haircuts. Now he said, "We had a fellow who'd been a professional barber on one of the Cunard liners. He had his barber's instruments with him when he brewed. No one can cut hair properly with shears." He laughed.

Wallingford laughed too, but Andy didn't join in. The presence of these two friends did not give him any pleasure.

"Just a milk run," said Wallingford modestly. He accepted the hostility that many officers showed toward irregular formations, especially one commanded by a naval officer.

"The Hun has come to a stop at present," said Piggy, in another effort to promote a friendlier atmosphere. "He seems to be digging in all along the front. It's just as well; we're not in good shape to counter another strong push."

Andy brought his cane up like a golf club. Then he swung it round expertly, to hit a small stone that bounced away into the scrub. Without looking at them, he said, "Rommel will have another go before the hot weather starts. He'll stake every bean he's got on getting to Tobruk. He needs those harbor cranes to bring in his tanks, eighty-eights, and ammunition. Without a port close to his fighting front, he's always going to be on short rations, hand-to-mouth."

"How close is the Hun?" asked Wallingford. "Do you think he'll push this way?"

"No. Work it out for yourself," said Andy. "Rommel has got to go by the shortest route: that means the coastal road. He's moving all his good stuff to the north. Even when he attacks us, there won't be much happening this far south. He's thin on the ground and pulled well back, with just a few guns to discourage us from finding out his dispositions."

"Wally needs to know what's out in front of us; he's pressing on tonight. He's going out along the *trigh*," said Piggy, who couldn't hide his admiration. "I invited him to eat."

At first Andy made no response. Then he looked at his watch and said, "Let's go have a beverage." The three men started walking over to the tent the officers used as a mess. "Sun's over the yardarm," said Andy. "Have I got the dark-blue terminology right, Wallingford?"

"Spot on," said Wallingford.

Piggy said, "Wally brought a case of Johnnie Walker for the old man."

"The old man's had it," said Andy, with that fierceness that men sometimes use to conceal their true feelings. "He copped a packet trying to stage a one-man rescue of headquarters company."

"Your Hun has a remarkable aptitude for placing his guns," said Piggy, as casually as he could. "He digs them in damned deep and sites them with such care that you can't see the buggers until an eighty-eight comes whistling past your earhole. Even then you can't see the buggers."

"You said the colonel went into a minefield," said Wallingford.

"He was dead by that time," said Andy categorically. The colonel's armored car had burned for a long time, and Andy did not want to think about what might have happened if the crew were not already dead. "His driver too, probably. His car had shed a wheel and was going round in circles. It was his burning car that got all their attention; that's why we got away."

"Where do you want your crate of whisky?" Wallingford asked.

Andy didn't answer.

As they reached the tent, Piggy lifted the flap for them to enter. The sun shining through the canvas flooded the tent's interior with green light, rippling and dappled like the clear water of an aquarium. At the end of the tent stood five folding chairs and some ration boxes that were placed to be used as footstools, or as places to put drinks. A long folding table was positioned where there was maximum headroom. It was covered with a checkered tablecloth and set with cutlery and glasses and some bottles of captured Italian wine that had gone a little cloudy with the heat. Their deceased colonel had always been very keen to preserve the niceties of dining in the mess, no matter what rigors the environment provided.

"Set an extra place, corporal," Piggy called to a man who was closely studying a large unlabeled can. "What filth are you giving us for lunch?"

"I don't know what's in this tin, sir," said the soldier. "I think it's either bully beef or bacon rashers."

"Unlabeled tins," said Andy. "Yes, we have a Standing Order from GHQ Middle East about that. To discover the contents of an unlabeled tin, corporal, you open it and look inside."

"Yes, sir," said the corporal mournfully. He'd heard the joke before.

"And bring us three bloody big whiskies."

The plates and place settings went only halfway along the table. Wallingford was about to remark upon this when he realized that the regiment had suffered heavier casualties than anyone was keen to talk about.

"I'd better send someone with you for the first half mile or so," Andy told Wallingford, as if regretting his hostility. "The *trigh* is not so easy to follow now we've fought across it. In some places you'll never find your way without help. We'll get you half a mile along the main track. After that you're on your own."

Wallingford nodded. It was a decision. He judged it better not to say thank you.

The ever-worrying Piggy said, "Take care, Wally. The Huns may be thin on the ground out there, but their gunners have the track zeroed in. If they hear anything moving along, they have only to press the button and they'll blow you to buggery."

"That will be something to think about while I'm tootling along in the soft sand," said Wallingford flippantly.

"I'm just trying to warn you," said Piggy.

"Yes, you're a good type, Porkers. I appreciate it." Piggy had been Wallingford's junior at school. Although there was less than two years' difference in their ages, their time at school had defined the relationship between them in indelible terms.

The drinks arrived in silver-plated mugs. Wallingford said, "Cheers."

"Cheers," said the other two men dourly and drank their whisky without relish, as if it were medicine.

"It's nothing you could do on foot?" Piggy asked.

"Our party tonight? No, it's nothing we could do on foot, old boy."

"You'd get through more easily on foot. Those trucks make a lot of noise at night."

"More than in the daytime?"

"You know what I mean, Wallingford."

A whistle was blowing short blasts from somewhere nearby. "Air raid," explained Piggy and went on drinking, studiously avoiding any sign of concern.

Wallingford went to the tent flap and stooped to push his head outside. Now he could hear the engines of some distant plane. Drink still in hand, Piggy joined him. "He comes over about this time every day," Piggy said.

There was too much haze for the plane to be clearly seen, but the noise of its engines increased as it turned in a lazy circle to come back toward them again.

"Recce plane," said Piggy. "They're building up a photo-mosaic ready for their push."

As he finished the sentence there were half a dozen loud explosions from a couple of miles to their left as the "photo plane" let fly with a stick of bombs.

Both men ducked their heads instinctively. They resumed the upright posture and Piggy smiled sheepishly.

"Well, it sounded just like the photo plane," said Piggy. He sipped his drink, his hand trembling slightly as he held the mug to his mouth. Wallingford glanced back inside the tent; Andy was staring at him, as if blaming him for whatever misfortunes beset them.

Wallingford went back and sat down to drink the rest of his whisky. "I needed that."

"The Indians must have caught that lot," said Piggy. "I suppose their camouflage wasn't good enough."

"Yes," said Wallingford. He realized that Piggy needed a reason to hope he wouldn't be bombed in the same fashion.

Anderson said nothing; he just went on sipping his whisky as if he were all alone.

Lunch with the other officers was a wake. They'd all been in the line too long. Their limited stamina had almost been used up. The loss of a popular commanding officer had dealt their morale a savage blow. It simply wasn't fair, they seemed to be saying. They'd chased Rommel across Africa to El Agheila, and just when they were beginning to think the job was done, Rommel had given them a resounding counterblow and chased them back. Here they had stopped, but that was more because Rommel had paused than because they had halted him. Now Wallingford saw around him an unexpressed but all-pervading feeling that they would not be able to hold the Germans when the next big attack came, as assuredly it would as soon as Rommel had built up his strength once more.

There was little conversation. Flies tortured them all through the meal. At this time of year it was impossible to get through a daytime meal without eating dozens of them. No matter how much one waved a hand over a morsel of food the flies would remain upon it. Most of the men smoked, but the smoke did not deter the flies. One of the officers draped a piece of netting over his head and ate from his plate inside this little tent, but even he consumed his ration of flies.

The afternoon went past slowly. The cars had been out on patrol four nights in a row, and there were few men who didn't want to spend the afternoon sleeping and girding themselves for another night of activity. When dinnertime came, Wallingford ate with his own people. He was surprised to discover that he felt more comfortable with them.

"I was glad to get out of there," said Wallingford to Percy that night as his two trucks, loaded with the men of the IDT, crawled westward along the desert track. "That crowd are battle-happy; they were beginning to give me the creeps."

It was dark. The corporal who'd helped them find the path through the minefield disappeared from sight as he went down

the other side of a rocky mound to return home. They were free
to speak. Wallingford climbed into the back of the truck and
said, "From now on, we leave all the talking to Percy. If we are
challenged, no one else is to say a word. Understand?"

"When we get through the German line—" said one youngster.

"Will you people listen to me?" said Wallingford testily. "We
are not going through the bloody German line. We are going to
a little village just along this track. Chances are we won't even
get a sniff of the Germans. From what I saw on the map, there
are miles and bloody miles of empty desert between the box we
just left and the nearest German. Where we are going is only a
mile or so from here, and Percy knows the route like the back of
his hand. Don't you, Percy?"

"Yes, sir. I do."

"What are we after, sir?"

Wallingford sighed. "Don't you stupid bastards ever listen?"

"I forgot."

"Optical goods. Percy's store of optical goods: binoculars,
cameras, range finders: the sort of stuff they fight to buy from us
in Cairo. This is the big one. Got it?"

"Yes, sir."

Wallingford always said "This is the big one," but when the
accounting was done, the share-out was never the sort of big one
for which they all kept on hoping.

"There are some huts on the track . . . just ahead of us there,
sir."

At the end of the nineteenth century, when this region was
first surveyed by Europeans, there had been almost two hundred
dwellings in the village now shown on the army's maps as Bir el
Trigh: the village on the track. Even in the nineteen twenties, it
had been a watering place on the long east–west desert trail. But
as the wells failed one by one, the population shrank. The little
mud huts tumbled into dust. It became no more than a campsite

for traveling caravans and then, when the fighting came, not even that.

It was Percy who went forward on foot to take a look. The others got out of the trucks, crouched in the sand, and waited. Some of the houses were sound, and Percy approached the place with great care. It was the sort of place that both sides sometimes chose for observation, or for intermittently manned outposts.

Only when Percy came back along the track and waved both arms in an agreed signal was there a concerted sigh of relief. The engines of the trucks started and they drove on into the open rectangle of flat hard earth that had once been the center of a thriving village. Some of the mud buildings still bore traces of the old days. There were shop signs and enamel advertising plates still embedded in the walls of a house where goods had once been traded and money exchanged.

By local standards it was a grand house, rising a few feet higher than its surroundings and with a low wall that had once protected a small date plantation.

Percy knew the place. Before he had deserted, during his time as a lieutenant on Rommel's staff, he'd come here as an aide to a colonel from the quartermaster's department of the high command. He'd never forgotten that visit.

"This way," said Percy authoritatively. He pushed against a sheet of corrugated iron and climbed on a low sill to gain entrance to one of the houses. "There'll be no booby traps," said Percy. And to demonstrate his confidence he kicked at the empty boxes and old German-language newspapers that littered the earth floor. He led them to one of the back rooms and cleared the rubbish away with the toe of his boot. Then he kicked the loose soil to reveal a straight line.

"Here," said Percy. He reached down, found a metal ring, and heaved at the floor until a square section of it came loose and a heavy wooden panel swiveled on a creaky hinge. A trapdoor. "Where is the flashlight?"

A big lantern was held over the black void. Its beam moved over the sheer edges of the pit, but it revealed nothing at the bottom.

"There's nothing there," said Wallingford, voicing what Percy for a moment feared.

"It is all right," said Percy. "I'll show you. It is all hidden. There is no ladder. Hold the rope, so I can lower myself down."

The men watched while the invincible Percy abseiled down into the darkness. When his head was about fifteen feet below floor level his feet touched the uneven earth.

"Now give me the light," said Percy.

They tied it to the rope and let it down. Percy switched it on and, with head bent low, moved out of sight along a crudely cut tunnel, which sloped steeply downward.

"Is it there?" called Wallingford anxiously. There was no answer. "Do you hear me, Percy?"

From Percy there came a yelp of fear—*"Scheisse!"*—and some more colorful oaths in rapid German. Then Percy's flashlight was extinguished and there came a sound that might have been Percy being knocked unconscious, except that Percy came back along the tunnel holding the broken light and asking for another.

"What the hell's happening?" said Wallingford.

"A snake," said Percy. "Two or three snakes, in fact. They moved too fast. I smashed the light. I am sorry."

"What sort of snake?"

"I did not ask it for its papers," said Percy irritably. "Come down here and see for yourself."

Wallingford had no great desire to go down into the cellar, but his authority was at stake. He held the rope and scrambled down in the same abseil style.

He couldn't see the light. "Where are you, Percy?"

"It is all right," called Percy. "I have found the generator."

Wallingford very gingerly reached out with his hands into the darkness, touching the roof of the tunnel and testing its dimensions. Then, moving very cautiously, he went in the direction that Percy had taken.

"Come. It is good," said Percy. His voice echoed softly. Encouraged by Percy's words, Wallingford bowed his head and proceeded down the ever steepening slope, looking all the time for any uneven piece of earth that might conceal a snake.

His eyes became accustomed to the gloom. There was a dull yellow light coming from the flashlight Percy was using at the far end.

Percy had put the light on the ground to produce a golden glow from the hard red earth that formed the walls of the tunnel. By the time Wallingford reached him he'd opened the door of a fuse panel fixed to the wall. He fiddled with the switches and fuses and then went back to bend over a small portable generator. "Stand clear. This should do it," he said.

He gave the starting handle a fierce tug, but the engine didn't catch. He tried again and again. On the fifth attempt the engine fired. There was a flurry of smoke and a clamor of sound echoed in the confined space as the engine came to life.

"You'll suffocate us," said Wally.

"No," said Percy and laughed. "You will see." He opened the door of the fuse panel again and pulled the main switch.

A hundred or more little red worms, dangling from the roof, turned orange and yellow, and then the filaments glowed brightly so that the whole place was lit up.

"Wow!" said Wallingford. It was a surprising sight. The little entrance tunnel had brought them down to another larger one. Its rocky sides were worn shiny. It was well over twenty feet high and in places twice as wide as that. And it snaked out of sight to both the right and the left of them.

"This was the bed of the underground river that fed the wells," said Percy. "Now it is just a dried-out cave."

"You left optical gear down here?"

By way of answer, Percy walked across and touched one of the packing cases. They were piled one upon the other. With

German practicality they had all been stacked so the labels were visible and right way up.

"I mean, will it still be in good condition?"

"Perfect! The air down here is cool and dry. Our captain was an old man, a mining engineer in civil life; he made no mistakes about such things."

"Why hasn't it been moved back behind the lines?" said Wally, who wanted to hear the answer repeated.

"I told you. They were Twenty-first Panzer Division. I was with them, driving back north. They all died at Sidi Rezegh, fighting the South African Brigade. That was when I got the South African paybook and started walking east to make a separate peace. The colonel I had been escorting went back to Berlin. Believe me, I am the only one left. The paperwork went: everything. There is not another living soul in Africa who knows all this stuff is here."

"It's wonderful," said Wallingford. Using his flashlight, he went close to read the labels on the sides of the packing cases.

Percy followed him. "I have committed most of the inventory to my memory."

"Wonderful," said Wallingford, and he stroked the packing cases lovingly.

"We will not be able to take all of it," said Percy. "You will have to decide what is the easiest to dispose of."

"Hamburg," said Wallingford reading from the labels. "Zeiss-Ikon, Dresden; Mauser-Werke A.-G. Oberndorf; Schneider Optik, Kreuznach; Voigtlander, Leitz binoculars. A microscope. Look, a case of movie cameras!" He was excited. These were magical names for him. These were the words that would work their spell on customers who coveted these expensive toys. "Yes, the air is very dry, Percy. Very dry indeed." And Wallingford laughed shrilly, and with a note of hysteria, so that for a moment Percy was alarmed.

"What a tragedy that men should be killing each other," said Wallingford, his mood suddenly changing to one of tense-voiced drama. "What madness! Man should be building the things the world needs—bridges, ships, roads, and houses—not tearing them apart. That's why I got out of it."

Percy was not listening. He'd heard Wallingford's mawkish rationalizations for deserting, and taking up his criminal life, many times before. But Wallingford was not the sort of man who let his emotions take over for very long.

"Damn, there's a fortune down here, Percy. An absolute bloody fortune. All we have to do is to get it to Cairo."

"Yes," said Percy soberly. "That is all we have to do."

The two men did not climb back up through the trapdoor. They followed the winding course of the underground riverbed until they found the place where this wonderland of optical stores had been delivered and unloaded by the Germans.

At the side of the natural tunnel a big wooden door had been fitted. They opened the bolts from inside and forced the lock. Then, with both men using all their strength and weight, they levered the door open. The sudden draft of night air, deflected by the walls of the wadi, was cool and refreshing. Here was where the underground river had once emerged. They clambered outside and up the side of the wadi. Even from this close, it was not easy to see the doorway. Wallingford saw why Percy had wanted to enter through the house interior and the trapdoor. It would have been a demanding task to find the door at night. Great skill had been brought to camouflaging the entrance.

"Clever bastards, those Krauts," said Wallingford.

"*Jawohl,*" said Percy.

Wallingford needed a moment to take it in. He sat down and lit a cigarette, carefully shielding the flame in his hands. Once lit he puffed smoke and gave a sigh of appreciation. "Will Rommel get there?" He picked up some small stones and threw them into the wadi, trying to hit a small rock.

"To Cairo? Probably."

"You seem damned confident," said Wallingford.

"I was on his staff." Percy had been the lowest of the low—a signals *leutnant*—but he was proud of that appointment.

"Yes, you told me."

"He knows every move the British make. Your generals decide to send a tank brigade somewhere, and Rommel knows the destination before the tank commanders are told they are moving. As a field commander, Rommel is nothing special—he's not a Manstein, not a Guderian—but when you know what your enemy is doing, you are likely to win. Yes, Rommel will get to Cairo. And beyond."

"You know all about it," said Wallingford, without showing much interest. He kept throwing the small stones down into the wadi. At last one of them hit the rock and bounced. Wallingford waited for Percy to say something about his marksmanship, but Percy was lost in his thoughts.

"Yes, I know all about it. One day I will write about it. I will tell your stupid British generals who was 'Rommel's spy' in Cairo."

Watching a stone roll down the slope, Wallingford was struck by a sudden fear. "Can we get the trucks down into this wadi?"

"We did it once," said Percy, but there was a touch of doubt in his voice. He never said anything without the tacit implication that German skills were exceptional. "We will have to walk back, now, and find the place where the sides of the wadi give access."

Wallingford tossed away the rest of his stones and got to his feet.

"Better put out the cigarette," said Percy.

Wallingford ground it underfoot; Percy used the toe of his boot to bury it. Then they walked along the wadi edge. Only in these remote regions of the earth does the clear air provide such a display of stars. To the north there was an occasional flicker of light along the horizon: artillery fire, too far away to be audible. As they walked, Wallingford peered into the gloom ahead, nervous of snakes and booby traps. Suddenly he grabbed Percy's arm and brought him to a halt. Percy looked at him quizzically. Wallingford nodded to where someone was stretched full length in the scrub that followed the wadi's edge.

"It is nothing," said Percy. "Just an old corpse."

He walked over and kicked it. It was little more than a bundle of bones. The dry heat had desiccated the flesh like a mummy from the tombs. The face was staring straight up to the sky: eyes missing, skin darkened and stretched tight enough to open the mouth. The clothes were bleached and ragged. Only the high-laced army boots identified the man as a German.

"A long time ago by the look of it," said Percy. He kicked the body again, staring down at it, as if half expecting it to disprove his words and move.

"You're a callous bastard, Percy."

"Yes, I am. That is why you need me. The rest of the men are uneducated, unmotivated, and useless to you."

"We need each other," said Wallingford warmly. He was lucky to have found the German deserter and recruited him into his gang. The other men didn't approve, but it had been a wise decision.

"I think not," said Percy. "I might leave you after this one."

A feeling of alarm came upon Wallingford. Percy was his right-hand man. Percy was the man who made everything go right when the others were trying to muddle through. Walling-ford remained outwardly calm. "What will you do?"

"I will push on toward Palestine . . . perhaps India. I would like to get well away from the fighting. With a bit of money I could set myself up in business."

"What sort of business?"

"Germany cannot win the war, not now that the United States is fighting us. Germany is finished, and I am too old to go home and watch an occupation army strutting about in my homeland."

"There's a lot more money to come," said Wallingford, determined to hang on to Percy at all costs. "Another year and you can clear off with a fortune."

"It becomes more and more dangerous," said Percy. "The military police are bound to get us one day; these men of yours are stupid. They drink too much and talk too much."

"Bigger and bigger convoys from America will bring phenomenal loot to the Canal Zone, Percy. You've seen the American tanks and trucks; that's just the start. Now that the Yanks are in the war they'll be sending better and better equipment. I want to concentrate our efforts on the docks; that's where the real money will be made next year. We'll be able to cut out all this scavenging on the battlefield."

"For you it will be easy," said Percy. "English is your mother tongue. For me it will not be so easy. I have blond hair; I have an accent."

"All for one, one for all, Percy. We'll look after you, you know that."

Percy didn't believe him. This was another of Wallingford's regular pep talks. It wasn't much different from some of the optimistic views Wallingford had confided to him before. But seeing how badly Wallingford was taking the idea of his leaving, Percy decided to lower the temperature. "I will not be doing anything for a while," he said.

"No. You'll need your money," said Wallingford.

Now Percy was sure he had made a bad move in confiding his future plans to his boss. If Wallingford decided that money would liberate Percy into leaving the gang, Wallingford would make sure he got none. Percy smiled. "Maybe I just need a strong drink," he said.

"How long will it take to get this stuff loaded?" asked Wallingford.

"You will have to select exactly what you want to take."

"I can do that in five minutes," said Wallingford.

Percy looked at his watch. "We may not be ready to move before daylight. And in daylight we are sure to be spotted. It might be better to find some good place and just lie low until tomorrow night."

As if to emphasize the need for such caution, there was the soft sound of distant aircraft. "Let's get back to the others," said Wallingford. "They'll be getting worried."

"They are all idiots," said Percy.

"They are all individuals," said Wallingford.

"Individuals like Tommy Mogg and Sandy Powell?" said Percy sardonically.

"Those two did all right," said Wallingford warmly. "When they saw that Siwa Oasis was full of policemen, they cleared out quickly and warned us. That was just what I told them to do."

"Yes, they have a good nose for policemen," said Percy. "A rapist and a thief."

"You're being hard on them: Sandy should never have been trusted with the mess funds. He went to the Gezira races and was unlucky on the horses. I feel sorry for him."

"And do you feel sorry for Mogg? And sorry for the girl he raped?"

"They did all right at Siwa."

"Very well. So what are you going to do now? You cannot go in there and get the Berettas with the police waiting for you."

"I'm going to sell the Berettas to the Jews. Cash and carry. They pay me. I tell them where to find the guns, and they arrange their own collection."

"Will they fall for it?"

"They need the guns."

"The Jews will get caught."

"They might or they might not: I'm going to get that idiot Darymple to help with some paperwork. But if that doesn't work, and Solomon does get caught, at least we'll have the money. Stick with me, Percy old lad. I have a head for business."

"Solomon will betray you if they catch him. He will describe all of us to the police."

"Why should he suspect us?" And when Percy didn't answer, Wallingford added, "Solomon will not turn informer. I'm a good judge of people: Solomon hates the British. That's the beauty of it. Solomon won't give them any help at all."

=16=

Peggy West had seen very little of Prince Piotr until Solomon had told her to spy on him. Now they'd become friends.

"If we went round the clubs one evening, we'd probably run into the royal entourage," said Piotr. He said it casually and went on to talk of other things, but he knew that Peggy, like so many other Cairo residents, was fascinated by King Farouk and everything he did.

"How would we know which club?"

"I could discover that from someone at the palace. The king has his favorite establishments, which change constantly. He's like a child in some respects. I could find out where he is likely to turn up."

"I saw him one night last week," said Peggy. "Everyone knew he was coming because the police cleared the streets, the way they do lately. He was in a big red Rolls with motorcycle outriders, and a truck of infantry, and then more cars with plainclothes policemen."

"He likes a lot of fuss," said Piotr. "Arabs all like show, you must know that by now. I used to have a silver and black Wraith, a Mulliner drophead coupé. I loved it, but the king sent the word to me to get rid of it. He didn't like being upstaged."

"How stupid. You should have refused."

"I have a French passport," said Piotr sadly. "These are sad days. That passport makes me very vulnerable to the authorities."

"Why?"

"You know why. The French were fighting the British in Syria last summer. Now the Japanese have attacked the British using French bases in Indochina. The British hate the French. They would love an excuse to kick me and all other French passport holders out of Egypt. Where would I go then, Peggy? Where would I go?"

Peggy was tempted to say Syria, but taking Piotr's rhetoric literally always led him on to worse bouts of self-pity. That was something she'd learned the hard way over the previous few weeks. "Everyone loves you, Piotr. Cairo would never be the same without Prince Piotr. You know they would never ask you to leave."

He brightened. Peggy knew exactly what to say. "Then you'll come dancing one evening?"

"I've nothing to wear," said Peggy.

"I'm disappointed in you, Peggy," he said archly. He was back in form now, his worries temporarily forgotten. "I thought you were a woman who rose above the hackneyed cliché."

"You're right, Piotr. I have plenty to wear. Dresses I haven't tried on since the war began."

"What about that low-top pale blue dress? That was so becoming."

Peggy looked at him; he could always produce another surprise for her. The only time he could have seen that dress was when she'd worn it at a party some twelve months ago. "Yes, I could wear the pale blue if you think it would be suitable. It's a short dress."

"Suitable? You'll look ravishing. No one wears long dresses at the clubs any more."

"I have matching shoes," said Peggy, as she tried to decide how to have her hair arranged.

"I know what! I said we'd have a birthday celebration and have some chums along. Let's do it in style."

"That's a wonderful idea, but it will be awfully expensive."

"I only have a birthday once every ten years. It's time I celebrated properly."

"You're very generous, Piotr."

"With a cake and lots of candles. It will be fun."

It worked as planned. They even saw the king. They were at the Tutenkhamon, a grandly named and fashionable nightclub on Sharia Muhammad Ali. The street had been built as an attempt to reproduce the Rue de Rivoli in Paris but it was not a comparison that leaped to the mind, especially for anyone at the Opera House end, which had, since the war, become an unofficial meeting place for black-market salesmen and their customers. The nightclubs and drinking places here had largely come under the control of Arab racketeers, notably an aged Nubian who spent most evenings at the gaming tables and his days at the races.

Piotr had decided that his acquaintance with the king should be witnessed by his closest friends. Alice's corporal being unavailable, Robin Darymple had volunteered to escort her. The other guests were Sayed and Zeinab el-Shazli. They were delighted at the opportunity to dress up and spend an evening in such company. Sayed had, in the past, expressed polite doubts about whether Prince Piotr was actually a friend of the royal family. This evening they would discover the truth, Sayed told his sister, as they stood together in front of the mirror with him dressed in a dinner suit he'd borrowed from a friend of his father's. The suit was not a perfect fit, and Sayed was worried at the way the trousers bunched slightly at the waist under his jacket. But Zeinab reassured him that he looked very English.

They all arrived at the Tut early enough to have the "luxury French cuisine" dinner that was advertised as an important part of its attractions. Sayed showed caution as he studied the menu, fearing he would eat something forbidden by the Muslim code. Finally he had the spinach soup and roast pigeon. It was not adventurous, but it was safe. His sister laughed at Sayed's reluctance to try new dishes. Placing herself in Prince Piotr's hands, she daringly ordered the lobster thermidor and the lamb cutlets in mustard sauce. Sayed looked at her sternly; he didn't approve. Neither did he approve of her accepting the offer to sip Robin Darymple's freshly poured champagne. Sayed could never get used to the idea that his sister was a grown-up woman who did not have to take his advice or follow his example every minute of the day. She tried to make her brother laugh, but he was not to be coaxed so easily from his anger. She decided he was worrying about the ill-fitting trousers and turned away from him and pulled her chair closer to the prince. If her brother was determined to be bad-tempered all the evening, so be it. She looked around her and smiled. She was determined to have a good time.

The three women all looked particularly attractive this evening. Piotr's invitation had given them a chance to dress up in a way they seldom did these days. Peggy was wearing a pale blue dress, decorated with bugle beads. Zeinab had seen it before. Peggy had shown her her entire wardrobe one evening after Zeinab had offered to lend her a pair of silk stockings. In Cairo silk stockings were rare.

Peggy had pulled out all the stops for this evening: her diamond earrings, a necklace, and a small gold brooch in the shape of a *P*, as well as a gold wristwatch. She knew now that she had overdone it. She always overdid things. Perhaps she had overwhelmed Karl with her plans and her hopes and her aspirations. She thought of taking off the necklace and the brooch and putting them into her evening bag. But if she did it now, someone would notice. Piotr might even tease her about it. Peggy looked at Alice. She envied Alice, not because of her youth but because of her effortless restraint. Alice never had to stand in front of a mirror taking things off and putting them on and trying to decide what was right. Alice always got things right.

Alice was wearing the plainest of cocktail dresses: black silk with a high silk-braided front. Her mother had ordered it from Harrods by mail just before the war began. Her only accessories were a double string of pearls that her father had bought in the Gulf and a simple gold wristwatch. Apart from pale lipstick, she wore only a touch of makeup. For tonight's celebration she'd had her fair hair cut shorter than usual, so her ears were revealed.

"These Arab women," Darymple told Alice in a discreet whisper that put his lips close to her ear. "They may end up fat and wrinkled, but when they are young they can be spiffing." He'd been eyeing Zeinab with great interest, as if seeing her for the first time.

"You'll spoil my makeup," said Alice, as he succumbed to the temptation to nuzzle her ear. She brushed her hand across her ear as if chasing away a midge. Leaning across the table she said, "That's a wonderful dress, Zeinab."

"It is my mother's, on loan for this evening only."

"You look wonderful, doesn't she, Captain Darymple?"

"Robin, please. What? Yes: wonderful."

Zeinab was looking particularly beautiful that night. Her dress was a colorful local print, such as only the very young can get away with. Her makeup was formal and quite heavy. She'd carefully applied heavy eye shadow and used a base that made her skin very pale. Zeinab at her most beautiful had that solemn quality that young Egyptian women can muster. And yet it was easy to make her erupt into laughter that transformed her into a very young woman, if not a child.

The restaurant was crowded, as all Cairo restaurants were that year. Peggy saw several people she knew, including Theda Borrows and Jeannie MacGregor. They were with two wounded Hussar officers who were going back to their unit next week. They all knew Peggy and waved to her. Perhaps this evening Jeannie was celebrating her assignment to an Advanced Surgical Center. There she would be as near the fighting as women ever got. Peggy had arranged the move, as Jeannie had no doubt guessed, but she'd not complained about it. Jeannie MacGregor seemed to have got over her caustic anger, and Theda Borrows had recovered from her inconsolable grief. The very young are made of rubber, thought Peggy. Perhaps it was better to express your emotions than to bottle them up all the time the way she did. And yet what would happen at the hospital if the sisters and senior staff went round shouting and sobbing?

"A penny for them?" said Robin Darymple.

"Those girls I work with: should I remind them that tomorrow they are both on early shift?"

"I wouldn't do that, old girl. They look like they are thinking of other things."

When the royal entourage arrived, the club's management cleared a dozen or more customers from three tables directly alongside the dancing floor. Not all the customers relinquished their places with good grace. A party of four merchant navy officers angrily took their chairs and went and sat amid the dance band.

The king liked to have a view of the room. Fresh tablecloths were fluttering like flags, flower arrangements came to the royal table, and ice bucket stands—each bucket containing some expensive wine—were arrayed like trench mortars.

King Farouk himself did not arrive until the rest of his party was standing by the table waiting for him. His entrance was stately. He looked around him with a grim smile on his face, obviously enjoying every last gasp and gabble of the commotion he caused. There was a harsh chord before the six-man orchestra bravely battled their way through the Egyptian national anthem. Then the king sat down.

It was the first time Peggy had been so close to the king. The lights from the dance floor gave her a chance to see him clearly. She'd not expected him to look so very young, although of course he was only twenty-two. His skin was soft and white. He was distinctly overweight, but his evening dress fitted him so perfectly that her first impression was of an attractive young man.

As the king's staff began ordering food and drink, the orchestra and the floor show tried to resume their performance. They played "I Want to Be Happy," and a man with oiled biceps, baggy silk trousers, and a whip began an acrobatic dance with two young girls in skimpy shiny costumes. The act was billed as Ivan's Slave Market, and the posters outside the club said Ivan had come straight from Beirut, Lebanon. There were not many towns for such cabaret acts to tour, now that the war had sealed off Europe and the whole of French and Italian North Africa.

After Ivan had cracked his whip for the hundredth time and a juggler, a belly dancer, and a Spaniard with castanets had performed, the floor was cleared. The orchestra set aside the sheets of unfamiliar music that they'd had to learn for the visiting acts. Now they played the tunes they always played for the customers to dance to, and the sound of this music made everyone more relaxed. Soon it was possible to forget that the king was sitting just a few yards away.

The manager himself brought Piotr's birthday cake to the table. The band played "Happy Birthday to You," and Piotr smiled and said it was all a surprise. He cut the cake, and after tasting it Peggy said no one would have guessed that sugar was rationed in Cairo. Robin Darymple had a second slice.

No matter that his style was somewhat dated, Prince Piotr danced very well indeed. He told Peggy that his mother had insisted upon his being given dancing lessons when he was very young. "Quickstep. Fox trot. Waltz. Tango. I can do them all," said Piotr.

"Then we shall tango at the first opportunity," said Peggy.

"It is agreed."

It was as they sat down after dancing a quickstep that one of the king's party came to their table. He was a man of about forty, with a military bearing and the square-ended jet black mustache that so many Egyptian army officers wore.

The aide bowed to Prince Piotr and conveyed to him, in elaborate terms, the king's compliments and good wishes on the occasion of his birthday. Piotr gave a smile of satisfaction and looked around the table to be sure that everyone understood this gesture of friendship from the king.

The aide gave a perfunctory bow to Sayed and then spoke to Zeinab. He introduced himself as an aide to the king and then, looking directly at Zeinab, said, "The king sends you his compliments. He would like to dance with you." He glanced at Sayed. Sayed looked back at him with no change of expression.

Zeinab got to her feet.

The aide said, "Not here, not in public. The king would like to dance with you in private."

Zeinab looked at her brother. Sayed stiffened and for a moment looked as if he was about to speak. But although the aide waited politely, Sayed sat still and said nothing.

"Please thank the king for his compliments, but I can not leave the party," said Zeinab. "I am the guest of Prince Piotr."

The aide was used to dealing with such hesitation. "The king's car will be waiting outside at ten thirty," he said. He bowed to her, to Sayed, and then to Prince Piotr. Then he went back to the table and sat down. He said nothing to the king, who looked as if he did not know anything about the conversation.

It was already ten fifteen. All Piotr's guests were looking at each other. For a long time no one spoke; then Peggy West said, "Tell him to go to blazes."

Prince Piotr, seated next to her, put a hand on her arm in a gesture of restraint. Quietly he said, "Sayed will be arrested if she doesn't go."

"Are you serious?" Alice Stanhope asked him. She glanced around to see if the Shazlis were listening, but they were just looking at each other.

"Alas, I am," said Prince Piotr. He dropped his voice lower. "Just before Christmas, the wife of an American was propositioned in exactly the same way. The American told the king to take a running jump into the Sweet Water Canal. Nothing happened, of course. The king was frightened that it would get into the American newspapers. But Sayed, alas, is not an American."

"The little bastard!" said Peggy West, looking over her shoulder to where the king was sitting. She caught a glimpse of him through the movement and blur of the couples dancing. The orchestra was playing "Smoke Gets in Your Eyes." A mirrored ball hung from the ceiling and revolved slowly. Flickers of light reflected from it, falling on the dancers like snow. Everyone was smiling; everyone on the dance floor seemed to be having a good time. Everyone, that is, but Robin Darymple. He was on his feet and standing well away from the table. He looked acutely embarrassed. He reached into his pocket for his gold cigarette case and lighter. He lit a cigarette and blew smoke in a way that revealed his agitation. Soon he edged away and wandered off.

"But Sayed is not American or British," said Piotr again.

"And what about Zeinab?" said Alice, trying desperately to conceal the full extent of her anger. "Doesn't Zeinab have a say in whether she wants to go to bed with that stupid king?" Having said it, she took a deep breath. Only a few minutes ago Alice would have rebuked anyone being so rude about the monarch in a public place. Now she was shocked and furious in a way she'd never before been.

"Please keep your voices down," said Sayed. They all looked at him. He seemed to have aged ten years.

"I must do as he says," said Zeinab, looking at them all.

Sayed reached out and touched her arm.

"It is better that I go with the brute than that I make bad trouble for my family," said Zeinab.

"I regret to say I agree with you," said Prince Piotr. "For any Egyptian to defy the king is very dangerous."

"Don't go!" Alice was adamant; her voice showed the others how strongly she felt. Piotr raised an eyebrow. So this was the real Alice Stanhope.

Peggy West was concerned about Alice, frightened that she was going to make a scene. "We can't advise them, Alice. This is their country and their king."

"But we run it," said Alice. "We run it and let this rotten corruption flourish: bribes and threats and injustice. How can you say we must stay out of it?"

Peggy was calm; she had the clinical restraint that is part of being a nurse. "It must be their decision, Alice. Let Sayed and Zeinab decide for themselves. Our comments only make it more difficult for them." The music stopped and the dancers left the floor. There was some well-mannered applause, and the orchestra took a few minutes' break.

Alice said, "Can't you do something, Prince Piotr?"

Piotr looked at her and slowly shook his head. "I wish I could. You know that. Zeinab and Sayed are my friends."

Alice saw that by choosing a woman at Prince Piotr's table the king was challenging him to interfere. Perhaps the king's choice was in some way influenced by animosity between the two men. Or perhaps such personal circumstances increased the king's sadistic pleasure, or his lust.

"Where is he?" said Peggy.

The king's party were still sitting at their specially positioned table at the dance floor, but the king was nowhere to be seen. Prince Piotr watched Peggy craning her neck to see the whole floor. "His Majesty will have gone," he said. "I know him. He is like that sometimes. He comes in to look around."

"To find a woman?"

Prince Piotr gave a weary smile. "Yes."

"What a pig!"

"Shall we dance?" said Piotr.

Peggy was about to decline, but it was no use railing at Piotr. Robin Darymple had returned and asked Alice to dance. Obviously Piotr wanted to give the Shazlis a chance to talk in private. "I'd love to," said Peggy. It was a slow waltz. Peggy could see Alice across the dance floor with Darymple, her face composed and beautiful, as if her spasm of anger had never occurred. The Shazlis were still at the table. Sayed had brought his chair closer to his sister.

"I'd love to," mused Prince Piotr as they moved smoothly over the dance floor. "Why do we keep to these absurd expressions? When I first went to England I used to say, Pleased to meet you. All my friends laughed at me. But why should How do you do? be better than Pleased to meet you?"

As Darymple danced past them, he called "Wotcher mates!" and grinned at them. His face was flushed. He'd had a lot to drink.

"It's a silly language," said Peggy.

"No, it's the language of Shakespeare and Milton and Wordsworth."

"Yes. Only the people are silly."

They danced in silence. Perhaps, she thought, Prince Piotr hated returning to Sayed and Zeinab as much as she did. They kept dancing for the next dance too. So did Alice and Darymple. When they returned to the table, only Sayed was there.

"Say nothing," he said. "I don't want to talk of it."

They all sat down. Prince Piotr ordered another bottle of champagne, but despite all the effervescence of the waiter, they sat there like mourners round a coffin.

Soon Prince Piotr proposed that they leave and go back to the Magnifico. "We will have one last drink in my apartment," he said.

But when they got back to the Magnifico no one wanted a last drink. The evening had been devastating for all of them. There were elaborate good nights and thank-yous before they made their polite excuses and went to their own rooms.

Only Sayed had something more to say. He pulled Alice aside and took her into the dining room, the same place she had sat with her corporal on that evening in January when she'd first arrived at the Magnifico.

Sayed switched on the lights. There was a faint smell of disinfectant. Bentwood dining chairs were standing on the tables, as if some mad prankster had arranged the room. Over each table there was a light fitting—a green glass shade—with a sticky flypaper suspended from it. On the wall there was a heavily retouched sepia photo of the late Signor Magnifico and a large colored litho of the Bay of Naples in a decorative ebony frame. Silver-plated pepper and salt pots were lined up on the counter in a straight line. So were some bottles of tomato ketchup. The fanlights that surmounted the windows were slightly open to provide a movement of air. From outside in the street came the sound of male English voices singing in a discordant drunken way, "My old man's a dustman. . . ." The voices faded as the soldiers lurched off back toward the bright lights of Sharia Kasr el Aini.

Alice faced Sayed and waited for him to speak. He looked at her and then looked away again. She knew she must give him time to collect his thoughts, however long it took.

"Miss Alice," said Sayed formally, "tomorrow I want to talk to your friend Bert." As if craving some sort of displacement activity, he grabbed a dining chair from the table. He placed it on the floor, so that Alice could sit down, and then got a chair for himself. As if feeling the necessity to explain the strange arrangement of the chairs, he said, "They are put on the tables after dinner each evening so the floor can be swept and mopped."

"Yes, I know," said Alice.

Once Alice was seated, Sayed sat down in the other chair. He clasped his hands, wringing them in a torment that the fixed expression on his face disavowed. "I will—" He stopped and there was another silence.

"Yes?" said Alice.

"I will work for him . . . work for the British . . . anything. I will do anything you wish." He wet his lips. "The king! That beast! That such people rule my country. It is a disgrace. Even the British do not do such things to us."

Above his head a flypaper hung from the ceiling. Upon its sticky surface, a fly was beating its wings angrily, trying to break free. "Perhaps you should think about it tonight, Sayed," Alice said. "Perhaps we should speak again tomorrow."

Sayed laughed as if she had made a good joke. "That you should say such a thing! You are not supposed to say that. You are supposed to welcome me to work for you in secrecy and be your agent."

"Yes, I suppose I am." She touched her pearl necklace, only with difficulty resisting the inclination to twist it in her fingers; her mother was always nagging her about that bad habit.

"Strike while the iron is hot. Is that not the expression?"

"Yes, it is. Your English is very good, Sayed."

"Then strike while the iron is hot, Miss Alice. I know your friend Bert is in the British Secret Service. . . . I will join him. I will tell him everything."

"No, no, no—"

"It is no use saying no, Miss Alice. I say yes." He hadn't moved. He sat in his chair, staring at her. "You will tell him?"

"I will tell him, Sayed." He was seated at the table with a hand propped under his chin.

Suddenly, Alice recognized that this was an important moment in her life. For this moment she had defied her mother, argued with her father, and coaxed and wheedled family and friends to get herself an interesting and important job in the Cairo administration. Now, amazingly, she was actually being given a chance to influence events. She was recruiting a man who would spy upon the revolutionary movement that the Egyptian army officers had formed. She must stop being the little girl her mother had created and become a woman of account. She must be professional, the sort of police officer Bert Cutler would approve of and respect.

In a new brisk voice, she said, "Very well! I don't want to risk your being seen and recognized in the police barracks, Sayed. Better that Bert comes here. What time shall I try and arrange it for?"

Sayed seemed not to notice the change that had come about in Alice. He looked down at his hands for a couple of minutes, as if considering what was at stake for the very first time. This was of course the point of no return. After this he would not be able to change his mind or laugh and say that Miss Alice must have misunderstood him. He raised his eyes so that he looked at her directly. "As early as possible."

"I'll get a message to him. Come and have a cup of tea in my room. Say, eight o'clock tomorrow morning?"

"Eight o'clock," he confirmed dolefully.

She stood up. She didn't want to give him time to modify his decision. "It's settled, then. Good night, Sayed. Get some sleep."

"Good night, Miss Alice." Politely he got to his feet as she stood up. She wanted to put her arms round him and comfort him. She loved them both. What could she say that would adequately express her feelings? It was the most tragic thing she'd ever seen.

They stood there awkwardly. He guessed that Alice was waiting for him to leave, so she could phone the night duty officer at the military police barracks. He bowed, turned, and left the dining room without adding another word.

Alice gave him a few minutes to walk upstairs before going into the lobby to use the telephone. She closed the door of the booth carefully so she could not be overheard. "Hello? Hello?"

It was never easy to get through on an Egyptian phone. She tried several times, then sought the help of the operator. A newspaper had been left behind in the booth. She glanced at it while she was waiting to be connected. There had been a big naval battle in the Java Sea with "severe Allied losses." The newspaper account gave few facts, but apparently the Japanese invasion force had got through. Soon, it seemed, the Dutch East Indies would fall. The official communiqués were obviously preparing the public for the next lot of bad news. Everywhere the Allies were losing the war.

She pushed the paper aside and flicked the phone rest a couple of times. The operator seemed to have abandoned her. She dialed the barracks number again. After two more tries she heard the ringing tone. Sergeant Ponsonby was acting as NDO; she recognized the voice.

"Night duty officer."

The police and the military were on twenty-four-hour alert. There had been extra shifts of duty ever since the night when, according to the legend that was now well established, British tanks surrounded Abdin Palace and the king was held at pistol point.

Alice was guarded in her conversation. She knew Bert would understand her cryptic message, even if Ponsonby failed to. "He must have breakfast with me at seven thirty in the morning. He must. You must find him. Tell him it's very very important. He mustn't be a minute late." She would have to speak with him before he saw Sayed; that was imperative.

Ponsonby refused to be moved by the urgency. Dolefully and slowly he said, "Seven thirty hours ack emma. Affirmative. I will get a messenger and make sure Major Cutler gets your communication within the hour." Ponsonby was being especially pompous tonight. Alice decided he'd been drinking.

As she went upstairs she passed the apartment that Sayed and Zeinab shared. She thought she heard someone sobbing, but it might have been the water pipes. The plumbing in the hotel was very old.

When Andy Anderson occupied the little room on the second floor, he'd fixed up shelves and installed an electric cooking ring and electric kettle. So equipped, he could make tea in the middle of the night and shave in the mornings without going to the bathroom down the hall.

The sun was shining brightly, falling across the card table upon which Alice had put a cloth and set out an English breakfast. Andy had used the table for his poker games, which had often continued into the small hours of the morning. Andy supplied booze for his friends, but he himself preferred tea. He was somewhat addicted to tea. Some said that tea drinking was the secret of Andy's good fortune at card games. Despite the drunken parties held in his room, no one had ever seen Andy drunk or even slightly tipsy.

Now that Alice Stanhope was occupying the room, she had transformed it with colorful curtains and a new rug. The Wedgwood tea set, cut-glass marmalade jar, and much else on the table had been borrowed from her mother's apartment in Alexandria.

"I'd always wondered what it would be like to breakfast with you, Alice," said Jimmy Ross. He was dressed in khaki drill with his white corporal's chevrons on the short sleeves. He found it easier to move about on the streets, and do the things he wanted to do, dressed as a ranker. Anyway, he didn't want to suddenly abandon his disguise; the Magnifico residents had come to know him as Corporal Cutler.

Alice looked at him sharply but she couldn't be sure there was no innuendo. He smiled, and she poured tea for him.

"No milk," said Sayed, and shielded his cup with his flattened hand. "It is good of you to see me, Bert."

"I'll have the grapefruit," he told Alice, "but for breakfast in Cairo I draw the line at hot porridge."

"Then I'll eat it all myself," said Alice. "Sugar?"

"I am in charge of the secret intelligence," said Sayed quickly, blurting it out so there could be no going back.

"For the Free Officers?"

"So you know of us?"

"It's not a closely guarded secret," said Ross. "But I didn't know you were the intelligence chief."

"I handle it. We do not have an intelligence chief."

"You'll have to give me names," said Ross. It was probably best to start with the hardest bit. When a man passed his friends' names to you, his allegiance came with them.

"Yes, I understand."

"I'll give you a code name. Your real name will never be

written down. Only the three of us will ever know of this meeting."

Before Sayed could respond, there was a light tap at the door. Peggy West stuck her head in and let out a gasp of surprise. "Alice! Sayed! And Bert Cutler!" said Peggy. "Whatever are you doing here?"

"What is it, Peggy?" Alice was trying to remain calm, but it wasn't easy. She hadn't allowed for the possibility of Peggy's barging into their meeting. She always met Peggy downstairs in the lobby.

"And what lovely china!" said Peggy, coming into the room to look more closely at the spread on the table. "I wanted to remind you we should leave for work at eight thirty sharp. All the shifts are being changed."

"I know. I'm almost ready," said Alice.

Peggy remained standing there as if expecting to be asked to sit down and take breakfast with them. But no one invited her to sit down. They had been surprised, and it showed. "I hope I'm not interrupting something important," said Peggy.

Alice got her hat and put it on carefully while looking in the mirror. For a moment she could think of no response. She stared at her reflection, a hat pin held in her mouth. Then she recovered herself, fixed her hat into position, and said, "Not at all. It's just a little celebration for Bert." She paused, and in the silence realized they were expecting her to explain further. Desperately she searched her imagination for something to acclaim. "He's being made a sergeant," she said.

"That's wonderful, Bert," said Peggy. "Congratulations." It was impossible to know from her tone of voice if she believed Alice's explanation. Peggy was obviously wondering why Sayed would be included in such a celebration.

"Zeinab will go back to her mother and live there. I asked Sayed to have breakfast," Alice explained.

Peggy West stood there, looking at Sayed and trying to think of some appropriate solace, but no words came to her.

"We'd better be going," Alice told her. "I'll let you two finish breakfast in peace."

As soon as the door had closed upon them, Ross took from his shirt pocket a plain sheet of paper that had been folded twice. He passed it to Sayed, and with it a wooden pencil. "Write the names," he said.

$=17=$

"It's hush-hush. Top damned secret, old boy." Wallingford grinned at Captain Robin Darymple. "The whole point is I can't tell you anything about what I'm doing. Or what we're going to do."

The two men, together with Percy, were in an office in Gray Pillars, the large stone building that was GHQ Middle East. From this curious example of Italian Fascist architectural style, Britain's war was fought. From here the orders went out to British forces as far away as Ethiopia, Iraq, and Palestine and to the fighting front in the Libyan Desert.

"Yes," said Darymple. Doubt was in his voice. He wondered how he'd explain why Wallingford—without written authorization from anyone—had taken possession of a large office next to his and equipped it with chairs and desks, filing cabinets, typewriters, and even two female secretaries. "But what will I tell the others?"

An attractive woman of about thirty-five came in, carrying some files. "Give them to Percy, Babs," Wallingford told her. He turned to Darymple again. "Tell them that what I'm doing is secret. S-e-c-r-e-t. It's not their bloody business. That's all they need to know." He winked at Babs conspiratorially. She smiled and handed the files over to Percy. Then she left the room with that exaggerated care about disturbing them that was impossible to ignore.

Darymple watched her and thought about his predicament. He wished he'd never mentioned to Wallingford that there was an empty office next door to his. And he wished he'd got into the building early enough to forestall Wallingford's seizure of it. Darymple didn't relish the idea of telling the sort of people who might inquire that Wallingford's unauthorized occupation of one of the most desirable offices in Cairo was none of their business. And yet, as things were, he was in no position to antagonize Wallingford. "How long will you need the room?" said Darymple.

"No telling. The way things work with us, we might get an 'action this day' telegram from the War Cabinet in London and be a thousand miles away, tackling the Japs."

As far as Darymple could see, Wallingford was not joking. "The War Cabinet?"

"Once, a few weeks back for a special show, the boss got a note signed by Winston himself. Winnie calls us his pirates." Wallingford looked Darymple in the eye and grinned. He'd long since discovered that in wartime you simply couldn't go too far. The more absurd and extravagant the stories you told, the less you divulged, the more willing people were to believe you and do as you wished. Wars were like that.

"Those two secretaries you have working for you," said Darymple. "One of them is the wife of Colonel Smythson, a damned fiery little staff colonel at British Troops in Egypt."

"Well, of course she is, old bean. You don't think I selected her for her secretarial skills, do you? When she came in this morning I asked her to type a letter for me. After she'd been seated motionless behind that bloody machine for ten minutes, I asked her what was the matter. She said, "I don't know how to type capital letters." Can you beat that, Robbie? She didn't know how to type capitals." He laughed. "I'll bet even you can type a capital letter if you put your mind to it. Am I right?"

"Stop acting the bloody fool, Wally. Suppose some admin bod comes checking out the office space? They do sometimes. How am I going to explain that you have taken over this office—and the secretaries—when we've got majors on this same floor cramped three to a room?"

"Stop worrying. We'll get Mrs. Colonel to chase them away. She can be fierce at times. You should have heard her on the phone getting those desks for me."

"I hope you know what you're doing," said Darymple.

"Look, Robbie, old sport. Let me explain the facts of life to you. These officers' wives are avoiding the evacuation order. They all should be on the boat to South Africa or home. The only way they can stay with their husbands is by getting a job with the army. Hell, I had the choice of a dozen or more women as soon as I said there were jobs going. So who do you think I chose? I'm not batty. I chose two women whose husbands have enough clout to get us out of trouble. Get the idea, old son?"

"I see."

"And of course they love the idea of working for a secret outfit like ours."

"Yes, of course."

"So hands off Babs and her friend." Big smile. "I don't want any added complications."

"But I—"

"Just a word to the wise, old fruit. Hands off my two girls."

"I'll just say the commander in chief knows all about you."

"Wonderful! That should bring inquiries to a full stop. Now bugger off and let me get on with my work."

"Okay, Wally. But there's something else I want to talk with you about."

"Really?"

"That money your Arab friend loaned me."

"Mahmoud. His name is Mahmoud. Is he chasing you for it? These Arabs get a bit emotional about money sometimes."

"I don't know what to do, Wally."

"You'd better pay him, Robbie. It was only a short-term loan as I remember. Just a few days, you said. They can get nasty."

"I haven't got it."

"Get it! You'll have to pay him. You know what these Arabs are likely to do if you don't pay them."

"No. What?"

Sometimes Darymple could be exasperatingly dense. "He won't take you to court, Robbie."

"You don't mean he'll . . . ?"

"Yes, he'll cut your balls off. Pay him. Borrow the money or go into the red with your bank."

"I'm already in the red with my bank. Look here, Wally. He's your friend. You said he was your friend. You could talk to him."

"I never mix business with pleasure. And in any case, they wouldn't listen to me. What would I say to them, Forget about the money my chum Darymple owes you? I'd get a royal raspberry in reply, wouldn't I?"

"Should I go see him and explain?"

"Be your age, Robbie."

"I can't pay!"

"Don't get excited, old boy. If you are really in a spot, there might be a way I can help you."

"I'll do anything, Wally," said Darymple solemnly.

"Tonight I'll sit down and draft out a few notes. I'll see if there's not some clever way in which we could fix it. Get you off the hook."

"I'll do anything."

"I'd be sticking my neck out for you, Robbie. You wouldn't go back on it afterward, would you?"

"Of course not." Darymple went over to the window. He was on the third floor, looking down into the street. It was noon and packed with vehicles, animals, and people; people all concerned with nothing but their own affairs. What a madhouse! The traffic had all been brought to a halt by the collapse of some wretched camel. Expediently, the animal had been slaughtered on the spot and was now being butchered. A child driving sheep across the intersection had lost control of them at the scene of the butchery. The smell of blood had sent the frightened animals in all directions. A soldier leaning from the turret of a newly painted armored car was shouting at someone out of sight, and behind him the rest of the traffic had come to a halt.

In the doorway of a seed merchant, a Scots sergeant, complete with tartan kilt, was bargaining with an old man who had six heavily laden donkeys roped together. A bearded Arab carrying a live baby goat was trying to get into the back seat of a tiny dented Fiat. At that moment Darymple would have willingly changed places with almost any of them.

As if reading his friend's mind, Wallingford said, "We're all here to better fight the Hun, Robbie. I'm just short-cutting all the red tape, so we can fight the bad men. Right? Nothing wrong with that, surely?"

Robin Darymple was a shallow personality, but he was not stupid. It was in failing to make this fine distinction that many of his acquaintances went wrong. Darymple knew now that Wallingford was not interested in fighting the Hun. Wallingford was deeply involved in some highly illegal racket that lined his own pockets. Wally had always been a cheat. He'd cheated his way through school exams. Darymple now felt sure that Wallingford had deliberately trapped him into taking the cash loan from his Arab cronies in the souk. Wallingford was no friend, he was a scheming bastard! But no matter how many times Darymple went back over the events of that day, he could not think of any alternative. He'd needed the money that day or Lucia would have thrown him out of the Magnifico.

Darymple had always needed money. Even at his prep school he'd never been able to manage his pocket money so it lasted the whole term. Finally his father had arranged for the matron to give him an allowance each week. Even then he'd ended every term owing money to the other boys.

"Okay, Robbie. Push off now. I've got work to do."

Darymple smiled. He knew Wally was being deliberately offensive. Or, rather, Wally was establishing what would in future be the relationship between them: Darymple would be the little boy who "pushed off" when Wallingford had man's work to do.

When Darymple had gone, Wallingford went to the connecting door and called. "Percy? Come in here a minute."

Percy was wearing clean pressed khaki drill; that was normal for all pen-pushing soldiers in the GHQ that the fighting men called Muddle East.

"He bought it," said Wallingford triumphantly. He sat down behind his desk, leaned back in his swivel chair, swung from side to side, and grinned.

"He did not have much choice," said Percy.

Wallingford looked at his German colleague. Percy was a practical, pragmatic fellow. Given Darymple's situation, Percy would have given in, just as Darymple had given in. Stamping and signing bits of paper so that military stores could be stolen did not seem such a difficult decision. "You don't realize what this means, my dear old Hun. With the right bits of paper, we can go into any depot we like and load up what we want. We can go into the base; we can go into the docks. These pen-pushers rule the world, Percy. And now we'll have a blank check that will get us whatever we fancy of it."

"Yes, I understand," said Percy.

"You're not exactly delirious. You're not singing the Horst Wessel song or heiling the Führer. What is it you chaps do in Krautland when you're happy?"

"We invade somewhere."

"Exactly. And that's what we're doing to this GHQ. So let's have a big smile, my old sour Kraut."

Percy looked at him and didn't smile. Although Percy always tried to hide it, his feelings about Wallingford were not everything a number one should ideally feel about his chief.

Wallingford was an excellent example of the effete English upper class that Percy's history teacher had told him about. "Your friend Captain Darymple—"

"Spit it out, Percy. What about the noble captain?"

"He's not your friend." When Wallingford frowned to indicate his puzzlement, Percy said, "Not a good friend. I think he doesn't like you. Suppose he went and reported us to the authorities."

"Chaps like us, Percy, have to take our friends as they come. We can't be too choosy. I know what you mean, though. The noble captain is a bit miffed because Mahmoud is chasing him for the money he borrowed. Plus interest: I don't think he's completely understood all that yet. He thinks I should do something about it."

"And will you?"

"In good time I might. But he'll have to do his bit to help us first."

Percy nodded.

Wallingford said, "Get on the blower to the police barracks. Tell those buggers we're staging a little show and we have to collect a consignment of Beretta machine pistols that are secreted away for us at Al Jaghbub."

"And who are *we?*"

"The usual: Independent Desert Team—number three. Tell them we'll push the paperwork through in a day or two."

"Can you do that?"

"Babs will draft out something that looks convincing on GHQ notepaper. Then I'll get the noble captain to sign it and bash a few rubber stamp marks across it. There will be no problems."

"Eventually there will."

"Eventually we'll be away from here. Isn't that what you said you wanted?"

Percy looked at Wallingford, trying to see if there was some other meaning in the question. Percy was sure Wallingford would do anything to prevent his going away. "Yes, you are right."

"While you're getting things moving here, I'm going to drift along to Cleo's Club early. I was there yesterday. You should have seen their eyes popping out at the prospect of cameras and binoculars. I've told them we have to be paid in gold, U.S. dollars, or Swiss francs. We've got to start getting rid of all those Gyppo bank notes, just in case we wake up one morning and find your pal Rommel thumping the counter in Shepheard's and asking for a room with bath."

"The sooner we get all those things out of the warehouse, the better. Any time at all, one of your gang will break into the cases and start selling them piece by piece. They all keep talking about the Leica cameras."

Wallingford noted that it was *his* gang rather than *our* gang. Percy was an outsider and determined to remain one. "Yes, and now that it looks like we'll be able to supply the necessary paperwork, I want to get some alternative buyers lined up for the Berettas too. If that fellow Solomon starts arguing about the price for these popguns, it will be nice to have someone else in the bidding." Wallingford put on his sailor's cap, looking in the mirror as he settled it on his head. Then he gave Percy a salute. "Take over, Percy. The office is all yours."

"Be careful," said Percy quietly. He usually called Wallingford "sir" in front of the others, but when there was just the two of them he saw no reason to do so. There were no ranks among outlaws.

That morning Jimmy Ross had gone into his office very early, in order to get some extra work done. The brigadier was coming at eleven o'clock. On such visits he liked to be able to say truthfully that there was no unnecessary backlog of work.

The brigadier was late. This was to be expected. His aide, Lieutenant Spaulding, had gone on a course in Palestine. Without his aide, the brigadier was apt to get his appointments mixed up and arrive late everywhere.

Furthermore, when he did arrive, there was another symptom of Spaulding's absence: the brigadier, always somewhat talkative, was positively garrulous. He threw his cap on a chair in the corner with a careless flourish and greeted his major with a warm smile. His cap slid to the floor.

"This secret stuff you're getting on the Gyppo officers is absolutely first rate," he said. He went to the filing cabinet and pulled open a drawer. Without a glance at its contents, he slid it shut again. It closed with a loud clang. "Have you got someone inside their cabal?" He was in a good mood, and the brigadier's good moods were apt to be manifested in displays of surplus energy. "What do they call themselves, the Free Officers or something?"

Ross decided to sit down. When the brigadier started charging around the office like a demented water buffalo, it was better not to get in his path. "We can't be absolutely sure there are no other organizations or plotters," he said.

"Who is it, a secretary, or have you bribed one of the little buggers?"

"It's quite delicate, sir."

"Mind your own bloody business," he said with measured joviality. "That's what you mean, isn't it?"

"Not at all, sir." Ross was cautious. He knew these euphoric moods could suddenly change, to be replaced by voluble expressions of extreme dissatisfaction. But whatever the consequences, he had no intention of telling the brigadier that the reports were coming from Sayed el-Shazli. That would entail a very real risk of the brigadier's blurting something out when dining with the embassy people. Everyone knew the brigadier was indiscreet at times, and Ross had decided that Marker was right about the British embassy: it was a nest of lazy, gossiping old women.

"To get really good information we have to offer something

in return, sir. I wonder if I can ask you about that?" Ross was nervous, and it showed.

The brigadier sat down. He hadn't encountered his major's conspiratorial tone before. "Shoot."

"There is a suspect with a murder charge hanging over him. If I could offer him a full pardon—"

"No, no, no," said the brigadier.

"Or even a deal."

"I said no," said the brigadier with unmistakable finality. "Forget deals. I know that sort of thing happens in civvy street. But the army's first task is to maintain discipline. Even solving crime is not more important than that."

Ross was crushed by disappointment. For several days he'd cherished the idea that he might one day get a pardon for the murder with which he was charged. He had waited to get the brigadier in a good mood, but all to no avail. "I thought that perhaps in very exceptional circumstances—"

"No, Cutler. No." He smiled mirthlessly and tried to reestablish the former rapport. "Did I ever tell you about the time when my uncle was acting chief constable? I went with him on his inspection tours. I know all about coppers, Cutler. And I also know the way they jealously guard their sources of information."

Ross gave up on his hopes of a pardon. "GHQ Middle East have taken over responsibility for the Beretta guns that were hidden at Al Jaghbub. Did you see my message, sir?"

The brigadier unbuttoned his breast pocket, brought out the message sheet he'd received, and read it again. "It was just a phone call, was it? We'll have to get this in writing, Cutler. I don't rely on phone calls. Any Tom, Dick, or Harry can dial a phone and say: I'm speaking from Ten Downing Street; hand my messenger a five-pound note."

"That's true, sir."

"Yes, I know it's true, major. What about it? What did you do to confirm its origin?"

"I didn't take the call personally, sir. My sergeant spoke with them."

"Sergeant Ponsonby?" The brigadier nodded approval. He shared years of prewar regular army service with Ponsonby. They'd encountered each other in British army outposts in Palestine and Iraq and on garrison duties in peacetime Cairo. Ponsonby and the brigadier shared an arcane camaraderie that a wartime soldier would never understand. Ponsonby and the brigadier were members of the real "regular" army. "And what happened?" There was always a story behind anything Ponsonby did. The brigadier got ready to enjoy it.

"He told GHQ we couldn't act on telephoned instructions. He said something very much along the line you have just taken: about being in Ten Downing Street and so on."

"Um," said the brigadier. He had perhaps overworked that illustration about telephoned instructions.

"Ponsonby expressed his skepticism very clearly. He told the secretary that she might well be a spy for all he knew. But the lady at the other end recognized Ponsonby's Yorkshire accent. It was Mrs. Smythson, Colonel Smythson's wife. She's working in GHQ."

"To avoid the evacuation order?"

"I imagine so."

The brigadier screwed up his face for a moment before laughing heartily. "That old bitch! I'll bet she gave Ponsonby a flea in his ear."

"She did indeed, sir."

"He told Colonel Smythson's wife she was a spy!" As the full import of this struck the brigadier, he slapped his knee briefly and laughed again. "You've made my day, Cutler. Good old Ponsonby. I knew he'd meet his match one day. I'd love to have heard it."

"She was very upset."

"Yes, that's a good one."

The brigadier got to his feet and went to the filing cabinet.

This time he didn't open it. He leaned an arm on it while he gazed across the square to the railway station. The square and gardens in front of the railway station—Midan al Mahatta—was one of the most frantically lively places in a frantically lively city. That's why the military police had chosen to be so close to it in the first place. Not all the people in the midan were travelers. There were some men in khaki and some military policemen, but mostly the crowd consisted of natives: porters and men selling beads and souvenirs and brightly colored drinks, snake charmers, conjurors, jugglers, pickpockets, whores, and thieves. It was a distracting sight, and the brigadier found it difficult to take his eyes away from it.

"What a place it is! It never stops, does it. I don't know how you ever get any work done, Cutler."

"It's not easy, sir," said Ross feelingly.

"Ever look at that statue?" said the brigadier, waving vaguely in the direction of the station.

"Statue? I don't believe I have, sir."

"Egypt awakens. Kitchener was going to haul the statue of Rameses Second all the way from Memphis, but someone stopped him. Now instead we've got a statue of Egypt awakening." The brigadier screwed up his eyes as he looked at it in the distance. "A woman getting up from a chair. Do we want her to awaken? That's what I ask myself, Cutler. And what will she do when she's awake? Boot us out. That's what she'll do, Cutler, she'll boot us all out."

Ross decided he'd rather not comment one way or the other upon the woman in the statue. He nodded.

In one of his inexplicable leaps of thought, the brigadier said, "Do you have any daughters, Cutler?" He turned to face into the room again.

"No, sir. I'm not married." He'd discovered that Major Albert Cutler was not married from a close reading of his diary.

"Girls are a worry, I can tell you. I've come to a point where I almost dread to open the letters from home. My eighteen-year-old doesn't want to go on studying; she wants to join the army—the ATS. I ask you, Cutler. What the hell does she think she's playing at?"

"She probably wants to help win the war," said Ross, without thinking too much about his answer.

"That's exactly what she said in her letter." The brigadier looked at him, amazed at his prescience. "Stupid girl. What am I supposed to say in reply? If I tell her to stay with her studies, I'm not patriotic; if I tell her to join the army, she gives up all she's worked for."

"It's very difficult, sir."

"She's supposed to be studying law. It makes me livid. God knows who's been filling her head with all this patriotic balderdash."

Ross gave a sympathetic sort of grunt.

"It's no place for a decent girl," said the brigadier sullenly. Then he looked up and, in another sudden change of course, said, "What are you doing about the Jews, Cutler?"

"About the Jews, sir?"

"Spaulding has gone to Tel Aviv to be briefed on the activities of the Jewish nationalists in Palestine: the Haganah, the Stern gang, and so on. The word was that they'd put all this Jewish homeland stuff on the shelf until after we'd beaten the Hun. But not all Jews are prepared to play by the same rules, it seems."

"The Jewish population here in Cairo is small and law-abiding," said Ross.

"Well, wouldn't anyone be? They're outnumbered ten thousand to one by the Arabs. Of course they're law-abiding. But what about secret activity?"

The brigadier could be exasperating at times. "They are successfully keeping that secret," said Ross.

The brigadier looked at him and for a moment seemed as if he would react angrily. But instead he tugged at his belt and said, "Jesus was a Jew. You know that, don't you?"

"Yes, sir."

"And Jesus clearly stated that 'not one tittle' of the laws of Moses, the Torah, should be changed. Have you ever given that a thought, Cutler?"

"Not for a long time, sir."

"Saint Paul was a Jew too. He was a Pharisee: that's a select school of Judaism. Paul was a disciple of Rabbi Gamaliel, an important Jewish leader. Apparently it was this fellow Paul who created the whole Christian business: the whole rigmarole." The brigadier stopped suddenly. "Not religious, are you, Cutler?"

"Not excessively, sir."

"Good. Don't want to step on your toes. Yes, Saint Paul ignored what Jesus had said about not changing the Torah. Paul put together a religion that would suit as many people as possible. He incorporated into Christianity every old sect and religion, every pagan myth and legend he came across. He said he'd make it all things to all men—those were his very words."

"I didn't realize you were so interested in religion, sir." In their previous encounters, the brigadier had not shown such passion.

"It wasn't until Spaulding briefed me on all this that I got the picture."

"Lieutenant Spaulding. I see." That explained it.

"You don't like him, I know, but he's a brainy fellow, Cutler. The modern army needs all the brains it can muster. I've never been one of these chaps who tell soldiers they are not permitted to think."

"No, sir." He thought the brigadier's fervor had run its course, but after a moment for reflection he started again.

"Jesus had always preached God the Father. It was Paul who started to put all this emphasis on Jesus Christ. In effect, he laid Christianity open to the charge of having several gods, like the Hindus and so on. That's why the Muslims look down on us."

"I didn't know they did," said Ross. Out of the corner of his eye he saw the door open a crack and then close again; surely that was Captain Marker making his escape to the canteen.

"Spaulding says they do," said the brigadier, evidently regarding that as the decisive word on the matter. "Spaulding told me the ancient Roman occupying army found the Jews to be the only ones strongly resisting their rule. The Christians didn't give much trouble, and if they did they were thrown to the lions, right?"

"I believe so, sir."

"When Rome became Christian, the Jews were isolated as the only opponents of the rule of Rome. *Roma locuta est*—Rome has spoken—meant no opposition would be tolerated. That was how anti-Semitism began. Did you do Latin at school, Cutler?"

"French and German, sir."

"*Roma locuta est:* Rome has spoken."

"Yes, sir."

"I know you don't like him, Cutler, I can tell that when I see you together, but you could learn a lot from Spaulding."

"This matter of the Jews, sir. Was there something specific?"

"So you see what I'm getting at? I thought you would." The brigadier found the view irresistible and went back to the window and stared out.

"I'm not sure I do, sir," said Ross, when he realized the brigadier was going to leave it at that.

The brigadier turned his head toward him. "Occupying army, Cutler. We are the occupying army, aren't we?" He smiled knowingly.

"But there are not many Jews in Cairo, sir."

The brigadier was staring out the window again, totally absorbed by the activity around the railway station. When he spoke it was as if his thoughts arose from the sight of the crowds. "It makes you wonder if the Jews weren't right, Cutler. It makes you wonder what Paul was up to, worshiping Jesus Christ, cobbling together all this pagan stuff and so on. Christmas is a pagan feast; you know that, I'm sure."

"Did Spaulding say that?"

"Everyone knows that, Cutler. Candles, robins, and fir trees and all that heathen nonsense. And the resurrection is pagan too: the coming of spring after the death of the soil in winter. Easter is an old pagan feast too."

"It's hard to see that the Jews offer any threat to the army here in Egypt, sir."

The brigadier came back to his desk, tapped a finger on it, and said sadly, "We can't afford to be complacent, Cutler."

"No, of course not, sir."

"When Spaulding gets back from Tel Aviv he'll have all the latest gen. I'm going to push through a promotion for him and put him in charge of a new department that will be monitoring this dimension. Religious Subversives, I'm going to call it."

Ross suddenly saw a warning signal. It was as if the brigadier was flashing on and off and emitting an intermittent shriek. The prospect of Spaulding's being promoted was bad. He'd come here, be given a department, and come sniffing and snooping in everything. That was danger. "You'd miss him, sir. Spaulding is a systematic organizer and awfully reliable."

"Um," said the brigadier. He looked up quizzically. "Well, I haven't made my mind up yet."

"I understand, sir."

"I think I'll cut my next appointment, it's nearly lunch-time." He looked at his wristwatch and then shook his fist as if wondering if it had stopped. "I'm lunching with a general who is going back to London. My guess is he'll get some good number in the War Office. I want to make sure he knows what we need over here. Sometimes you can get more done over lunch than by the regular channels."

"Yes, sir."

"Where did you put my hat?"

Ross picked it up from where the brigadier's careless disposal of it had left it on the floor and dusted it off before handing it over.

"What's it doing on the floor?" said the brigadier. He looked at his hat suspiciously and then put it on as if it might explode.

"I can't imagine, sir."

"Germs get everywhere, Cutler. That's how these diseases spread. You can't be too careful in a place like this."

"No, sir."

"Well, press on with this business and keep it all to yourself for the time being. Understood?"

"Of course, sir."

He escorted the brigadier through the door onto the open balcony that connected all the offices. The brigadier stopped and looked down at the parade ground. A platoon of impeccably turned-out military policemen were being inspected by their officer.

"You never saw anything like that in Glasgow, did you, Cutler?" said the brigadier proudly.

"No, sir, indeed I didn't," said Ross.

When the brigadier went downstairs, Ross returned to his office window to watch the brigadier get into his car and drive away. He wanted to be quite sure he'd departed.

"Ponsonby!" he called very loudly as the car pulled away in the busy traffic that swirled around the Midan Bab-el-Hadid.

"Yes, sir. A cup of tea coming up, sir," said Ponsonby, putting his head round the door.

"Where's Marker?" he yelled as Ponsonby withdrew.

"Captain Marker, sir?" said Ponsonby, as he entered bearing a large steaming mug of tea.

"How many Markers have we got in this office?" said Ross, venting his wrath upon the unfortunate Ponsonby.

Captain Marker came in. He had heard the commotion from where he was: along the balcony in the radio room, avoiding the brigadier and talking on the phone to one of his many "contacts."

"Hell, Lionel. Must you always be missing when the old man pays us a visit? I have to invent reasons why you're not here."

"Sorry, major."

Ponsonby came in with a second large mug of sweet tea, placed it in front of Marker, and withdrew without a word.

"You missed a tirade of monumental proportions."

"A tirade?" Marker's legal training had left him with the infuriating habit of taking such words at face value.

"That's not the right word. He's been pacing around the office analyzing just where Saint Paul went wrong in inventing Christianity."

Marker sipped tea. From the parade ground came the staccato cries of a drill sergeant. Marker went to the door and pulled it closed, but this didn't much diminish the sounds of the men marching up and down.

"He's become obsessed with the Jews. He seems to want us to find out what they are doing. No, worse than that." Ross corrected himself as he remembered more far-reaching aspects of the brigadier's plans. "He's sent Spaulding to some conference in Tel Aviv, and that wretch is going to come back and stamp his heels all over us."

"The Jews?"

"Someone has obviously put a bee into his bonnet. Spaulding, I suppose. The brigadier said something about getting him a promotion and creating a department to deal with 'religious subversives.' "

"I think I know what's happened, major."

"What?"

"I was just on the phone to Colonel Stevens, the first viol—"

"The first who?"

"The quintet, major. We're rehearsing the Mozart K.516 for next month. Stevens says the second violin has been posted to Khartoum. It's dreadful. Stevens thinks we'll never be able to replace him, and he's probably right." Marker stopped as he realized his major had very limited interest in the problems of GHQ's amateur string players. He collected his thoughts. "Yes. Stevens is on the political staff of the C in C. They're all in a flap

about an article that was just published in a Washington newspaper. It was written by that American fellow who was sniffing
around at Al Jaghbub, Harry Wechsler; he's a big name in America, they say. He goes into a lot of detail about the Haganah: the
secret Jewish defense organization in Palestine. The article says
the British army used units of their Palmah, the Jewish military
arm, for intelligence and sabotage operations behind the lines in
Lebanon and Syria as far back as 1940, long before we fought the
Vichy French there."

"Is that true?" Ross sipped his tea. He was really getting to
like Ponsonby's strong brews with condensed milk. He wondered
how many other awful things he was getting used to.

"Probably. They'd be able to supply people who can pass
themselves off as natives. Where would we get people like that,
if not from the Palestine Jews?"

"Is that what got GHQ excited?"

"No. The article went on to say that the Haganah are now
asking for guns and other military equipment in return for all the
help they provided. The writer of the article said the British were
reneging on their promise. They were denying the Jews a chance
to defend themselves against the Arabs. So the Jews had sent
men into Egypt to get German and Italian armaments that were
to be found abandoned on the old desert battlefields."

Marker had expected his major to react to this complication
in some demonstrative way—to groan or swear—but he sat
there and sipped tea and for a long time said nothing.

When he did speak, he spoke quietly and soberly. "I'm going
to start a religious subversion desk, and you will take charge of
it, Marker."

"Yes, sir," said Marker, as he thought about what such a job
would entail.

"I'm supposed to be worrying about the general leakage of
high-grade intelligence: 'Rommel's spy,' as I hear it called everywhere. I'm determined not to let up on it."

"Set up a department before Spaulding gets back? Is that wise, sir? If the brigadier—"

"It will be enough to spike Spaulding's guns. Even if the brigadier takes complete leave of his senses and gets Spaulding a captaincy, you'll have unassailable seniority." He sipped more tea. "And I'll ask the brigadier to put you in for a promotion too. Get some files and reference material together. If they want a Jewish conspiracy, let's have a few big fat files to prove we have been thinking about it before saying there isn't one."

"It's just a newspaper story, sir. I'm sure there's nothing in it."

"How did Wechsler get this story through the censor?" said Ross.

"GHQ say the censor's office swear it was never submitted. He must have found some way of getting it out without using the telegraph service. It's what newspapers call a think piece; it wouldn't matter if it was delayed a few days. It had Wechsler's name on it but no dateline. His editor will just say it was written before Wechsler arrived in Egypt. In any case, I can't imagine even Winston Churchill would be reckless enough to get into a row with a U.S. newspaper."

"You'd better get a look at this newspaper article and then see if you can find Wechsler. I should have given him a grilling when we found him poking around at Siwa the other day."

"Yes, sir."

"Don't make any contact with Jewish religious leaders or anyone of that sort. If you must talk to Wechsler, watch your step. I've seen him in action; he gets somewhat emotional. If there are any Haganah people in this town, they are probably keeping well away from him."

"I'll be very circumspect, major." Marker got up to go.

Ross said, "Anything on that naval bod?"

"Is Wallingford his real name?"

"Sure to be. That other little tick Darymple knew him at school."

"Then we've drawn a blank. No lieutenant commander of that name, they say. That's the trouble with having navy records at Alex. You have to rely on someone else to do the search."

"At Alex, of course. Perhaps that's why he likes to wear a navy outfit."

"There is that possibility, sir."

As Marker reached the door, Ross said, "I thought you told me you didn't play German music."

"Wagner. I said I wouldn't play Wagner." Marker recognized this as another of Ross's attempts to trap him into admitting he was a hypocrite. Although the two men had become friendly, Ross felt his impersonation would be imperiled unless he showed that measure of disdain which all policemen have for lawyers.

"What's Mozart got that Wagner hasn't got? They're both Germans, aren't they?"

Marker wet his lips. "It's a musical decision, major. For a violinist, Wagner is not important. He didn't write any great works for violin: no violin concertos, no chamber music, nothing I would want to perform."

"I'd thought your Wagner embargo was a political decision," said Ross with a grin.

"Wagner was a giant of twentieth-century music. But his music was a slave to the drama of the opera stage. He said so himself."

"I'm glad you cleared that up for me, Captain Marker. I hope you soon find another violin player."

"Thank you, sir. By the way, Bert." He paused. "Perhaps I'd better remind you that I am Jewish." He stood there in case this revelation caused a change of plan.

"Exactly," said Ross. "That's our trump card, isn't it? That wretch Spaulding can't top it."

Marker nodded and opened the door. The drill sergeant's voice pierced the air. Marker said, "You're right. Even Spaulding is likely to draw the line at getting himself circumcised."

$\equiv 18 \equiv$

"Alice says you have been thinking of going to Palestine," said Captain Lionel Marker.

Peggy West didn't answer immediately. She looked at Alice and then back to Marker, wondering just how much Alice had told him. Then she took a black olive, shiny with oil, and bit pieces from it until only the pit remained. Delicately she put it on the edge of her plate and wiped her fingers. "I have thought about it from time to time," she admitted.

Marker smiled at her. He understood her caution; he was a policeman. "There's no law to prevent a British subject from going to Palestine, Peggy."

"No? You'd think there was, if you were a female civilian trying to arrange it."

"We all suffer from the paper-shuffling brigade," said Marker. Marker had chosen this little Arab restaurant, hoping she'd like it. It was in a shadowy alley on the edge of the Muski district. The food and the decor were authentically Arab. Yet it was so near the places that tourists liked to go that surely no European would feel out of place. He'd ordered the sort of simple meal that almost everyone in Egypt ate, if they could afford it: *tamia*—chick-peas ground into a garlicky paste, flattened, and fried—with red kidney beans, black olives, *hummus,* and raw onions. Best of all there was *aish balady*—peasant's bread—

large flat loaves, charred in places and swollen with hot air, that came straight from the primitive oven at the back of the dining room.

"Yes, my husband is in Jerusalem. At least, I think he's still there. He's been away for over two years."

"Is he a British subject?" Marker tore a piece from the loaf and chewed it. He had resolved to reduce his weight, but tomorrow would be soon enough.

"Canadian father and Italian mother," said Peggy. "He was born in Palestine."

"I mean, does he hold a British passport?"

"Yes, he does now."

"He acquired it after marriage to you?"

"Yes," said Peggy grimly. Put like that, it always sounded as if Karl had married her to get a British passport. Especially when someone used a word such as "acquired." Such words put her on her guard. And yet Marker seemed a warm and friendly man. Perhaps she was being too defensive. Women on their own got like that; Karl said so. She took another olive and chewed it carefully.

"So you'd be giving up your job at the hospital?" Marker asked. He could see that neither of the women were enjoying the food he'd ordered. He waved to a passing waiter and ordered lamb kebabs. That was more ordinary and would be more to their taste.

"I suppose so. I keep changing my mind. I worry about getting a job when I get to Jerusalem. People say it's not so easy getting work there."

"Why?"

"In Egypt there is plenty of work for nursing sisters who specialize in surgery." She said it brutally. In her handbag she had a postcard from Jeannie MacGregor, who was now serving with one of the Advanced Surgical Centers near the front line. *Lots of hard work here, Peggy,* she'd written. *This is real surgery—you can save a leg or an arm—sometimes save a life. I've never worked so hard but I love every minute.* It made Peggy feel guilty at even talking about leaving her job.

Marker looked at her. "Yes, that's regrettably true." The tough interrogative attitude he'd adopted toward her when searching Solomon's boat, and the way he'd taken her back to the Magnifico to get her passport, now militated against him.

"What does your husband say? About your living there, I mean."

"Karl never was a letter writer."

"He's not expecting you?"

"If I wait for Karl to suggest it, I will never go. I don't know where he is. He was in Iraq, but now he's gone to Palestine. I have to find him. It's my marriage, captain—Lionel, I mean. It's important to me."

"Yes. Forget the captain: Lionel. In civvy street I was a solicitor. One day I'll be a solicitor again. And that's why I urge you to get advice before doing anything so drastic as giving up your job and your room at the hotel. What does your friend Solomon Marx say?"

"Oh, yes," said Peggy. "Of course; you know Solomon, don't you?"

"I've met him once or twice. We have to check all the boats. What does he say about your husband?"

"He'll say don't go, I know he will," said Peggy.

"Why are you so sure about that?"

Peggy realized that she was on the edge of discussing Solomon and the way he brought money for her. "I don't know Solomon well enough to discuss it with him."

Marker offered the women the plate of *hummus:* they did it so well here. But neither wanted any. "I'm sorry, I thought you'd like Arab food," said Marker.

"I do," said Alice.

Peggy smiled. She hated Arab food. It was all right for Marker, who probably got unlimited varieties of English cooking in his officer's mess. For people like Peggy, variations on this sort of food were a necessary part of eking out the budget. Over the years, she'd come to associate it with her lack of money. What wouldn't she give right now for a slice of cold salmon with English garden tomatoes and a salad made from one of those soft green lettuces her parents used to grow! Just thinking about her parents made her sad. She missed them more and more as she grew older. And as she grew older she understood more about them, and the things they'd said to her.

The kebabs came. They looked wonderful: charred and sizzling, straight from the charcoal fire. The waiter took a fork and removed the cooked lamb pieces from the skewers, releasing the juices of the meat and the smell of scorched cumin seeds.

"Eat up," said Marker.

Peggy was hungry, and the grilled lamb was excellent. She tore off a piece of bread and used it to pick up a piece of meat and eat it in the Arab way. "How clever of you to find this curious little place."

Marker nodded. The tiny room, with its smells of bread baking and charred meat, was filled with the smoke of the open grill. Fierce sunlight came in at a steep angle to make swirling bars of pearly light. The chairs and tables were of all shapes and sizes, and the plates and dishes were old and worn.

Marker thought about it as he spread *hummus* on his bread. "Look here, Peggy. There is another way of doing this."

"How?"

"The department for which I work has a regular courier service that leaves here on a Tuesday morning. A lorry, or sometimes a car. It goes to Tel Aviv and up to Haifa, usually. Sometimes right on to Beirut, according to what has to be delivered. I dare say we could square it with the driver to take you to Jerusalem."

"But—"

"A bottle of whisky for the driver would do it. You could stay a week and return with the following courier."

Peggy looked at him suspiciously. She knew Marker was

some sort of military policeman, or spy, or something mysterious in the army. Was he the sort of man who would offer such a spontaneous act of friendship without ulterior motive? "I'd still need papers to cross the border," she said.

"No. The paper the courier carries gives him and the vehicle the right to go through the frontier without inspection. If you are on the manifest, you go through too. You'll just have to show your passport to prove your identity."

Peggy brightened. "The Hoch would give me a week off, wouldn't he, Alice?"

It was a rhetorical question. Peggy knew the senior surgeon better than anyone: she worked with him every day. She was just looking for reassurance. "Of course he would," said Alice. "And I could rejig the schedule to give you an extra day or two if you needed it."

"You're sweet," Peggy said softly and automatically, as her mind examined all the implications. Then she turned to face Marker. "You've made me feel a fool, captain—Lionel."

"How have I done that?"

"I'm sitting here talking to you as if I had no will of my own. You're asking me what my husband thinks, you're asking me what Solomon thinks. It's my life, isn't it?"

"Yes, of course it is."

"I want to go. If my marriage is finished, it's better that I know it now."

Marker was pleased to hear that her marriage was at the heart of it. He glanced across at Alice, but she didn't meet his eyes. She was watching her friend. He tried to think of an appropriate response to Peggy's cri de coeur but decided to occupy himself with the food for a moment or two.

"Have you ever been to Jerusalem, Peggy?" Alice asked her.

"No. Never."

"It's unique. My father took us all one year. There is so much to see. Daddy said every Christian should make a pilgrimage there at least once."

"My father was a Jew," said Peggy.

"Jerusalem has even more significance for Jews," said Marker hurriedly.

"Yes, it does," said Peggy.

Alice was grateful to Marker for saving her from what she felt had been a foolish gaffe.

"I'm not religious," said Peggy. "My mother sent me to the local Catholic school. It was nearby: only at the end of the road. The girl next door went there, and she got a scholarship to Oxford. My father had doubts, but he said going to school with Catholics would be better than being with pagans in a Protestant school."

She paused to remember it. Alice shot a glance at Marker, but he was sprinkling salt on his bread.

"My first day was a nightmare. I'd never seen a life-size crucifix before: the tormented Christ and his gaping wounds, shiny red and dribbling blood. I was terrified; I couldn't take my eyes off it. Then the other girls said they had to eat the body of Christ and I would have to do the same. I ran all the way home crying." Peggy smiled as she remembered it, but the smile was a bleak one. "Now, for me, all religion is just a lot of mumbo-jumbo. Just a ritualized way of dumping the hard work onto women, while the men spend all day praying."

Marker hadn't expected such a confession. And now he was pleased at a chance to chuckle at her joke.

Alice said, "All religions are dedicated to male supremacy, Peggy. The men spend their time thinking about complex theological problems, while the women sweep the floor for them, cook their food, and have their babies."

"Are you two ribbing me?" said Marker.

"Of course not," said Alice. Peggy grinned at her.

There was a change of mood, thought Marker. Whatever might have caused it, Peggy had become more relaxed with him. He could see it in the way she started eating her lamb kebabs.

"Um, this tastes good," said Peggy. "Yes, I would appreciate it if you could arrange for me to go to Jerusalem. I'll arrange time off and then get back to you."

"Good," said Marker.

"I'll tell the Hoch. I dare say the hospital can manage without me for a week or two. Especially now, with Rommel brought to a standstill in the desert. Thank you. Thank you very much."

"I'll arrange it," said Marker. "Thank Alice. It was her idea to get us together."

When Captain Marker got back to his office, Ponsonby was as near to being excited as he ever became. "Bull's-eye, Captain Marker!" He said it again. "How did you guess?"

"Start at the beginning, Ponsonby. I've left my crystal ball in my other suit."

Ponsonby gave a brief smile to acknowledge the little joke. "You asked the Field Security office in Tel Aviv if they had any records on a Karl West."

"That was rather a long time ago."

"They don't hurry themselves," said Ponsonby. "You know what Records are like." Seeing an almost-missed opportunity, he added, "I sent them reminders from time to time, of course. Lots of them, and phone calls too."

"Of course."

Ponsonby riffed through the battered file that had arrived from Palestine the night before. "So you've seen the file already?"

"I was here last night when it arrived."

"And you were right, sir. He's one of these revolutionary people. Karl West, or Wieland, or Weiss: he's used a lot of names. He's wanted for all kinds of crimes. He's been working for the Haganah for ages." He flicked through the papers expertly. "Twice he's been arrested, and each time he's escaped. There's a warrant outstanding. If you know where he is, we can pick him up."

"No, I don't know where he is. I'm not even sure I know where he's going to be."

"He was in Baghdad during the Rashid Ali rumpus. Tel Aviv think he was there to contact the Germans."

Marker could not resist a smug smile. It was not often that a routine inquiry like the one he'd lodged after searching the Solomon boat came up with such a startling result. "We'd better put this man Solomon under twenty-four-hour surveillance. Tell that police inspector—Khalil—to find a couple of bright lads for me. He knows what we want. Make sure he understands: twenty-four hours. Solomon isn't the type who goes to bed when it gets dark."

"I'll get right on it, sir."

"Can you drive, Ponsonby?"

"No, sir. Might I ask why?"

"We have a regular courier service leaving every Tuesday. It takes secret papers to Haifa. Next week, when it makes a side trip to Jerusalem, a civilian passenger will go along."

"A courier service? Do we? I've never heard of it, sir."

"Of course you haven't. I've just decided to start it. I'll need a reliable man who can drive. . . . By the way, do we have anyone reliable in Jerusalem?"

"Of course. We have—"

"Let me rephrase that. I want someone who looks like a native and can sit in the dirt in the street and watch what's happening without attracting attention. Someone who can wear a dirty galabiya and speak all the local languages."

"What are the local languages?"

Marker leaned forward and whispered, "Arabic, Yiddish, Hebrew, and German."

"I'll find someone," said Ponsonby.

"And Russian too. To watch a woman. I wonder if we could find a female agent to do that."

"To watch what woman?"

"His wife. She'll lead us to him, Ponsonby. You mark my

words. She'll track him down wherever he might be hidden."

"Will she, sir?"

"That's the one thing I discovered in my law practice," said Marker reflectively. "A woman doesn't need any detectives to help her find her husband."

"Yes, sir. Well, I'll find someone to watch her, sir."

At that moment Jimmy Ross arrived. His face was tense and he was biting his lips, as he did sometimes when anxious.

"Are you all right, major?" Marker asked. Ponsonby gathered up his papers, opened the filing cabinet, and began putting them away very slowly, as he did when he wanted to eavesdrop.

"I've just come from Gray Pillars. The brigadier and the provost marshal were there."

Marker said nothing. His major was apt to pause between sentences, and he was not pleased if anyone butted in.

"That MP detachment guarding those guns at the Siwa Oasis got into a shooting match. Arabs arrived brandishing bits of paper from GHQ. They wanted to collect those damned Berettas."

"But GHQ rescinded that order," Marker said. "Mrs. Smythson—Colonel Smythson's wife—phoned me. She was in a bit of a state about it. It wasn't properly authorized or something."

They both looked at Ponsonby, who was continuing to file his papers as if he'd not heard the conversation. "What do you know about that, Sergeant Ponsonby?" said Ross.

"I did make a few inquiries about it," admitted Ponsonby. "But it's not our pigeon." Ross looked at Marker, who gave an almost imperceptible grin. Mrs. Smythson had made the fatal mistake of reprimanding Sergeant Ponsonby, a founding member of that secret society of senior NCOs who held Cairo's military activities in an iron grip. So Ponsonby had shifted responsibility elsewhere; he seemed to have a sixth sense about trouble.

Ross said, "The Arabs went out there to get the guns and wouldn't take no for an answer. When their documents weren't accepted, they tried to help themselves to what they came for."

"And?" said Marker.

Ross hung his cap on the peg. "Those boys have been out there too long. They were trigger-happy, I suspect."

"Is that all we know?"

"GHQ only just heard about it," said Ross. "It's nasty. Six dead and eight injured. A couple of our people wounded."

"Gyppos or desert Arabs?"

"Gyppos," said Ross. "Egyptians, all of them."

"And there was no hint of this from your Egyptian army informant?" persisted Marker.

"No, it's something of a mystery."

"How did the brigadier take it?" said Marker.

"He was very decent. He admitted that the stakeout was all his idea, so for the time being there's no heat on us. But Spaulding has persuaded him to keep that MP detachment out there."

Ponsonby closed the filing cabinet drawer. "Don't you worry, sir. Someone will turn up, all right. Guns have a fatal fascination for quirky people, I've noticed that."

"Yes," said Marker. "They call those quirky people soldiers."

"That's a very good joke, sir," said Ponsonby solemnly. "Now, what about a nice hot cup of tea?"

"I hate your bloody tea, Sergeant Ponsonby. You put all that filthy condensed milk in it."

"Sergeant major's tea, that is, sir. The British army was weaned on tea like that. The brigadier always asks for one of my specials when he comes here."

"But he doesn't drink it," said Marker. "Have you ever noticed that? He leaves it on my desk, and I throw it down the sink."

"The major keeps him too busy chatting, sir."

"But I'll have one just the same."

"Yes, sir. I've got it all ready for you. And for you too, major."

Ross looked at Marker. Marker sighed. No one ever got the best of Sergeant Ponsonby.

≡19≡

"It will soon be time to move on," Solomon told his partner, Yigal. He had chosen to impart this news as a casual aside, while driving across Cairo for an evening meeting with old Mahmoud.

"Why?" said Yigal. He wondered whether the decision had come out of restlessness, necessity, or as orders from Tel Aviv.

"The reason does not concern you."

Solomon had become a different man over the six months that Yigal Arad had been with him in Cairo. Despite all his energy and inventiveness, despite the stories he liked to make up and embroider about his father and the big house in Cairo, Solomon's moods of ever-deepening despair were becoming more and more evident.

Despite Solomon's obsessive secretiveness, Yigal was coming to know him very well. It was impossible to live in such close proximity, and share the secret work they did, without learning a great deal about each other. He knew Solomon's moods and sudden unexpected enthusiasms. He had even learned to recognize the terrible fits of anger that Solomon could hide from most other people. Today Solomon's wrath was evident in the way he was driving the car. Sometimes he could be a careful driver, who double-clutched and treated the gears with care bordering on reverence. This evening he was spiteful and careless in shifting. Spiteful and careless, too, in the way he treated the pedestrians, honking and driving straight at them to make them run.

Something had deeply upset Solomon today. Yigal did not know exactly what, but a messenger had arrived in the early afternoon. It was a young Arab speaking with the harsh accent of the Hatay, a small coastal region of Syria. Yigal guessed it was a message from Tel Aviv. It was a spoken message, and that was further confirmation, for the men in Tel Aviv did not commit important commands to writing. Crossing the border, and the roadside checks that the British military police inflicted on all road users, made carrying any sort of contraband too risky.

But Yigal had no evidence to support the idea that a move was anything but Solomon's whim. Among his closer friends and acquaintances, Solomon was famous for his intuition. Yigal wondered if this was another example of that nervous art.

"The houseboats have become too damned conspicuous," Solomon said. "Drunken parties and black-market people. There are always cops hanging around. We'll hold on to the boat for the time being—at least until the end of the month—but we must have somewhere else . . . just in case."

"Somewhere in the city?" said Yigal.

He knew Solomon's highly regarded intuition was often based on intelligence he had picked up in his normal course of duties. Yigal did much of the legwork, moving across the city to pick up the reports and pay the men who kept Solomon and, through him, Tel Aviv well informed about what Cairo was thinking and doing. But Yigal did not get to read the reports. Yigal was number two. Solomon had got to his present position by keeping his subordinates in their place. And he'd stayed alive so long by confiding only as much as he thought he must. But Yigal had noted the words: just in case.

"In case of what?"

"Rent somewhere," said Solomon. "You know the sort of place we need. Two or three rooms over a shop. Exit back and front. Doors not too easy to kick down. You know."

"What are you expecting?"

"I don't know. Nothing."

"It's that bastard Wallingford, isn't it? He knows too much about us."

"He's a deserter. He won't spill anything," said Solomon. "He won't help the English."

"He *is* English. Rich English. I know them. Deserter or not, if he has to choose which way to jump he will jump the way his school friends jump."

"I've done business with him before," said Solomon. He wanted to allay Yigal's fears. Yigal detested Wallingford. Yigal had a utopian dream that the Jewish homeland could be built without dealing with any kind of crooks, deserters, or anti-Semites.

"I know you have."

"You've got to bend with the wind, Yigal. Rommel is preparing his big offensive. He'll probably start before the hot weather comes. This time he will get all the way to Cairo."

"You think so?"

"What is there to stop him? You get around more than I do. You've been out into the desert. The soldiers are demoralized, the officers are unreliable, and the British equipment is not good enough to stop the Germans. You said that. I'm not making it up; you said it."

"You seriously think the Germans could do it?"

"Take Cairo? Sure."

"And British power collapse right through the Middle East?"

"Right."

Yigal thought about the consequences. "They'd lose their oil. They lose their routes to India, Burma, Singapore, and Australia. They'd lose their naval presence in the Mediterranean. If the Germans followed it up with an invasion of England, it would mean the end of the war."

"Now you're getting the idea," said Solomon.

"I haven't seen you as low as this before, Solly. Where

would our people go? How would they survive?"

"Don't ask me, Yigal."

"Does Tel Aviv think Rommel will take Cairo?"

"What do they know? They rely on *my* reports to *them.*"

Yigal said nothing. Tel Aviv had a thousand other sources of intelligence, but Yigal had no wish to be needlessly provocative.

To break the silence, Solomon conceded a fraction. "I'm not in the business of making prophecies; in battle there is always an element of luck. But the British will need a hell of a lot of luck to beat Rommel once he starts moving."

"And that's when we leave?"

Solomon scowled. "No, my friend Yigal, that's when our work really begins. I am setting up a line of contact with Tel Aviv that we'll still be able to use when the Germans are here. Additionally, they are sending a powerful radio transmitter. The place you must find is where we will be living when the Germans arrive. We will have new identities, new papers, new everything. Oh, yes, and get a top floor. We can get out onto the roof if we have to run, and it will be needed for the radio antenna too."

"Now I understand, Solly." Every time Yigal was ready to dismiss his superior as an overrated has-been, something came along to prove that he had lost none of his skill. "We'll disappear."

"No, we won't exactly disappear. Men who disappear excite too much attention. Search parties and tracker dogs are sent out for men who disappear. Our departure for Palestine will be witnessed and documented. Everyone will know where we have gone."

"Have you decided to abandon Wallingford's guns?" He was hoping they'd never deal with Wallingford again.

"The Berettas? No, our people need them. That's what is delaying us. Tel Aviv has found a dealer in Transjordan with another million rounds of Italian ammunition that would fit them. No, the Berettas are number-one priority. That's why I've hung on to the houseboat all this time."

"I don't understand."

"For transhipment."

Solomon slowed and leaned out of the window to see where they were. Satisfied, he turned into a narrow lane, negotiating the deep potholes with care. When he spoke again, his voice was quiet but he gave great emphasis to his words.

"I saw Wallingford last week. We had dinner at Cleo's Club. He wanted us to collect the guns. He offered to adjust the price by ten percent if we went out to Siwa Oasis and got them. Cash and carry, he called it. He said he had other urgent business to do and is short of transport."

"Ten percent? I don't like the sound of that; he's giving away too much."

"You should have seen him the other night, spilling over with charm and consideration. That wonderful English courtesy and sense of humor. French champagne and rare Burgundy. There were even two girls at the bar waiting for his invitation to join us. We both got very drunk. Oh, yes, Yigal, I was given the full Wallingford treatment. After the war, Wallingford will be a successful capitalist businessman."

"He's a *shnorrer*," said Yigal.

"A *gonif*," said Solomon. He got a certain perverse pleasure from provoking Yigal into angry comments about Wallingford. "When he was very drunk he fell down in the urinal. I helped him to his feet, and he started shouting that he knew all about Rommel's spy—this one they say is feeding priceless intelligence to Tripoli."

"It's him," said Yigal.

"What?"

"The spy. Rommel's spy. It must be Wallingford. He moves around all the time out there in the desert. He's always wining and dining officers here in the city. He seems to know everyone." Yigal was excited as he thought about his theory. "It all fits together, doesn't it? Wallingford is a spy for the Germans. They probably finance him. That fellow Percy—his sidekick, aide, and ever-present assistant—is probably a trained German agent. Percy is his master."

"Don't get carried away, Yigal. Wallingford isn't Rommel's spy."

Yigal was miffed. He was sure he was right. "Why do you say that?"

"Don't shout at me, goddammit! I say it because I know I'm right. He's a thief—a *gonif*—like I said. He's not a spy. I've been in the business; I know who might be a spy and who could not be. Wallingford is not a spy."

"Percy is not a South African," said Yigal petulantly.

"Okay: Percy is a German. But that doesn't make Wallingford a spy, and it surely doesn't make him this superspy who is helping Rommel with his battle plans."

For a long time Yigal was silent. It was always like this. Solomon always treated him as if he were a small and stupid child. "Did you agree? About the Berettas. Did you agree to collect them?"

"Wallingford has disappeared into the blue. There's no telling when he'll be back. We have little choice."

"When do we go?" said Yigal.

"We're going nowhere. It's far too risky. The following morning I made a deal with Mahmoud. He sent his people out to Siwa. It was easier for his men. Arabs can sink into the sand and disappear out there."

"And you paid him for that?" said Yigal.

"Eight percent. Perhaps I am getting old, and old men become suspicious. I saw it happen to my poor father. Our people in Tel Aviv are saying I'm too cautious. They constantly complain about the money I'm spending. This time it's true I may have been extravagant, but it is better always to be cautious."

"Mahmoud collected the guns?"

"Yes. It was all as Wallingford said, but I still don't trust him. Our boat will be loaded before daybreak. Then we can breathe again."

"What boat? Have you got a boat ready?" It was exasperating that Solomon did not keep him informed.

"A felucca is coming up from the south. Mahmoud's men will do the loading." Solomon stopped the car at an imposing old archway. Set into a high wall was an ancient door studded with metal stars and supported on ornate hinges. At their approach, an Arab squatting by the door jumped to his feet and pulled at the bell rope.

"I wish we didn't have to do business with these Arab crooks," said Yigal as he looked at the Arab guard and at the doorway.

"Our people in Tel Aviv like it this way," said Solomon.

"What do you mean?"

"Tel Aviv can't spare any more gold or U.S. dollars or Swiss francs. They say the gold for the Berettas is the last they have. They say I must bargain. They won't understand that things have changed. Smart thieves don't want British pounds sterling or Egyptian notes any more. They're getting their money out of the country and clearing out before Rommel comes."

"And Mahmoud will take anything?"

"He owns a bank. He deals with the top people: Egyptians and British too. Don't make any mistake, old Mahmoud is a mighty big man in this town. We'll pay him his markup because we're paying in Egyptian notes, but he'll have that changed into anything he fancies within an hour or so."

"How?"

"Discounts to British army pay corps cashiers who put the balance in their pockets."

The big wooden door opened. A servant bowed low to them and ushered them inside. The door gave onto a tiny courtyard, its walls lined with lovely old oriental tiles, and green with plants growing from tall decorative pots. They crossed the yard and went through a low door set in a thick wall and then into a long cool whitewashed room.

Mahmoud and Tahseen were there: the banker fat and grinning alongside the slight, serious figure of his chief cashier. They courteously went through the rituals of "Allah be with you" and "May Allah lengthen your days." Then they all sat down on the array of cushions while servants brought steaming-hot mint tea and tiny cakes.

The tea was sweet, but Solomon drank it greedily. The sugar seemed to ease the tenseness and stress that the prospect of the meeting had brought upon him. First it was a time for small talk and compliments. Solomon dutifully admired the furnishings and the collection of carved ivory that was arrayed round the room. Ivory was one of Mahmoud's many interests, and one by one he had his prize examples brought for Solomon to stroke and esteem. The carving techniques had to be explained and the dates and places discussed. Business would come in due course.

Mahmoud was a more relaxed and elegant figure here, in his home, than he was in the carpet shop in the souk. The noisy extrovert manner he always displayed with Wallingford and his cronies had gone. Here in his home he was a man of culture and breeding. His galabiya was of fine material, his face newly shaved, and his hands manicured. As always he hid his eyes behind dark glasses, so when he spoke it was not always easy to discover his mood.

Mahmoud sipped his tea and said in a lighthearted manner, "Did you think I would go into the desert and bring back the guns for you personally?"

Solomon treated it as a joke. "Yes, of course. The desert is lovely at this time of year."

"Too hot for a picnic," said Mahmoud.

Tahseen joined in the questioning. "Was it Lieutenant Commander Wallingford who suggested that we collect the guns for you?"

Solomon sensed danger. "No. That was my idea." He took a

pastry and bit into it, only to find it was filled with date paste. Solomon did not like dates; he'd eaten far too many in his deprived and wretched childhood. He put the uneaten half in an ornate silver ashtray. A servant swooped in and replaced the ashtray with another even more ornate.

"And what about Captain Darymple?" said Tahseen, in his clear and perfect English accented voice. "Did he want to involve us?"

"Why? What are you getting at?" said Solomon.

"Please tell us," said Mahmoud. He got up and went round behind where Solomon was seated. There was something threatening about this movement, and when he felt a hand pressed upon his shoulder Solomon flinched.

"I believe Darymple arranged some of the paperwork," Solomon said. "He countersigned something for Wallingford. He brought them to him in Cleo's last week. But Wallingford is his own man, you know that."

Mahmoud adopted a new voice. "You see, Captain Darymple owes me a large sum of money. Mr. Wallingford arranged it. He said he'd buy the debt from me. I think he wanted to have Mr. Darymple under his control."

"That's nothing to do with me," said Solomon. He was beginning to suspect that they wanted him to repay this debt of Darymple's and find some way of deducting it from his payment to Wallingford. Solomon was determined to resist any such idea.

Having let the idea sink in, Mahmoud said, "It is a time of calling in the debts. All over the city, it is a time when debts must be paid."

Solomon looked at him. What did such extravagant talk actually mean? Did the artful pair know that he worked for Tel Aviv? A cold smile on Mahmoud's face suggested that they might.

Solomon took the black leather case he'd brought and put it on his knees. He opened it carefully. It was packed with new

Egyptian ten-pound notes. "I've brought what we agreed. I have no margin for bargaining."

"There is always a margin, Solomon. We have to allow for accidents." Solomon knew now that something had changed in his relationship with the old man. Always before they had found common ground in doing business. Until now Solomon had seen no animosity in these men. But tonight it was different. Tonight Solomon was being made aware of the fact that he was a Jew. He was a Jew naked and unprotected in the City of Gold, the ancient and sacred center of Arab life. For the first time Solomon felt vulnerable.

"Take it or leave it," said Solomon bitterly.

"We are in a strong bargaining position," said Tahseen sadly, as if he almost regretted it.

Solomon looked at them. The faces of the two Arabs were completely blank. If they held the consignment of guns he had no leverage. They would just keep the guns. "Let us not quarrel," said Solomon.

The two Arabs drank tea and said nothing. Solomon shut his case and put it on a side table.

"You can't make me pay another man's debts," said Solomon.

"Admit the truth, Solomon. You are all in it together. You, Wallingford, Darymple. Perhaps others too."

"No, you're wrong, Mahmoud. I am alone in this."

"I was hoping you'd be sensible," said Mahmoud. He took off his dark glasses and dabbed at his eyes with a handkerchief. The eyes were red-rimmed and dilated. The lights caused him such discomfort that he turned his head away from them. Solomon knew the signs of addiction. Mahmoud was said to be a dealer in drugs, but now it was evident that he sampled his own wares. His mercurial mood this evening was explained, and Solomon became more wary than ever.

"It is a matter of honor," said Tahseen. "A bank cannot allow a customer to flaunt its rules. The word will get out . . . you understand?" Solomon noticed that Mahmoud had drained his glass of tea. He did the same. No one poured more for him. The mint leaves, sticky with sugar, were glued against the side of the glass.

"Wallingford and Darymple are nothing to do with me," said Solomon again.

Mahmoud got to his feet suddenly. "Perhaps we should talk again tomorrow, when your blood is cooler. In this way we can part good friends and you can have a night to reflect upon what I have told you."

Solomon got to his feet too. He was angry. "Tomorrow the answer will be—"

Tahseen put his finger to his lips. "It is still the morning of our discussion. Tomorrow all will be well." Tahseen was always the moderator; that was his role.

The servant brought Solomon's hat and handed his bag to him. Mahmoud and Tahseen came to the door with them and bid them good night with all the care and courtesy that Arab hospitality requires.

Only when the big outer door closed did Yigal speak his mind. "They're going to keep the guns. Those bastards are going to hold on to our guns."

Solomon didn't reply. He got into the car and started the engine. As he did so a British officer leaned in through the window and said politely, "I'm sorry to intrude upon you gentlemen, but this area of the city has been closed to civilian traffic. We'll have to search you and your vehicle. Would you please get out of the car?"

Desperately Solomon tried to accelerate away, but his car rocked violently without moving forward. The engine revved loudly and backfired. "There are blocks against your wheels," explained the officer. "And my men are armed. Don't do anything silly." In the darkness it was now evident that a dozen or more men—military policemen armed to the teeth—had blocked off the alley.

Yigal and Solomon got out of the car. "I'll take your attaché case," said the officer. "My sergeant will help you into the truck. We're going to the Bab-el-Hadid barracks. One of my drivers will bring your car there. You will probably not be detained very long."

"That bastard Mahmoud!" Yigal could not contain his anger.

"Be quiet," Solomon told him. "Yes, of course, captain. We'll do whatever you say. We have nothing to hide."

The next morning Alice went to give her weekly report to Jimmy Ross and found the SIB offices in a turmoil. Solomon and Yigal had been arrested late the previous evening, and Marker had been up all night, interrogating both suspects. Alice Stanhope's activities were hardly worth reporting in the circumstances: Sayed, the innocuous activities of the prince, and so on. The only development was that Darymple had packed his bags and disappeared. She went quickly through her report with Ross and then started typing it out.

While she was doing this, Captain Marker returned from a lengthy interrogation session.

"Well?" said Ross.

"Not much," said Marker.

"You showed them this?" He picked up the cellophane-wrapped brown sticky treacle and dumped it down again.

"I showed them. It did no good."

"And?"

"The younger one obviously didn't know what it was. The other one—Solomon—laughed and said that Mahmoud must be getting feebleminded to plant six ounces of raw opium on him when even the small dealers are handling it by the hundred-weight."

"Why do you think Mahmoud shopped them?" said Ross.

"We are not sure he did, are we?" Marker looked at Alice in

case she had brought some fresh news. She met his eyes and shrugged.

Ross was sitting with his feet up on his desk, his hands locked behind his head. "Oh, he covered his tracks with great care, but that's what makes me so certain it was Mahmoud. It's obvious what happened. Mahmoud sent his men out to Siwa and they got shot up. He sits around brooding about it and decides it was all part of some conspiracy that Solomon and Wallingford have hatched."

"A lot of funny things are happening as Rommel gets nearer," said Marker.

"But not that funny. Did you get anything out of the younger one?"

"At least he replies when you talk to him. The trouble is he doesn't know anything. He's very much the junior partner. He's kept in ignorance of their day-to-day work."

"We'll hold them for a few days. Solitary. Unless they start talking, we'll have to release them."

"The young one did say something."

"Yes?"

"He's got the idea that Wallingford, the navy deserter, is Rommel's spy."

Alice stopped typing; she wanted to hear.

"Did he say that?"

"Yes," said Marker. "In those same words. He seems to think that Wallingford and Mahmoud are in league. He thinks Wallingford tipped us off and had them arrested last night. He thinks it's all part of Rommel's planning."

"Wallingford. Yes, I'd like to talk to Wallingford." Ross swung his feet off the desk and flipped open the Solomon file to look at it.

Marker watched him. "He said Wallingford is a deserter and runs a gang of deserters. He moves around all the time. It makes sense."

"Well, that much may be true. But the brigadier has actual

intercepts of the messages going to Rommel. If you'd seen that stuff, you'd know that Wallingford isn't our spy. It's not gossip from Cleo's Club. It's top-level stuff: strategic ideas, evaluation of weapons, appreciations, comments on morale and intentions. Arrival of convoys and what they are bringing. Unit movements are known before they are even started. A clown like Wallingford doesn't move in those circles."

"No. Well, I knew it was absurd," said Marker sadly. He'd been secretly nursing a hope that he'd cracked the war's biggest secret.

"Go back and try some more," said Ross. "Keep the pressure up. If there is an effective Jewish network operating, we must find out all about it."

Marker looked at his watch. He'd planned to have a wash and a shave and perhaps even an hour's sleep. But this was their big chance to spike Spaulding's guns by showing they already knew about "religious subversives." "Whatever you say, major." He swigged back his tea, got to his feet, and left the room. Ross returned his feet to their place on the desk and leaned back in his chair.

"Wallingford," Ross mused aloud. "I wish I could believe it."

Alice was watching him. She hadn't resumed her typing. "But you do think he's a deserter?" Alice asked.

"Wallingford? Probably. I asked navy records to do another complete check on him. But you know how long it takes to get anything from those people in Alexandria."

"Why are you so interested in Wallingford when you don't think he's the spy?" said Alice.

"I don't know." He gave a brief laugh to admit that Wallingford was on his mind lately. "He's about the only suspect we've got left."

"Isn't the blood on the bank note evidence enough to charge him with murder?"

"Not really. It's completely circumstantial. But it's enough to bring him in for questioning." She looked at him. He said,

"You're right, Alice. Perhaps the time has come to sit Walling-ford down and shine the bright light in his eyes." He resolved to concentrate on the SIB work: that was the best way to stop himself worrying.

"What will you do if you catch the real spy?" said Alice. She realized how much better it would have been to say *when* you catch the spy, but by that time it was too late.

He swung his head around to see her. "It would have to be something very drastic," he said. "Maybe I'll punch the brigadier on the nose and ask you to marry me."

She smiled and started typing again. She could see he was very very tired.

≡20≡

Robin Darymple was happier than he had been for months. The sand crunched under his feet and there was clear air to breathe. He was enjoying that feeling of well-being that greeted men when they arrived here. Darymple couldn't believe his good luck. He was back in the desert with the fighting men. Not only that, he was with a decent battalion. It had all been easier than he'd ever supposed. He'd heard about men who discharged themselves from hospital, got back to their units, and carried on there without suffering any consequences. It was when he forged those documents for Wallingford that he thought of fixing himself up with some sort of paperwork to get up to the fighting line. Authority, it was rumored, did not punish men who went and fought.

Certainly there seemed no reason for him to worry right now. No one was paying much attention to him. Men were crawling all over the old armored cars, greasing them and checking the transmissions, the suspensions, and the wheels. They were cleaning the guns and adjusting the telescopic sights. They were tuning the radio sets. Into the bins they were stowing spare parts and tools and extra rations. Everywhere around him there were shells, machine-gun ammunition, flare cartridges, water, and food. "Bombing up," they called the process. Darymple watched them with pride and affection. These were the men with whom he felt comfortable: simple, straightforward men, unlike Walling-ford and the hard-eyed ambitious pen-pushers he knew in Cairo.

They were tired, of course, but this was an efficient unit. Darymple had a theory that a battalion's discipline and morale could be judged from the camouflage netting overhead. Units like this one tightened the nets so that the cover made was flat and taut. Slack and sloppy units had slack and sloppy camouflage netting, and one was constantly ducking the head to avoid brushing against it.

Darymple looked at the armored car nearest to him. The name BERYL had been stenciled on its side. Darymple grabbed at the wheel guard and climbed up onto the front armor plate. The metal was hot to his hands, and he could feel the heat through his shoes. For a moment he stood on the hull looking down through the open hatch into the driver's compartment. He re-membered this car Beryl. He'd been given command of it briefly when it first arrived from the workshops. It had arrived from England complete with its name. Was Beryl the wife or girlfriend of its former commander? They would never know, but by com-mon consent the name remained. Crews believed it was unlucky to change a name. Yes, he knew Beryl very well but, like the soldiers around her, Beryl had changed. Layers of encrusted paint had dried and scabbed, like makeup on an aged face. Poor old Beryl; her age could not be concealed. There were half a dozen scars on her armor plate, some of them deeply gouged by 5cm or even 7.5cm high-velocity shells that, striking only a few inches lower, would have turned Beryl into scrap metal and incinerated her crew.

It was a hot day. Darymple could smell the inside of the car. It was an odor in which sweat, urine, excreta, oil, rubber, and cordite could all be detected. It was not a pleasant one, but it brought the past back to him with a suddenness he'd not ex-pected. He stroked the metal armor and looked down at torn leather, the dials—speedometer, rev counter, and pressure gauges, their glass hazy and fractured—the gear lever, and the brake lever, now worn shiny by the driver's caresses.

Darymple wriggled around the turret and perched himself on the little leather-topped commander's seat that he'd sat upon so often. It was cramped. The gunner's seat was close against his leg, so there was scarcely room for another human frame to fit there. Now he could smell the sweaty foam rubber pad that the gunner's face rested on as he sighted the gun. Darymple reached for the traversing wheel to touch it lightly.

From this position on the turret, Darymple could see the "soft-skinned" echelon vehicles. They were being loaded with extra ammunition, food, and petrol. Each day they came forward bringing replenishments. The echelon men had a rotten job; enemy gunners liked to pick off these vulnerable vehicles, which usually succumbed to the first hit.

Darymple kept looking for old friends to greet, but few of the soldiers he'd served with six months before were still here. All around him were fresh-faced newcomers, some of them little more than children. It was now May 1942. The war had been going for nearly two years: long enough for youngsters drafted after the war began to be trained and arrive out here in the desert. Pimply schoolboys, faces flushed by their first exposure to the harsh sunlight, were driving armored cars, firing the guns, and tuning the radios. Many such kids had even got stripes on their arms. All of them were noisy and active, spending recklessly the energy and confidence that is the currency of youth.

Not so the old-timers. The men who had been with him in what was now called "the old days" were difficult to recognize. Almost all of them had aged in a way that only stress ages men. Lined faces, thin unconvincing smiles, and troubled eyes set deep in their sockets were as much a mark of front-line service as were the dark tans, faded uniforms, and such fashions as suede desert boots and fancy sweaters.

Darymple was not unduly troubled by the depleted battalion he now found himself with. Darymple was not a particularly sensitive man and certainly not sentimental. It was a soldier's job to fight and die. That the battalion's men had been doing that troubled him not at all. His only regret was that he had missed so much of the action while sitting behind a desk in Cairo.

The desert was glorious in May, still not unbearably hot. From his vantage point on the car he could see sprawling patches of desert flowers that had sprung up from the winter rains. Crushed by tank tracks, heavy-duty tires, and boots, the green patches gave off a scent of wild thyme. The hot springtime winds were late this year, but soon they would come. The flowers would shrivel and disappear overnight. At last he spotted someone he knew: Lieutenant Copeland. "Piggy!" Now it really was grand to be back.

His friend Piggy came strolling over to him. Taking off his peaked cap the lieutenant scratched his head. "Are you still in love with Beryl?"

Darymple smiled self-consciously. He knew he was making a fool of himself by such evident pleasure in returning to his own people, but he could not subdue it. He slapped the armor. "She's a lucky old bitch."

"It's true. Beryl always seems to pull through. By-the-by, did I tell you that Wally came through the other day?"

"Wallingford?" Darymple felt a sudden jar.

"He said he'd seen you. Lieutenant commander and a DSO and all! How the devil does a chap get into one of those independent mobs? Mind you, Wally was always a lucky swine at school, wasn't he?"

"I suppose he was," said Darymple cautiously. He was expecting to see Wallingford today, but he wasn't looking forward to it. When one day Wallingford was caught—as surely he would be—Darymple wanted to be completely disassociated from him. "I've seen him once or twice. He wasn't in my house."

"No, not in your house, but you were on the school eleven with him. You went around together, didn't you?"

"Sometimes. I forget. It's a long time ago."

"A long time is right. I think I'm going to end the war still a bloody lieutenant. Do you know how long I've been out here now?"

"It's probably just the paperwork," said Darymple. "Your promotions will all come thudding through together, and you'll be jumped to general or something."

"Can I have that in writing?"

"What's that?" said Darymple. He pointed to the west. In the distance a wall of fine brown dust was moving slowly toward them. It looked solid, and only his common sense told him it couldn't be. The wall must have been three or four miles across and reached high, perhaps five hundred feet, into the air. "It's not the khamsin?" said Darymple, who knew it wasn't like any dust storm he'd ever seen before.

Piggy followed his stare. "No, it's the Hun. He's been stirring up dust almost every day for the past week. He kicks up that dust wall when he moves his tanks and vehicles. He must be concentrating a hell of a lot of armor down to the south of us."

"Well, it won't be long then," said Darymple.

"No, it won't be long," said Piggy.

As if to confirm these words, Darymple heard the drone of engines and looked up to see a lone plane flying a steady straight line across their front.

"That's Hermann, photographing our positions. He must have enough photos by now; he comes over almost every day."

"Maybe it's part of a plan to keep us twitchy," said Darymple.

"Then he does it well," said Piggy. "It gives me the jitters to think the Hun can plot the position of every tank, car, truck, and dump we've got here."

"It's the coastal railway they're interested in," said Darymple. "Our chaps are pushing the railway out as far as Tobruk."

"You fellows in Cairo are the only ones who know what is going on," said Piggy without resentment. "We never get to know anything out here at the sharp end."

"And there is a water pipeline too. They say the Corps area will have as much water as it can use."

"I'll start washing again on a regular basis," said Piggy. "I just dry-polish, the way the water ration is right now."

"Who the hell is that fellow?" said Darymple, and the urgency and indignation in his voice startled Piggy.

"Who? Where?"

"That bastard!" He pointed.

"Oh, he's some major from Cairo who came up here to powwow with Andy. Hush-hush, Andy said."

"I know that swine," said Darymple. "He's a bloody corporal. I know him!"

"Steady on, Robbie, old boy."

"I tell you I know him. He's a bloody little corporal. He's running around with a gorgeous girl who lives in the same hotel I did."

"I say, what a nerve," said Piggy, without displaying much emotion.

"Well, what are you going to do about it? He's gone into the officers' mess."

"It's almost time for lunch."

"Don't be a bloody fool, Piggy. He can't eat with us. You'll have to get some police and put him under arrest. He's impersonating an officer. On active service and all that. He's probably adrift, a deserter. False papers and so on." To himself, Darymple added softly but fervently, "I knew it. I knew it all the time. What a crook!"

Piggy looked at Darymple, trying to decide if this was another of Darymple's jokes. At school he'd been quite a joker; he'd been beaten before the lower school for sending the house master one of the school kitchen's indigestible meat pies through the post. He'd written the address and stuck postage stamps on the pie crust, and it had arrived still intact!

But this was evidently not one of his friend's jokes. Neither was there much sign of Darymple's excitement abating. And since Darymple was a captain he had to be obeyed. "Whatever you say, old boy. Here! Corporal!" he shouted to a passing NCO. "Go and tell the orderly room sergeant that we've identified a deserter and that he's to come here and bring an armed escort."

"Yes, sir," said the corporal. He smiled. This was certainly something to liven up the day's proceedings.

"At the double!" called Darymple.

"Yes, sir," called the corporal over his shoulder as he started to run.

The arrest of the visiting police major was remembered vividly by those who witnessed it. There were four officers in the mess tent at the time. The visitor, wearing cloth major's crowns on khaki drill, was standing drinking a whisky. Three lieutenants— one an elderly ordnance officer—were seated at the table wolfing an early lunch before getting back to work.

With Darymple there was Lieutenant Piggy Copeland, a sergeant assigned to orderly room duties, and Sergeant Butcher of the Royal Corps of Military Police, a man the orderly sergeant had chosen to bring on account of his physical strength and unyielding dedication to King's Regulations and the army's way of doing things.

It was Darymple who made the running. "You!" he shouted to Ross. "What do you think you're up to, man?"

Ross had already spotted Darymple but was hoping to avoid him. Now, as he came into the mess tent yelling, Ross was unable to still a deep feeling of anxiety.

"Cutler, or whatever your bloody name is, come here at the double." When Ross did not obey this command, Darymple turned to the sergeant and said, "There's your man."

Military Police Sergeant Butcher hitched up his webbing belt and revolver, which he'd put on hurriedly without adjusting the shoulder strap properly. Then he pulled the peak of his red-topped cap low over his eyes and approached Ross. As he stood confronting him, his stance reflected a certain measure of uncertainty.

Ross smiled. It was a nervous reaction but it didn't seem like one. It further incensed Darymple and prompted Sergeant Butcher to ask Cutler for his identification papers.

Ross handed these over with what Darymple thought an impudent flourish. This, and the fact that his adrenaline was flowing, caused Darymple to snatch the papers—"Forgeries, forgeries; one glance is enough to show anyone that"—and stuff them into his pocket. "That will be important evidence. Arrest him, sergeant. I want him handcuffed." To Ross he said, "You'll not give me the slip this time," which gave onlookers the impression that he'd had the same man arrested on some previous occasion.

"Pull yourself together, Captain Darymple," said Ross. His heart was beating furiously, but he kept telling himself that this didn't have to be the end. He had only to keep calm. Ross knew his identification pass was authentic: he must make them look at it. "Look at my SIB pass. I'm a major. I'm here to talk with Colonel Anderson."

"*Colonel* Anderson?" said Darymple loudly. For one brief moment, the news about Anderson's colonelcy crowded everything else from his mind. "*Colonel* Anderson?"

"Yes, Captain Darymple. I came here to talk with Colonel Anderson."

"What about?" said Sergeant Butcher gruffly. He'd seen many military impostors; they all seemed to want to dress up as majors. It was a good rank: most military police were nervous about challenging it, while it was not high enough to attract the wrong sort of attention.

"Security," said Ross and realized immediately that in answering Butcher so civilly, he'd confirmed that man's suspicions. Ross had met dozens of men like him during his time in the ranks. Butcher was the sort of man who used his own rank to bully people and could not easily envisage others not using their rank in the same way.

"You're under arrest," said Butcher. He was a big man, and he twisted Ross's arm to snap a handcuff onto the wrist. He quickly pulled the other arm round to the back and completed the handcuffing, so that both of Ross's hands were pinioned behind him.

"Look at my identification." His first terrible fears had been replaced by indignation, as he realized that this confrontation was simply caused by Darymple's mistake. Ross began to feel a fool as more officers came into the tent for lunch and stood around enjoying this bizarre scene.

"Just explain to me why you were dressed as a corporal. Explain that," said Darymple triumphantly.

"I don't have to explain anything to you, Captain Darymple."

"Now, now, laddie. Don't make a fuss. We'll sort it out," said Butcher. He'd learned how to quell arrested men with soft words and extravagant promises. He grabbed Ross by the arm and began to move him from the tent.

"Get your Field Security people here immediately," Ross told Butcher. "And take these handcuffs off at once. Look at my papers. I'm permitted to wear any uniform I choose. And any rank."

"Calm down, laddie," said Butcher. "They all say that sort of thing."

"You're a bloody fool, Darymple! If you don't order this idiot to release me at once I will see you court-martialed for impeding an SIB officer in the execution of his duty."

Partly in order to reassure himself, Butcher said, "If you were really an SIB man you'd carry a card saying you are permitted to wear any uniform you wish."

"But I'm dressed in the uniform of the rank I hold," said Ross. "I'm not here in any sort of disguise. You have my identification, and you have refused to look at it."

At this moment Colonel Anderson came into the hut. Leading him was the orderly sergeant who, seeing how the row was brewing up, had decided to play safe by bringing the CO.

"What's going on here?" Anderson said loudly in his broad Yorkshire accent. When no one answered, he said, "What's happening, Major Cutler?"

"Mr. Darymple has instructed the MP sergeant to arrest me," said Ross apologetically.

Anderson looked at Darymple for a moment. The bottled-up resentment he felt about the way Darymple had treated him in the past overcame his restraint. Pausing between each word, he said, "You are a stupid prick, Darymple. You are an idiotic, officious, pretentious halfwit. Major Cutler is my guest, as well as being here on official duties. Get your arse out of the mess before I forget myself and punch you in the head."

"But I know this soldier," insisted Darymple, but his resolution was flagging.

Anderson looked at him, as if wondering what to do next. "Did you look at his identification papers?"

"I thought they were forgeries," said Darymple, handing them to Anderson. "I'm sorry, sir." He looked at Cutler and tried to say, "I'm sorry, Major Cutler," but the words came out as a croak.

"Take your meals somewhere else until I tell you you can come back and eat in the mess. I hate the sight of your stupid face."

By this time, Sergeant Butcher had released his captive from the handcuffs and was standing rigidly at attention. His face had gone bright red. Butcher realized he was in trouble.

Anderson's scarred puglike face could be frightening when he scowled, and he was scowling as he put his face very close to Butcher's nose. "I'm going to find some work for you, Butcher. I'm going to find some job for you that will keep you so busy you won't have time to put innocent people under arrest and listen to scandalous rumors, idiotic accusations, and unsubstantiated hearsay instead of examining evidence." He waved Cutler's identification in the air before handing it back to its owner.

"Yes, sir," said Butcher.

"Meanwhile, you are on a charge."

"Yes, sir."

"For conduct to the prejudice of good order and military discipline in that you invaded the officers' mess without permission and without proper reason. And take off those stripes before I see you again. Now get your fat arse out of here."

Sergeant Butcher blinked and cast a glance around him to see if any lesser ranks had heard what was said. The two mess waiters were standing behind the mess table with broad grins on their faces. There was no doubt that Butcher's error of judgment, and the dressing down he'd got for it, would be known to every soldier in the vicinity within an hour or so.

"It might be better if we took lunch in my tent," said Anderson, watching Butcher and Darymple depart. "It's a shade more private." He signaled to a waiter and led Ross outside.

"Bloody Darymple," said Colonel Anderson, when they were seated in the commander's tent. "He came crawling back here with some tale about his orders being mislaid."

"Don't be too hard on him, colonel. He'd seen me dressed as a corporal. It was probably a shock to see me in this uniform."

"What's wrong with being a corporal?" said Anderson. "Can you honestly tell me that if Darymple had joined as a ranker he'd have ever been made up to corporal?"

Anderson was just testing the ground. Ross said nothing. There was a deliberate noise of the tent flap being opened, and Anderson's orderly arrived with a large gin and tonic on a platter. Anderson took it and sipped it. "What will you drink, major?"

"A beer would be most welcome, sir."

Anderson nodded to the soldier. "Well, I'll shove the bugger back to GHQ if his official orders don't arrive by the end of the week. Now tell me what you want, and I'll do whatever I can for you."

"I'm looking for a naval bod named Wallingford," said Ross. He took the beer the mess waiter brought. "Good health, sir."

"One of those Independent Desert Team gangsters. Yes, he comes through here now and again. What is it you are after?" As he said it, the engine of a low-flying plane was heard. Anderson didn't move a muscle. The roar of the plane grew louder and louder. Anderson's studied calm was the sort of bravado that front-line soldiers liked to demonstrate to visitors from rear areas.

Ross had seen action, and his inclination was to dive under the table and take cover from what might be a strafing run, but he did nothing as the ear-splitting crescendo passed over.

"Our flying friends," said Anderson, and smiled bleakly as the sound dwindled away and the RAF fighter pilot continued on his way home. "Beating up" the army was a favored entertainment of homebound RAF fliers.

Ross said, "You have probably noticed that the Hun is remarkably well informed about everything we have, everything we do, and most things we plan."

"Where's he getting it from?"

"To be absolutely frank with you, no one knows. But this fellow Wallingford might be able to help us. He is probably a deserter—"

"Is he, by God!"

"Yes. He runs a gang of thieves."

"One of those," said Anderson wearily. The army was being picked to the bone by theft. "Yes, he's been through here. I've let him sign chits for food and fuel and stuff. What a fool I am."

Ross said, "He's a smooth talker and very convincing. I saw him once."

"He's even eaten in the mess with us. Yes. He's a crony of Darymple. He's a navy type, a lieutenant commander with the DSO."

"We're still running checks on him. It was a bright idea to use navy uniform. Not many RN policemen in the desert. Or even in Cairo, come to that. He stays away from Alex, where the navy lives."

"Is he the spy you're after?"

"Perhaps."

"Only perhaps?"

"We arrested two men in Cairo. Wallingford was boasting to one of them that he knew who the spy was."

"Is that enough to go on?"

"The arrested men had had dealings with Wallingford. One of them gave us a statement implicating Wallingford in deals in stolen arms. We also have evidence to show that Wallingford was present when a sergeant major was murdered in El Birkeh last January. I have a bloodstained bank note with what are probably his fingerprints on it. If I can find Wallingford, I'll hold him on a murder charge and see what I can squeeze out of him."

"You think he'll talk?"

"I'll make him talk."

"With a murder charge over his head, isn't he likely to remain silent and yell for a court-martial?"

"I'd do what I could for him, of course."

"For a deserter . . . a crook?"

"Colonel, this spy is a real threat to us. I'd give evidence on behalf of Adolf Hitler if it meant nailing the person who's sending our secrets to Rommel."

"Well, of course I'll do anything I can to help you."

"He's probably heading this way. He sticks to the same route as a rule; we think he has contacts. We've alerted military police units. The navy rank badges make him a bit easier to spot, but he wears khaki and will no doubt change uniform and disappear if he hears we're after him. I got a plane ride so that I could get here ahead of him. I'd like to sniff around and ask a few questions." He looked at Anderson. Seeking the commanding officer's permission was only a formality, and both men knew it.

Anderson looked at him for a moment without answering. He did not welcome the idea of mysterious SIB men coming up here and "sniffing around" his officers, but there was no alternative. "Yes, of course. Let me know what you need."

"Thank you, colonel. If Wallingford arrives with his gang, I will need your help."

=21=

"This is my favorite time of year," said Wallingford suddenly, and for no apparent reason. Wallingford was driving the big Matador truck. It bumped over some slabs of rock and down to a great lake of sand as white, flat, and unwrinkled as a freshly starched tablecloth.

Percy, jolted out of the seat alongside him by the bumps, grunted. Percy was not easily fooled. He suspected that Wallingford was not enjoying anything. Wallingford had had too much of the desert. Eventually the euphoria that comes with the clarity of the air and the magical nights of star-filled skies is replaced by a feeling of lassitude, a weariness brought about by the absence of any visual stimulus. These featureless vistas—without buildings, trees, roads, or grass—eventually dulled the mind and made a man retreat into himself in the way that Wallingford was doing more and more often.

"You take unnecessary risks," said Percy. There was no admiration in his voice.

"Just one more trip," said Wallingford with forced cheerfulness. "Think of those cameras."

"I don't want to think of them." Percy was hot and sweaty and thinking only of how much he'd like a cold beer.

"Then think of the money," said Wallingford angrily. "Think of getting rich."

"I try to," said Percy. "But I keep thinking of getting shot or getting arrested."

"Not you, Percy. You're like me; you're a survivor and as hard as nails."

"Taking unnecessary risks is stupid. These front-line areas are more dangerous for people like us than Cairo could ever be."

"Why?" said Wallingford mildly. He always regarded any arguments against the way he did things as the product of weak nerves and inferior courage. It was Wallingford's powerful personality that held his gang together. He tried to keep them all cheerful and optimistic, but sometimes that was difficult.

"They shoot deserters in the front-line areas."

"Don't be silly, old boy. The British don't shoot deserters; they just lock them up."

"You're a fool," said Percy.

"How are we doing?" They were passing one of the cement-filled barrels that had been positioned throughout this part of the desert. Percy looked down at the map on his knees and compared the number and map reference with the markings on the barrel.

"It is okay." They were on course.

Soon they spotted an armored car. It was stationary, positioned hull down behind a mound. They kept to the well-marked track and approached the car with respectful care. The enemy often employed captured tanks, trucks, and cars; identification was no guarantee of safety. They continued along the well-marked trail. They saw two more cars and recognized the markings. This was the regimental B echelon leaguer of an armored outfit. These trucks went back for supplies and ran them up to the units at the front. They worked by night. Nearby there were the tents of the supply echelon personnel, together with regimental fitters, ambulances, and a couple of mobile workshops. They'd start work again when the sun went down. It was afternoon, a time when most of the soldiers were sleeping. Here and there men were to be seen doing their laundry, and others were writing letters home.

They passed right into the loosely formed leaguer. The vehicles were all widely spaced, as was the practice in daylight; at night they were moved closer together. Soon they reached the place they were looking for: regimental HQ. The ground was hard and uneven. A sentry was standing on the top of a tank so that he could see across the stony plain on all sides.

Wallingford waved to him. The sentry waved back. There was no threat likely from soft-skinned vehicles like this one. When the Germans attacked, they came in tanks.

The truck was bouncing across the hard rock when Wallingford spotted Captain Darymple. He was standing near a tent at the very edge of the encampment. He looked like a veteran in his bleached shirt and ragged trousers, but his nervousness became evident as he ran forward and greeted them.

"Wally! Where have you been?"

"I'm dead on time. What's wrong?"

"We've got to talk." Darymple had been standing in the hot sun; his shirt was black with sweat and clinging to his body. His face was wet too. A film of dust covered his perspiring flesh, so that it looked as if he were made of sand. He hauled himself up, swung into the driver's cab, and slammed the door. Then he said, "Keep going along the track. Get away from here."

"We're sleeping here, you twit," said Wallingford.

"No, Wally. Something's happened. Keep going, just keep going."

"Jesus Christ, Robbie. You look like you've seen a ghost. What is it?"

For a moment or two Darymple just sat back in the seat and caught his breath. Then he said, "I *have* seen a ghost, Wally. That's exactly what I have seen—a bloody ghost!"

"Spit it out, man. What is it?" Wallingford was becoming irritated by this melodrama. He was tired. He wanted a drink and a chat and a sleep. He didn't want Darymple pulling faces and trying to tell him where to go and what to do.

"It's that little Corporal Cutler. Did you ever meet him?"

"I might have done. Yes, I think I did: the pianist. What about the little sod? Is it something to do with that smashing girl of his? You're sweet on her, aren't you? I knew you were."

"Cut it out, Wally. Listen to what I'm telling you. That little corporal isn't a little corporal."

"No, he's Napoleon Bonaparte."

"Listen, Wally, damn you. That little corporal is a major. What's more, he's a major in Field Security or one of those army Special Investigation outfits. You know. He's a bloody Gestapo man, Wally."

"Is he here?"

"Very much so. He's with that sod Anderson. Anderson's been made up to colonel, if you can believe it. And this jumped-up little bugger is with him. They're drinking and laughing together."

"Never mind all that crap. Get to the point. What's all that got to do with me?"

Darymple looked at Wallingford with resentment. It was typical that Wally was only concerned with himself. "I thought he was a deserter or something when I saw him parading around with crowns on his shoulders, so I arrested him."

Wallingford turned his head slowly as the words sank in. As he came to face Darymple, his face lit up in a big smile. "You arrested him?"

"I thought he was a deserter."

"You arrested him? And he's a Special Investigation Branch major? That's rich, Robbie!"

"I was in the right."

"Of course you were," said Wallingford. He laughed again and hammered the steering wheel with his fist.

"He's after you, Wally," said Darymple, more to stifle Wallingford's laughter than because it was his considered opinion.

Very casually Wallingford turned to Percy and told him,

"Go back and see if everything is all right with the others, Percy. Tell them not to get out. We might be moving on."

Percy knew he was being got rid of. He put on his hat and slowly climbed down out of the truck.

Only when he'd gone did Wallingford say, "Why would he be after me?"

"I walked past the CO's tent a couple of times. I could hear what they were saying. He's got a Gyppo bank note with blood spots on it and your fingerprints. He says it will get you done for murder."

"The hell he does!" Then he was calm again. "Any more gems, Robbie?"

"He's trying to find out who's leaking all these secrets to the Hun."

"Is he, though?" said Wallingford reflectively.

"Oh, yes, that's his real job. He said he's got to plug the leak of secrets. He said he'd get Adolf Hitler off with a reprimand, if he helped solve that one. Or words to that effect," Darymple added, as he realized he hadn't heard it in full.

"Even Adolf?"

"It was a joke, of course."

"Yes, I thought it might be, Robbie." Wallingford waved flies away.

Darymple watched his face, but he couldn't tell what effect the news had brought. "What are you up to?"

Wallingford shifted in his seat until he could see the distant figure of Percy reflected in the exterior driving mirror. "If I told this Gestapo man what he wants to know, Robbie, would he let me off the hook, do you think?"

"You're joking," said Darymple and gave a nervous smile.

"No, I'm not. Have you got a cigarette?"

"You know?" He found a pack of Players with four cigarettes. "Keep them all if you want them."

"That's right; I know." Wallingford lit up a cigarette and inhaled deeply before blowing smoke. "Bloody flies!"

"You know who's given the Hun our secrets?"

"That's it."

"Jesus! How long have you known that?"

"Never you mind, old boy. I have a tame Hun who knows all the answers. He used to be on Rommel's signals staff."

"Percy, your Hun?" Now Darymple twisted round to catch sight of the German deserter as he walked back to the second truck.

"The point is, will your SIB chum do a deal with me?" Wallingford said.

"How should I know that?"

"Go and talk to him, there's a good chap."

"I'm not in a good position to talk to him, Wally. I told you; I arrested the little blighter."

"Talk to him. Just say you know someone who knows what he wants to know. But I'd want to come out of this as clean as a whistle. Make sure he knows my conditions. Do that for me, will you, Robbie?"

Darymple seemed doubtful.

Wallingford said, "It's what he so desperately wants to discover, isn't it? He'll welcome you with open arms, old boy."

"I suppose he might. Okay, I'll talk to him."

"No names, of course. All for one, one for all. That's how it always was."

"And always will be, Wally." Once again the Wallingford charm had worked its magic. All Darymple's hoarded resentments and hatreds had evaporated. Once again Wallingford was the star of the school cricket team and Darymple his faithful admirer. "What will you do now?"

"We'll push on to the squadron area. Do you know where the box ends?"

"Keep going on the marked track. You'll see the tire marks of the echelon vehicles where the going gets soft. Then there's a line of barrels and a sign. Thunder is in charge up there. He'll look after you."

"Jump down, Robbie. Thanks for the tip-off, old sport. And by the way, don't go back to Cairo. Old Mahmoud has put a price on your head."

"What?"

"I can't explain it all right now. But stay out here in the blue, and you'll be all right. I'll fix it when he's calmed down a bit."

"Good God, Wally. Are you serious?"

"I'm serious, old boy, and so is Mahmoud. These Arab johnnies get very touchy when you don't pay your debts. It's not like going into the red with your local High Street bank in Blighty."

"Can you straighten it out, Wally?"

"See what you can do for me with Sherlock Holmes. If he says he can give me what I want, you send a message to me up at squadron. Okay?" Wallingford touched the accelerator to show he was impatient to pull away. Darymple climbed down from the running board.

"I'll do anything that will help," said Darymple.

"And I'll keep Mahmoud off your back," said Wallingford. "One for all and all for one." He leaned his head out of the truck. "Come along, Percy, I'm waiting for you!" he bawled, and flicked the cigarette butt so that it whirled away to land in the sand.

They drove ten miles forward before finding the squadron area. It was an armored unit placed at the forward position, as far west as the lines stretched. Wallingford spotted someone he knew. The young lieutenant was seated on an armored car with one bare foot twisted, so that he could trim his toenails. He was dressed in a ragged shirt, a greasy beret, and shorts. His skin was tanned dark by the sun, and his face had not been shaved for a few days. His name was Rodney Benton, but at school his personal habits had given him the name of Thunderbum. In course of time this had been modified to Thunder and its origins almost forgotten.

Benton was another of the regular contacts by means of

which Wallingford navigated through the desert. He gave himself a minute to put on his cheery manner. Then he waved a bottle of scotch out of the window and called, "Hello, Thunder. How are you?"

The lieutenant brightened and quickly pulled on his long woolen socks and slipped into his battered suede desert boots. Wally had cemented friendships everywhere by his cheery manner, his funny stories and Cairo gossip, and his judicious gifts of whisky and brandy.

The armored cars were carefully spaced out and camouflaged with netting. Apart from Thunder, the crews were sitting under the netting in the shade of their cars. It was a hot day. Most of the soldiers had cast off their shirts and were clad only in shorts and shoes or boots. Some of them were eating and others, having finished their meal, had stretched out and were asleep.

Thunder greeted the newcomers and took them over to the tent where the radio was set up. The tent was dug into the sand so as to be invisible to enemy aircraft and patrols. To get inside it was necessary to stoop down almost on hands and knees. Once there, an excavated floor made it possible to stand up. When he did so, Wallingford discovered they were not the only visitors to this forward area. In the tent he found Harry Wechsler and Chips O'Grady.

"We have another visitor," announced Thunder. "And he's brought whisky."

Harry Wechsler was washed and carefully shaved. His bush shirt was clean. He got up from the ammunition box he was sitting on and shook hands with a firm grip and hearty pumping action. "Good to see you again, lieutenant commander," he said.

Wallingford nodded but gave no sign of having met him before.

"Whisky," said Thunder again. Harry Wechsler smiled at him and wondered whether he was being told that all visitors were expected to bring such gifts.

"Mr. Wechsler writes for American newspapers," said Thunder. "He's come here waiting for Rommel to attack."

There was an unmistakably sardonic tone in Thunder's voice, but Wechsler gave no sign of recognizing it. He said to Wallingford, "These guys think Rommel is going to sit on his ass out there, waiting for you all to get ready."

"And you don't?" said Wallingford, watching Thunder pour whiskies for them all. It was hot inside the little tent, and there was a ceaseless buzz of flies.

Wechsler said, "On past performance, Rommel will hit you early and in the place you least expect it. That's what he did at El Agheila in January. It's what he's always done before, so why not now?"

"The Germans aren't supermen," said Wallingford, calmly providing the official point of view. "Rommel has done his bit of dashing and advancing. Now he needs time to refit and regroup. Maybe he'll be ready to attack in a month or so—July or August—but by that time we might have done a bit of attacking ourselves."

"I've got to get back to my chaps," said Thunder, downing his drink. "I can hear the echelon vehicles arriving early. I must get them unloaded and away again. I'll leave you to discussing Rommel; after you've agreed on what he's going to do, you can let me know." He grinned. "We'll be sending a patrol out later, Mr. Wechsler. You're welcome to come and have a shufti at the way things are done."

"Thanks, kid."

"Aren't you supposed to have a conducting officer with you?" Wallingford asked them when Thunder had departed.

"We're let off the rein every now and again. Even conducting officers need a little rest and relaxation." Wechsler winked. "Chips here knows the ropes. He's been working this beat since before the fighting started."

"Good luck," said Wallingford and sipped his whisky. He approved of men with independent spirit.

"Maybe you don't remember me," said Wechsler. "We met at Prince Piotr's apartment. There was a party. Remember?"

"Yes, I do." He waved flies away from his face. To some extent one got used to them, but they were always trying to settle upon the moisture of the mouth and nostrils and eyes.

"A guy with navy gold on khaki isn't forgotten easily."

"I suppose not. And do you still think fighting Rommel is a sideshow?"

"Is that what I said?"

"You said that the real battle . . . the real battle is the fight for the Jewish homeland. You said the Jews in Palestine must be given guns to fight it."

"Did I say that?"

"Yes, you did."

Wechsler laughed without revealing if his views had changed. The laughter stopped abruptly as Thunder came scrambling back into the tent. They turned to see his crouched figure framed in the glaring sunlight of the open tent flap. He seemed to relish their attention. "First prize for crystal-ball gazing, Mr. Wechsler," he said breathlessly. "Our friend Rommel seems to be on the move."

"What?" said Wechsler. "Now, this is the development I needed." In some instinctive and nervous reaction to the news, he pulled a pencil from his pocket and put a thumb upon the point of it to see if it was ready to write.

"I'm glad you're pleased," said Thunder and immediately added, "But that means I'm getting you gentlemen away from here. Civilians are not supposed to get mixed up in the more sordid and personal aspects of warfare."

"Tell me how much you really know," said Wallingford calmly. "Have you spoken with Battalion? With Division?" When Thunder didn't respond he said, "I'm the ranking officer here, I think."

"We are not at sea, Wally," said Thunder primly. "This is the army's patch, and I'm running the show." Having said that, he became more conciliatory. "Those echelon vehicles we heard. They weren't arriving. They were vehicles that left here this morning. They were coming back."

"Coming back empty?" said Wallingford.

"They were fired upon," said Thunder. "By German tanks and field guns . . . probably tracked artillery. They didn't hang around to identify exactly what it was. One of the water-tank wagons was lost. Can't blame them for doing a quick about-turn."

"To the east of here? Could it have been a mistake, friendly fire?" said Wechsler.

"We're not likely to start firing at ourselves deep behind our own lines, Mr. Wechsler."

"It has happened," said Wechsler.

"Perhaps. But this time I think we have to believe their story. There are Germans or Italians, or both, on the track to our rear. To get this far, Rommel must have started moving last night."

"To the east?" said Wallingford. "That's impossible. There are minefields along this front, all the way south to Bir Hacheim."

"I wish it were impossible," said Thunder.

"They would have to have swung miles to the south and then north," said Wallingford, leaning over the map that Wechsler had opened and spread out on the ground.

"Oh, boy!" said Wechsler softly, as he realized what distances were involved and how fast Rommel's men had moved. "Rommel swung south last time," he said. "He went through Msus and panicked your Armored Brigade into flight."

Thunder didn't look at the map. He didn't want to be reminded of that disaster. He said, "I can't get anyone on the air, and the land line has been out of action for almost a week."

"So what do you propose to do, Thunder?" Wallingford asked. "Will you try to get everyone back to Regiment?"

"Too many soft skins to fight our way back. Normally, I

would leave our odds and ends to their own devices, but having Mr. Wechsler here changes everything. I can't leave him, and neither can I leave you here, Wally."

"We'll take our chances," said Wallingford. "If we move off after dark, we'll have no trouble slipping right through the Hun."

"And that goes for me too, buddy," said Wechsler. "It will be a great story. We'll be all right, won't we, Chips?"

"Ah! Sure we will," said O'Grady.

Thunder looked at one and then the other.

Wallingford said, "I'll take responsibility for Mr. Wechsler and Mr. O'Grady, if that gets you off the hook, Thunder. You get in your sardine cans and give a hand tormenting yonder Hun. We'll wait here until it gets dark. Then we'll move down the track very quietly and slowly until we get to Regiment. Don't worry, we'll be all right."

Thunder stared at them and then shook his head slowly. "No. Better we all go together. We'll abandon the echelon vehicles and everything else we don't absolutely need. After dark, we'll form up my cars with three of the best trucks inside the formation. If they spot us, my cars will divert their attention, while the trucks push on."

Wallingford saw it was a strategy Thunder had decided on before coming into the tent.

Gently Wechsler said, "I think we would have a better chance to get through without your armored cars, lieutenant. I've got a specially strengthened four-by-four. It will go anywhere."

"I can't take that risk, sir."

His gentle persuasion having failed, Wechsler became more forceful. He said, "There is no good reason for you escorting us in your damned cars, except that you're scared of getting a rocket for leaving us."

"Perhaps you are right," said Thunder coldly.

Encouraged, Wechsler said, "You know we'd have a better chance on our own. What's more, if Rommel's boys start lobbing ordnance at us, you fellows in your armored cars will be safer than us out in the open."

"We could argue all day and all night," said Thunder. "But the fact is that I am in charge. It doesn't matter what you think. You two are both civilians, and Mr. Wallingford is not in the army. I'm running this show. I've made my decision, and that is it. Be ready to move off as soon as the sun goes down. We'll have to crowd people into all the cars and trucks, so you can't take any baggage except your typewriter and camera."

"My chaps need something to eat," said Wallingford.

"Tell them to forage around the cookhouse. We'll be dumping everything before we move off. No brewing up, though. For the time being I don't want any fires." In the distance could be heard a loud continuous rumble. They scrambled outside the tent to hear it more clearly.

Wallingford said, "That's to the east of us."

None of them spoke. Anyone still hoping that the echelon vehicles had run into nothing more than some long-range enemy patrol now gave up that hope. What was happening to the east of them was a real battle.

For the last few days Thunder and his men had seen little or no air activity, but now, high overhead, two fighters crawled across the deep blue sky toward the gunfire.

"I need another scotch," said Wechsler, as he watched the planes disappear over the rocky skyline. "It might be a long time between drinks."

"What do they do with captured war correspondents?" said Wallingford affably.

"Jewish war correspondents?" said Wechsler, taking the cork from the whisky bottle. "I'll drop you a postcard and tell you."

Wallingford smiled. He suddenly had the thought that Wechsler's friendship might be a valuable asset when it came to an encounter with authority. "You won't go into the bag," he told Wechsler. "Stick with me. One of my chaps speaks fluent

German. In the dark, we'll bluff our way through."

Thunder had already sent two cars out to recce the surrounding desert area, while avoiding the vast marked minefields that stretched out on both sides of them. They prayed that the Luftwaffe spotter planes would be needed elsewhere; in that respect, at least, their prayers seemed to be answered.

Thunder's convoy was formed up, briefed and ready, well before darkness. They started out early so that the drivers would all find the marked track, and be able to get compass bearings, before complete darkness closed in on them. No lights were permitted anywhere, and Thunder had strictly prohibited brew-ups and smoking. It was a demanding journey. Only a few veterans among the men had much experience of navigating across the desert by starlight. The vehicles straggled.

Harry Wechsler was in the front seat of his Ford station wagon, with O'Grady driving. In the rear seats were nine soldiers, rear-echelon men who'd abandoned their vehicles. All Wechsler's expensive kit and equipment had been left behind to make room for them. Wechsler had argued and complained but Thunder proved adamant. His only concession was to promise to come back and get it all if the German attack fizzled out.

They'd been going about an hour and a half when Thunder—leading the procession in his armored car Ping-Pong—halted to take a look around and get a compass bearing. The desert air was cool and refreshing after the stifling heat of the armored car.

Once his feet were on the desert floor, Thunder knew where he was. It was always like that. Standing in the car with one's head poking out the top—or, worse still, peering through the tiny visor slits—he always had the feeling of being lost. But there was something so reassuring about having one's feet on the ground that problems disappeared like spilled water.

He could see everything through his binoculars. The ground sloped away. Lit by hazy starlight, the track stretched out in front of him for a mile or more. The tire marks were easily seen, for the supply trucks had been using this track for weeks. There was a marker barrel only three hundred yards away, and he didn't have to check the map reference to know where he was. The barrel was splashed with paint, where some nervous soldier had fumbled while painting the reference numbers. The splash looked like a seagull in flight, at least it looked like that to Thunder, and that's why he recognized it so easily. From here the track led over a ledge and then down and across a hard flat limestone stretch. Beyond that was the place where they'd find warm food, a drink, and a welcome. Regimental HQ was home. It was where he kept his spare kit and his precious little hoard of reading matter: four paperbacks, a neatly tied bundle of letters, and ancient hometown newspapers. By now perhaps more mail would have arrived.

Thunder started them off again and waved the accompanying armored cars through. The way was clear, but it was better to keep to the Standing Orders: armored vehicles in the van, soft-skin vehicles protected. At the rear of Thunder Column, as one of his sergeants had named it, came Wallingford's two trucks and then a final armored car manned by Thunder's best crew.

Thunder was reassured to have Wallingford at the rear. Wallingford was experienced and had always taken a perverse pleasure in swanning around way out there in no-man's-land. Wallingford seemed to court danger but, like most such men, he was always on his guard too. It was necessary to have someone experienced and alert as "ass-end Charlie." In France in 1940 the gunners of both sides had always targeted the leading vehicle first. In the narrow roads and confined spaces of northern Europe that was a way of bottling up the vehicles following, so that they could be destroyed one by one at the gunner's leisure. But desert fighting was different. Here gunners picked off the rearmost target first, in the hope that the loss would not be noticed before a couple more were knocked out. So he wanted someone reliable there.

As Wechsler's station wagon passed him, Thunder waved. Behind Wechsler's big Ford came another armored car, Dog's Dinner. The car commander was a corporal. He flicked Thunder a salute that was almost a wave of the hand.

Thunder slapped the metal of his own car, as a signal to ready his own driver, and then clambered up onto the top and slid inside. The skein of cloud opened and the moon came into view, as he started down the slope. The track was well marked here. Although the ledge was hard and rock-strewn, there were enough soft sandy patches for there to be tire tracks. This was where the supply convoys liked to rendezvous with squadron.

Thunder remained in his vantage point, reviewing the convoy as it trundled past him. But they didn't look like a parade, more like a train of refugees. Even the armored cars were half hidden under amazingly large bundles of kit and boxes of supplies that they didn't want to leave as a gift for the advancing Germans.

As the big truck passed, Wallingford gave him a broad grin. Thunder waved to him, picked up his microphone, and told his driver to get going again. "Let's go, Yo-yo."

He'd never been able to understand Wallingford. Wally had submerged himself in the war; he never mentioned going home. Neither did he ever speak of his family or say anything about England. Wally had immersed himself so deeply he didn't want to talk about the navy, his promotion, or his desert teams, or even about booze or women. Wally had become an outsider.

Thunder's car moved easily down the line of vehicles, overtaking them one by one. All the time, Thunder was watching the horizon with quick sweeps of the head, the way he'd been told to do at training school. But in fact he knew there was no chance that any enemy forces would be squeezed into the strip of land that now separated the retiring car squadron and its regimental home.

The moonlight came and went. In the gloom Thunder's driver was careful. The man had been assigned to Thunder at a time when he was considered the best driver in the regiment. Now there were other better, more experienced men who had been posted from other units, broken up by casualties. But Thunder was content with Lance Corporal Yeomans. Yo-yo had the same sort of care and—let it be whispered—caution that was a part of Thunder's makeup. Like Thunder, Yeomans would take any risk that was a necessary part of a fighting man's duties, but he had no ambition to earn a medal for valor—especially a posthumous one. He picked his way forward slowly.

As his car got near the head of the column, Thunder had his head sticking out of the turret and was admiring Wechsler's Ford. He would love to own a vehicle like that. It ran smoothly and quietly; even after they'd crowded all the extra men into the rear seats, its big V-8 engine had purred and it had pulled away effortlessly.

So Thunder was watching the Ford when it came to grief. The flash seemed to light up the whole landscape. Thunder felt the hot wind on his face and swayed with its force. Pieces of the Ford's bodywork came flying past his head, playing a dissonant musical chord as the sharp-edged pieces of metal sang through the air. Only then did the sound of the explosion start going round inside his brain.

The car following Wechsler's station wagon swerved to avoid the cloud of smoke that came rolling up and hid the wreckage. "Get on! get on!" Bodies—some of them ablaze—came rolling across the sand as men were thrown out of the car. "Get on!"

What would have been an agonizing decision, about whether to continue on and risk more casualties on the trail, was solved by Thunder's instinct and his automatic reaction to the danger. "Keep moving! Get on!"

As the smoke drifted away, the bent frame of the station wagon came into view. It could have been the victim of gunfire, of course, but after so many months of fighting, all who saw it knew it had hit a mine. It was a Teller mine: a large steel dinner plate with an ignition device fitted into the upper pressure plate. Most of them were set so that a man, or even a motorcycle, would fail to trigger them. Only the pressure from something worth destroying would make them explode.

The Germans had laid the Teller mines across the track, four meters apart, in the usual pattern that avoided a domino effect. Then some artful German engineers had rolled a British tire across the center of it, to leave its distinctive tracks. It was an old trick, but like all old tricks it worked well enough to be repeated time and time again.

Thunder jumped out of his armored car and ran to the burning wreck. The front off-side wheel had taken the blast. The men who'd been crammed into the rear seats had been strewn across the desert. Miraculously, most of them were still alive. It was not easy to see them in the darkness. All of them were burned, their clothing scorched and tattered. They were huddled together, like men carefully arranged for group photos. Three were sitting in the sand, nursing their legs and moaning softly. Two others were standing over them, cuddling themselves in postures characteristic of broken arms and cracked shoulder bones. They all looked dazed, as casualties do as they endure the first few minutes of a lifetime of being crippled.

Thunder ran to the car. The flames had died out but the wreckage was hot, and there was a nauseating smell of burning rubber and scorched oil. The two men in the front seat were still there. They were done for. O'Grady was the lucky one; he was dead. Wechsler's lower body was crushed by the dismounted engine, and a steering wheel spoke had pierced his stomach. His head was flopping to one side, and he was groaning through chattering teeth.

"We'll get you out," said Thunder. He'd seen it all before. They'd never get him out; both men were jammed tightly into the jungle of twisted metalwork. "Just hang on for a minute or two."

Wechsler seemed to have heard him. His hand moved a fraction, and he gave a soft yelp of pain. A corporal medic appeared from nowhere and Thunder stood aside. The man was a gunner from one of his cars. A kennel boy before the war and without any proper medical training or experience, he'd become the unit's only first-aid man. While rummaging in his shoulder bag he gave a glance at O'Grady. It was enough. Without hesitation he pushed the needle of a disposable morphia syringe into Wechsler's arm, squeezing the tube tight to give him as big a dose as possible. Then he turned to Thunder and shrugged.

"Get back to your car, corporal."

"It's gone, sir."

"Climb up onto my car then. It's not far to go now."

"I'll stay with the rest of them, if you don't mind, sir."

Thunder hesitated. It would mean one car without a gunner. On the other hand, the injured echelon men deserved some sort of first-aid treatment. "Okay. I'll send someone back for you before it gets light."

"We'll be all right, sir."

Thunder nodded. The gunner was risking his life, and yet his manner was matter of fact, as if he was doing no more than wait for the next bus. Thunder wondered sometimes if the men really understood the consequences of the risks they took. And yet this man was staring those risks right in the face.

"Good man," said Thunder. It was things like this that racked him with a guilt that piled up higher and higher. One day it would be piled so high he'd not be able to go on. Thunder tried to push it out of his mind as he climbed back up onto his car again. He gave a quick look around and saw Wallingford.

"It's not your fault, Thunder," Wallingford said.

Thunder looked at him. Wallingford had always had the uncanny knack of reading his mind. Did his face always reveal his every feeling? "Yes, it was," said Thunder. "The tire tracks were too fresh. Look at them. The bloody Hun engineers rolled a British tire between their mines. I should have been at point."

"There was no way to be sure. The Hun likes to use British

trucks. Everyone knows that, although I've never figured out why."

Thunder answered him mechanically, as he answered questions from his men sometimes. "The double tires on their Opels clog with sand. They like British wheels and tires; they're more open treaded." He got into the car and picked up the microphone and tried to push the guilt out of his mind.

"You learn something every day," said Wallingford, with an assumed brightness that was not convincing. Like Thunder, Wallingford could not help but see the deaths of Wechsler and O'-Grady as some sort of dire omen.

"Let's go, Yo-yo," said Thunder quietly, and his car moved forward. He twisted his head for one last look at the casualty. He could see the corporal medic inspecting the injuries of the huddled men. Over his microphone he said, "Put your foot down as much as you can, Yo-Yo; we'd better be leading the parade when the old man spots us. We'll have to send someone back here to collect these odd-bods."

The driver gave nothing more than a click on the intercom to acknowledge the order. They plowed onward for what seemed hours. The promise of dawn was turning the eastern sky purple when they saw the outer sentries and guard tanks that shielded the regimental leaguer.

"Home sweet home," said Yo-yo. With Thunder leading the little column, the vehicles crawled into position, coming into their parade formation. For a moment everything seemed normal and calm. The tanks were sitting in tight groups, as they always were at night. A few men emerged from their tents, blinking in the moonlight as they watched them arrive. But the men moved in a curious way, and there was not the sort of activity that was normal in a unit preparing for dawn stand-by.

As Thunder climbed down from his turret, he saw it all more clearly. The regiment had taken a beating. Armored cars and tanks that from a distance seemed so sound and intact could now be recognized as wrecks. In such poor light the appearance of a tank does not change much after a high-velocity armor-piercing shell has traveled right through it, making hamburger of its crew and iron filings of its engine.

Jesus! said Thunder to himself. They've been clobbered. There's no one left. He was reminded of those scenes from Hollywood Westerns after the Indians had scalped everyone in the fort.

More men came to stand and stare. It was not as bad as it looked. The newcomers greeted their friends and stood about exchanging accounts of what had happened. Casualties had been relatively light, but the German armor had picked off many of the tanks. The dumps had gone up in smoke. As an armored unit, the regiment's potential was severely depleted.

Staggering, swaying, and uncertain, still deafened by the artillery barrage, men emerged from their shelters to look at Thunder's Column and the survivors it had brought. Colonel Andy Anderson, his uniform dirty and torn, grabbed Thunder, took him aside, and listened impatiently to his report. Then, with a typical example of Anderson showmanship, he ordered his own driver to jump into the Matador and go back to collect the men stranded in the desert.

Wallingford looked around nervously. He saw Darymple's car, Beryl. It had survived the attack and even nailed some of the attacking force. "What happened here, Robbie?"

Darymple was grinning. It was action, the very thing he'd wanted so badly while sitting behind that Cairo desk. "The Hun came in from the east side of the box, and we weren't ready for him. He was knocking us all over the field by the time any of the engines were started. He'd got his guns up close. We were sitting ducks. It was a massacre: like facing a bloody firing squad. Bang! Bang! Hand the gentleman a coconut! I got Beryl hull down and let the blighters have a taste of their own medicine. The show was all over in an hour, and their armor pushed off somewhere to the northeast. There are still plenty of Huns along our perimeter. Infantry and antitank guns. Just for the moment they have us pinned down. We're out of contact with Brigade. Wireless out of action, precious little drinking water, and ammunition is strictly rationed until we make contact with echelon. We've spent the last three hours of darkness mopping up and getting the bodies buried." He looked at his wristwatch. "I must make sure my chaps get something hot to eat."

Two men from the cookhouse arrived with a big bucket of hot sweet tea for the newly arrived men. "Listen, you people!" shouted Anderson. He stepped up onto an ammunition box so as better to see the men around him. "Get yourself some tea and don't waste time. I want you back reporting to your sections inside five minutes."

He turned to Wallingford and his men.

"You men with IDT badges, close up and listen to me." The men shuffled forward and surrounded him. "We know all about you. You're all thieves and deserters. You stink! You let down your friends, you let down your families, and you let down your country. I despise the lot of you."

At this disconcerting greeting, some of the men looked around and saw regimental police, their rifles at the high port and ready to use.

"Well, you're lucky. Now you've got a chance to redeem your self-respect. We're expecting another attack by the Huns, and then another and another. So I need all the men I can find, even rotten scum like you. The chaplain is with me here. He'll take a note of your name, rank, and number, your unit, and the approximate date of your last pay parade. I don't want you wasting his time with any bloody fairy stories. Fairy-story time is over; get that into your thick heads! Give him your correct details, then draw a rifle from the armory sergeant. You'll be assigned to a place on the perimeter. Move from it one inch, and you'll be shot dead by the Field Security police. I'll be watching every one of you, and so will your comrades."

Wallingford's men took this news with mixed emotions. Some were horrified, some were frightened, some were relieved.

"Is that all right, Mr. Wallingford?" Mogg asked.

Before Wallingford had a chance to reply, Anderson said, "And cut those IDT badges off your shirts right away. You're under my command now. Your mister bloody Wallingford won't be giving you any more orders. He's a deserter, a crook, and no better than you lot. I'm taking him along for interrogation. Now, pretend you are real soldiers again; form a line for the padre."

As the men started to line up in front of the chaplain, Sandy Powell called, "Will you put in a good word for us, colonel?" The others turned to hear the reply.

Anderson stared at him indignantly. "When we repair the wireless and regain contact with army HQ, I'll tell them I've got you deserters on my ration strength. I'll list your names so that your friends and relatives back home will eventually get to know you were here, fighting alongside real soldiers, who know how to do their duty. It's our job to hold out as long as we can. That's what I mean to do. The only thing I can promise any of you miserable bastards is a Christian burial."

Ross had kept Wallingford under observation from the moment he arrived. He'd even guessed what Wallingford's greeting might be, "Can we make a bargain, major?" But Wallingford's proposal surprised him. "One of my men knows what you need to know—about the spy and so on—but I don't think you'll squeeze it out of him without my help." He puffed on his cigarette.

"It took you a long time to see where your duty was," said Ross.

"Better I talk to him first. I know how to handle him. He's called Percy. He's a German deserter. He was a cipher clerk for Rommel. He knows all about the intelligence stuff Rommel is getting from Cairo."

"You're a fool, Wallingford. One of your mistakes was awarding yourself the Distinguished Service Order. I couldn't trace you through naval records, but when we checked the list of DSO winners it took only half an hour to confirm that you were a phony."

"I can—"

"Go and get yourself a rifle and be a man instead of a thief. I don't need your help, Wallingford. I'll find your pal, Percy. This is my show."

Jimmy Ross had no trouble in finding Percy. He was standing in line where the rifles were being handed out. Ross walked up to him and, without a word, grabbed him by the throat and said, "I want to talk to you—"

But Percy had recognized what was in store for him. He'd prepared for this moment a thousand times. He ducked his head and lashed out to strike Ross's face with the edge of his hand. Then Percy was running. At first it seemed as if he might be heading to the tent where Anderson had set up his command post, but then he headed toward the German lines and went scrambling up the sandy embankment. It was a dune of wind-blown sand, steep and soft. He slipped but persevered, grabbing at the sand with both hands and feet, so that he climbed like a spider. He looked around and, seeing Ross running after him, scrambled more frantically.

When he reached the top Percy stood up. Although the landscape was lit by a bright moon, he showed no fear. It was as if he believed himself invulnerable to the shot and shell of his own people. He ran along the ridge in full view of the Germans manning their forward positions. Ross, equally exposed, chased after him.

But now Ross changed direction. By risking a more exposed route, he could cut Percy off. Jumping over the top of the ridge, Ross skidded in the sand, toppled, and nearly fell. Shots were fired. His sudden movement attracted a stream of machine-gun bullets. He heard them spitting and hissing in the sand near him and rolled over to go head first down the incline. Now he was completely exposed to the German fire. Ahead of him there was a flat stretch of limestone and, beyond it, Percy. Ross jumped up and sprinted across the hard slippery surface, while bullets chipped off pieces of ground and sent them singing away in all directions.

At the far side of the flat stretch he got to a wide gully, created by a flaw in the rock. He threw himself down flat and for a moment felt safe. He made his way along the crevice, using the knees-and-elbows crawl that does not have to be taught to men being shot at. As the gully tapered to nothing he was again spotted, and he heard bullets passing close as he ran the final few yards.

He could see Percy now; he was running across soft sand. The guns paused as the Germans stared and tried to understand what was happening. Lungs bursting, Percy came to the ridge and an abandoned Bren gun weapon pit. From here there was a clear view of the German positions. The nearest ones were about six hundred yards away, marked by sprawling figures, spread-eagled grotesquely like rag dolls. They were dead British soldiers, tumbled out of their slit trenches to make room for the new owners.

Percy started to run again, but he was moving more slowly now. Every intake of breath burned his lungs. He slipped and skidded down the far side of the slope, but each step pained him. Ross had now encountered the soft sand and found it heavy going, as Percy had done. With each step he went in to the ankles and sometimes deeper, so that he felt like a fly on sticky paper, trying to get free.

Now a few Germans were also standing up. One of them was on the top of a dune and using binoculars to see better. Then some German sniper opened fire. Single shots came very close. Ross dropped flat and Percy did too. They both got up, but Percy was slower in recovering.

Half a dozen more shots were fired before Ross reached Percy. He charged into him, shoulder forward, knocked him full length, and landed on top of him. The two men rolled down the slope in a cloud of dust. By the time they stopped rolling, Ross was uppermost and had his captive pinned down. Here in a piece of dead ground they were lost to the sight of anyone. Ross hit him hard and Percy went limp.

Squatting upon him, Ross said, "I swear by God I'll kill you. . . ." He stopped and tried to get his breath. "You're going to open up about your lousy signals intercepts, or whatever they were."

There was no answer. Percy was winded too.

"Do you hear me, Percy, damn you?" He slapped him to provoke a reaction. Percy had his eyes tightly closed. He gave a grunt that might have meant yes or no. The firing had slackened and stopped. Then came the distant sound of an engine starting. Someone was sending a vehicle to investigate.

Ross turned Percy over roughly and, holding the back of his head, banged his face hard down into the sand. "You're for the high jump, unless you talk, Percy. So get it straight in your mind: you are going to talk. And talk. And talk. And talk." He smacked him across the side of the head.

Percy couldn't breathe. Close to death by asphyxiation, he struggled and finally twisted his face clear of the sand. He spluttered, spat sand, and gulped. "Let me go. Please! I will tell you."

Ross let Percy move a little and let him free his arm. Percy twisted, reached up and rubbed his throat, and shook his head as if trying to clear his mind.

There came the sound of more shots. But the two men couldn't be seen from the German lines. The shots went overhead, and they heard them hitting nearby rocks. The Germans were becoming alarmed, fearing that what they'd seen was the precursor to some kind of counterattack. As Ross was taking his weight off his victim, half a dozen mortar shells landed with a dull thump. One after another, in close succession, they exploded deep in the soft sand, so that they made tall columns of dust and smoke and deep craters. The sand and smoke drifted across them so that Ross could taste the cordite. There was some artillery fire off to the north. Everyone was getting jumpy. Were these incidents all part of the overture? Was this a softening up that would soon become an attack in strength? More thumps of mortar fire sounded.

And then the sound of the engine became much louder. Ross looked at Percy and Percy grinned. But when the sound got close it was not a German tank that came rumbling over the sand and rolling down toward them, it was Beryl.

"The armored car will give us cover," said Ross. The first light of dawn was making long shadows in the sandy landscape in which they were hidden. "While he's with us, we're going to scramble back along that gully and up the dune and get back to the British position. Crawl with me and keep with the car. And don't try anything stupid."

"Tell me again," said Ross.

They were sitting on the ground in the shade cast by a wrecked tank. It was late afternoon, and so far the threatened German attack had not developed. There had been more false alarms. The Germans were trying to keep them jittery.

"How many years did you say you were in Signals?" he asked Percy. It was a question designed to test the consistency of Percy's story. Ross was getting the hang of this interrogation game. It was just like an audition. Easier really, for no one could tell better lies than an actor who wanted a part.

"Always. I read electrical engineering at the Technische Hochschule in Berlin. I immediately became a lieutenant, and I was assigned to Lauf, the radio intercept station."

"All right. Don't go all through that again." He looked at his notes. "So the messages came in; then what happened?"

"The intercepted messages were stripped of their superencipherment by the cryptanalysts on duty."

"How long did that take?"

"A short message, less than an hour."

"And then you sent it to Tripoli?"

"No. I told you. The messages had to be translated into German, by someone who understood British military terms, equipment, and the way the British army works. Then they were rewritten so that no one could guess where the stuff was coming from."

"But your people in Tripoli would have it within a couple of hours?"

"More like three hours. It varied, of course. The black code was easy for us."

"Tell me about the black code." He offered Percy his cigarettes and matches.

Percy took a cigarette and lit it. "Black is the American name. It is called black because the bindings of the codebooks are black." Percy leaned back against a sprocket wheel of the tank and drew on his cigarette. "In Rome, an agent of the Servizio Informazione Militare stole it from the American military attaché. He also got the superencipherment tables. The SIM gave it all to us."

"Us?"

"The Abwehr."

"You said you weren't in the Abwehr."

"I was signals staff attached to the Abwehr," said Percy, pleased to have won the exchange.

"When did you first get the code?"

"Last summer: August or September."

"Good stuff right from the start?"

"Supply shipping, morale, evaluation of enemy tactics and weapons. Everything Rommel needed to know. Numbers, units, dates. It was wonderful material."

"It sounds like it."

"Sometimes it could tell us of British intentions: a raid, or an attack, or how a certain unit would be employed when the right time came. And there were comments, very frank comments, about the training state, morale, and readiness of the British units."

"And then, when you came to Africa, you were on the receiving end?"

"I worked as an assistant to Rommel's Staff Officer Operations. Sometimes I was in Tripoli, but Rommel likes to move around, and usually I went where he went."

"In his car?"

"I was not that important. I was in a truck with my immediate superior, a signals *Oberleutnant,* and the maps and radios and so on. We worked even while on the move. Rommel is tough."

Gently Ross steered him back to the messages. "So you saw the messages in the first raw state?"

"Exactly as they were sent. I could speak and write English. Sometimes they would ask my opinion about a word or a phrase that puzzled the interpreters. But since the difficulties were usually technical British army words, I could not help very often. I told you that. I saw the originals. That is why I know where they came from."

"Tell me again."

"The messages are coming from the American embassy, from the military attaché in Cairo. They are filed through the Egyptian Telegraph Company, Cairo, for radio transmission to Washington D.C. Each message is marked MILID WASH: that means the destination is the Military Intelligence Division, Washington."

"And we've been looking for a spy all these months."

"Yes."

"The American attaché is shown everything," said Ross, remembering Harry Wechsler's stories. "The instructions are to show the embassy staff anything they want to see. Every tank and gun, down to the last nut and bolt."

"Rommel's staff knows everything you do," said Percy simply. He looked around him at the wrecked tanks and the tents as if seeing it all for the first time. "You will be overrun before nightfall." He said it without gloating, as if it were a self-evident fact.

"I must get you back to Cairo. I must tell GHQ."

"You must let me go," said Percy.

Ross stared at him in disbelief. "Are you completely mad? Don't you know what your playmates will do to you if they find out that you've betrayed their greatest secret."

"It is a gamble," said Percy. "When they overrun the box, you will be my prisoner. If they do not overrun it, I will be your prisoner."

"I'm not making deals with you," said Ross.

Percy didn't respond. He knew no one would want to transmit such a story over the air. Rommel's monitoring service would be sure to pick it up. Even without that happening, a sensational story like this would be sure to leak out among the British signals staff.

Ross said, "Colonel Anderson has generously offered me a car and crew. I'm going to try and get you through the lines tonight. With luck we'll get to Cairo. Cooperate, and I'll see what I can do for you."

As he said it, they heard whistles blowing and there was a sudden heavy salvo of gunfire. Then there was the curious popping noise of smoke shells. Anderson came out of his command post and called to them. "This is it, major. The Hun infantry is coming over in open order, a lot of them. They have a sprinkling of tanks. We may not be able to hold them."

"I'll need your man," said Ross.

"He's coming," said Anderson. "Butcher is the man for the job." He went back into his tent. There were more explosions and more sounds of Spandau machine guns.

"What does that mean?" Percy asked.

"I'm giving my notes of what you've told me to a runner. He'll depart in a few minutes' time. We'll leave tonight, if we haven't been overrun by then. Meanwhile, should your people break into the compound, Colonel Anderson has assigned a reliable man to shoot both of us."

=22=

Alice got the news from Peggy West. Peggy had spent fifteen minutes preparing herself for the ordeal. She went into the office. Alice was alone there. Thank heaven for that; it would have been unbearable to tell her with others present.

"Alice, I have to tell you something," she said. Her tone was somber, and she paused to let the words sink in. "It's not entirely good."

"It's Bert?"

"Yes, it's Bert. He went into surgery. I was on the team. But he's strong; he'll be all right."

"What happened?" Alice was on her feet. Her face was drained of blood, and she was holding some pages of typing with both hands, holding them so tightly they were beginning to tear apart.

"He'll be all right."

"Tell me the truth, Peggy."

"Burns on his legs, mostly. Shock. Exposure too. He was unconscious for a bit. He had a couple of nights and days out in the sun before they found him."

"Will he . . . ?" She couldn't bring herself to look at Peggy. She looked out the window. She could see the Kasr el Nil barracks. There was always a crowd of Egyptians there. They watched the daily activities of the British soldiers with the passive curiosity of visitors to a zoo.

"No, he'll be all right," said Peggy. "He'll be on his feet again in a couple of weeks or so. He'll be scarred, of course, but he's lucky to come through."

"May I see him?"

"The brigadier has been up there with him. He's brought back some important news. He was demanding to see the brigadier before he went into surgery, but the Hoch wouldn't delay."

"The Rommel spy?"

"Yes, something like that. No one was allowed up there while the brigadier was with him."

"Are you sure he'll be all right, Peggy? How soon may I see him?"

"Come up with me. I'll get you in there, brigadier or no brigadier."

Alice smiled nervously. "I do love him, Peggy."

"Of course," said Peggy.

As they were going along the corridor they met the brigadier on his way out. Spaulding was with him, wearing shiny new captain's pips and looking comical in shorts. Under his arm he had a fat bundle of papers and a notebook. It was a hot day and Spaulding was suffering in the heat. Both men stopped as they caught sight of the women.

"Ah, Sister West . . . and Miss Stanhope!" said the brigadier. He took off his cap upon catching sight of Alice. "I was with your mother last week. Such a charming lady. She was at a cocktail party in Alex. We talked about you."

Peggy smiled. Alice nodded, and Spaulding looked from one to the other. He was standing in the exaggerated posture that he assumed when being photographed. He was very upright, with his peaked cap tucked under one arm. But today the effect was marred by the bundle of papers he was balancing.

"I just heard about Major Cutler," said Alice.

By now the brigadier had got over his initial surprise at seeing her and remembered that Alice Stanhope was on Cutler's staff. "If it's about the spy business, you can rest your mind. Spaulding has been taking notes during Major Cutler's verbal report to me." His face clouded over as he thought about it. "There is going to be the biggest damned scandal Cairo has ever known."

"If it gets out," said Spaulding warningly. He wiped his brow with a khaki-colored handkerchief.

The brigadier caught his eye. "Quite so. It mustn't get out. Top secret."

"I have to see him," said Alice, edging away to continue on her way.

"He's been under a terrible strain," explained the brigadier. "He was out there alone in the desert for two days."

"Yes, I know. Sister West told me."

The brigadier shook his head. "He was the only survivor of an armored car crew. It was a burial party that found him. Dead and dying all round the landscape apparently. Germans and British. The Germans had left him for dead. Goodness knows exactly what happened; Cutler will enlarge on it in the fullness of time, I'm sure. He had a dead South African handcuffed to him. What a terrible business. The chaplain with the burial parties thought Cutler was another corpse at first. He'd already buried half a dozen before looking at him."

"I must leave you now, brigadier. It's important that I talk to him."

"Why?" said the brigadier with the simple directness that rank affords. He gave her his most winning smile. He was in prime condition. The brigadier reveled in this hot weather. "Why?"

"I'm going to be his next of kin," said Alice.

When they knew the brigadier was coming, they'd given Jimmy Ross a private room. He was sitting up in bed there. The overhead fan was revolving slowly, bringing little change in temperature but emitting a regular squeak. Sunlight was streaming through the windows, striking a khaki uniform hanging on the end of the bed. Crowns had been removed from the shoulder flaps and new corporal's stripes had been stitched onto the sleeves. This handwork was that of Sergeant Ponsonby, who was sitting by the bedside.

"You gave your name as Corporal James Ross," said Ponsonby, shaking his head sadly. "That chaplain who found you wrote out a ticket for you in that name. You came in here with that name on your docket. It was Sister West who recognized you when they were preparing you for surgery."

"Tell me the worst," said Ross.

"I have all your documentation here," said Ponsonby. He opened a heavy brown envelope stuffed with official records. On the outside it said ROSS, JAMES. Over that a large rubber stamp mark said DECEASED. "Here's your death certificate." He held up a flimsy sheet of paper so Ross could see it.

"Nothing else?"

"I hope you never stood trial for that other business?" Ross shook his head. "Good. Good. That's what I thought: just charged, weren't you? It gives you a clean sheet, see. When a man dies, all charges against him are dropped. There is no alternative to that. You've come back to life, but they can't charge you again: that would be double jeopardy, wouldn't it?"

"You mean I'll be resurrected?"

"These things happen a lot out here. A man is captured and then escapes weeks later. Or he's left for dead and then recovers."

"And they all have any charges against them dropped?"

Ponsonby gave an artful grin. "Oh, no. They're all posted as missing. You were lucky; you were certified dead."

"So it's all over."

"You've been posted to India and they're sending you to some other hospital for recuperation. You'll have to recover first.

You should be able to fiddle some sick leave, plus the fourteen days' leave you usually get before embarkation. But they're in a hurry to get you out of Cairo."

"Why?"

Ponsonby paused for a moment before explaining it. "I spoke to the sergeant major in records. It would make it easier for them if Major Cutler died out in the desert two days ago. The brigadier is agreeable to that. In fact, he's recommended Major Cutler for a Military Cross."

"Wait a minute. For getting that stuff about the attaché?"

"Yes, I knew you'd be a bit ratty about that. But we can't alter the fact that Corporal James Ross wasn't there, and Major Cutler was."

"I earned that medal."

"That's not on. Military Cross is for officers only. You can't be a corporal and have an MC ribbon on your chest. Be reasonable."

"Why can't they put me down as Corporal Ross for the last month?"

"Because you've been drawing major's pay, son."

"Yes, that's right." Ross thought about it. A few days ago, all he wanted was to be pardoned and have the clock put back. It was only a piece of colored ribbon. "Corporal Ross, yes, I see. No charges of absence or desertion?"

"You weren't absent, were you? You were in the SIB office every day, working hard on behalf of law and order. Anyone standing up before a court-martial board saying you were absent could be made to look a right bloody fool. I heard Captain Marker explaining that in words of one syllable to some cocky lawyer from GHQ."

"Have you and Captain Marker cooked all this up for me, Sergeant Ponsonby?"

"Not me. I just do everything by the book. You know that."

"The brigadier, then?"

"He doesn't want to know. I talked with him, of course. But

he feels it better if he's not officially notified of this sort of detail."

"So I'm a free man?"

"No, son. You're in the bloody army."

At that moment Alice came in.

"Bert!"

"I was just leaving, miss."

The message for Peggy West came by phone to the Hotel Magnifico, very late in the afternoon. The caller gave the name of an Austrian dentist in Alexandria. It was not far from Garden City to the far side of the island. In the cool of a summer evening it was a pleasant walk.

"Hello? Hello?" Peggy West called more than once before going aboard, but there was no reply. Always before, the servant had met her even before she set foot on the gangway. This evening the boat was silent. The only lights to be seen were the small hooded ones along the deck. They shone on the woodwork and the dark water of the Nile that rippled past the hull.

She would not have been so tentative if she had not had the strong feeling that she was not alone. She looked around her and then called again. "Hello! Hello, Solomon!" She'd never called him Solly.

She knew the boat well by now. She knew the narrow companionway that led from the afterdeck to the galley and the lower deck. She went down the steep companionway. The door was unlocked, and she let herself into the salon, which was more like a drawing room, with big windows that looked out on the far bank. There was enough light coming through the windows for her to see that the furniture all seemed to be in its usual places. She found the light switch—"Oh!"

For one moment she thought it was a corpse that was facing her, slumped in the big armchair near the far door. Peggy had seen plenty of dead bodies, and although surprised she was not frightened. "Solomon! My God!"

The figure stirred. "Take it easy. Don't be scared. It's me. Walk across to the windows and close the curtains. Do it naturally."

She did as he ordered.

"The boat is being watched. I want them to think you are the only one aboard. Were you followed?"

Her impulse was to answer in some joking way, to say No, only whistled at, or something of that sort, to mock his melodramatic manner, but now, as she turned to look at him, the words dried up. She could see he was hurt. The usual stylishly dressed Solomon was unrecognizable. This man was dirty, his white linen suit stained and torn, and his face screwed tight with pain.

"What time is it?"

"Nearly ten. What's happened?" she said.

"I stopped a bullet." He wiped his lips and then dabbed at them with a blood-specked handkerchief. "Yigal is dead."

"How did it happen?"

"We shot Mahmoud, the banker. He was informing on us."

"Let me look at you." As soon as she opened his shirt she could see it was a serious wound. She wondered how he'd got this far, with his chest matted with blood and the huge blue bruise that a bullet causes at close range.

"Um!" He bit his lip, trying not to admit to pain.

She ran her fingers gently across his chest, speaking more to herself than to him. "I can't do much without instruments. I can't find the exit wound, but sometimes they are very small. I'll have to get you to hospital. I need—"

"I'm all right. I've got no time to go to hospital right now. I'm on the run from the law. Put on a new dressing for me." He rummaged in his pocket, found a fresh army field dressing, and gave it to her. Then he produced a small bottle of iodine.

"It's an open wound. This stuff will hurt like the devil," Peggy warned him.

"You sound like my mother."

She got some water and, kneeling beside him, cleaned the wound as best she could. There was a pistol in his pocket, but she pretended she hadn't noticed it. "It might have nicked the lung." She wiped his mouth and looked for fresh blood on the handkerchief. She found none, but that wasn't conclusive evidence. "You must be X-rayed as soon as possible." She ripped open the dressing and applied it. "You must see a doctor," she said, as she helped him back on with his shirt. "That's just a first field dressing. It's not designed for nursing work."

"Stop fussing. I've seen a doctor. I'll be all right."

"You won't be all right. You are badly hurt. You have internal damage. And it will go septic if you don't change the dressing every day."

"Don't fuss." Slowly and carefully he got a wallet from his inside pocket. He laid it on his knee and flipped it open. "Here's the money from Karl."

"Thank you."

"That's all you come here for, isn't it?"

This deliberate offensiveness was all part of his makeup: his determination to show he didn't need her, didn't need anyone. "What else would I come here for?" she said, and got to her feet with a sigh. She'd had a long day.

He smiled. "Rommel's coming, Peggy. What will your money be worth then?"

"He won't get to Cairo." She moved away from him, straightening her dress and touching her hair, as she sat down in a soft chair.

"I say he will," said Solomon. "He's taken Tobruk and crossed the Egyptian frontier. Hitler's made him a field marshal, and he's just a few miles along the road."

"He will need nurses," she said, with a calm she did not feel. "What time is it?"

"Why do you keep asking the time?" When he gave no answer, she looked at her watch and said, "Five past ten."

"I've missed the BBC news. A boat is coming for me."

"Are you going back to Palestine?"

She noticed the way in which he moved his hand very slightly so that he could feel the shape of the pistol under his coat. "I think they will try and grab me when the boat comes. But they won't get me."

"Who will?"

"This boat is staked out. I told you. We are being watched at this minute."

"Are you talking about the British, the Special Investigation Branch?"

"That bloody Cutler; he's a madman."

"You are both madmen. But Cutler is somewhere in the blue."

He shook his head. "You know that's not true, Peggy," he said good-naturedly. "Not any longer. They flew him back this morning. The rumors say he was chained to someone when they found him. It is also rumored that the British have had some sort of breakthrough about their security failure."

"How do you know all this?"

"What do you think I do in Cairo, twiddle my thumbs all day?"

"But how do you know about Cutler?"

"I have agents everywhere."

"Jews?"

"Some doctors and nurses have a proper sense of duty," he said, looking at her.

"I did what I could, Solomon. It's not my fault that Prince Piotr is just a windbag. I told you that, right from the start. I told you spying on him would be a waste of time."

He nodded. What she said was true. It was not her fault; it was his. "Perhaps I got that one wrong," he said.

She'd not heard him express such self-doubt before. Perhaps it was the chronic pain that had brought him down so low. "You did what you thought was right," she said vaguely. "You're not in the right condition to make important decisions."

He seemed not to have heard her. "Yigal always argued with me. He was always going on about helping the British. He liked to fool himself that fighting Hitler and the Fascists is the only important task for any Jew."

"You don't agree?"

"It's more complicated than that," said Solomon, as if he didn't want to pursue the question.

"Jews have a wide choice of enemies," said Peggy.

He touched the dressing she'd applied, as if trying to test himself with the pain. "Perhaps you think I should be trying to stop Rommel?"

"In your present state you won't do much to swing the balance."

"The British are collapsing. They're on the run in the desert. They won't fight."

"They'll fight," said Peggy. "You don't know them as I do. They will fight."

"Go up on deck. Take the flashlight. Watch for the boat . . . a felucca. They'll repeatedly flash a green light three times. You keep the light switched on."

She looked at him. "Repeatedly flash a green light three times." She repeated his exact words. How precise and how childish. He was always playing the conspirator. It was an essential part of his character; he should have been an actor. "I'll go and look."

She was glad to have some time to collect her thoughts. She stood on the deck, staring into the gloom. The coming of night had brought a sudden change of temperature, and a ghostly mist lay upon the water of the Nile. There were bats. They swooped through the lights on the other boats and across the water, down into the layer of mist, and through the bridge. She'd got used to them now, but at first the swarms of bats in Cairo had been one of her irrational terrors. There were so many things she had wasted time worrying about. Only now that her parents were dead could she start to see her life in some sort of real perspective. Why hadn't she settled down in England and got a good job, a good husband, beautiful children, and a comfortable house? Why had she spent her adult life working with second-rate surgical equipment and living in primitive apartments in hot, dusty towns? Had she been entirely self-indulgent, or was she after some romantic goal that didn't exist?

Solomon must have heard the approach of the boat or sensed it in some way. He was remarkably prescient at times. He appeared at her side in time to see the second lot of signals. She answered with the flashlight. It was a big lateen-rigged felucca, the sort of boat that has sailed African waters for centuries. But it was no ordinary felucca, judging by the soft sound of the powerful diesel engine. Its engine cut. It drifted on the current and discharged a rowboat, which moved across the water toward them. Solomon buttoned his coat, readying himself to climb aboard it.

"Do you have luggage?" she asked him.

He shook his head. "I have nothing."

She looked into his face. "Take care of yourself. You must see a doctor."

"You can have the houseboat," he said, as if it was a sudden impulse. "It's furnished. There is a bill of sale, signed and notarized; it's in the top drawer of the bureau. The mooring fees are paid up to the end of 1943. Sell it if you don't want it."

"Thank you, Solomon." She knew it wasn't an impulse. Solomon was never impulsive; he was a man for whom planning was sacred. Even when seriously wounded the plan—whatever it was—would have to be carried through.

"Karl is dead," he said, as if explaining his gift.

"Yes, I know."

"How could you know?"

"I guessed. You never brought anything that was in his handwriting."

"There were notes from him."

"Typewritten. Karl couldn't type."

"Perhaps he learned."

"Not Karl."

She expected him to say something fulsome about Karl, something about his dying bravely or giving his life for the Jewish homeland. But he didn't enlarge on what he'd said.

The rowboat missed the fenders and bumped against the hull as it came alongside. "Is this the city of gold?" said one of the men at the oars.

At first she thought it was a coded challenge, but then she remembered the houseboat was called the *City of Gold*.

"I'm here," said Solomon. He steadied himself by gripping her arm. Then, carefully, he started down the ladder from the stern. At the bottom rung he stopped and watched the rowboat bobbing on the water. With great difficulty, he stepped aboard it. His weight made the boat dip alarmingly. He swayed. For a moment it seemed as if he might tumble into the water. Then one of the men caught him and put an arm around him as he dropped onto a seat.

"Help him, he's sick," called Peggy softly. "Get him to a doctor."

Solomon slowly turned to her and, with a gentle wave of the hand that took in the houseboat, he said, "Where I am going, they are all doctors. Enjoy!"

She waved back but he had already turned away. As soon as he was aboard, the men pushed off. When the rowboat was alongside the felucca, willing hands helped Solomon aboard. Then, as it swung in the current, the felucca's motor started with a sudden burst of power that settled back into a gentle purr. There were no lights anywhere on it, and even the shape of its great lateen sail was soon swallowed by the gloom. The last she saw of Solomon, he was huddled in the stern and being wrapped in a blanket.

Peggy stood for a moment staring into the purple dusk. She felt sad, and yet she had never liked Solomon. There was about him a male arrogance that she did not find attractive. Sometimes she told herself she expected too much of men.

It seemed that only a minute or two passed between Solomon's departure and the sound of booted feet and the Egyptian police inspector's urgent warning: "Don't throw anything overboard, madam!"

She turned to see them clambering aboard with their rifles and steel helmets. "I wasn't about to throw anything overboard," said Peggy.

"I'm looking for the owner, madam," said the police inspector politely.

"I'm the owner," said Peggy. "This boat, the *City of Gold,* is mine. Someone just gave it to me."

More and more policemen came on board. Eventually Captain Lionel Marker appeared and gave Peggy a cheerful and informal salute. "Good evening, Peggy."

"What is it you want?" said Peggy, looking from one to the other.

"We wanted to be sure you were all right," said Marker.

"And you were after Solomon?" she suggested.

"Yes," he admitted. "We were also after Solomon."

"He's gone," said Peggy. She couldn't decide how pleased she was that Solomon had escaped them. She had never understood Solomon. She didn't know what he wanted or what he really believed in, but it was good that he escaped. She didn't like the idea of anyone being locked up.

"Yes, we were just too late," said Marker solemnly.

They stood there for a moment, as if their previous friendship had never existed. The Egyptian police inspector came up to Marker, saluted, and said that his men had found nothing of importance. "Thank you, Inspector Khalil. You can stand your men down. The birds have flown."

"The boat went upriver," said the police inspector. "It was the one I told you about," he added with just a hint of admonition.

"Perhaps the navy patrol will pick him up," said Marker.

The police inspector saluted. The look on his face said he didn't think the navy would pick up anyone.

Peggy watched the policemen as they clattered across the gangplank, climbed back into their truck, and drove away.

Peggy said, "He gave me the houseboat."

"Yes, I heard you tell the inspector. Congratulations."

She stroked the rail. "I've never owned anything before." She looked at him. "I didn't work for him, if that's what you're thinking."

"I was only thinking nice things, Peggy."

"If you want to come downstairs, I can offer you a drink," said Peggy. This boat was almost the last in the line nearest the bridge, so they could see traffic moving on the road from Giza. Every vehicle from the entire Western Desert had to cross the English Bridge to get to Cairo. Only horses and mules went through the Delta. Now they watched the blinkered headlights of trucks crossing the bridge. Nose to tail, a long convoy. It was coming from the desert, and it was made up entirely of army ambulances. At the hospital tomorrow there would be another day of grim hard work.

They both stood watching the convoy as if it were some formal parade, as if turning their attention away in search of a drink would be disrespectful to the bloody, mutilated men from some distant battlefield. Only when the last ambulance had given place to a noisy demonstration, of students shouting slogans about welcoming Rommel, did they move.

"Did you say a drink?" said Marker eventually.

Once in the comfortable cabin they relaxed a little. Marker tossed his cap onto the rack and sank down into a soft armchair while she boiled a kettle and made a pot of tea. Marker preferred something stronger.

She searched through the bottles. "Whisky, cognac, gin, or vodka, Captain Marker?"

"Lionel. A very small whisky with water, please, Peggy. Half and half." She poured it carefully, as if measuring something in the hospital pharmacy, and handed the glass to him. He held it in the air and proposed a toast: "Congratulations, Peggy. Here's to the *City of Gold*. God bless all who sail in her."

"The *City of Gold*," said Peggy. She smiled, sat down, and poured out her tea. "It's a city of brass really. I've always thought that. The brass trays, vases, and cheap ornaments they sell in the souks—most of them made in Birmingham, England— the brass bugles that wake everyone up every morning, the brass buttons on the uniforms of the British soldiers, and the brass hats who act as if they own the whole country."

"In my father's part of the world, brass was a word meaning money," said Marker.

"It shines like gold, but it's only an alloy. If you don't keep polishing it every day, it goes green, doesn't it?"

Marker watched her. She was unusually philosophical to-night. With masculine simplicity he decided that she was feeling rejected. "Were you planning to go with Solomon?"

"Yes, I was." It wasn't true, but she wanted to see how he took it.

"To Palestine?"

"To visit my husband."

"I thought you were going with our courier."

"You don't have a courier. I made inquiries about it." In fact she'd asked Alice, and Alice had innocently admitted the truth: they had no courier to anywhere.

"You're right." He held up his hands in a gesture of surren-der.

"You don't have a courier, and I don't have a husband any more. There is no point in my going anywhere."

"I'm sorry." He knew Karl was dead. She could tell that from the way he reacted. He must have got official word of it through the police.

"Don't be sorry, Captain Marker," she said. "It all happened a long time ago. He's dead. I think he only wanted the British passport. Perhaps I've been a fool."

"Call me Lionel. Anything I can do? I'm off duty now. This is strictly off the record."

"Lionel, yes. Can you tell me of a good place to get drunk, Lionel?"

"Getting drunk is not a course I'd recommend," said Marker seriously.

"Can you think of something better to do on a Saturday night in Cairo?"

He looked at her for a long time. She was a very attractive woman; he'd thought that from the moment he first met her. "Pursuant," said Marker, who was likely to resort to legal jargon in moments of tension, "pursuant to a good dinner with a bottle of wine, I might well be able to recommend something."

She laughed for the first time in a long while. She realized then that Lionel Marker had deliberately let Solomon escape him. Marker was his own man. She liked that.

Tomorrow she would be back on duty. She could hear the rumbling sound of more ambulances crossing the English Bridge. There would be lots of hard work for the surgeons and the theater nurses, for many days and nights to come. They'd stop Rommel, she had no doubt of that, but they'd pay the butcher's bill.

He was watching her carefully. He saw her frown and said, "What is it, Peggy?"

"Perhaps I'll have a drink with you," she said. She got up and poured herself a whisky and water. No ice; she didn't like ice in it. She looked at him and raised her glass. Tonight was hers to do as she wished. Suddenly she felt free. Tomorrow she'd change the name of this damned boat. The *City of Brass,* that's what she'd call it.

Postscript

The American military attaché in Cairo was suddenly recalled to Washington in the summer of 1942. "And when the new military attaché there began using the M-138 strip cipher, which defied all Axis attempts at solution, it cut Rommel off from the strategic intelligence on which he had so long depended. The loss occurred just as he was crossing the frontier into Egypt and seemed to have the pyramids and victory almost within his grasp. The British 8th Army fell back to its fortified positions at El Alamein."*

So Rommel and his Afrika Korps never got to Cairo. Deprived of his most valuable source of information, Rommel went on the defensive. In October the British offensive began. It was a complete surprise to the Germans, who suffered a defeat that marked a turning point in the whole war. Rommel's Afrika Korps began a retreat that ended with its being pushed right out of Africa. Said Churchill, "Before Alamein we never had a victory; after Alamein we never had a defeat."

*David Kahn, *The Codebreakers* (London: Weidenfeld & Nicolson, 1966).

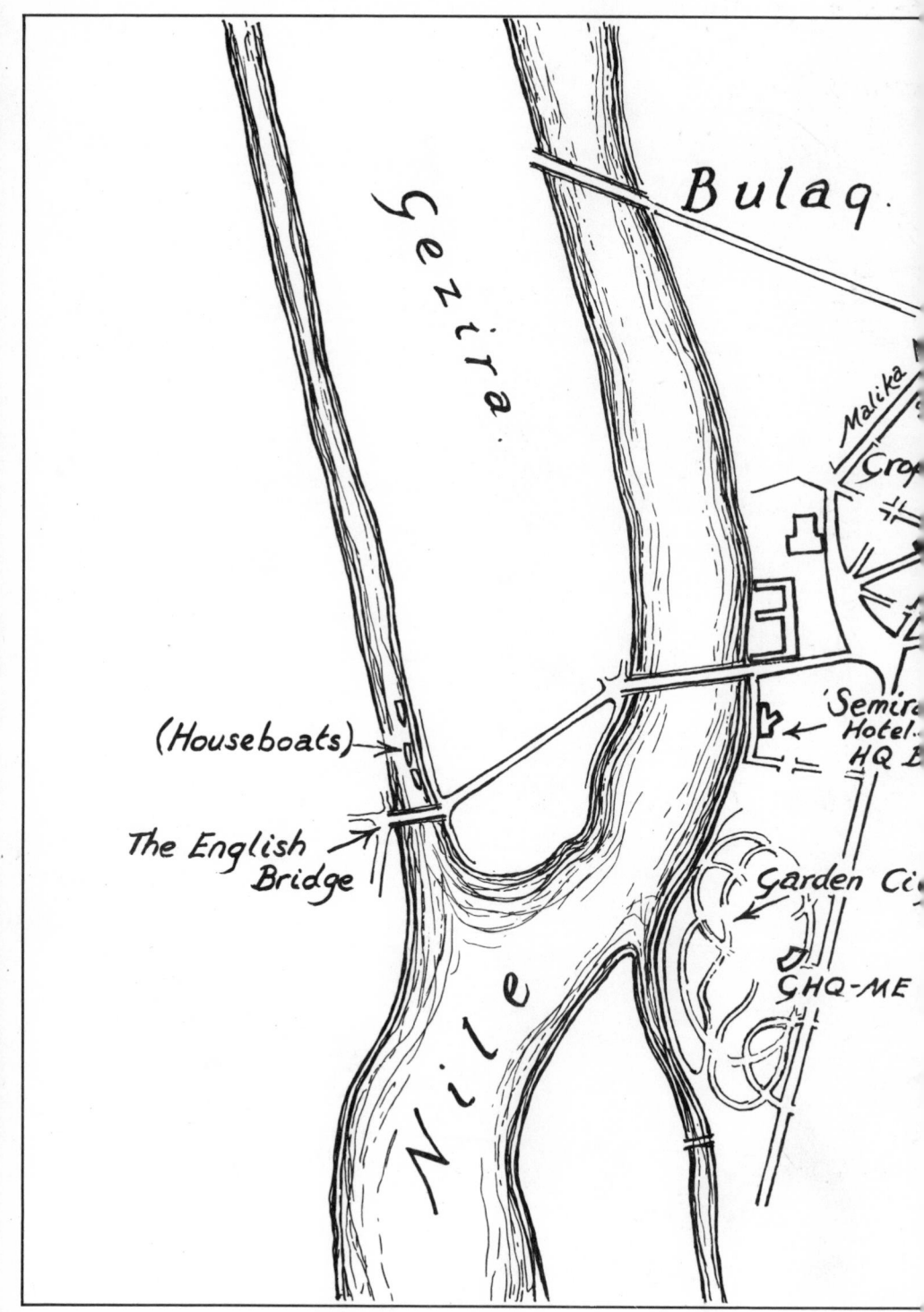